"That's all right. Y[...] You're about to be fed[...] can come later."

He gave Tanny a sn[...] eyes on Tanny's face. So far, he'd managed not to take too close a look at the skinny body. He didn't want to until it was offered to him. It sure was tempting, though.

"Are you sure someone doesn't pay you? I mean, as a professional do-gooder?"

Laughing, he shook his head. "No, Tanny. I'm doing this because I want to."

"My head's cold," It had to feel better, though.

"I've got a bandana somewhere. I'll go find it while you dry off and get dressed." Billy patted Tanny's shoulder and left to find the bandana.

It was in his dresser drawer, behind his socks and underwear. It was blue and white and he grabbed it, heading for the kitchen. He could eat.

"I... Are you in here?" Tanny wandered in, eyes *huge* without the filth to detract from them.

"Yeah. I think it's about time for our tacos." He spent a moment admiring and then grabbed a couple of plates and napkins. He passed a plate and the bag to Tanny. "Help yourself."

"Thanks." Tanny took a taco, bent to eat it.

"Go ahead and sit." He sat at the table himself and snagged one of the tacos, taking his time eating it.

"Thanks for the taco. It's so good."

Found

This is a work of fiction. Names, characters, places, and incidents either are the product of the author's imagination or are used fictitiously. Any resemblance to actual events, locales, organizations, or persons, living or dead, is entirely coincidental and beyond the intent of either the author or the publisher.

Found
TOP SHELF
An imprint of Torquere Press Publishers
PO Box 2545
Round Rock, TX 78680
Copyright © 2009 by Sean Michael
Cover illustration by S. Squires
Published with permission
ISBN: 978-1-60370-746-6, 1-60370-746-8

www.torquerepress.com

All rights reserved, which includes the right to reproduce this book or portions thereof in any form whatsoever except as provided by the U.S. Copyright Law. For information address Torquere Press. Inc., PO Box 2545, Round Rock, TX 78680.
First Torquere Press Printing: June 2009
Printed in the USA

If you purchased this book without a cover, you should be aware that this book is stolen property. It was reported as "unsold and destroyed" to the publisher, and neither the author nor the publisher has received any payment for this "stripped book".

The Hammer Novels

Bent

Forged

Spoken

Found

Found

Found
by Sean Michael

www.torquerepress.com

Found

Chapter One

It was a miserable night.

It had been grey all day, but now it was cold and rainy and dark.

Billy should have arranged to meet Ollie at the club instead of the toy store. It would be a miserable walk from Playing For Keeps to the Hammer. Of course, the man was already there, beneath the awning, wearing a red rain coat, austere face made almost stark by the streetlights.

"Oliver. Good to see you, man. Could be a better night for it, though."

"Indeed. This weather isn't fit for man nor beast." The older man waved at him, smiled. "I'm sure this was your idea, of course."

He cackled and thumped Ollie on the back. "You might be right at that." He nodded at the door. "Come on, let's get out of the wet and find some fun stuff to torture your boy with."

Ollie smiled, looking happy. "You know how he loves to scream, hmm?"

"You guys got a cigarette to spare?"

Billy looked over at the ragged man with black dreadlocks and a gaunt face who just stared at him. Jesus, the man looked... haunted.

Hunted.

This was no night to be out on the streets. "Wouldn't you rather a hot meal?" He surprised himself with the words, but once they were out, he didn't take them back.

"I can buy me one for a fiver, man, if you got one to spare..."

"Don't encourage him, Bill. They just use cash for drugs."

"Then I shall buy the meal myself, and I'll know that's where the money's gone." He peered into the man's eyes. "What do you say to that?"

They were so dark, nearly black, and desperate, fierce. Needy. "I could eat."

"Bill." Oliver looked at him. "You can't save them, my friend."

"Yeah, asshole. Fuck you. I don't need saving."

"Tsk. I'm not saving anyone. I'm hungry, he's hungry. We're going to eat. Where's the saving?" Billy patted Oliver's back. He knew his friend didn't understand this, but he'd had a hard life growing up and now he was well-to-do with too many blessings to count.

Oliver's eyes met his, worried. "You'll call me? After your meal?"

"I'll be fine, old friend." He was strong, stocky. This gaunt, starving man would not hurt him. Could not. "We'll do this another time. I'm sure you already have plenty of things to make Jack scream with until then." He gave Ollie a wink, hoping to ease his friend's worries.

Oliver nodded, and the kid stared at him, one eyebrow lifted. "Where to?"

"You like burgers and fries?" Dominico's was only a half block down and there wouldn't be too many raised eyebrows at his companion's dress.

"That's cool. You sure you don't have a smoke?"

"I'm sure. It's a nasty habit." He pushed his hands into his pockets and headed into the rain, glad Dominico's wasn't that far—it really was a bitter night.

The guy walked behind him, silent as a ghost, filthy hair dripping. He wanted to ask if the man had somewhere to go, somewhere to get out of the rain. He had a hunch the question would be better received after their meal rather than before it.

When they arrived at the little informal restaurant, he held the door for his companion.

"Thanks, man." The guy ducked in, the girl at the counter immediately coming up.

"No, Montana. You can't hide out in here no more. The boss'll kill me."

Billy pushed up from behind the lanky man—Montana, he had a name now. "He's with me, actually."

"Yeah? For real? No weirdness in the booths, now."

Montana snarled. "I'm not a fucking whore, Lisa."

"No, but still..."

Billy puffed up; he might not be the tallest man on earth, but he was beefy. "Excuse me. Do you want my business or not? I can easily spend my money somewhere else."

"No. No, come on. I'm sorry. I just... Damn it."

Billy put his hand on Montana's lower back and led him to a table in the window. Let her put that in her pipe and smoke it. Billy didn't give a shit what other people thought of him, so he was more than happy to sit in plain view with Montana at his side.

Montana sat, fingers drumming on the table. The nails were long, cracked, dirty.

"I'm Billy." He held out his hand for Montana to shake.

"Tanny. Thanks for supper."

"You're welcome, Tanny. I like the burgers here, and

the fries are some of the best in town. Do you know what you want?" he added as "Lisa" came over with her order pad in hand.

"Whatever you're having."

"Two hamburger specials and two Cokes, please."

Montana was quiet, hands and legs in constant motion, eyes flicking back and forth.

"So what do you do?" *Why are you living in the streets?*

"Nothing much. I haven't been here long."

"No? Where are you from?"

Their Cokes came and Billy unwrapped his straw, stuck it in the glass. He watched Montana while he did it, picking up more details of the man's face in the better light. The man was obviously Native American—at least partly. Montana's skin wasn't as dirty as he'd first thought—it was a lovely shade. The hooked nose and hawk-like face could have come from a hundred different Old West photographs.

"Arizona. I lived on the res there."

Ha. Right. "Why did you leave?" Billy found himself really wanting to know. He wasn't just paying lip service here, making conversation. No, he wanted to know.

"I had an accident and needed out, so I came West. You know, to see the sights, the ocean. I'm just saving cash to get back."

"This is a terrible place to live with no money."

Their food arrived and he gave the girl a nod, but his focus was all on Montana.

"Anywhere's terrible without money, man." The man fell on the food like he was starving.

Billy's lips tightened as he imagined that Montana probably was starving. He grabbed the salt and added some to his fries and then he popped one in his mouth. God, they were perfect.

Someone tapped at the window—a little rat-faced man staring in, shaking a bottle of pills. "I got it, man!"

Montana stared out, a pure, desperate hunger in that gaunt face.

Billy shook his head. Montana wasn't going to get back to Arizona if he was taking shit. In fact, he wasn't going to go anywhere but into the gutter.

He felt the pull to make sure that didn't happen.

Montana flashed a hand at the guy, mouthed 'one hour'.

Perhaps the lure of a hot shower could delay the inevitable. Billy didn't say anything right then, choosing to eat his burger first. It only took Montana half a dozen bites before the food was gone. Billy ate more slowly and offered over half his fries. "I love them, but I had lunch not that long ago."

"I... Would you mind if I took them? For a snack later."

"Go for it. But only if you'll share dessert with me." They did a mile high chocolate cake here that was nearly as good as the fries.

"That... sure. I... I meant it, what I said before. I'm not a whore. I mean, if that's what the offer's for."

Billy shook his head. "I'm not interested in fucking you. No, that's a lie. I'm interested, but not unless you're clean and sober and I have informed consent. And I'm sure as hell not paying for it."

"I. Okay." Montana looked at him like he was utterly insane.

He just grinned and raised his hand to get Lisa's attention. "A large slice of your ridiculously high chocolate cake, please. And two forks. Coffee?" he directed the last at Montana.

"Sure. Sure, yeah. That'll be warm."

"And two coffees, please."

Found

He watched her go and then smiled at Montana. "Speaking of warm—how would you like a hot shower? I've got a washer and dryer at my place and some sweats that, while very short, should still fit you." *Come out of the cold for an hour or two, maybe even a night.*

"I..." Those near-black eyes shot outside. "No offense, man, but unless you're going to do something bad to me, you got no reason to invite a junkie loser to your place."

Billy didn't take offense. He wouldn't have trusted him either under the same circumstances. "I didn't start life as a well-off queer, but I had a lot of people give me a boost when I needed it. They never asked for anything in return. I try and pay 'em back in kind."

"That's what all the pretty axe murderers say."

Billy snorted. "Then it's a good thing I'm not pretty."

Montana looked at him, chuckled a little. "Oh, I don't know. You're on the pretty side..." Uh-huh. Right.

"I'm built like a bull and I've a face to match." He might not be an axe murderer, and Montana might be cautious, but a good con would be, too, and Billy wasn't born yesterday or taking any more chances than Montana. Still, he didn't really believe Montana was trying to con him. The guy was just... lost, was his guess.

The cake came with the coffee and Montana drank the cup quickly, even though it had to be burning the man's tongue.

Billy caught the waitress' attention and mimed getting a refill before he passed over one of the forks.

"Thank you. The coffee's great here."

He took a sip. It actually was marginal, at best. He added some cream. That helped.

Billy took a few bites of the cake and then sat back, patting his belly. "Now that is a decadent dessert. I think I'm done."

"You didn't eat very much of it." Montana took a bite,

moaning softly.

"We can take anything we don't eat now with us. I love the cake, but it's not something I ever order on my own—it's huge!"

"It is. You're a good guy, man. Thanks for the food."

"You're welcome. Now keep me from feeling guilty and let me take you home so you can get that shower."

"I..." Montana shook his head. "No, thanks. I got a friend to meet and I'll just get soaked again. Thanks for the offer."

"Fair enough." He wasn't going to push. If Montana would rather be out in the wet getting high and sleeping in the gutter, there wasn't a lot Billy could do about it.

He pulled a business card out of his back pocket and handed it over. "Call if you change your mind. I'll accept charges, and I have an SUV. I can come pick you up no matter the weather."

"You're sweet. I... If you ever need someone to share a meal with, I stay under the boardwalk."

Jesus. It was all he could do not to order Montana back to his place right now. "I'll keep that in mind."

Montana slid out from the seat, as soon as the waitress brought over a doggy bag for the fries. "Can I have a to-go cup of coffee, Lis? Please?"

"Sure, Tanny. How 'bout you, sir? You want one, too?"

"No, I'm good. But make sure his to-go cup is on my tab. Oh, and he needs the cake wrapped up, too, please." Billy stood as well and held out his hand again. "It was nice to meet you."

"Yeah, I'm charming as fuck. Thanks for the do-gooding. It made my night." Montana shook his hand, offered him a quirky smile.

Billy chuckled and leaned in the smallest bit. "I know you won't believe it, but you've made mine as well."

"Hey, who am I to argue?" Montana chuckled and took the cake as well. "Have a good night, man."

"You, too." Even as he said it, Billy was pretty certain that his would be much better than Montana's.

It sort of had to be.

Chapter Two

Fuck, he was cold.

Tanny shivered, looking over at Mark, shivering too. He'd given up his food, his coffee, his coat, and his last eight dollars. In return he wanted the pills.

There were three of the reds and that would keep him for two days, maybe three.

"Quit fucking around, man. I gave you what you asked for." Please. He was miserable and he just wanted to go to ground and watch the ocean.

"I find out you're holding out on me and I'll come take it out on your hide." Mark looked at the eight bucks in his hand and his mouth twisted. Then he handed over a little baggie with the three pills.

That was when the fucking siren went off, police lights flashing.

"Fuck!" He turned and ran, busting it hard toward the beach. Fuck. Fuck. Fuck.

His feet dug into the sand and he scrambled, air burning in his chest, his aching, scarred back miserable.

"Freeze, asshole!" Shit, the cop sounded close.

No way.

No way.

He sobbed, sliding around a car.

"God damn it!" He was clipped as he went around the

car and then pushed up against the next vehicle, the cop right behind him, hand pushing his head down onto the hood. "I said freeze."

Fuck. He swallowed the pills all at once, knowing that all they could do was get him for running.

The cop got his hands behind his back, putting the plastic cuffs around his wrists before patting him down. He didn't have anything. Not a fucking thing but a couple of sheets of paper towel, that dude's business card, and two quarters.

"Fuck off. Leave me alone."

"Screw you, asshole. We're taking you in." The cop pulled him up into a standing position and started walking him back toward the police car.

"For what? I didn't do anything! You ASSHOLES!"

"We saw you make a buy, tough guy." He was pushed into the back seat, the car door slammed behind him.

"With what? I ain't got jack shit!" Tanny kicked the back of the seat, screaming.

They pretty much ignored him after that, making stupid fucking small talk during the ride back to the precinct like he wasn't even there. The drugs were coursing through him by the time they had him fingerprinted and thrown in the drunk tank.

Fuckers.

"FUCKERS!"

"You want your phone call or you want to just sleep it off?"

"Who the fuck am I supposed to call? What are you fucking holding me for?"

"You're high. We'll hold you until you're sober, unless there's someone willing to come pick you up."

"I. There's a guy. A card. I got his card. Dude, I got his card. His fucking card."

The cop held up a small plastic bag with his paper

towels, quarters and the little card. "This?"

"Yeah. Yeah, that one. He'll come."

Maybe.

Or not.

But still.

The cop gave him some quarters, the card, and opened the door, pointing to the pay phone on the wall.

He dropped the quarters six times, hands shaking violently, but he finally managed, dialing the number and praying to whatever gods were around.

"Hello?" The voice was deep, husky, but he was pretty sure it was the right guy's.

"I. This is. Tanny, you remember, from the diner? I'm in jail and I just need someone to pick me up, and then I'll go and I swear I'll never bother you again but I gotta get me out of here, you know?"

"Which jail are you at?"

That was it. No demands, no recriminations, just, "Which jail".

"Uh. Downtown. By the park. Please, I'll do anything, just come get me. I won't bother you no more..."

"Give me fifteen minutes to get down there. We can talk about where you're staying tonight after I've got you out."

He hung up the phone, stared over. "He's coming. Now."

Fuckers.

"You can wait back in the tank." The cop grabbed his arm and pulled him back over to the cell.

He shoved in, sliding across the floor. He found a corner, arms wrapped around himself. At least it was dry.

Dry.

Right.

Dry.

Found

Fuck.
Dry.
Tanny closed his eyes, hiding in the noise in his head.

Chapter Three

Billy stood in the reception area of the police station downtown, waiting for them to bring Montana out.

They'd told him that Montana had been picked up after a drug bust, that they were keeping him for being under the influence of an illegal substance, and that they expected him to keep the guy off the streets for the night.

He could do that. As long as Montana finally took him up on his offer of a hot shower.

Tanny was short one coat, looking very much like a drowned rat, with huge, jittering eyes.

Good lord, he was high as a kite.

Billy didn't say a word, though. Instead, he took the little baggie of 'personal effects'—right, like some Kleenex and a couple quarters were personal effects—and nodded to Tanny. "Car's right outside."

"Cool. Thanks. Bye, guys." Tanny waved and bounced out, stopping at the bottom of stairs. "You are my hero, man. Thank you. I swear I'll never call again. Never. I just... Thank you, huh?"

Billy nodded toward the car. "Go on and get in. If you trusted me enough to call me from jail, you can trust me enough to get a hot shower, some clean clothes and a bed for the night."

"I... For real?"

"Yes."

"I... I haven't slept in a bed since... shit, I think I spent a night in the shelter last Christmas."

Jesus. It was almost Halloween. "Then it should be a nice treat for you." Billy held the car door open, trying hard not to show how appalled he felt.

"Yeah. Yeah. It's. Yeah. Wow."

Once they were both in and seat-belted, Billy headed home. "It sounds like life's been dealing you some blows lately."

"No more than usual. It's cool. I'm cool." The kid was jittering, legs going ninety to nothing.

"What are you on?" And how much had Tanny taken?

"Reds. Uppers. I like to go. Keeps you warm. I had to take them all, 'cause the fuzz came, and you know, that's bad. Mark took all my cash and my food and my coat, so it's good that I'm warm, because damn, huh?"

"Shit, kid, you're not going to need that bed—you're going to be up all night." He'd bet Tanny crashed hard when the drugs wore off, though.

"I. You. You don't have to let me stay. It's okay. It's cool."

"Shut up and accept my offer, Tanny."

"I. Yeah. Sure. Okay. I'm okay. It's cool."

Billy chuckled and turned the heat up. It was a little hotter than he liked it, but he figured Tanny needed it, even if he wasn't feeling the cold right now.

"Where... where do you live? Do you have an apartment?"

"I own an apartment in a big old house that's been converted. I have the top floor." It was an awesome place with a turret and sloped ceilings, a little hideaway attic.

"Wow. That's cool. Do you have good neighbors?"

"Yeah, actually, it's starting to be less uptight. I see 'em once a year at the back-yard barbeque."

"That's... nice?"

Billy chuckled and nodded. "Yeah, it is actually." He turned onto his street. "I've had overly friendly neighbors before and I can live without them."

He wasn't a curmudgeon or anything, he just usually found his interests different from most neighbors'.

"Oh. I. I have... well, Rat Man stays under the same bridge."

Rat Man. Excellent.

"It's going to be cold under that bridge in the coming months." Spring and summer were one thing, especially for a boy from Arizona.

"Yeah. And Mark has my coat, but it's cool. Maybe I'll head south. I like south. Although San Francisco's north and I hear good things about it."

Frankly, he thought Tanny needed to get clean before he made any more big decisions.

"This is the place." He pulled into the driveway.

"It's pretty. I. I shouldn't come in. Your neighbors might see. I might be too loud. I might talk, you know?" Tanny tugged at the foul dreadlocks. Billy wasn't sure those were salvageable.

"I don't care what my neighbors think, Montana. Come on up. I've got a bottle of shampoo and copious amounts of hot water." He got out and headed for the door; Tanny didn't really have anywhere else to go but his place, or the street.

Tanny followed him in, arms wrapped around himself, bouncing from foot to foot, eyes flickering around.

"I'll give you the tour after. For now, let's get you clean and warm." He grabbed a pair of his sweatpants that were tight and his robe.

later. He didn't look, he knew. He just shrank into a smaller ball and ignored it.

He knew how bad the scars were.

He'd crashed the bike going seventy, had slid flat on his back for half the length of a football field. He knew.

"What happened?" Billy asked. No sugar coating, no dancing around the subject, just, "What happened?"

"I had an accident. Almost three years ago. Wet street. Motorcycle."

"God damn, that's quite the accident. Does it hurt?" Billy had come to stand next to the shower, looking at him through the gap where the shower curtain didn't meet the wall.

"Sometimes. It's ugly. I know."

"It's amazing you survived." He thought he felt a feather light touch and then Billy was stepping away. "I'll get these in the washer. Take your time. Wash your hair."

"I can't. But okay. Sure. Thanks."

A few minutes later Billy came back. "You want some help, Tanny? With your hair, with your back?"

"I'm okay." He watched the dirt drip onto the tub. "I don't think there's enough water to get me clean now."

"Oh, I imagine there is. Look, if you won't let me cut the dreads off, at least let me shampoo them. They'll come clean, but they're going to need more washing than one person can manage on their own."

"You don't understand." They were so tangled and torn and infested and... Bugs. Jesus. Bugs everywhere and he just needed to get the hell out of here and walk. Maybe he could walk down the coast for, like, forever. Maybe just walk into the water and go and go and go.

"No, you're right. I don't. Look, do what you can and then come into the living room and have something to eat and you can do a monster movie marathon on TV or something. We need to talk once you come down."

He nodded, and let the water pour and pour, scrubbing himself gently at first, then brutally, tearing off layer after layer of dirt and a few layers of skin.

Then, finally, he crawled out of the tub and jittered around the bathroom, dancing a little to the constant drumbeats in the back of his head.

There was another knock at the door and Billy put his head around. "Dry yourself off and get dressed before you catch your death."

"I was just enjoying being bare for a second. A minute. A while."

Something.

He wrapped himself in the towel, moaning happily.

Billy chuckled. "I guess that's allowed. Go ahead and take your time. I'll be in the kitchen when you're ready."

The door closed again.

So nice.

"So nice." He liked the way the words felt in his mouth, so he said them again and again as he slid the clothes on.

The sweats were way too short and a little loose at the waist, but there was a drawstring which he pulled tight. The robe was thick and soft and felt amazing on his skin. He didn't look at himself in the mirror, he didn't want to know. He headed out, curious to see, to know what happened next.

Billy was sitting in the kitchen. "Hey, how about a cup of hot chocolate?"

Oh. Oh, wow. Fucking A. "Man, are you real?"

"I am. Is it me or you we're supposed to pinch to prove it?" Dark green eyes twinkled at him.

"Me. No one's just nice. No one."

Billy reached over and pushed up the sleeve of the robe, pinching him. Hard.

"Ow!" He gasped, then started laughing hysterically.

Chuckling, Billy guided him to a chair and put a steaming mug of hot chocolate in front of him. A couple of muffins on a plate were also set near him on the table.

"Oh. Muffins." He reached out, stroked the top of the muffin. Soft. Sticky. Cool.

"I have butter if you want. For the muffins." Billy waited by the counter for his answer.

"I. It's okay. I probably can't keep this down. I ate so much earlier." His hands were shaking, touching the sweet. Maybe he could save it.

"How about a few bites, then, and you can have more in the morning?" A couple bottles of water were also set in front of him. "That'll help work the drugs out of your system."

"I don't want them out, you know? I like buzzing." He tore off a bite, moaning over the sweet, buttery taste.

"There are other things that can give you a buzz. Legal things. Not blow your mind out things." Billy sat down across from him.

"That's what people who think speed is wrong say."

"I didn't say it was wrong—I said it was illegal."

"Well, yeah. Lots of things are—lots. Even not bad ones."

"So tell me why you left Arizona. Was it because of the accident?" Billy grabbed the corner of one muffin and began munching on it.

"Yes. I mean, yeah. The bills were so much and everyone was so mad, you know?" He leaned back, curled into the robe. "There's all this blame and screaming and then hatefulness and I'm useless, so I left."

"That sounds pretty rough."

"It's okay. I didn't belong there." He didn't belong here either, but he knew, if he kept wandering, he'd find that place where he did.

Billy met his eyes. "Well, maybe you belong here."

"I wish. I like this part of the coast. It gets colder than I thought it would, though. I'm thinking Thanksgiving will be bone-cold." Pretty eyes. Such pretty eyes.

"It will be. Especially if you're used to a much drier climate." Billy licked his lips and then nodded, as if he'd been trying to work something out. "I've got an offer for you. You don't need to answer right now, or even tomorrow. You can stay here until you've made up your mind."

"Huh?"

"I'd like you to consider staying here with me. Clean up, find work, and once you're on your feet again, we could see if there was anything between us."

"Why?" That didn't make any sense. No sense at all.

"Because I like you. I like how you look." Billy shrugged and seemed really casual, but Tanny could tell there was something deeper there. "Because there's something in your eyes that I recognize. A need that maybe I can fulfill."

"I. Dude, you're too cool to be real and I appreciate it, but... I'm bad news. I know me. I'm a fuck up. I can't help it. I 'm trouble, looking for a home."

"You mean you're a challenge." Billy grinned and winked. "Look, I said you shouldn't decide right now and I meant it. You can stay here while you make up your mind—a day, a week, however long you need. Though we're going to have to do something about the bugs in your hair if you don't want me to cover the guest bed in plastic."

Okay, the guy was creepy. Nobody wanted to be nice to him, for no reason. No one. "What's your angle? I'm not looking to deal or anything."

"My 'angle' is that when you're in a place to make a decision, I'll want to discuss entering into a relationship with you. I'm not interested in anything from you while you're high or desperate."

"Okay. Sure. We can talk when I'm better. Sure." Psycho. He was going to get his clothes back and get out, at first light. No one that nice could be sane.

"Excellent!" Billy finished his hot chocolate and went to the sink to wash the mug. "Did you want to watch movies or something?"

"Sure." He itched. Everywhere. Mark was out there, somewhere, with his coat.

Billy got up and headed into the front room. The place had sloped ceilings, a wide window seat looking out over the road, and a fireplace. It was really nice. As was the huge couch with poofy pillows and the huge HD TV. "What kind of stuff do you like?"

He sat on the window seat, looking out. "I don't know. Uh. I like funny stuff, mostly. I sneak in and watch movies sometimes. In the back."

"Let's see. Comedies are here. You can choose." Billy indicated an area on the bookcase that was jam-packed with DVDs.

"I..." He went over, fingers trailing over the backs, the colors swirling. He pointed at one, randomly, not able to focus enough to read the spine.

"The Three Stooges Collection. You're into the classics?"

He grinned. Oh, cool. "Yeah. Yeah, them and Andy Griffith and Lucy and shit. My gran watched them on the rabbit-ear every day before she died."

"Oh, cool. I've got most of the oldies there. You can have a marathon."

He nodded and headed back over to the window. Unease was riding him hard. This wasn't right, having this stranger welcome him in. It wasn't right. It didn't make sense. It couldn't be real and it was probably dangerous.

Billy settled in the big easy chair and, within about twenty minutes, was snoring softly.

Tanny waited for another hour, then crept to get his clothes out of the washer. He put them on wet. It was still pouring; it wouldn't matter. Then he folded the sweats and the robe up carefully and slipped his sneakers on.

He left a note on the kitchen table, on a paper napkin that the muffin had been on.

"Thanx. You rock. Tanny."

By the time he was cuddled under the boardwalk, the sun had lightened the sky up to gray.

Chapter Five

Billy drove down to the boardwalk and parked near the walkway.

The Saturday shoppers were all out, hurrying here and there, as well as folks strolling along the boardwalk and enjoying the sunny day after all that rain. He had Tanny's note in his pocket and he kept touching it, as if it was his only link to Tanny.

He supposed he should have known the man would run as soon as his own eyes closed, but with no coat and wet clothes, he'd bet Tanny was freezing, even with the sun being out.

He wasn't sure what he could say that would make Tanny stay with him, but he wasn't going to make it an order. That kind of thing needed Tanny to be clean, sober, and making his own way. Billy wouldn't take on a sub who was also choosing a roof over his head and a hot meal.

Hell, he couldn't quite understand why the hell he wanted Tanny safe so badly. He did, though, and he had to believe that little voice that had him up and moving. If there was anything the last ten years of meeting and losing and loving subs had taught him, it was that he needed to trust that voice.

Billy locked up the car and headed for the area under

the bridge, hoping Tanny would be there.

There were a few people walking their dogs, walking around. The bridge was dank and moldy beneath, piles of cardboard and blankets stuffed underneath.

He saw Tanny, curled up in a lee away from the wind.

"Hey, Tanny," he called out. He figured the man would be coming down pretty hard at this point and might be more willing to have a warm, clean place to stay.

"Hey, Hero-Man." He got a weak smile.

"Hey." He went over and crouched next to Tanny, trying not to breathe in too deeply. "You look cold."

"You don't. Did you sleep good?"

"I slept fine. I was a little disappointed when I woke up, though. I thought you'd decided to take me up on my hospitality."

"I... I couldn't. It was too nice. People do things they regret, huh? You're too nice to do that to."

"The only thing I regret is you leaving. Why don't you come back with me and warm back up, come down in peace?"

Tanny looked up at him, dark eyes confused. "People like you aren't real. Don't you know that?"

"I know I'm real. You want me to pinch you again to prove it?"

"No. I'm fucked up, don't you get it?"

A beer bottle winged out of the darkness, hitting Montana in the jaw and neck. "Shut UP, you little fuck, or I'll slit your goddamn throat!"

Tanny winced, shrank back a little before shaking himself and standing. "Come on. You'll get hurt. Let's walk."

"I'll get hurt? I'm more concerned about you." He let Montana lead him away, and headed them in the general direction of his car. "You can't keep living like this, Tanny.

I don't want to find out you've been murdered in your sleep or died of exposure."

"Are you like one of those TV angels?"

Billy started to laugh. "I'm no angel, Tanny. I'll tell you, though. All these people out here. None of them see you. But I do. I see you."

"Why? Why me? Why not see somebody pretty?"

"You're not twinky pretty, but you're striking, quite beautiful in your own way. And..." Billy shrugged. "You pull me to you."

He hadn't been looking for anyone. Hell, when he'd first invited Tanny for supper, it had just been to get the poor guy out of the rain and put something hot in his stomach. Then he'd seen the scars, the strength right there, painted on the surface. He wanted to test that strength, to temper Montana into the beautiful, sensual man he knew was hiding there.

Tanny kept walking, hands in his pockets, head down. "I could be violent. A thief. Diseased."

"Someone looking to hurt me wouldn't have left last night." He slowed down as they drew near to the parking lot where he'd left the car, foot playing with the sand.

"I couldn't just stay. I felt... I felt bad for you, having me there, in your house where it's so... normal."

Billy chuckled. Normal. Him. He'd have to share that one at the next Dom night at the Hammer. "It looks normal on the surface, doesn't it?"

"Yeah." The wind blew and Tanny shuddered. "Yeah. Look. I... I gotta go. I don't got any money, and I'm gonna need at least twenty to get my stuff."

"Look, come back with me. You can help around the apartment to earn the roof over your head and we'll look at what else you can do. I just hate to think of you out here with the weather so bad." He rested his hand on Tanny's arm. "Come on. Trust me for twenty-four hours, and then we'll take it from there."

Tanny reached up, rubbed the growing bruise on his jaw. "I. Okay? For a little while."

"That works for me." He nodded, smiled and pointed at his chair. "Come on, then. Maybe we can hit a drive-through on our way home to my place."

Tanny's stomach growled, those big eyes staring at him. "You're like my hero and shit. It's weird."

"Maybe." Billy shrugged. "I'm just doing what feels right."

"I do that a lot. Do what feels right."

"There you go—we already have something in common, then." He opened the car door for Tanny and then went around to his side.

He looked Tanny over—the man was in his early twenties, maybe older. He'd looked younger last night.

"What kind of fast food do you like?" He aimed the car to detour through drive-through lane.

"You mean my favorite? I love tacos."

"Taco Bell it is." He'd take Tanny to a proper Mexican place when the man had new clothes and didn't have a head full of buggy hair.

"I'll work it off. I promise."

"Yeah, we'll work something out. I was thinking of doing some redecorating, but the idea of doing it myself has kept me from actually doing it..."

It would give Tanny something to do, let him feel like he was earning his keep until he was cleaned up enough to find himself a job.

"I used to..." Tanny stopped. "I'm no good at fancy shit."

Billy turned into the Taco Bell drive-through. There were only a couple cars ahead of them. "What did you used to do?"

"I. Didn't. I. I was a painter. Not pictures. Houses."

Found

"Oh, cool. So you're the right man for helping me." He gave Tanny a smile and then leaned out the window. "A half dozen beef tacos, please, and two Cokes."

Tanny moaned, the sound oddly sexual. "Tacos."

He chuckled. "As many as you can eat." He moved up to the window, paid, and accepted the bag from the pimply-faced teenager. Billy passed the bag over to Tanny. Tanny's hands were shaking, rattling the bag.

"You have anything that helps with the coming down?" he asked gently.

"More uppers." Tanny winked.

Billy laughed and turned the car toward home. "Okay, you've got the caffeine there in the Coke. That's the best I can do for uppers."

"It's okay. I got Mark for that."

Not if he had anything to do with it.

"You can start if you want." He nodded toward the bag in Tanny's hands.

"I can wait. It's okay. It's warm."

"You going to let me wash your clothes again and stick them in the dryer this time?" His old sweatpants were getting quite the workout.

"Uh-huh. They're clean this time, at least."

He was hoping to take Tanny shopping in the next couple of days. Get him set up a little.

They made it back the house without incident, Tanny humming softly under his breath.

"Here we are again." He smiled over and grabbed the Cokes.

Tanny looked, shaking a little. "It's so pretty."

Billy's heart went out to Tanny, but he knew the only way to get past the shakes was to go through them. "Yeah. I like it. You haven't even seen the best bit yet. My bedroom has the turret."

"What's that?"

He pointed to the round column at the back end of the house. "A round room. Well, the one end of it is round, the rest is a regular square."

"Oh, wow." Tanny took a step forward, stumbling a little bit.

He put his hand around Tanny's arm, guiding him up the stairs. Billy figured between coming down off the high, the lack of sleep and the fact that the only food Tanny'd eaten yesterday had been a burger and some fries, Tanny had to be feeling pretty dizzy, weak.

"Come on; let's get you upstairs and sitting down."

"I'm okay. I just. Wow."

Billy smiled, leading Tanny up to the third floor. "The guest bedroom looks out over the back garden—it has lovely picture windows. I think you'll like it."

"Am I a guest?" Tanny blinked at him.

"You are. For now. That was the agreement, wasn't it?" He wasn't expecting Tanny to share his bed.

"Yeah, I think. I mean. Fuck. Fuck, my head hurts, man."

"Food, caffeine, and aspirin. And then maybe some sleep, hmm?" He unlocked the door and ushered Tanny back in.

Tanny climbed into the house, shaking hard, the clothes clammy and awful under his hand.

"Shower first, huh? Get you warm again." He all but dragged the poor man into the bathroom and took the bag of tacos, setting them down on the counter. Then he started stripping Tanny.

"I. Uh."

Oh, God. That hair smelled... God.

"Let's face it, Tanny, your fingers aren't exactly working, so just let me do this." He made short work of the clammy clothes and then started the shower and pushed Tanny into it.

Tanny moaned, face lifting to the water.

Billy stared at the scarred back for a moment, fingers itching to trace the scars, to discover the thing that had so changed Tanny's life. He finally pulled himself away and put the clothes in the washer. Again.

Grabbing the scissors, along with the old sweatpants and his robe, he made his way back into the bathroom.

Tanny was resting on the floor of the tub, soaking in the water.

He set the clothes on the counter and went to crouch next to his guest. "Tanny? I'd really like to get rid of the bugs making a home in you hair."

"I would, too. They bite."

"So let me cut the dreads. And then I'll shave you right to the skin. That'll be at least as good as all those dreads in keeping people away." Though, really, he imagined Tanny would be very striking bald.

"I... I'll be hideous."

"It'll grow back, Tanny. Healthy, clean, bug-free."

"No, it won't. There'll be bugs again."

"If you go back out on the street. And if so, then at least you'll have had some time free of them."

"I'm going to be the ugliest man on earth. Ever."

"I don't believe that. With your bone structure you'll be stunning. And it will grow back." He showed Tanny the scissors. "It won't take long and you can stay here while it grows back."

"This is the weirdest situation, ever."

"Really? Weirder than living on the streets?"

"No one ever wanted to shave my head in exchange for tacos, man." Tanny looked over at him. "What's your name again?"

"William Harker, but you can call me Billy. And it's more in exchange for letting you rest your head on my guest bed, complete with pillows and new sheets."

"Billy. I... My head will freeze out there, without the hair."

"We'll keep the heating on inside and buy you a hat for outside." He was determined to have an answer for each of Tanny's objections on this one.

"My own hat, hmm? Can it be blue?"

"Any color you want."

It weighed heavily that having his own hat could be such a big deal to Tanny. It wasn't right.

"I know it's stupid, but... I mean, I'm not a kid. It's just..." Tanny closed his eyes and took a deep breath. "Just do it, man. It's worth it for a night out of the rain."

"Maybe even more than one." He picked up the scissors and began to hack at Tanny's dreads. Such an interesting mixture of mature and bouncy, of curious and quiet.

It had to hurt—the huge logs of filth were tight, but Tanny never said a word. That fortitude and strength in a scene would be intense, mind-blowing. It was all Billy could do not to moan at the thought.

Tanny seemed to relax as it went on, leaning into the pain. A natural, then. So lovely.

Billy cut away as much as he could, bagging the dreads along with their bugs and tying the bag off. He'd take it out as soon as they were done here. Then he picked up his razor, put in a new blade, and grabbed the shaving cream. "This might feel a little cold."

Tanny shrugged, nodded. "I'm okay."

"Okay." He pushed the showerhead over a little, so water wasn't falling directly onto Tanny's head anymore and rubbed the shaving cream into Tanny's scalp. Then he began shaving Tanny bald.

Tanny closed his eyes, almost asleep, and Billy hummed softly, working quickly, but carefully. He ran his hand over Tanny's head once he was done to gauge where he needed to come at Tanny's scalp at a different angle.

The lack of hair made Montana's features look fierce, pointed, the cheekbones sharp. Billy felt a surge of something far deeper than lust go through him.

That was his mark on Montana's body.

"I look like a freak, don't I?"

"No, Montana, you don't look like a freak at all. You look like... a fierce warrior."

Tanny have him a half-smile, the look tremulous. "A warrior?"

"A warrior—strong and fierce." He cupped Tanny's cheek and let his thumb run over the sharp cheekbone.

"I don't feel very fierce right now."

"That's all right. You're warm. You're clean. You're about to be fed and sleep in a bed. Fierce can come later."

He gave Tanny a smile and stood, keeping his eyes on Tanny's face. So far, he'd managed not to take too close a look at the skinny body. He didn't want to until it was offered to him. It sure was tempting, though.

"Are you sure someone doesn't pay you? I mean, as a professional do-gooder?"

Laughing, he shook his head. "No, Tanny. I'm doing this because I want to."

"My head's cold," It had to feel better, though.

"I've got a bandana somewhere. I'll go find it while you dry off and get dressed." Billy patted Tanny's shoulder and left to find the bandana.

It was in his dresser drawer, behind his socks and underwear. It was blue and white and he grabbed it, heading for the kitchen. He could eat.

"I... Are you in here?" Tanny wandered in, eyes *huge* without the filth to detract from them.

"Yeah. I think it's about time for our tacos." He spent a moment admiring and then grabbed a couple of plates and napkins. He passed a plate and the bag to Tanny. "Help yourself."

"Thanks." Tanny took a taco, bent to eat it.

"Go ahead and sit." He sat at the table himself and snagged one of the tacos, taking his time eating it.

"Thanks for the taco. It's so good."

"Have as many as you want. I got six." He figured Tanny was good for at least a couple. Leftovers could be reheated later.

Tanny needed some meat on his bones just to not be too skinny.

"You're being nice to me again."

"More pinches, or should I stop?" he teased.

"No pinching. It's just a little weird. What do you do for a living?" Montana winked at him, laughed quietly.

"I write—I have columns in several magazines and newspapers."

"Wow. So you're smart. That's cool."

He chuckled. "Thank you. It pays the bills." It more than paid the bills, actually.

"Yeah. Me? Not with the smart."

"No? There's different kinds of smarts, though, aren't there?"

"I guess. I'm pretty street-smart."

"I would imagine you'd have to be to survive on the streets." Billy finished his taco and took a second. Hoping to encourage Tanny to eat more, he passed the bag over. "What would you like to do?"

"With what?" Tanny took one more, picking this one apart.

"With your life. Didn't you want to be something when you grew up?"

"I wanted to be a race car driver. I like speed."

"I guess your accident put an end to that, eh?"

Tanny's eyes met his, flashing with the first true emotion

he'd seen. "It put an end to a lot of things."

Billy nodded. "I'm sorry."

"I'm over it."

Oh, he could see that. "You want any more of those? I have cookies somewhere for dessert."

"No. No, I'm okay. I'm done." Tanny was beginning to shudder again.

He put the other two in the fridge. "Feel free to grab them when you want them. How about some coffee?" The caffeine would help. "Or maybe just bed?"

"Coffee. I... I probably have to go. I can't... I'm nervous. This is... I like coffee."

He reached out and put his hand on Tanny's shoulder, squeezing. "Deep breaths, Tanny. Your clothes are still in the washer and I'm not letting you leave in them soaking wet again. We'll let them dry, and you can rest and be clean and warm and fed for awhile."

"I don't know how to do this. I don't know how to do this with you."

"I've never done this before, either. I say we just go with it. Do our best, hmm?" If he was Tanny's master, he'd make it happen, make it work for Tanny.

"My best. Okay." Tanny stood, started wandering a little, fingers sliding over this and that.

"Did you want to just wander, watch a movie, tell me to leave you the hell alone?"

"I. It's so nice in here, so many different things to touch."

God, this man was going to be the most sensual person. "I like surrounding myself with nice things." He shrugged. "And I'm lucky enough I have the money to indulge myself."

"Yeah. It's good to know when you're lucky."

"I do appreciate everything I have. It wasn't that long ago I depended on the kindness of strangers myself." He heard the washer ding and went out to switch Tanny's clothes into the dryer. "We could go for a walk once your clothes are dry. If you're feeling stir crazy."

"You don't want to be seen with me." Tanny's hands rubbed the bald head, moving restlessly.

"No, that's not true. I don't mind being seen with you at all."

"I mind being seen with me."

"Because I shaved you bald?"

"No. No, because I'm... unsavory."

"You look savory enough for me. I took you out for supper, didn't I?" He wasn't ashamed when the people he chose to be with weren't 'upper crust'.

"You did. It was the best."

"I'd like to do it again sometime." He headed into the living room, figuring Tanny would follow.

"Only if I can pay. I'm trying to get a job somewhere."

"Having clean clothes and no more dreads should help with that. You can use this place as your address, too." He knew most people wanted a fixed address for their employees.

Tanny looked at him, eyes hot. "What do you want? What is all of this going to cost me?"

"I want you to get clean, become independent. You get yourself in a good place, and then I can talk to you about the things we might both want." Because he hoped it wouldn't be one-sided. He hoped Tanny wouldn't freak when he found out about the way Bill liked to play.

Tanny stared him down, or tried to. The man couldn't hold his gaze.

"I promise you that I will never make you do anything you don't want to do." Of course, he imagined there were a lot of things that he could think of that Tanny would think he didn't want, but that really, he did.

Found

"Can we sit, now? Just sit and watch TV for a minute."

"Sure thing." He grabbed the remote and settled in his chair, leaving the couch for Tanny. Maybe the man would sleep. Tanny settled on the floor in front of the sofa, Billy turned on the television and started clicking. "What do you feel like?"

"Anything. Anything that's noise."

He found the TV Land channel, which played old black and white sitcoms, and *I Love Lucy* was on. "There we go."

"It's cool." Tanny rested his chin on his knees, holding tight.

Billy watched Tanny more than the show, finding himself imagining what Tanny would be like during scenes, obeying orders. Being a sub. There was this amazing strength, this stillness, then there was an answering fury, a stubborn streak. Tanny would be a challenge. A delicious challenge.

He couldn't wait and reminded himself to be patient. Let Tanny come to him clean and sober and able to stand on his own. It would be all the sweeter for it.

Tanny dozed off, rocking unconsciously, comforting himself.

Billy turned the sound a little lower so it didn't disturb Tanny and grabbed his laptop to work on his latest column.

Chapter Six

Tanny was warm, curled into something soft and cushiony, the scent of bacon in the air. Bacon and toast and tomato soup. Oh. Oh, yum.

"Gran?" He stretched, trying to remember how he'd gotten home.

A low chuckled sounded. "Not quite."

His eyes popped open and he jerked, falling on the floor with a thud. Oh, fuck. Oh, fuck. Wait.

"Oh, Tanny." Solid, warm hands patted his arm and then slid into his pits, helping him stand.

"Sorry. Sorry. Did I fall asleep? I'm sorry. It was warm. I know better. Just dopey, I guess." Where was he? Oh. Right. Hero-man. Yeah.

"You can sleep as long as you like here. It's safe." Billy waved at the food on the coffee table. "Of course you can eat, too."

"Oh. Oh, wow. I smelled bacon." Bacon sandwiches. Yum. He reached up to scratch his head, belly tightening as his fingers met skin.

Right.

Right.

He didn't want to think about that.

"Yeah, tomato soup and bacon sandwiches. Comfort food, you know?" Billy gave him a smile and handed over

Found

a spoon.

"Thank you..." Comfort food. Yeah. Of course, any food was comfort food.

"You're welcome." Billy handed him a couple of paper napkins and settled back in the big chair with a bowl of soup.

He was going to get spoiled. "I haven't had two meals in a day in a while."

"You know you can eat as often as you like here, right? I mean, if you're hungry go ahead into the kitchen and take what you want out of the fridge or the cupboards."

"I can't do that. I can't just act like this is mine." He was a bum, not a... a... a thief.

"I guess I'll just have to keep asking you, then."

He shrugged and ate his sandwich, the bacon still warm and salty and crisp.

Billy chuckled and kept eating his soup. "Do you like games, Tanny?"

"Games? Like Monopoly?"

"Sure. Or card games."

"Yeah. We play poker by the beach. Or dominoes."

"Oh, I like dominos. And cribbage—that one's my favorite." Billy finished his soup and began to eat his bacon sandwich.

"I've never played that one. I'm good at cards, though. I could learn." There were lots of things he was stupid about, but not cards.

"Excellent. It would be fun to play some games together."

He nodded. If Billy wanted to, sure. It was the least Tanny could do.

"What else do you like to do?" Billy sounded like he honestly wanted to know.

"I like to walk on the beach. I make things sometimes. I like to hang out outside the bars and listen to the music."

44

Normal shit.

"Oh, I like music, too!" Billy took the remote back up and pressed a few buttons until light jazz was playing. "What kinds of things to you make?"

"Just stuff. I get bored."

"So would you call that a hobby, then?"

"I don't know. Hobby's for people that need shit to do that's not their job, isn't it?" He found shit in the trash and made stuff that tourists would buy or that other street people would need.

"It's things people do for fun, yes. Some people make their hobbies their jobs." Billy gave a little shrug. "I'm just trying to figure out what you'd like to do with you time, is all."

"I make things from trash. I mean, dolls or books or jewellery. Tourists buy weird stuff. I make things for people like me, too. I made an umbrella out of sacks and hangers."

"That sounds pretty ingenious."

"It's handy. I make money." He shrugged. "One day, I'm going to own a store and sell handmade things."

"That's an excellent goal. Would you sell things for other people as well?" Billy hadn't made fun of him.

"Maybe, if they didn't suck and didn't try to steal from me. People steal a lot."

"Trust is a precious commodity always, isn't it? No matter what sphere of influence you come from."

"If you mean that everywhere there are people that suck, then yeah." Man, Billy used a lot of words to say simple things.

"There're good people everywhere, too, though."

"Yeah. I guess. I got some friends here." Mark was kind of a friend, when the man wasn't dealing.

"I hope you'll count me as a friend."

"I think you are, sort of. I mean, you don't know me

and I don't know you, but you're nice."

"We'll get to know each quite well, I hope." Billy nodded toward the bookshelves. "There are games there, if you wanted to play something."

"Do you want you? I mean, I can. I don't have anywhere to be." Tanny wouldn't go back to the bridge for a couple of days. He rubbed his jaw, the bruise there aching.

"Neither do I. Let's play dominos or cribbage."

"Okay." He smiled, nodded. "I won't play for money, though." Not without any in his pockets. If he had cash? Damn.

"No, I've got something better than money to bet with." Billy gave him a wink and stood. "You pick the game. I'll be back in a minute."

"Oh. Okay." Weirdo. Nice weirdo, though.

Billy was back a moment later with a huge bag of M&Ms. "The only thing better than playing for chocolate is playing for clothes, but as most of yours are in the dryer, I figured chocolate would be more fair."

"Okay. Okay, that's cool." He clapped a little, laughed.

Yeah.

Nice weirdo.

Chapter Seven

They spent the whole afternoon and evening playing cards for chocolates. Tanny was quick, picking up the object of cribbage no problem. Tanny certainly had more of the M&Ms than he did. When he started snacking on his, he realized maybe it was time to have some supper.

"You like pizza, Tanny?" He was not in the mood to cook; he could make something Tanny healthy tomorrow.

"Sure. Doesn't everybody?"

"No, I'm quite sure there are people who don't. Of course, they're weird." He waited a half second before continuing. "What do you like on your pizza?"

"Anything. I'm easy."

Billy chuckled and tried not to read anything into Tanny saying he was easy. He was going to have to pull himself together and not read innuendo into things Tanny said. Patience, he reminded himself. "How about a Greek pizza then? With olives and feta cheese?"

"Okay. I haven't had that before, but I'll eat anything."

Yes, he imagined that Tanny would. Even things that most people would consider inedible. "Maybe I'll get a couple of smalls and we can have some of each, try a few things out."

"What... what do you want me to do?"

"It won't take me long to order, why don't you see if I have any paper plates left? I think they're in the cupboard over the sink."

"Sure." Tanny moved quietly, careful not to touch anything. The paper plates were found, brought out, and placed on the counter.

By the time Tanny was done, he'd ordered three small pizzas: one with all cheese, one meat lovers, and one Greek.

He was going to fatten Tanny up if he had to constantly tempt the man with food. Three meals a day were the norm, not a rarity. Or at least that was the way it should be.

Tanny went to the dryer and pulled his... oh, God. They weren't clothes anymore. "Shit, I'm sorry, Tanny." On the other hand, this gave him an excuse to buy Tanny new clothes. "I'll replace them—it was my fault they're nothing but rags now."

"I." Tanny stared at his clothes, pale. "I. Um. I."

He went over and patted Tanny's arm, and then pulled the man into a hug. "It's going to be all right. I'll replace them, I promise."

Tanny went stiff, pulled away. "I. What. I mean. I. Guys don't hug."

Billy snorted. "Sure we do."

"Since when?"

"I hug my friends all the time." Whether or not they were gay or he was interested in them.

"Yeah? Things can be weird in California."

"Yes, I'm sure that's it." He chuckled and went and found Tanny a T-shirt and sweatshirt from the folded laundry in the basket, waiting to be put away. "Here, these might work better than the robe. If you give me your size, I'll go out first thing in the morning and get you something to wear that actually fits."

"We can stop at the Goodwill. They have three-dollar T-shirts and seven-dollar jeans."

"That fit?"

"I don't know. I mean, T-shirts are T-shirts."

"I'll just buy you something at Target." Properly fitting clothes would help Tanny in the whole looking for work thing, and he'd feel better knowing Tanny had them should Tanny decide to take off again.

"That's nice of you... Are you sure you don't want something? I mean, in return."

"Sure I do. I want you to get clean. To find a job doing something you love that still puts food on your table and a roof over your head." He wanted plenty, but first he wanted for Tanny to get off the street and off the drugs.

"Maybe one day. Maybe. I come from a long line of losers."

"Stop that. Stop putting yourself down."

"It's not putting myself down when it's true."

"Then you be the one who stops the trend. You be the one who isn't a loser. You have it in you, Tanny." He was going to beat Montana's ass long before it was time if the man insisted on considering himself a loser.

"Jesus, are you always so goddamn... uh... self-help guru-y?"

"Nope." He went to the fridge and pulled out some soft drinks, put them on the table.

"Uh. Good?"

Poor Montana—the man looked completely out of his element. He patted Montana's shoulder. "You'll get used to me in time."

"You think you'll want to be friends after I'm back on the street? It's bad for a guy's rep, you know. Your other friends will be mad."

"I'd prefer you weren't back on the street." He'd keep saying it until it sank in, until Tanny started considering not living on the street as an end result.

"Well, I don't have a place to stay. I mean, you've been good to me, but..."

"I want you to stay here, Tanny. And when you have a job, you can start to pay me room and board. I'm not offering charity—I'm offering a leg up."

Those black-black eyes met his, bright as a bird's. "Why?"

"I told you before that I had help when I needed it, people who gave me the same leg up I'm offering you. And I am interested in having a relationship with you, but I'm not going to do it while your choices are me or the street. You get back on your feet and I'll make my move." He'd already told Tanny that, but he wasn't sure the man even remembered.

"Don't bullshit me. You don't know me."

"I'm not fucking bullshitting you!" That made him mad, that Tanny thought he was lying. "You think I'm going to wait until you go to sleep in the guest bedroom and then jump you? If I'd wanted to hurt you I could have done it already a hundred times over."

"Then why haven't you? I'm a fucking loser! There's a thousand people out there—a hundred thousand that need you and are good people!"

"Because you're the one who called to me. You're the one who asked me for change that day. I believe in following where the universe leads me and right now it's leading me to you." Now Tanny would no doubt believe he was a whackadoodle.

"Your friend told you I couldn't be saved."

"He didn't see what I see." He loved Oliver dearly, but they were not the same at all.

"I can't... I can't think about this. I haven't had my

stuff. I just don't think I can deal."

"That's why I keep saying I want you to get clean, get yourself back on your feet before, well before anything else. This is a safe, warm place, Tanny. I'm not going to hurt you or ask for favors. You can pull your weight helping keep the place clean, helping me with the renovations and stuff. And once you're feeling better you can find work and stuff."

"I don't know how to deal with you."

"Just take me as I am?"

"You're asking me to just turn away from everything I know about people."

"I'm asking you to trust me because I haven't been anything but good to you. Aside from washing your clothes into rags."

Tanny's mouth opened and closed and opened. "I... You got lots to lose."

"You mean my stuff? It's all replaceable."

"Your stuff. Your rep."

"I'm not worried about either." His friends wouldn't dump him if this turned out to be a stupid mistake.

"Okay?" Montana chewed his bottom lip, nodded.

"Okay." The bell rang. "That's our pizza."

"Okay. I'll stay in here."

"Sure." He paid for the pizzas and brought them back into the kitchen. "I hope you're hungry."

Tanny was standing by the window, staring, fingers still moving over his bald head. He was stunning, and Billy stopped for a moment, just staring.

"What? What? Am I hideous?" Tanny asked.

He had to clear his throat. "No, just the opposite."

"What's the opposite of hideous?"

"I was thinking stunning. You have an amazing silhouette."

"Don't be silly." Look at that grin.

"I can be silly, but I'm not being silly about this." He put the pizzas on the table. "Come on and eat and I'll try not to be distracted by how striking you are."

"Right. Right. God, it smells good."

"It does, doesn't it?" He grinned and grabbed one of the plates. Opening the top box, he helped himself to a piece of extra cheesy pizza. Tanny took a piece of the same, sat at the table and bent to it. Billy had a million questions about Tanny's life, but he figured he'd better keep his mouth shut for tonight—Tanny had agreed to stay for a while; one battle at a time.

Montana started dozing after his second piece of pizza, nodding at the table. Poor man.

Billy put away the extra pizza and quietly did the dishes while Tanny slept. It would likely be awhile before Montana had a 'normal' schedule. He wondered if he should encourage Tanny to attend meetings or something. He knew he didn't want Tanny to leave for the streets. Maybe Tanny wouldn't stay here, but the man needed something besides the streets. If he had to, he'd talk to Oliver, find out who was looking for a roommate.

In the meantime, he had to encourage Tanny to eat, sleep and stay off the drugs.

He hoped his heart wasn't leading him completely astray.

At this point, though, he figured it was already too late if it was.

Chapter Eight

He'd tried.
He had.
Billy was dear and fun and clever and now Tanny had two pairs of jeans and briefs. T-shirts. Socks. It was amazing.

But.

Montana sat in the window box, rocking himself, looking down into the street. Mark was out there, somewhere, with a fix. Just waiting for him.

Maybe worrying.

If not worrying, at least curious.

The front door opened and Billy came in, laptop bag in one hand, mail in the other. "Hey, Tanny."

"I. Hey. I." Damn. He should have gone. He couldn't be nice and go now.

"How's your afternoon been?" Billy had gone just before lunch for a meeting with an editor or something.

"Long. I. I have to. I'm sorry, but. I got stuff to do." He'd made ten little toy airplanes out of the soda cans in Billy's trash. They'd go to the tourists for five apiece.

Billy frowned. "What kind of stuff?"

"I got some stuff to sell. I need... I need to see a guy."

"Even I know that translates to buying drugs. How about we go sell your stuff together and then we find you someone to talk to about the drugs, or a meeting or something?"

"I'm not going to some fucking meeting." Still, the guy didn't even suggest that he'd stolen anything. That meant something. "You wanna see what I made?"

Nodding immediately, Billy smiled. "I do."

"I made little planes. You can hang them outside." They took two cans each, but they were cute. He used one can for the plane body, the second for the wings and propeller. "If I had toothpicks and bottle caps I could make wheels."

"Oh, look at that. How clever!" Billy examined one of the planes from every angle. "Maybe with some of the money you get from these you can buy toothpicks and bottle caps. For the next batch."

"I... I know you don't get it, but the pills cost. There won't be any left, and I can't wait much longer."

"We agreed, no more pills, Tanny."

"I don't. I can't. I'm sorry, man. I have to." He didn't have a choice. He needed them.

"No, you don't." Billy grabbed his arms and shook him slightly. "I'll help you, but no more drugs."

"I have to. I'm sorry. I am, but I can't do without." No one who wasn't hooked could understand.

"Tell me what you need to help you. Because you *can*. Others have."

"I'm not macho. I need them." He was going to get snarly.

"It's got nothing to do with being macho. It's about strength. And the man who survived what you survived can kick the habit."

"No, I can't." He started gathering up the planes.

"I don't believe that."

"You don't have to." His hands were shaking, now.

Billy grabbed his hands and pulled him back to the

window seat, sitting across from him. "I'm right here. I'm not going anywhere."

"But I am. You don't understand. It's waiting for me."

"You don't need it." A hard note had crept into Billy's voice.

"I do too." He was getting pissed off.

"No, you don't!"

"This isn't going to get anywhere if you just keep yelling at me!"

"I'm not yelling. I'm being firm."

"So am I." He wanted the Reds.

"I can't let you, Tanny. You'll be happy you pushed through this later on."

"How do you know? How do you know that the high isn't the best fucking thing ever? That flying isn't better than anything?"

"Because I know another kind of flying, Tanny. Another way to get higher than even the drugs can get you." Billy looked like he believed it, too.

Of course, that intrigued him. What if there was something better out there? "What? What's better? Are you taking something designer?"

"No, I'm not talking about anything you take."

"You're not making any sense. I've got to go do this. I... It's been days. Almost a week."

"So don't waste that week by giving in now."

He was going to scream in pure frustration. "You don't understand."

"No, I don't. So explain it. Make me understand." Billy was still holding his hands, keeping him right there.

"It's like... it's like racing again, you go and go and you can't breathe, you can't stop, there's nothing you can do but give in to it, go and go and go." His cheeks flushed, he could feel himself getting hot.

"I know a few things like that. Like the speed, like the drugs, but an all-natural high."

"I haven't found anything like that." He tugged a little at Billy's hands.

"But I have." Billy's hands tightened on his, not hurting, but not letting go.

"I... Let go of me."

"No. I want you to stay right here with me. I'm not letting you go back out on the streets."

"You can't stop me." He couldn't help himself from moving closer.

"I can help you, though. Whatever you need, Tanny. I'll hold you or run the shower for you, or lock you in your room. Whatever. Just tell me how I can help."

"I need it. I itch. My head hurts. I have bugs." He was going to keep fighting until Billy understood.

"Show me what itches and I'll help you scratch. I have aspirin for your pain and we got rid of your bugs when we shaved your head, Tanny." Billy seemed to have an answer for everything.

He held out his arms, showed the deep, red scratches that were almost open wounds.

"Oh, Tanny." Billy stood, drawing him up. "Come on."

"Where are we going?" He followed, though.

"Bathroom." Once there, Billy pulled down a first aid kit and took out the gauze. "We're going to cover that, so when you scratch, it doesn't tear your skin."

He watched, just a little fascinated. "I don't know how to handle you."

Billy laughed softly. "I can live with that."

"I'm scared."

The laughter faded, Billy nodding. "Okay. That's all right. You can hold on to me."

"It's not all right. The answer's out there on the street."

"No, the answer is right here." Billy pressed a hand against Tanny's heart. "Here."

"Don't bullshit me! I don't believe in all that! I only believe in what I know, what I can see. You're a good guy, Billy, a good-good guy, and I'm a fuckup."

"A fuck up who's spend nearly a week not fucking up. Come on, Tanny. You might not believe in it, but I've seen your back. I've seen how terrible it must have been and you made it through that. Don't give up on yourself now."

"Yeah. I lived through it, and everybody hated me." Katy had died and everyone—everyone from his mom to his aunts to the cops to the neighbors—had said it should have been him.

"I'm not going to hate you, Montana. I promise you that." Billy began to wrap the gauze around his arms. "This is a new place. You have a chance for a new start. Take it, Tanny."

"You might." His hands opened and closed, over and over.

"I won't." Billy's hand slid over his head. "Tell me what else you need, what I can do for you?"

"I don't know. I don't know what to do." He was lost.

Billy's arms wrapped around him, pulling him up against the solid, square body. "Then we'll just stand here as long as we need to."

"I can't... I don't know how... I..." He couldn't decide whether to fight or give in.

"Shh. Shh." Billy held onto him; he could feel the strength in Billy's muscles.

"I don't know what to do..." He couldn't breathe.

"Come on. Let's sit in your window seat and we can watch the world go by. Be nice and warm and safe."

"I. Okay? Okay?" He needed some help.

"Okay." Billy wrapped an arm around his middle and led him into the living room, over to the window seat. Sitting, Billy drew him down and close.

"Why are you smiling?"

"Because you're staying. You've decided to trust me."

"Is it that cool?" He didn't understand Billy, not at all.

"It is. It totally is."

"Totally." He chuckled. "Are you sure you don't want to go... meet my friend Mark?"

"I'm very sure I don't want to do that. I'm happy just getting to know you better."

"There's nothing exciting about me." He was bald, sad, skinny. Boring.

"Sure there is. Your striking looks, your strength, the fact that you survived something so terrible. I see so much potential in you."

"You're a little crazy." He leaned against Billy, eyes closing.

"Maybe a little." Billy rubbed his arm soothingly.

That made him chuckle, and he leaned harder. "My head hurts."

"Would you like something for it? I've got Tylenol and aspirin. We'll make this as easy as we can."

"I want a Red, but Tylenol would be good, I guess."

Billy patted his arm. "I'll be right back, then."

He sat there, looking out, willing himself not to move, not to get up and run. Billy came back a moment later with a glass of water and two little white pills. He was so tense, he couldn't even reach out for the pills.

"Open up," Billy held the pills up to his lips.

He did, his jaw creaking. "I need to go out."

"We can go for a walk." The pills were placed on his tongue, the water pressed to his lips. He drank deep, grasping the hope that he might find a hit.

Billy put the glass on the coffee table when he was done and then came back, sitting with him again. "You want to just sit or you want to go for that walk?"

"I want to go out. My friends will be worried."

"Can you go out and see them and not get high?"

"No." He had no problem being honest. Lying was for pussies.

"Then we can go for a walk around here, but not down at the beach or anywhere else you used to hang out."

"Don't you like the beach?"

"I do. A lot. But if the temptation's going to be too much, then we shouldn't go right now."

"Okay. I. Okay." He didn't quite know where to look, what to do.

"Come here." Billy pulled him close again and held him.

"This isn't natural." It was warm, though.

"It's as natural as breathing, Tanny."

"I don't know about that... " He pressed closer, snuggling in. He'd never been held like this. It was... weirdly addictive. Billy relaxed against the wall, holding him easily. His eyes closed, his worried mind skittering from thing to thing to thing to... He liked this, being warm.

Billy began to hum, the sound a deep baritone. It kind of rumbled from Billy's chest to his own skin. He was sinking, entire body relaxing, melting. Billy didn't say anything, just held him like he could do this forever. Eventually, he dozed off, quiet and happy and right there. At least for right now.

Chapter Nine

Billy held Tanny most of the afternoon and into the evening. Then he made grilled cheese sandwiches and more tomato soup; it was his own favorite comfort food. After they ate, he sent Tanny to take a shower, hoping it would help ease the man's need.

He did the dishes and made coffee, set out a couple of slices of cake and went to rescue Tanny from becoming a prune. He could hear the water running, hear Tanny singing idly, the tune random and restless.

He knocked on the door and went in. "Tanny? How're you doing?"

"I'm..." Tanny turned a little, showing him the horribly, violently scarred back. He wanted to touch it. Lick it. Learn it. "Good, thanks."

He stared, trying not to will his prick not to get hard. "Good to hear. I have cake and coffee when you're done in here."

"Oh, okay. I was soaking." Tanny reached for a towel, exposing a bare chest, a nearly bare cock that was long, thin. Tempting.

Billy swallowed and turned away, forcing himself to leave. He went back into the kitchen and took a few deep breaths.

He heard the slap of Tanny's feet on the floor. "You

okay, man?"

"Me? Fine. I'm just fine." He took another breath and turned to smile. He pointed at the table. "Cake and coffee for two."

"You spoil me. It smells good."

"Something tells me you're due a little spoiling. It's mocha cream. My favorite."

"Mocha cream? Wow. My favorite is apple crisp."

"Oh, I can get into that, too. I'm not fond of apple pie, but make it a crisp and add some ice cream and I'm there." He waited until Tanny sat and then he poured out the coffee and sat, too.

"Thank you for not freaking out with me."

"That's a rule here, you know. Only one person is allowed to freak out at a time."

Montana blinked up at him, then started laughing, the sound rich and honest and oddly beautiful. He found himself smiling at Tanny, enjoying the joyous sound. There needed to be more of that in his life. In Tanny's too, he suspected.

The laughter died down and they settled in to dessert, Tanny's fuzzy head bent over the coffee. His fingers itched to reach out and touch; he wanted to feel the scratchiness of the short hairs tickle his palm.

Big black eyes met his. "You okay?"

"I'm good." And that was twice in the last few minutes Tanny had asked him that. He needed to get himself under control. There would be no pressure on Tanny from him. Not until Tanny could handle it. Of course, there was a tiny voice inside him noticing that, if Montana was this sensitive to his moods now, as a sub, the man would be amazing. It had him smiling more naturally at Tanny. "How's the cake?"

"It's good. It's not as sweet as some. I like that." In one of those quick changes he was getting used to, Tanny asked. "Do you dance?"

"Not really. Sort of, maybe." He chuckled and thought about it a moment. "It depends on what you mean by dance, I guess."

"You know, get out on the floor and shake it. I love that—with the lights and the crowds and all."

"Oh, I can do that. I don't do anything fancy, though. Just the shaking."

Tanny chuckled. "Yeah, well. No one does, not really."

"Oh, some of the members at the Ham—the club I belong to are quite accomplished at waltzing and doing that slinky Latin stuff."

"Oh, I could never do that. I just jerk and wiggle."

Now didn't that give him a happy picture to imagine? His prick certainly thought so. "I'd like to see that."

Tanny chuckled. "We'll have to go out sometime."

"I'd like that. I know a little place…" Somewhere that Tanny would be safe. When Tanny was more ready to be introduced to the lifestyle.

"Yeah? Where do you party? I like Trashcan Alley." God, that was a dive—cheap booze and back alley blowjobs.

"I like the Rainbow Bar and Grill. I also belong to a private club."

"Well, I wouldn't be in a club that would take me."

This constant negativity had to stop. "I want you to stop that."

"Stop what? Eating? You said I could have a piece."

"I wasn't talking about the eating—I was talking about the putting yourself down." It wasn't helping Tanny at all.

"What?" Tanny looked completely confused.

"Saying things like how you're a loser or not good enough or how you wouldn't go to a club that would let you in, either. I want you to stop talking about yourself like that."

"People in hell want ice water." The words were bitter and ugly, and Tanny looked surprised at himself.

He kept his face impassive. "We're not in hell, Tanny. And you can have ice water any time you want it."

"I... I don't know how to respond to that."

"Tell me you'll try not to run yourself down so much. And I'll point it out every time you do." He'd make it so Tanny hated hearing him point it out so much that he'd stop.

"I'm a bum. What am I supposed to do, be proud?"

"See? That's what I'm talking about. Stop that." He shook his head. This, he suspected was going to be as hard as kicking the drugs. "You are not a bum."

"I am too."

"Are not."

"Am too." Those black eyes twinkled.

He chuckled, shook his head. "Not infinity."

"Not infinity, squared." Tanny blinked. "Wait."

Billy laughed. "Oh, no! No waiting. You just agreed with me."

"I didn't mean to!" Tanny was chuckling, shoulders shaking with the sound.

"I'd like to think maybe some part of you did." He reached out and squeezed Tanny's hand.

"I wish I could understand why you're good to me, so I could keep doing it."

"I can't see entirely past your armor, but what I can see makes me want to see more."

"Armor? I don't even have hair. I have... fuzz."

"That's a great word." He reached out and ran his hand over Tanny's head. He did it without even thinking about it. Oh. Soft. Oh, fuck. That could be addictive.

He drew his hand back before he gave away just how

much he enjoyed touching it. "It's great fuzz, too."

"It'll grow, huh?" Tanny stood, going to pour them both another cup of coffee.

"It will. Hell, it's already grown in quite a bit from when we shaved it." He wondered if it would still be as soft as it grew longer.

"Yeah. No bugs yet."

"You keep it clean and there won't be. There's this newfangled invention that can help with that called shampoo."

"Fuck off, man. I know that. There ain't showers in the places I hang."

"I was just teasing," Billy pointed out softly.

"Yeah. I know. I'm sorry. I just... I keep waiting for the other shoe to drop, and I know you're going to say there isn't another shoe, but there is, there always is." Tanny started fluttering some, pacing, eyes on the door.

"Have you ever considered that the other shoe might be something good?" He got up and went to the little radio he kept in the kitchen. Maybe some music would distract Tanny.

"Huh? No. It's never good, is it? I mean..." Tanny followed him, staring, touching him, pulling on his own clothes.

He found some dance music and turned it up. "You want to dance, Tanny?"

"I. What? Here? Now?"

"Why not?"

"Because we're in a kitchen?" Tanny was moving to the rhythm, though, hips swaying.

"All that matters is the music and shaking it, right?" Billy wasn't the most graceful dancer, but he could 'shake it', so he did. He figured if Tanny were distracted and moving with a purpose, it would make things easier. Of course, Tanny stepped closer, rubbed against him, then stepped back, muscles working.

He swallowed and told himself they were just dancing, and that's what you did when you danced. He tried not to watch Tanny too much, but his eyes were drawn to the lovely body over and over. Tanny moved beautifully, completely into the music, eyes closed, hips rolling. Billy closed his own eyes and thought about ice down his pants to keep his arousal down.

The music slowed and Tanny stepped closer, bringing their bodies together. His arm slipped automatically around Tanny's waist. He could smell Tanny, the clean, male scent of him.

"Mmm." Oh, damn. That was... Pure temptation.

He forced himself to put a little space between them and angled his hips away from Tanny. He could lose himself so easily in this and rush Tanny long before the man was ready to make any decisions at all, let alone one like what Billy was going to ask.

"Sorry." Tanny stepped away, eyes closed as the man lost himself in his own world.

"It's fine. Everything's fine." And if his voice was a little husky, he certainly wasn't going to point it out.

Tanny nodded, turned from him a bit, moving slower. He could do this all night; it was a good place to be. He was fascinated by the way Tanny moved, and he could see those scars moving, where the T-shirt exposed them at Tanny's nape.

He could imagine making love with Tanny and watching the scars move and writhe.

"So, you're queer, right?"

He blinked, focusing back on Tanny's face. "Yes. I am."

"Cool. So, what kinda guy do you like?"

Well, this was an... unexpected turn of conversation. "I don't know if I have a type, exactly. What about you?"

Because saying 'you' was no doubt going to send Tanny back out into the streets.

"I don't really do long-term stuff, but I like guys."

He was going to change that if he could. The long-term part, not the liking guys part. "You have a type?" The little voice inside his head told him he was playing with fire.

"I like... I like strong guys, you know. Ones that know what they want."

Damn, it was almost too good to be true. Billy just nodded. "I know what you mean."

"You too? It's sort of an addiction, huh? That strength."

"Strength in any form is addictive."

"Yeah. I've got a serious addictive bone, you know " Tanny leaned against the counter, watching him.

Billy chuckled. "I would have guessed you did. Pills, speed. Hot men." Me.

"Booze, for a while. I switched to the speed."

"And now you're switching to nothing."

"No. No, I have to have something to jones on." Tanny stretched, belly rippling.

Jesus Christ, this was pure torture. "I might have an idea or two for that."

The smile he got was wry, bittersweet. "I bet I've done wilder things than you can imagine."

"I've got quite a vivid imagination."

"I've had a crazy life."

"I live a bit of a crazy lifestyle." He gave Tanny a grin. "Why don't you try me?"

"I lived on the ocean for eighteen months, making stuff out of trash." Tanny grinned at him, daring him to play.

"I ate burnt toast for breakfast for three years straight starting when I was twelve." He'd managed to convince himself if he ate Mrs. Daisy's burned toast she wouldn't send him away like the other foster parents he'd had.

"Why?" Tanny hopped up on the kitchen counter. "I ate a cockroach on a dare."

"Just the one?" He laughed, starting to enjoy this game. "She was the best in a long parade of bad mothers. I've had barbeque crickets at a dinner party once."

"On purpose? My mother hates me. I don't blame her. I had an orgasm racing a bike once."

"Yes, on purpose—believe it or not, they were the most edible choice at the table. My mother gave me up when I was two. I don't think she hated me; I think she was too high to care. And really? On purpose?" He was having a ball. Honestly.

Tanny shook his head. "Well, I mean, yes really. Not on purpose. It just happened. Is that why you're anti-drugs?"

"It's one of the reasons. I've seen them ruin a lot of people's lives."

"They haven't ruined mine." Tanny's heels banged on the cabinet door.

"No? You don't think you could have a better life without them?"

"No. They make..." Tanny's lips went tight. "It doesn't matter. Whose turn is it?"

He could imagine how that sentence would have been finished, and he was determined to prove Tanny wrong, to prove that his life could be better without the drugs. "Yours, I think."

"I, uh, I came to California to see the ocean. When I got here, I jumped in with all my clothes on."

Billy laughed. "I hope it was a warmer day than today!"

"No! It was raining and so cold! I froze my nuts off."

"And was it worth it?"

"Yeah. Yeah, it was. I was so fucked up and so sad, and I needed something huge." Tanny nodded at him, grinning ear to ear.

"Cool."

Just look at that smile, the pleasure in those dark eyes.

"So?" Tanny reached over, poked him. "Your turn."

"Hmm... something shocking..." He might never have a better opportunity to slip it in. "I'm into BDSM."

"Like beat me, whip me? Really? Dude."

"It's a little more complicated than that, but essentially, yes." He couldn't tell if Tanny was shocked, amused, repulsed, or interested.

"Huh. You pay people to hit you? I've met men who were into that. It's an expensive hobby."

Billy chuckled and shook his head. "No money changes hands, and I'm the one who does the hitting. And like I said, it's more involved than that."

Tanny hadn't run screaming into the night yet. He was taking that as a minor victory.

"No money? No shit. Huh." Tanny grinned. "I stole an apple from the grocery store every day for eight months without getting caught."

"The same store?"

"Yeah. I was quick."

"You sure the owner wasn't just being nice?" That was a lot of days to steal something and never get caught.

Tanny nodded. "Pretty sure. She sure was pissed when she caught me. She hit me with a stick."

"Oh, now, that's only fun if it's consensual on both sides." He gave Tanny a wink.

"I don't know, man. I think that's a little mean, to hit on someone."

"It's not all about the hitting. Hell, many a couple never goes in for that side." He gave Tanny a nod, ready to change the subject for the moment. "I believe it's your turn, and you haven't shocked me yet."

"I killed my sister."

Billy's eyes went wide, and he couldn't stop his gasp. "You're making that up."

"No." Tanny jumped back off the counter and walked away.

Billy headed after him. "You can't just throw that out there and not explain." He couldn't believe Tanny had done something like that deliberately.

"What's there to explain?" Tanny headed to the window seat, curling into himself.

He went and automatically wrapped himself around Tanny, seeking to comfort. "What happened?"

"She wanted to ride with me. We were on my bike and... I hit a slick spot. I landed on my back. She landed on her head. I don't want to talk about it."

"Oh, God, Tanny. I'm so sorry." Now it all made sense, the way Tanny said everyone hated him. He suspected no one hated Tanny for it more than Tanny himself. He held Tanny tight.

"Yeah. I'm okay, huh? I lived."

"Yeah. You did."

Only now Tanny was doing his level best to throw his life away. Or at least he had been.

Billy didn't say anything else, he just held on. It was all he could do for now.

Chapter Ten

The hallway looked good—a pale, pale green that caught the light from the big bay window. Tanny pulled the painter's tape down off the baseboards and ceilings and pulled up the floor drape before carrying everything back downstairs to the storage shed that was Billy's to use.

There was a rich, deep blue paint for Billy's room—two cans, to account for the turret—and dove gray for the guest room. After he was done with those, he'd start working on the kitchen. That was going to be a lemony yellow.

When he returned upstairs, he found Billy in the kitchen, tapping away at his laptop and muttering to himself. The fading sun glinted off his dark hair, making it shine. Billy was a good-looking man, broad-shouldered and solid-chested. Too bad the man wasn't interested in him. Well, Tanny knew Billy was interested in that good Samaritan, white knight sort of way, just not in that oh, fuck me now way.

He crept around the table, staying quiet so as not to disturb, and headed for the guest bath to wash up.

Billy looked up before he made it out into the hall. "Tanny! Hey. How's it going?"

"Hey. Good. Hall's done and cleaned up. Didn't mean

to bother you."

"You didn't. I was looking for the distraction." Billy smiled, closing his laptop. "Are you hungry? Would you like to go for a bit of a walk with me and then out to dinner?"

"I... Sure. I could. I mean, I haven't been out to sell anything yet..." He didn't know how this worked.

"How about I pay for dinner? After all, you've been working your tail off painting my house."

"I... How about you have dinner, and I'll keep you company? I'm not hungry, but I could so hang out." See him. See him be cool.

Billy snorted and started him down. "Of course you're hungry. I'm not giving you cash for the work you do, not yet, so I think this would be a good start toward paying you in kind for what I owe you."

"You sure? I..." He grinned. "I'll pay you back."
Someday.

"I know you will. And yes, I'm sure. Go on and get cleaned up; I want to change my shirt. Can you be ready in ten minutes?"

"Sure." He could take a quick shower. He knew how.

"Excellent. I'll meet you by the front door in ten." Billy gave his shoulder a squeeze.

"Sure." He hurried off, bouncing a little. Two weeks. He hadn't been out in two weeks.

Billy was waiting for him when he arrived at the front door, looking fucking hot in tight black jeans and a red button-down shirt. There was a smile all for him when Billy saw him, too.

"Wow." He grinned at Billy. "Look at you! You'll get laid tonight, man."

Billy chuckled. "I'm just looking to have a good time with you. And you clean up very nicely yourself."

"Right." He rubbed his stubbly head. "I'm a charmer."

"You've charmed me." Billy smiled, eyes warm, and then opened the door and motioned for him to go ahead.

"Thanks." He headed out, smiling up into the sun.

Billy wandered along next to him, guiding them toward one of the touristy parts of town. "There's a little store along Luna Avenue called Rainbow Artists; have you heard of it?"

"No. No, nobody in that part of town wants somebody like me there. The cops get snarly." Shit, hanging out on that side got you popped in jail overnight for loitering.

"They don't want drug addicts, no, but that's not you anymore." Billy chuckled, hand landing in the small of his back. "I promise the cops won't arrest you."

"They might." He grinned over, winked. "So, what's this rainbow artist thing?"

"It's a collective of gay artisans, artists, craftsmen. They have a studio-slash-storefront where they work, sell their goods. None of them could afford the place on their own, but all together..."

"Oh, that's cool. It's a way to make things work." They headed down the street, walking slowly. "Do you shop there a lot?"

"I always go there first if I'm looking for something for the house or a gift. They've got a wide range of things. Your airplanes would fit right in..."

"What? No. I make trash for tourists. That's arty shit." He was a bum that made crap.

Billy made a little growly noise that was really kind of sexy. "You might use trash to make your things, but that is art. There's even a name for it—found art. You ask the people at the Rainbow."

"No. No, that's cool." No fucking way was he going to embarrass himself in front of arty-types.

There was that growl again, low, almost subvocal.

Tanny just ignored it. Billy had some weird hang-ups.

They turned onto Luna, the lights starting to come on in the store fronts, making it merry and bright.

"It's pretty, huh?" He wrapped his arms around his belly, warming himself up.

"It is." Billy steered them into a menswear store a half a block down. "I wanted to go in here."

"Sure." He was easy and he liked to look. "I'm yours. I mean, whatever you want." God, he was in a dorky mood.

Billy chuckled and they went in. "Oh, look at the coats. These are nice."

"Mmmhmm." He nodded, looking idly. There were nice jackets, warm-looking sweaters.

"This would look great on you." Billy pointed to a rack of full-length dusters.

"You think? I'm short, and they're expensive. You ought to try on the blue sweater. It's soft and warm and nice." He'd buy a new coat from Goodwill after he got a job.

"Look, dinner won't cover what I owe you for what you've painted so far. Let me buy you a nice coat—it doesn't have to be that one—and we'll be even."

"What? No. No, Billy. That's too much. You buy yourself something. I'm fine."

"It would make me feel better to have you paint the rest of the house, if I knew you'd accepted full recompense for the job you did with the hall. Please." Billy's shoulders had a stubborn set to them.

"Billy, this stuff is expensive. You'd pay me what? Twenty bucks to paint the hall?" He couldn't do that.

"I'd pay you a lot more than twenty bucks. Besides, I'm not paying you in actual cash so it's not an exact exchange."

"Billy." He shook his head. "Maybe later, huh? I owe

you a lot. People will think badly of you." He was a bum, not a... a... mooch.

"A sweater, then. You'll be cold on our way home from supper." Man, Billy didn't just look stubborn.

"I... if there's one on sale." He could compromise.

Billy's lips pursed, but he nodded. "Yeah, okay."

"Okay. Let's look at the clearance."

They went over to the clearance racks, Billy going through the jackets and sweaters there. "Some of these are nice. Which ones do you like?"

"I like soft ones. They're good for sleeping in, you know?"

"I like the comforter better." Billy gave him a wink.

"Mmm. The comforter on the guest bed is great."

"Mine's pretty good, too." Billy pulled down a forest green sweater. "You want to try this one on?"

"Sure." He tugged it on over his T-shirt, modeled it. "How's it look?"

"It looks good. Does it feel as nice as the comforter?"

"Nicer." He ran his heads down his belly.

"It looks better on you, too." There was warmth in Billy's eyes, admiration.

"You've never seen me in the comforter."

"True. I have a good imagination, though."

"Right. Like you imagine my skinny ass." He chuckled, swatted Billy's arm before he tugged the sweater off.

He thought he heard Billy muttering, but by the time he had the sweater right off, Billy was going through a rack of leather pilot jackets.

"Oh, those look great. You should get one. Leather jackets always smell so good."

"They do, don't they?" Billy didn't pick one out, though. Instead, he came back and nodded at the sweater. "Is that the one you'd like, then?"

He checked the tag. It was on clearance for twenty

four dollars. "Yes, please."

"Good. It looked wonderful on you." Billy took it from him and headed to the cashier. "Did you want to wear it now?"

"Yeah, it'll be nice with the wind. Thank you, man. I appreciate it. I'll pay you back."

"I thought we'd agreed this was in exchange for you painting the hall?" Billy handed a credit card over to the cashier and asked her to remove the tags.

"Well, you feed me." The sweater was handed to him and he tugged it on. Oh, warm. Soft. Sensual. He liked it.

"I think we should just wipe the slate clean, yeah? We can work out some exchange for room and board and your painting as of tomorrow." Billy smiled and held the door open for him as they went back out onto the street. "It's not like I need to get all that much more to feed you as well as myself."

"My hero." He bounced a little, eyes on the lights, on all the people.

Billy chuckled, pointing out gag T-shirts in one window and the display in the bookstore, as well as a couple holding hands, both men with bright red hair.

"I should bleach my hair and dye it... I bet I'd look neat as a blond. Maybe with green."

"That would certainly look... startling."

"Startling is cool. Dangerous, you know?" He liked that idea. "In that, don't fuck with me, I'm scary way."

"I, for one, would love to see your hair long, only how it looks naturally, not all matted and dreaded."

"It's straight and black, I bet." He'd never had it so long as when Billy cut it.

"Yeah, I imagine you're right." Billy chuckled and stopped suddenly. "Here's the Rainbow Artists."

"Yeah?" He looked in, curious and jealous all at

once. There were beautiful pieces in there—rainbows and statues, paintings and cloth and shit. Wow.

"Come on, let's go in. We can talk to the artists. My friend Margaret wanted to meet you."

"I... I don't think so." What was he going to say? *Hey, I'm Billy's pet project. I make shit out of trash. Please be nice to me, because I'm a junkie trying to get clean.*

"They heard about the things you make and wanted to meet you, Tanny. Come on, don't be shy."

Oh, God. "I'm not shy. I don't belong in there."

"I would think the artists themselves would be the judge of that. And they asked to see you." Billy took his arm and opened the door, urging him to go inside.

He went in, head down for a few steps before he lifted his chin. He wasn't going to apologize for being a fucking loser. Billy's hand had somehow come to rest at the small of his back; he could feel its warmth through his T-shirt and the new sweater. It felt surprisingly good, sort of calming.

A woman sitting near the back at a table covered in little bits of glass smiled at them. "Bill!" She chuckled and stood, hurrying toward them, her auburn curls bouncing around her face.

He took a step back. He wasn't an artist.

Billy gave her a hug. "Helena, how nice to see you. And this," Billy turned to him, "is Tanny. He's the young man who made the airplane I showed you."

"Oh! That was so clever. It's so good to meet you." She came toward him like she was going to give him a hug as well.

He stepped back, held out one hand. "Hey."

She shook his hand, the grip firm, her fingers dry and rough with cuts and calluses. "Welcome to Rainbow Artists."

"Thanks. It's nice." Jesus, this was weird.

"So, Billy tells me you do more than just the airplanes?" She looked genuinely interested.

"I just make stuff from junk to sell to tourists. Nothing that's art or nothing."

"Are you kidding? Found art is huge right now. People love that it's earth-friendly, and they love seeing things they use every day worked into something new, something fun."

Billy was nodding.

He didn't know what to say, what to do. What to think. He was a loser. A fucking loser.

"Would you be interested in letting us sell some for you on consignment?" Helena gave him a gentle smile, her eyes bright. "You'd get thirty percent of anything of yours we sold. We'd keep the rest, cost of shelf space and expenses and all. And if they sell well, we can discuss bringing you into the collective. There's room at the back to work, we all help out with manning the place, so to speak. Well, that's all details and would depend on whether or not your stuff sells." She laughed. "I'm always getting ahead of myself."

"I. I. You want my ugly planes?" This was a favor for Billy. He knew it was.

"The one I saw wasn't ugly. And they sell, right?"

"I sold them to tourists on the beach. Five bucks each. Ten for the fancy ones."

"So, we'll put them out for a little more than that, because we each want good money, right? Let's say a two-week trial?" She patted his arm. "Don't look so worried, honey, if they don't sell, we'll give them back to you and won't ask for more. We're here to help each other make money."

"Okay. I mean, I guess so. You've seen them, right?"

"Yes, Billy brought us one. We all thought it was great and would sell well. Bring in what you can by, say,

Monday? If you do more than just the planes, we find that variety sells well." She chuckled. "We've found people like buying more than one thing."

"Monday. Right. Okay." Maybe he'd sell one. Maybe. Or not. "Thank you."

"Oh, good." She clapped her hands, but anything else she might have said was interrupted by someone coming in. "I gotta go, but I'll see you on Monday."

Billy nodded as she waved while hurrying over to greet the paying customers. "Did you want to look around or head to the restaurant?"

"Let's go." He was unnerved. Aggravated.

"Sure." Billy led him out and pointed to a place called The Purple Spotted Dick. "I thought it would be fun to eat there. They've actually got fairly good food and the name's good fun."

"Cool." He was a poser. He didn't belong here.

He and Billy went into the restaurant. It was about half full, everyone casually dressed. It smelled really good, actually. He saw three or four people he knew—two waiters, one guy that was into prostitutes, another guy that bought meth... Tanny was careful not to make eye contact, just in case.

"So what do you feel like?" Billy asked him, passing over the menu.

"What are you going to have?" There was a lot of stuff. Lots. He saw the burger, and he settled on that. It would be cheap, simple, and he knew about burgers.

"I think the battered fish and fries. They're good here."

"Yeah? I used to like fish sticks..."

"Only used to?"

"I haven't had them since I was a kid."

"No? Maybe I should pick some up the next time I go to the grocery store."

"Oh, you don't have to. I mean, if you like them you can. I mean, you can do whatever, I mean. Fuck." He needed to get out of here. "Where's the restroom?"

"Down at the back." Billy pointed it out.

"Thanks." He headed back there, feeling like everyone was watching him. He slipped into the room, staring as himself in the mirror, trying to calm down.

One of the waiters opened the door, followed him. "Dude, Tanny. It is you. Dude, you have no hair!"

"I know." He gave the guy, whose name he didn't know, a smile. "How're you?"

"Okay. Wish I was high. How about you?"

"I'm good." He wished he was high, too. This would be easier.

"You got anything on you? We could share."

"I don't. Sorry, man. I don't have anything..."

"Too bad. So who's the guy? You doing him?"

"No. No, he's just a nice guy. He's not into me. I'm working on his house—painting and shit." God, it sounded so normal.

"Yeah? So you're not hanging out down at the beach anymore?"

The door opened and another guy came in, glanced at them, and then went into one of the stalls.

"S... sometimes. On my days off."

"Yeah? Maybe I'll catch you down there next week. We can pool our resources. If you know what I mean." The waiter gave him a wink and headed out.

"See ya." He stood there, staring at his dark eyes in the mirror. He sucked.

A few minutes later the door opened again and Billy came in and went over to the urinal. "I was beginning to wonder what happened to you."

"I. Someone I knew came in." He shrugged, unwilling to admit how wigged out he was.

"Ah. It's not easy, is it? Making changes like this."

He looked over at Billy, surprised. "No. No, it's not. Not at all."

Billy finished up and came over to wash his hands. "One day at a time. I know it's a cliché, but you'll drive yourself nuts otherwise. Now come back with me before our waitress thinks we've left."

"Okay. Okay, Billy. I'm sorry. You know?"

"For what?"

"Freaking out. I feel like a liar."

Billy grabbed his arm and squeezed. "It's okay, you know. To have moments where you're not sure where you fit."

"I know where I belong. That's the problem."

Billy shook his head. "No, you belong where you want to be, and you have to want more than the streets and checking out of life." Billy glanced over as the man came out of the stall and Tanny's arm was taken. "Come on. I'm hungry."

"Yeah. Yeah, okay. Did you order already?"

"Yeah, you said you wanted the burger, so I went ahead and gave our order." Bill's hand rested against his back as they went back to their seats.

"Thank you." He sat, hiding in the corner.

"So what did you think of Helena and the shop?"

"I think she's nice." He thought he was completely out of his league. Hell, he wasn't sure he had a league.

"She is. They're a great bunch." Billy sat back, smiling across at him. "So if this works out, if you get a chance to save up, what's at the top of your list?"

"It won't." The words popped out of his mouth before he thought.

"You don't know that."

"I'm pretty sure. Aren't you? Really?"

"I am, actually. I'm pretty sure it'll sell. The artists at

the Rainbow are nice people, but they aren't going to give up shelf space to be nice. They are in a business."

"Yeah. But I make trash..." Trash from trash.

"No, Tanny. You take trash and you turn it into art."

He ducked his head, drank his Coke. There was no winning this argument.

Billy sighed. "Let's see if your stuff sells, hmm? And if it does, it must be art to someone. If it doesn't, maybe you're right."

"That's fair."

"Good. Oh, here's our food." Billy rubbed his hands together. "I'm starving."

"Oh, it smells good!" Tanny grinned. Jesus, the hamburger was as big as his head.

Billy had two huge pieces of battered fish that looked nothing like the fish sticks of his childhood memories, and they both had mounds of fries.

"It does smell good." Billy looked like he was going to start drooling any second.

"Yours looks amazing." He cut his burger in half, took a big bite.

"Yeah, I wouldn't kick yours out of bed either." Billy gave him a wink and then dug in, looking very happy with his meal.

Tanny chuckled, eating happily. He'd worked hard, all day, and was empty inside. They didn't say much as they ate, aside from "pass the salt" and "would you like another Coke?"

When he was done, Billy sat back with a heartfelt sigh and patted his belly. "God, that hit the spot."

"It was good. Thank you." He rubbed the back of his neck, eyes moving around the restaurant. "So, do you have a boyfriend? I never see you call one."

"Not at the moment, no." Billy looked like he might say more, but then didn't.

"Ah. Well, if you need me out of the house some night, you just have to say. My feelings won't be hurt."

"I appreciate the offer, though it's not at all necessary." Billy patted his hand. "How are you doing with the withdrawal?"

"I'm. I don't know what to tell you. I want it. Still."

"I want you to tell me the truth." Billy squeezed his hand. "Will you reconsider going to see someone? Either meetings or someone one on one? You don't have to do this alone, you know."

"No. I don't want someone telling me drugs are bad and to find God."

Billy chuckled. "I can understand that. Hell, I can tell you drugs are bad, you should go find God." Billy winked. "But I would like to help. Is there anything I could do that would make this easier?"

"I just... I'm going to need a hit, eventually. I can only wait so long."

Billy shook his head. "No, Tanny. That's the point. No more drugs."

"I can't do that. I can't just be like this forever." The drugs were a lie, but they were his lie.

"You need something to take the place of the drugs. I have a few suggestions, but I want you to feel ready to hear them, to feel like you're standing on your own two feet. Like if the thing with the Rainbow Artists works out."

"You need to know that druggies are always druggies. I'm an addict. I get off on flying, on the rush. I need it."

"Are you listening to me? I know a different way for you to get the rush. And the discipline you need."

"You keep saying that."

"I mean it. I just don't want to suggest it unless you've got a clear head." The man was fucking obsessed. Really.

"So what? You've got some drug? Some meditation or something?" Tanny wasn't into sitting and looking at his eyelids.

"I told you I was into BDSM, right?"

That always sounded like some weird corporate deal—IBM, EBSCO, BDSM, IRS, CIA, FBI. "Well, yeah, but what does that have to do with anything?"

"It can be like flying, Tanny. The biggest, best high ever. On either side of things."

Jesus. Right. "Billy, you're a good man, for real, but there's never been sex that's that good. Never."

"Then you've been having the wrong kind of sex."

"Man, I bet your lovers are tickled to have someone with your confidence." He relaxed back into his chair, sipped at his Coke.

"Would you like to find out?"

"What?" He choked a little bit. Surely Billy wasn't suggesting what Montana thought he was suggesting. Billy hadn't shown any interest at all.

"I hadn't meant to say anything until you had a job or your found art was selling well, but it seemed the right time."

"I don't need a pity fuck, Billy, but thank you." He grinned, reached over, and actually patted Billy's wrist. "You're such a nice man."

"That's what you think this is?" Billy actually looked fucking shocked.

"You don't want me, man. I've been watching, close. You're sweet and all, but you deserve to have someone you want."

"I didn't think I'd been hiding it that well. I've wanted you since the moment I saw your back and realized you were so much more than just a pretty boy."

"No, you haven't." Bullshit. No one looked at that mess and found it attractive.

"You don't get to decide what I feel when I see things. There is strength in you, Montana, that I find very arousing."

"I..." He didn't know what to think about that.

"If you're not ready to discuss this yet, I understand. I meant to wait..."

"I just... I don't know how to get it on with a fancy guy, man." He'd mostly dated girls, back home.

"I'm not fancy, Tanny. Come on, you know I put my pants on one leg at a time, just like you."

He shrugged, wrapped his arms around his belly. "You're not a royal fuckup, though. I'm not sharing blowjobs to stay warm."

"You're not a fuckup either, Tanny. How many days now have you stayed clean?"

"I don't know. A few. Too many."

Billy chuckled, hand sliding over his. "You're not a fuckup. You just need a little direction, something to anticipate every day. I promise you this much. If you stay with me, you will not be bored."

"You could have any man you wanted."

"And I want you." Billy met his eyes, gaze not wavering.

"Why?" Was he having this conversation?

"Because, though I've hidden it, I'm incredibly attracted to you. I want you to be my sub. I want to test your resolve, your will, your strength." The intensity in Billy's eyes increased.

"I'm not a sub. I'm not into kinky stuff."

"No? I think you could be."

"What if there's no chemistry?" There was chemistry.

Billy chuckled softly. "Meet my eyes and answer that truthfully. Is there chemistry?"

He looked at Billy, aching a little inside. If he was smart, he'd lie. He could see the heat there now, and Billy was either a really good actor, or the man wanted him. His cock jerked a little bit.

Oh, yeah.

Chemistry.

Billy smiled; he knew.

"I need. I think I should take a walk."

"Let me get the check and we can go."

"Okay. I'll wait by the door." He stood, tugged his sweater down to hide the bulge in his jeans. He caught the admiring look, the half smile on Billy's lips. Then Billy nodded and went over to the bar to pay for their meal.

His skin felt too tight; he was buzzing, just from those looks.

It was ridiculous.

There it was again, though, when Billy came through the door. He felt the man's stare before Billy said anything; he knew Billy was looking at him.

"Where do you want to go?"

"We could go straight home or we could take the long way around, maybe get some ice cream on our way?"

"Sure. I need to walk." He needed to breathe.

"This way, then." Billy pointed to the left and they headed off.

There were lots of people out and about; it was dark now, but surprisingly warm for the time of year, and the street lamps and store lights made things bright. His sweater kept him toasty and, as they walked, his tension eased.

Billy pointed out a few stores, telling tales of the owners, or about an adventure he'd had there. They were light and amusing, nothing heavy. Eventually they came to a little store front wedged between two others with a line up out the door. "It's not as bad as it looks—they can only fit about four people inside."

"What's your favorite ice cream?"

"Coffee bean. I've only ever found it here—it's a vanilla with swirls of coffee ice cream and little coffee bean chips. I've never had anything like it." Billy moaned a little, the sound almost sexual. "What about you?"

"I like cinnamon." He liked the sting and heat.

"Cinnamon's good for you, did you know that?"

The line was moving fairly quickly.

"Good for you? For what?"

"Everything from bad breath to the common cold. Prevents nervous tension, improves the complexion and memory. It's good for diabetics, too."

"I don't think it made my complexion any better..."

"I think that might be the addition of milk fat preventing it from doing so." Billy winked and bumped shoulders with him.

"Yeah, yeah, yeah." He looked away, grinned.

"What will you get if they don't have cinnamon here?"

"Dark chocolate. Vanilla. I'm really easy."

"I'll remember that." The words went right into him, left him a little shivery. So did Billy's smile. It was hot.

"Are you cold?" Billy asked, hands sliding up and down his arms.

"No. No, I..." He leaned into the touch a bit. That was nice.

"Good. I would have to go buy you a thicker sweater if you were." Billy gave him a wink, hands lingering, warming him even more than the sweater.

"Mmm. One sweater a winter. It's a law."

"I think that might be a law I've broken a time or two." Billy chuckled and let him go as the line moved forward enough that they could step into the little shop.

There was a counter with a dozen different tubs of ice cream. It smelled heavenly—sweet and rich, all at once.

"Two large cones, please. One coffee bean and one

cinnamon." Billy ordered for both of them, handing the money over to the girl before she started making their cones.

The cinnamon ice cream here had Red Hots in it, and the smell was amazing. He murmured his thanks, took his cone. They left with their cones, squeezing past the people in the doorway and then heading in the general direction of Billy's place.

"Oh, God, this is good." Billy's moan backed up his words.

"It is." His mouth was hot and cold, all at once. He licked all around the edge, catching the drips. When he looked up, he found Billy watching him while licking at his own cone. "What?"

Billy shook his head. "Nothing. You're just... nothing."

His cheeks heated, and he ducked his head, focusing on his ice cream. Yeah. They walked slowly, both licking at their ice creams. He could feel Billy watching him now and then. It was weird, but he didn't know what else to do, so he ate.

Man, he missed his hair.

"Would you like a taste of the coffee bean?" Billy suddenly asked, offering his cone over.

"I. Sure. You don't mind?" At the shake of Billy's head, he offered his to Billy. "Try mine."

"Sure." Billy's hand covered his, bringing his cone closer so Billy could take a long lick from it. "Oh, that's weird, the heat with the cold, I mean."

Then Billy offered his cone out again for him to try. He licked, tongue flicking around the edge. Oh, yum.

Billy groaned, and, unless it was his imagination, Billy's hand trembled just a touch.

"It's good. I like it."

"It'll keep me up late tonight, what with the bits of

actual coffee bean in it. Looks like it's movies for me."

"Movies are cool." They started walking again, turning off Main and onto Dudley Street.

"I think it's neat that we have the same taste for the old stuff. Especially the comedies."

"It's the good stuff." Tanny sucked ice cream out of his cone.

Billy laughed, the sound rather husky. "Yes, it certainly is."

"So, home? Your house?" God, he had to stop doing that.

"Yes. Home." Billy smiled as he said it. "It's your home, too, right now."

"No. I'm just staying with you because you're nice. Home is where they can't make you leave."

Billy peered at him. "Where is your home, then?"

"I don't have one. That's what homeless means, Billy."

"I want you to think of my place as home, Tanny. The only rule is no drugs, okay? I won't kick you out except for that."

"I can't promise that. I'm an addict. I do drugs." He would say it until Billy understood it.

"You can promise to do your best not to do them, though. And I want you to come to me, to tell me when things get so bad you're going to give in, okay?"

"Okay. I'll tell you." It wouldn't stop him, but it would make Billy feel better.

"Good, good." Billy did look happier with that, steps picking up to a quick walk as they got back to the big house where Billy's condo was. "Home again, home again. So which room are you working on tomorrow?"

"Your bedroom, unless you'd rather have me do the guest room."

"No, I have plenty of work to do. My laptop plugs

in anywhere, and God knows the big chair in the living room is the most comfortable place for me to work."

"Cool. I'll start tomorrow. It should be nice, masculine."

"Strong. Like me." Billy gave him a grin and held the door open for him, following him up the stairs.

"Yep. I'm painting the guest room gray." Like him.

"Sounds good." Billy let them in the front door. It was warm and it smelled good inside. Like Billy and like... him. Well, and a little like paint, too, but still...

Good.

"You going to stay up and watch some silly television with me?"

"Sure. Do you want me to get you something to drink?"

"I wouldn't mind a Coke, actually. Thanks."

Tanny nodded, heading to the kitchen to wash up, pour two Cokes.

Billy came in just as he was pouring the drinks. "I had a sudden yen for popcorn."

"Popcorn? That'll make the whole house smell good."

"Yeah. You want to share?" Billy put the popcorn in the microwave.

"Maybe a bite or two. Sure. I ate a lot of my burger." He handed Billy his glass.

"You could handle a little fattening up." Billy patted his belly and then returned to the cabinet he'd pulled the popcorn out of. "Do you want anything on it? I've got a number of those little flavorings here."

"Flavorings? Like butter?"

"Like salt and vinegar, or nacho cheese. Stuff like that. I've also got... pickle, jalapeno, and mustard—that one is not an experience I want to repeat."

"Mustard? In popcorn? For real?" That tickled him,

and he laughed.

"Yeah, I should have known better, but they made the flavor so I thought I'd give it a try." Billy shuddered dramatically and made barfing noises.

"Ew. Ew!" He cackled, laughing so hard he bent over his crossed arms.

Billy waited until he'd stopped laughing to enquire. "Did you want to give one of the other flavors a try or are you happy with just plain butter and salt?"

"Whatever sounds good to you. I'll try it."

"Well, I know the nacho cheese is good, let's go with that. We can share the bowl if we're having the same." Billy pulled out a large tub as the popcorn in the microwave began to pop noisily.

"Cool. I'm going to go put my sweater away so I don't mess it up." It was the nicest sweater.

"Sure. I'll meet you on the couch."

Tanny went to the guest room, took off his sweater, and put it with his two extra T-shirts and pair of jeans in the tiny dresser.

This was insane. Billy wasn't seriously coming onto him, right? It was just a game. A... a... diversion. Right?

Right.

Billy was sitting on the couch instead of the big chair when Tanny got back, a space obviously left for him next to Billy. Tanny went to sit, legs curled up under him, reaching for his soda. Billy gave him a warm smile and offered over the bowl of popcorn before starting the movie. It was *A Day at the Races* with the Marx Brothers.

Before he knew it, they were laughing together, munching away at the popcorn like they'd been friends forever. Their hands brushed now and then as they ate and Billy kept stealing the popcorn he was going after. It was... nice.

Weirdly comforting.

Something he could get used to.

And when Billy, despite his assertion that his ice cream would keep him up all night, fell asleep and wound up leaning against him, snoring softly, that was something Tanny thought he could get used to, too.

Chapter Eleven

Billy was going slowly out of his mind. He brought up his interest to Tanny ages ago, but he was beginning to think Tanny hadn't believed he was sincere. He supposed he could have made a move that Montana couldn't possibly misinterpret, but he honestly didn't want Tanny to think he had to put out or get out, so he'd kept things low-key, flirted subtly. All he had for his troubles were aching balls and a well-jacked cock.

His hands were getting quite the workout.

It was time to move forward before he completely lost it.

"Hey, Tanny." He found Montana in the kitchen, putting away a couple of tacos after a long day of painting the trim. "How about we go down to Rainbow Artists and see if you're making art or junk?"

He was praying the stuff was selling, because that would give Tanny a little independence from him. It would mean he could make an offer to Tanny. Or at least try for a kiss.

"I. Okay. But... what if nothing sold? What if they laugh at me?"

"Nobody's going to laugh at you, Tanny. Did they laugh when you brought the stuff in?" Tanny had taken in a dozen airplanes, a dozen birds, and half a dozen wind chimes, all made out of cans from the recycle bin.

"No. No. They were cool." Tanny had bitten his lips bloody that day, paced the floor all night long.

"Come on, then. Worst case scenario, you didn't sell even one. And then you're no worse off than you were to start." He was betting that they'd sold out of the little pieces of found art, each one slightly different from the next. People dug that sort of thing and the Rainbow Artist shop was just the place for it.

"Yeah..." Tanny's teeth sank into his lip. When Tanny was his, that would stop.

He grabbed Tanny around the waist and gave him a hard hug. "No matter what happens, I want you to know I'm proud of you for putting yourself out there like that."

"Thank you, Billy." Tanny almost hugged him back.

He let his hug linger for a moment, and then grabbed Tanny's arm and headed them toward Luna Street and the Rainbow Artists' store. "I bet they're all gone."

"I bet none sold."

He tried not to growl. "What do you want to bet?"

"Uh... I don't know. What do I have that you want?"

"How about a kiss?" He had another gift for Tanny, one of the leather pilot jackets Tanny'd been admiring at the clothing store. He grabbed it casually from beside the door as they went out.

"No." The word was flat, sure. "I won't bet that. If we do that, it'll be because we both want it."

He grinned and nodded. "Absolutely. How about this?" He held up the package. "If more than none have sold, it's yours."

"And if none have?"

"Up to you—what do you want if you win the bet?"

"I don't want to win the bet."

Billy laughed and clapped him on the back. "I don't

Found

believe you will."

"We'll see. Let's go, get it over with."

Billy nodded and led the way, sure it was good news. He wanted to see Tanny's face when the man realized that he had a talent for making things that people were willing to pay for. They didn't dither, just headed straight over to Luna.

They opened the door, and Helena looked up, squealed. "Montana!"

Tanny stepped back a little, hand on his arm. Billy patted Tanny's hand, beaming, pleased. There was no way Helena would be this happy to see Tanny if his stuff was still sitting on the shelves, taking up room.

"Montana. Are there more? They're gone and there's a couple of dealers that want to make orders!"

He knew it! Billy laughed and hugged Tanny. "You hear that? They're all gone and dealers want to make orders!"

"I. I. I." Tanny blinked, staring at him.

Billy laughed again, gave Tanny another hug. "I think maybe he needs to sit for a moment, Helena."

"I told you, didn't I? I told you that you'd be a hit!" Helena was bouncing, arms waving as she laughed.

Tanny blushed dark, then ducked under Billy's arm and bolted, heading out the door at a dead run.

Helena stared. "Billy?"

"I don't know. We'll be back." He turned and took off after Tanny.

The road had a crowd on it, with Tanny nowhere to be seen. God damn it. Okay. Okay, where would Tanny go? Where would he run?

Going on a hunch, Billy headed for the boardwalk, moving as quickly as he could.

He saw the dark stubbled head down by the shore, Montana's shoulders hunched, hands shoved in his pockets. He slowed down a little, catching his breath as he approached. "Tanny?"

Tanny didn't look at him. "Yeah."

"What's wrong?"

"Nothing."

"You ran out of the store because there's nothing wrong?" Billy snorted. If he had to guess, it was because Tanny wasn't sure what to do with success. Montana was so convinced he was a loser who made garbage that he was having trouble adjusting his world view.

"Yeah. I'm a fuck up. I need to take a walk."

"I'll walk with you." He did, too, keeping pace as Montana headed up the beach. "Are you scared of succeeding?"

"Don't analyze me. I'm not scared of fucking success."

"Then why are we down here instead of collecting your money and working out a deal with the Rainbow Artists?"

"It doesn't matter." Tanny's shoulders hunched more.

"Stop." Billy put his hand on Tanny's arm and turned him, looked into his eyes. "It does matter. You matter. You do."

"Stop it. You don't understand."

"Then explain it to me."

"I'll. I'll go back, if I do well. I'll go back."

He didn't understand. Not at all. "Go back to where?"

"The speed. I need it. If I have the cash, I'll do it."

Oh. Shit. "Then we'll work something out so you don't have the cash on hand. I can hold it for you—Helena can hold it for you. We'll work something out, Tanny. This is a good thing, trust me."

"It's not that easy."

"Why not?" He wasn't going to let Tanny run away

from this just because it was hard. What he wanted to have with Tanny wasn't easy, which was what made it so good.

"Because I fuck EVERYTHING up!" Tanny's cheeks were red, eyes glittering.

"Maybe you won't fuck this up. Maybe having people on your side will make a difference."

"I'll just make you hate me."

"Stop that right now. Stop putting yourself down, stop assuming the worst." He was going to beat self-confidence into Tanny if he had to spend the next twenty years doing it.

"Make me."

Now there was a challenge he could not refuse. "I will, Tanny."

Those dark eyes met his. "What?"

"That was a challenge. I accept. I'll make you stop putting yourself down."

"You can't." The full lips were actually pouting.

"I believe I can. I accept your challenge, Montana."

"I... I... I... But..."

Jesus, that was cute. He looped his hand in around Tanny's arm and walked them back toward the shop. "Let's go see what kind of deal the Rainbow Artists want to give you. This thirty/seventy cut in their favor won't do. You deserve a bigger percentage."

"But. I can't. I mean, I'm just... it's trash."

"No, we agreed that if none of them sold it was trash; if any of them did sell, then it was art. And not only did they sell, they all sold and people want more. I told you—found art. It's huge." He kept them moving back toward Luna Street.

"I can't go back in there."

"Sure you can. I'm right here with you, and Helena won't mind." He bumped Tanny's hip. "You artist types are supposed to be flighty and strange."

"Fuck you."

Oh, he wasn't sure how he felt about that. "I was just teasing, Tanny, that was uncalled for."

"I'm not in the mood to be teased. I want a goddamn hit. I need one. I can't do this shit. I can't be like real people."

"You are a real person and you don't need that junk." He kept walking them toward the store. If Tanny refused to in, they'd just go home and he could call Helena in the morning.

Tanny shivered, tugging at his hand just slightly. "I need it."

"You're not going to get it, though. Not tonight." Not ever, if he had his way, and in this he was determined that he would have his way.

They walked through the door of the shop before Tanny answered. Helena stepped forward, wringing her hands. "Are you okay?"

"I think Tanny is just a little overwhelmed. He didn't expect to sell his art here."

"Well, you did and I hope you'll sell more, honey. It was a hit." Helena didn't crowd Tanny, which he appreciated.

"I think maybe Tanny needs some time to think about it. Why don't you tell us your offer and that he can spend some time pondering it?

"Well, the dealers want a hundred for the Christmas rush, but they'd need them by the weekend before Thanksgiving."

He raised an eyebrow. That was a lot of pieces to be done in a short while. "And did you want more for the store?"

"I do. They are different, you know? Clever."

"Did you hear that, Tanny? The pieces are different.

Clever." He didn't wait for Montana to answer before going back to negotiations. "What kind of percentage are you going to want for the store and the distributor sales? Thirty percent to Tanny seems kind of low, now that you know he'll sell."

"It's our standard rate. In fact, the dealer sales drop to twenty percent, because they're only charged half cost."

"Really? Wow. All right. I guess thirty percent of twelve bucks a pop is better than a hundred percent of nothing." He knew the store was charging twelve dollars, but he wanted it said out loud because he didn't know if Tanny knew that they'd put up the price from what he'd been selling them for on the beach.

He looked at Montana. "Did you want Helena to keep the money for now? Or give me enough to buy you cans from the recycling depot?"

Tanny was going to need a lot of cans, more than they could drink. "I..."

"I have a check for you for fifty and I'd be happy to front you a hundred dollars on your shipment for supplies." Helena winked. "I know where to find you, after all."

"Montana doesn't have a bank account. Could you manage cash instead? And I don't think he needs the advance." He'd help out if the fifty didn't cover the supplies, though it should. Hell, they could ask to raid their neighbors' recycling for free to pick up more cans.

"Sure. No problem. Do you think you can make the order, Tanny?"

Montana nodded, swallowed hard. "I can. Yeah."

Billy was thrilled. They could work through the money and speed issue, and he could actually show Montana how much he wanted the man without feeling like a jerk. Tanny had options now and that made all the difference.

Helena took fifty dollars from the register, and Billy

put it in his wallet.

"Oh, Margaret wanted to meet you, Montana. She's a book binder and is looking for an apprentice. She wants to keep it in the family, you know?"

"What's a book binder?" Tanny looked like he was going to shake apart.

Helena went to a shelf and pulled down a leather-bound journal. "She does the binding by hand. Journals and diaries for the most part, but she also gets special orders in to bind actual books, sometimes from publishers or authors, sometimes from collectors. Her arthritis is starting to take it away from her, I'm afraid." Helena caressed the leather.

"Oh." Tanny looked, staring at the book. "I did something like that. Out of cardboard and the funny papers. For a little girl."

"There you go—you've already got some experience!" Helena dug into her pocket and pulled out a handful of cards. She looked through them until she found the one she wanted, handing it over to Tanny. "Give her a call tomorrow."

"I. I. Okay. I'll try."

"Good deal. Thanks, Helena." Billy shook her hand and then turned back to Tanny. "I think you're ready to go home now, aren't you?"

"Can I come to your house?"

"That's what I meant, Tanny." He slid his hand over Tanny's arm and tugged him toward the door. "I've told you to think of my place as home."

Tanny didn't answer, just followed him, teeth working his bottom lip.

"So what's on your mind?" he asked as they walked home. He couldn't wait to give Tanny his pilot's jacket. No, actually, if he was truthful, what he couldn't wait for was the right time to make his move.

"Nothing. I'm just walking."

"There's nothing at all going on in your mind?" He found that hard to believe.

"I want a fix. I'm nervous. I'm a little wigged out. I feel weird. I'm hungry. Is that enough?"

"Yes. Thank you for sharing that with me. The hungry I can certainly help with. I bought steaks." He'd been anticipating a bit of a celebration.

"Steaks? For me?"

"Do you not like steak?" That hadn't occurred to him.

"I love steak. I meant, did you buy them for me? For this?"

He smiled and nodded. "I thought it would be good news. And I wanted to celebrate."

"That's very sweet."

"I'm not sure sweet is exactly what I was going for." Billy chuckled.

Tanny's head tilted, eyes curious, but the look seemed warm. "No? What were you going for?"

"Strong, masculine. Maybe a little bit sexy."

"You're sexy. You know that."

"I do." He looked Tanny in the eye. "I want you to know it, too."

"That you're sexy?" Tanny shivered, nodded. "I know. I try to not focus on that."

"I've tried not to focus on how sexy you are, either. But now that you've been clean for awhile and that you have income, it's different."

"How?" Those pretty eyes looked so confused.

"Now, if I make a move, your response can be honest." If. Like there was any question in his mind that he was going to make a move.

"Why would you? I'm squatting at your house, eating your food."

"Because you're sexy and strong, and I'm so drawn to you that it's been torture not touching you these last weeks." He might as well lay it all on the line.

Tanny blushed dark. "You know I'm a junkie, don't you?"

"If you'll remember, I did pick you up from jail."

"I know. I was really fucked up." Tanny's fingers twined with his.

He squeezed Tanny's hand and slowed down, enjoying the moment. "You were. You told me you took your whole stash."

"I didn't want the police to find it. He took my food and my coat and all my money for the pills."

"Jesus, Tanny, that's just wrong." Tanny had considered this guy as a friend?

"It's what it costs. It takes everything away."

"It's not worth it, Tanny." He unlocked the door and they headed up the stairs.

"It was... important to me." Tanny followed him.

He leaned against the door to his condo. "Was?"

"Is, I guess. I don't know. I don't want to talk about it." Obviously Tanny did, or they wouldn't keep doing it.

He reached up and put his hand behind Tanny's neck. Oh, fuck. Warm, smooth, the scars fascinating—this was heaven. He slid his fingers, just touching, not taking the kiss yet that hovered between them.

"I got scars. I know they're ugly."

"They're fascinating." He tugged gently until their mouths were nearly touching.

"Are you going to kiss me?" Tanny's hands reached out, touched his belly.

"Yes." Now that the moment was here, though, he didn't want it to be over. He'd waited days. Weeks. Months.

"Is it going to be good?" Tanny was staring at him, lips parted.

"Yes." He licked his own lips, tongue reaching to touch Tanny's bottom lip. He could feel Tanny's heart pounding, beating against his chest. Eyes holding Tanny's, he brought their mouths together that last little bit.

Soft, warm, Tanny's lips felt good against his own. Tanny gasped, just barely, lips parting for him. Making a soft noise, he licked at Tanny's lips and slipped his tongue between them.

Oh, damn. Tanny tasted sweet.

There was nothing like the first kiss.

Nothing.

He kept his hand behind Tanny's neck, kept Tanny right there as he slowly licked inside the barely open lips. Leaning against his front door, he explored and tasted and felt everything he could. Tanny trembled against him, moaned into his lips as the kiss deepened. He loved the way Tanny's mouth opened to his as if it were the most natural thing in the world. It was hot and wet and better than he'd thought possible.

Those hands slid around his waist, Tanny stepping closer.

He encouraged it, enjoying the sensation of Tanny's slender body pressing against him.

"We... we shouldn't. Your neighbors will see."

"I have the whole top floor; no one will see. Besides, I don't care." He slipped his keys out, though, and unlocked the door.

Tanny followed him in, nudging the bag that was still on his arm. "So? What's in the bag?"

He handed it over. "It's for you. Congratulations on your sales."

"Really? It's heavy. What is it?"

"It's a present—you have to open it and see." He knew

Tanny liked the jackets—he'd been admiring them at the store when they went in for his sweater. Which Montana wore all the time.

The bag was opened, Montana's eyes huge. "Oh. Oh, dude. That's fine. It's too much. It's great."

"I love the smell of leather, don't you?" He held it out for Tanny to try on.

"Yeah..." Tanny shrugged into the jacket. It fit beautifully.

"You look fantastic." He slid his hands along the leather from Tanny's belly to his chest. "Very good."

"It's so pretty..." Tanny was hard, filling the tight jeans. God, that made his mouth water.

"So's the man wearing it." Damn, his voice had gone all gravelly with how much he wanted Tanny. Tanny's hand brushed over the short fringe of hair, and the man opened his mouth, probably to argue with him. Billy pressed his fingers across Tanny's lips. "I know what I see and it doesn't matter what you say—I'm still going to see it."

He felt the brush of heat as Tanny's tongue slid over his fingers. It made him groan and lean back against the hall wall. He was lost. Utterly lost.

"You okay?"

"Yeah. I want you, though."

"Is that bad?" Tanny stroked the leather jacket again.

"Not at all. At least, not if you want it, too. If you don't, just say so. It's not a price to stay here or for the jacket or anything. It's separate." That was important, that Tanny understood that. It was also why he'd waited for Tanny to be clean for awhile, for him to have his own money coming in.

"Shit, I want. I want." Tanny wrung his hands, stared at him. "I have to tell you, though. I haven't done a whole lot with guys, mostly girls. I mean, I've done some, but

Found

not lots."

"You're bi?" He shook his head. "Not that it really matters, as long as you're willing..."

"I'm not anything, I don't think. I just do it because it's what you do." Tanny backed away. "It's not like it's getting high or something, right? I mean, it feels nice."

"It feels great. And I want to do it with you. It doesn't matter if you've done very much. I don't care. We can just rub off, hands, mouth, asses. I'm easy." He smiled. "I once heard you say you were, too."

Tanny grinned at him, dark eyes twinkling. "Yeah. Yeah, I really am."

"Come to bed with me?" He held out his hand. He had lube and condoms if they needed them.

"Okay..." Tanny stepped forward. "I'm going to leave my shirt on, okay?"

"I don't mind your scars, but if you're more comfortable, you can." He gave Tanny a wolfish grin as they moved down the hall. "I don't promise not to push it up so I can get at your chest, though."

"My scars are awful. I hate them."

"They're a badge. They tell anyone who sees them that you're a survivor, that you're strong." One day Montana would let him explore them.

Tanny shook his head, hunched a little as they went into his bedroom. "Are you sure you want me?"

He took Tanny's hand and brought it to his crotch. "What does it feel like?"

Those beautiful eyes went wide, fingers moving over his cock, exploring him. He moaned, hips pushing forward; he'd be lost once they were naked. The heel of Tanny's hand pushed harder, worked him harder.

"Damn..." Groaning, he kept pushing into those touches. "Feels good."

"You're hard. What do you like? Do you like to be sucked?"

"Show me a man who doesn't. Whatever we do, though, this isn't going to be one-sided." Tanny nodded, head bobbing, hand still moving, over and over. "Okay, stop." He reached out and grabbed Tanny's wrist. "I'm too old to come in my pants."

Tanny had him close. Maybe it was because he'd been waiting so long, maybe it was just that Tanny was hot. Tanny's fingers curled, the soft moan addictive. Billy undid his top button. "Let's get naked together."

"Mmmhmm." Tanny stepped closer, eased his zipper down. He reached out to return the favor, popping the top button of Tanny's jeans. Tanny's belly was flat, warm, the dark curls above the man's cock just barely exposed. Groaning, he stroked Tanny's skin. He loved how it felt under his fingertips.

"Oh." Tanny stepped forward, leaking against his hand.

"Just feel that." He met Tanny's dark eyes and leaned in. He wanted another kiss.

"You feel good." Tanny's skin was heated, smooth, fascinating.

"Yeah, you, too." He took that kiss, slid his tongue along Tanny's lips.

The kiss went deeper and deeper. Tanny licked his lips, and those hands dragged him closer. Moaning into Tanny's mouth, he pushed down the man's jeans. His fingers slid along Tanny's hips as they were bared.

His knees went a little weak. Tanny's hips were pointed, the skin soft. Kissing as he went, he tugged Montana toward the bed.

"Billy, you taste so good."

"Uh-huh." He leaned back against the bed. Spreading his legs, he tugged Tanny close. Tanny pushed in; the man fit nicely against him. He wrapped a hand around Tanny's cock and slowly jacked it.

"Oh." Tanny stared at him, the look a little stunned, a lot dazed.

"Kiss me again."

"Mmmhmm." Hot lips pressed against his.

Oh, good, Tanny did follow orders. Smiling, he opened his lips and invited Tanny in. The kiss was sweet, slow, Tanny focusing on him, following the curves of his teeth, his lips. God, he could get used to this. He wanted to get used to it.

He kept pulling on Tanny's prick as his free hand crept up beneath Tanny's T-shirt, his fingers searching for the man's nipples. Tanny started panting into his lips, abs rippling under his fingers. Tanny was the sexiest thing he'd seen in... forever.

"This is... I... Damn." Tanny's eyelashes were so long they tickled his cheeks.

"I want you to come for me, Tanny. I want to smell you."

"Oh." Montana shuddered. "Just... just like this?"

"Yes." He didn't want to lose a moment of this caught up in his own orgasm.

"But what about you?"

"You're not going anywhere, right?"

"What? No. No, not unless you want me to." Poor Tanny, so confused.

"Of course not. But that means I can wait." He reached up and tweaked one of Tanny's nipples as he squeezed that hard cock, reminding Tanny of where they were and what they were doing. A cry split the air, Tanny stumbling closer.

Yes. Yes, come on. He jacked Tanny harder while playing with the little nipples that grew hard for him. Tanny cried out for him, those eyes wide and staring at him.

"That's it, Montana. Give in to the pleasure. Enjoy it."

His voice was ragged, his own need riding him.

"Billy. Oh, fuck..." Montana curled a bit, panted for him, and shot, heat spraying over his fingers. The smell of it was sudden and sweet. Moaning, he kept stroking Tanny's cock. Tanny moved, rocked into his touch even still.

"You gonna stay hard?" Billy asked.

"I don't know. I've never... usually it's just over, isn't it?"

"No, it doesn't have to be." Billy grinned. "I think we're going to have a lot of fun together, me and you." He kept sliding his fingers along Tanny's prick; there was no reason Montana couldn't stay hard.

"Fuck... You're good at that." Montana stepped closer, rubbing against his palm.

What kind of lovers had Montana had if a simple hand job was so good for him? Billy growled a little. Things were going to change for Tanny, if he had any say in it. Tanny responded to the noise, cuddling closer, hands moving to his skin.

"You like giving blow jobs, Tanny?" He'd love to see what that beautiful mouth could do.

"Yeah, it's okay. You won't choke me, right? That freaks me out."

Every word out of Tanny's mouth made him angrier at Tanny's former lovers. "You'll be in total control."

Tanny kissed his cheek, then settled between his knees, hands working Billy's fly open.

"I'm probably not going to last very long." He'd been wanting this too long. Shit, he'd been dreaming about it.

"That's okay. It's been intense." Tanny pulled his cock out, took it in those long fingers, rubbing careful. "You're thick."

He reached out and stroked Tanny's cheek. "I am. I won't hurt you, though. I promise." Not with a blow job and not with fucking, either.

"You won't. You're like a knight or something."

He almost laughed. If Tanny only understood. "I'm just a man who cares about you."

He slid his thumb along Tanny's mouth and then ran his palm along the soft, short hairs that covered Tanny's scalp. They weren't that short anymore. Soft lips wrapped around his cock, Tanny's tongue the hottest, wettest thing he'd ever felt.

"Oh, fuck." He might have whimpered; it felt so good.

"Mmm." Tanny moaned all around his prick, the sound happy and warm. So far, Tanny was proving to be excellent at giving blow jobs. Soft noises wrapped around his prick, vibrated the tip of his cock.

His fingers curled in the sheets and he spread his legs wider. He could imagine so many situations, so many scenarios. So many things they could do together.

"More," he growled softly.

"Mmmhmm." Tanny sucked harder, pulled fiercely.

"Oh, yeah." He kept his hips still, his thigh muscles shaking with the effort. Montana's swollen lips wrapped around the shaft, squeezing him tight.

"I'm gonna blow soon," he warned.

He felt Tanny's nod, all around him.

Moaning, Billy felt himself go, felt Tanny's mouth pull the pleasure right out of him. Montana swallowed, groaning, trying to take him in. He came and came, pouring his heat down Tanny's throat. When Tanny pulled back, the final spurt sprayed on Tanny's face.

Leaning down, he licked Montana's face clean. The look on Montana's face was pure shock, blended with a sweet need. He ended his licks with a kiss and they shared the flavor between them.

"You're. Wow." Montana looked up at him, blinked.

"Me? You're the one who just blew me, hmm?" He stroked Montana's cheeks.

"You noticed." Tanny winked at him.

He chuckled. "I did." Bending, he kissed Tanny again. "Come to bed with me."

"You're going to have to eat dinner eventually." Montana crawled up into the bed.

"We are, yeah. But I want to hold you for awhile first." He settled under the quilt, holding Montana close. Had Tanny ever enjoyed the afterglow? He'd obviously never had a twofer.

"Oh." Tanny wiggled a bit, then settled, snuggled around him and held on.

He stroked Tanny's arm. "Yeah, like that."

They could eat steak anytime; this was special.

Chapter Twelve

The steak smelled good.

Tanny sat on the counter, watching Billy cook, wondering if it had really happened. Had they really hooked up? Really? Billy came over and bumped against his leg. He was given an intimate smile.

Oh yeah, really.

He grinned a little, not quite sure what to do. "It smells good."

"It's almost ready. Are you hungry?"

"Yeah. Do you need some help?"

"You could set the table."

"Okay." He slipped down, gathered plates and glasses, poured Billy and him both a Coke, then got forks and knives. It was weirdly domestic. Billy dished up the steaks and put the salad on the table along with some rolls.

"Anything else?" He didn't quite know what to do now.

"I think that's it. Let's eat."

"Okay." He sat, suddenly, unaccountably nervous.

Billy gave him a warm smile and placed a hand over his. "Congratulations again. I'm very proud of you."

"For what? I haven't made them yet. I might not be able to." A hundred. A *hundred*.

"For selling them in the first place. For putting yourself

out there."

"You didn't really give me a choice, you know..." He still wasn't sure it wasn't all a set up.

"I'm not sorry for that."

"No? Aren't you supposed to be?"

"I don't care if I am or not. You needed someone in your corner believing in you." Jesus, Billy was stubborn.

"Have you ever noticed that you're very invested in what other people need? Not what you need?"

"Other people? You, yes. I don't want to think of you as 'other people'. You're a man, with a name, a background." Billy smiled and nodded at his food. "Eat, Tanny. You're still too skinny."

"You're going to spoil me." And when he ended back out on the streets, it was going to be hard.

"I'm treating you right. I hate that that's all it takes for you to feel spoiled."

He snorted. "You have an unreasonable idea of right. People are vicious."

"I'm not 'people' and I judge myself by my standards." Billy reached out and squeezed his hand. "Eat. Enjoy. It's your celebration dinner!"

"Right. Right, it smells great." He bent to eat, letting himself enjoy the meat.

Billy waited until he'd started to dig in.

They didn't talk much as they ate, which didn't surprise him. They didn't usually and they ate a lot of meals together. His thoughts zoomed from all he had to do to the fact that all the planes sold to the fact that...

They'd hooked up.

Him and Billy.

Jesus.

He looked up to find Billy smiling at him, watching him as he finished his salad. There was definite heat in Billy's eyes. "I hope you saved room for cake."

"Cake?" For him making fifty fucking dollars?

"Yeah, it's this lemon cream filling thing that I absolutely love. I hope you like it, too." Billy went to the refrigerator and pulled out a cake covered in bits of meringue.

"Wow. That looks like a party cake."

"They use real cream in the filling and it's the most delicious thing ever."

"Real cream?" He took the dinner plates to the sink, grabbed little plates. "Is that why it's in the fridge?"

"Yep. Plus it tastes better cold." Billy rubbed his hands together and got out the big knife. "I hope you have enough room for a big piece."

"Just a little one, in case I don't love it. That way you've saved more for you."

"Or we could share one big piece." Billy smiled, cutting the cake. "That way I get to feed you."

Tanny chuckled under his breath. "You're not serious."

"Oh, I am. In fact, why don't we take this piece back to bed along with a couple of glasses of milk?" Billy was serious.

He stared for a little bit, then nodded. "Okay. Okay. You aren't worried about crumbs in your sheets?" He grabbed two glasses and poured the milk.

"Some things are worth risking crumbs over. And a wonderful experience like this is one of them." Billy looked at him like he was dessert.

"Oh. Cool." Okay. That sort of rocked.

Billy led him into the bedroom again, put the plate of cake on the edge of the side table. He couldn't help but notice there was only one fork.

Then Billy stripped.

He slid his jeans off, left his briefs and his T-shirt on. "Is this cool?" He'd look stupid with his cock hanging out under his shirt.

"Sure. You won't offend me without your shirt on, you know."

"It's really ugly." His back looked like he was some sort of a weird monster or something. The first time he'd seen it after the bandages came off it was like he was put together out of hamburger or something.

"I've seen it. I know what it looks like."

"I. That was before we kissed."

"I swear to you, I will still want to kiss you, to make love to you, even after seeing your back again. Besides, you're going to be facing me."

He sighed and slipped off his briefs, then got into the bed and pulled his shirt off, making sure his back was on the pillows.

"Thank you," murmured Billy, fingers sliding across his belly.

"Yeah... yeah, okay." He tried not to freak out, not to let his muscles jerk and shudder.

Billy leaned in, bringing their mouths together.

"Oh." He scooted closer, lips open, begging for more. Hand pressing against his belly, Billy deepened the kiss, tongue slipping in.

He could get used to these kisses, to the way Billy licked at him, over and over.

Not to mention Billy's fingers, and the way they touched him, the way they stroked his skin like it was precious. His cock started filling, lifting, and he shifted, trying to slow himself down. Billy hummed, pressed closer and slid warm fingers along his prick.

"I. That's not going to make things slower."

"Are we trying to make things slower?" Billy licked all around his lips.

"I... Aren't we supposed to?" Isn't that what people wanted? Jesus, this was complicated.

"There's no protocol here, Montana. We're both consenting adults. We can do what we want, however we want." Billy's fingertips danced across the tip of his cock. "I know what I want."

"What?" He spread a little wider.

"You. I want you."

"I'm right here. Where else would I want to be?" He grinned over, winked. "You have the cake."

"Oh, I get it now. You want to slow down so you can have cake." Billy laughed. "Actually, it's worth it."

Billy grabbed the plate of cake and sat next to him. It smelled good—lemony and fresh and sweet. He reached out, took a fingerful of the sweet.

"How do you like it?" Billy watched his finger move toward his mouth.

He sucked his finger clean, eyes closing. "Oh, it's tart."

"A little surprise, but a nice one, hmm?" Suddenly Billy's tongue was on his fingers, licking at them.

"Billy." That was hot.

"What?" Billy took his finger and sucked on it.

"Nothing."

Chuckling, Billy held the cake out to him. "Take another fingerful—I want a taste."

"Okay." He could do that. He pushed his finger through the cake again and Billy leaned in, lapping at the cream before taking his whole finger in and sucking on it. His eyes rolled, lips opening and closing at the flush of pleasure, the pure rush of need. Oh, God. He hoped Billy wanted to eat the whole fucking piece.

When his finger was thoroughly, completely, beyond a shadow of a doubt, clean, Billy pulled off slowly.

Then the man slid his own finger through the cake and held it up to Tanny's mouth. "Your turn."

Tanny leaned forward, licking the bite off with

short, quick laps of his tongue. Billy moaned, the sound vibrating between them. "I don't think I'm going to need the fork."

"No. No, I don't think so." He was in so much wonderful trouble.

Grinning, Billy picked up a bit of cake with some meringue attached and offered it to him.

"No, it's your turn." He snapped the bite up, though, sucking and biting the tip of Billy's finger.

The sheet slipped and he could see Billy's cock, already hard, twitch as he worked Billy's finger. He was so tempted to slide onto Billy's lap, rub them together.

So fucking tempted.

Billy smiled at him and stroked the skin near the right side of his mouth. "What do you want?"

"What?" How did Billy know?

"Don't be shy, Tanny. I can see you want something." Billy's thumb slid across his lower lip. "Just tell me."

"Your lap. Can I?"

Billy beamed at him and shifted so that Billy had the pillows behind him. Spreading his legs, just a little, which left more lap open, Billy patted his thighs. "Come on, then. It'll make... feeding each other easier."

"Uh-huh." He climbed up, straddled Billy's thighs and snuggled in. "Hey."

"Hey." Billy said it softly, fingers coming up to trace his cheeks, his mouth and nose, even his eyes. He could feel the heat of Billy's erection, pressed against his own cock.

"You want another bite?"

Billy's eyes danced wickedly. "I want another bite of the cake, and then I want a bite of you."

"No biting." He winked, slipped a fingerful of cake into Billy's mouth. Billy murmured something around the cake and his finger, and then focused on sucking. He could feel the pull of each suck on his skin, and a moment later the sweet lapping of Billy's tongue.

Montana rocked, ass sliding on Billy's thighs. Billy moaned around his finger and then slowly pulled off. "God. This cake has never tasted better."

"Must be fresh." They could eat it every day.

Billy chuckled. "Yeah, that must be it."

Instead of offering over another bite, Billy wrapped a hand around his neck and pulled him in for a kiss. He pressed closer, their stomachs rubbing together. Billy's mouth opened, inviting him in as Billy's hands slid around his hips and grabbed his ass. He leaned in, and his tongue slid into Billy's mouth, fucking those sweet lips. Billy's hands opened and closed on his ass. The movements encouraged him to roll, to rub their cocks together, nice and slowly.

He didn't even worry about the fact that Billy's fingers were moving up toward his hips, his scars.

"You taste like lemon cream," murmured Billy, one finger finding his crack and sliding up and down it.

"I... I don't think... I mean. I'm not into that, I don't think."

"No? Have you ever tried it?" Billy's finger kept sliding, up and down and tickling his skin.

"No. No, I haven't. I didn't want to get AIDS. That's why I took pills. No needles." The whole dying thing seemed fucking overrated.

"That's what condoms are for. Does this feel good?"

"I don't know. It feels... different. It makes me a little shaky."

"Shaky can be good." Billy's fingers stopped, though, and one hand slid around to tease the head of his cock, the other slid up over his back, touching his scars.

He went still, waiting for Billy to freak out, waiting for Billy to tell him to get off. Billy didn't, though. Instead the hand on his back flatted over his shoulder and tugged him closer while the hand in front wrapped around both their cocks, sliding them together.

"They're horrible." He moaned into Billy's lips.

"What?" Billy frowned, looking down at their cocks.

"The scars." He joined his fingers with Billy's.

"Oh." Billy's head tilted, his hand sliding slowly down over his back, fingers spread. "No, they're different. Unique. Fascinating."

"Fascinating? Me?"

Billy's eyes met his. "Utterly, Montana. And not just because of the scars."

"I... I don't think I'm ready for that." To be special.

"Let's just make out and not worry about anything else. I want to come with you again." Oh, now that was a much, much better idea.

He grinned, nodded. "That's a good idea." His hand slid up and down Billy's cock.

"I thought so." Billy grinned, the look a little wild, a little feral. Hand tightening around his, Billy moved them faster.

Oh. Oh, fuck. Yeah. His eyes rolled back in his head.

Billy leaned in and began to suck on his neck.

"Billy..." Oh, don't stop. Don't stop.

A low growl vibrated his skin, Billy sucking harder. He could feel each pull of Billy's mouth matching each stroke of their hands around their cocks.

"You're going to make me..." He needed to.

"You can come, Tanny." Billy bit at his skin.

Well, of course he could. Couldn't he?

Billy bit again, thumb stroking the tip of his cock, and he shot, teeth rattling together.

"Mmm. I do love the way you smell." Then Billy did that thing where he brought his hand up to his mouth and started licking it clean.

He blushed dark, watched Billy open-mouthed.

Billy smiled and held the come-covered hand out to him. "It's even better if we both do it."

"Do you think I taste good?" He leaned forward, licked a part without much spunk, just in case.

"I do." Billy licked next to where he was licking, tongue playing with his. Billy wasn't like anyone else he'd ever known. No one.

Billy kept alternating between licking his hand clean and kissing Tanny, the flavors getting all mixed up together. He nuzzled up against Billy, knowing that the man had to need. A sweet groan was fed into his lips, Billy's free hand dropping restlessly down to his ass. Billy squeezed and released his ass cheek several times before pulling him closer. "Let me rub against you a bit."

"Yeah. Yeah." Billy'd been so good to him and felt so fine; he'd let the man do a lot.

Billy rolled, putting him beneath the strong body. Giving him a kiss, Billy started rubbing, cock sliding along his hip.

"Mmm." He pushed back, jonesing on the weight on him, the pressure.

"Feels good, doesn't it?" Billy kept peppering him with kisses, kept licking at his mouth.

"Yes. God, yes. It's exciting."

Billy's head dropped and his lips and tongue teased the mark left behind earlier.

"Oh, fuck..." His poor cock jerked, tried to fill again, but he ignored it, focusing on Billy.

"I love how you smell. How you feel." Billy's voice had dropped low, growly. It was hot.

Tanny blushed dark, staring up. "Good."

Billy leaned in and his tongue pushed in and out between Tanny's lips. Like fucking. Just like fucking.

So hot. He could feel Billy's hips speeding up, Billy's

hot cock like a brand on his belly. He wrapped his hands around Billy's hips, dragging him closer.

"Yeah. Fuck." Billy groaned, humping faster. "Yeah."

"Mmmhmm. You feel... this is good."

"It is. It's going to make me come. You are making me come."

He turned his head, lips finding Billy's earlobe, sucking on it.

"Montana!" Billy pushed hard and heat splashed between them.

He hummed, sucking happily, knowing how good it felt. Panting, Billy rested on him, body hot and hard.

"I have you." He patted Billy's ass.

"Mmm... you do. I like it."

"Me too." He liked it a lot.

"Good." Billy kissed him softly. "Sleep here tonight."

"You're sure?"

"One hundred percent sure."

"'kay." He nodded, cuddled in.

He could do that.

Chapter Thirteen

Billy woke up slowly, wrapped around a warm body. Oh. Montana. Smiling, he slid his hand along Tanny's hip and then tugged him in closer. Tanny was a natural snuggler, wrapping around him and pulling him tight. He was happy to snuggle in, fingers sliding on warm skin.

How long had it been since he'd last had a lover? Too long.

And Tanny was addictive, something he wanted to taste over and over. A drug. Tanny would find that amusing, he thought.

He nuzzled, looking for skin to kiss, to taste. Billy could look down Tanny's back from here, stare at the mass of scars, the fascinating patterns. One day Tanny wouldn't be ashamed of them. He slid his hand gently along them, learning them.

"Mmm." Tanny stretched, pushing into his hands. So sensual, Tanny made him want so many things. So many wicked things.

He kept touching the scars, Montana beginning to rock against him, one hand sliding down to cup Tanny's cock. He placed soft kisses on Montana's skin as he continued to trace the ragged scars. He felt Tanny's muscles twitch and jerk, shifting for him. How long had it been since

Tanny'd let someone touch him here?

He teased his fingertips along Tanny's spine. The twisted scars spoke of great pain. There was a smooth spot, right at the base of Tanny's back, just above the swell of his ass. Billy's fingers stroked there a moment; he was intrigued by the contrast.

"Oh. Oh." Montana jerked, still asleep. "Oh, fuck. Right there."

He wanted desperately to lick that spot, to tease it unmercifully with his tongue. He settled for stroking and rubbing and scratching at it instead.

Tanny jerked himself off with short, hard strokes. "Bill..."

"Right here, Montana." He dug his fingers into the sensitive flesh just above Tanny's crack.

Those near-black eyes popped open, Tanny coming, heat spreading over his belly. Billy moaned as the scent of Tanny's come rose up from between them.

Reaching down, he swiped his fingers through Tanny's come and then began to lick his fingers clean.

"I. Morning. Good morning." Tanny panted, blinking at him.

He chuckled and leaned in for a kiss. He took it, his lips lingering on Tanny's before pulling away. "Good morning."

Tanny nodded, staring at him before pushing close, kissing his collarbone. Humming, he raised his head and offered more of himself to Tanny's mouth.

"Mmm. Sweet." Tanny licked and nuzzled, kissing him lazily.

"All for you." His fingers kept sliding on Tanny's skin and he reached around for Tanny's back again. Montana stiffened a little, slid under the covers to hide.

"No, no. It's all right." He held onto Tanny's hip and tugged him back close.

"Yeah?" Tanny pressed in.

"Yeah. I—they're fascinating, Tanny. Truly." He slid his fingers up Tanny's spine and then traced scars on the way back down.

"You're a little weird, Billy."

He chuckled at that, not the least bit insulted. "I am, am I?" Billy didn't think it was a bad thing at all.

"Uh-huh. A little." Tanny's lips found his nipple, circled it.

He groaned, his hands going to Tanny's head, holding it at his chest. "So it wouldn't surprise you to hear that I want to trace your scars with my tongue?"

The suction stopped, Tanny's dark eyes peering at him.

"I'm serious."

"Really?"

"Yes, Tanny. I wouldn't tease you like that. I mean it."

"You don't think they make me look like God hates me?"

"I'd say it's more that he tested you than he hates you." Billy kept touching them, tracing them. He let his fingers wander down to the spot just above Tanny's ass, free of scars, where he'd stroked to make Tanny come. Montana's moan was sweet on his skin, then those lips wrapped around his nipple, pulling hard, His cock twitched and he pushed forward with his hips to slide his eager prick along Montana's skin. "I want to make love to you."

"Mmhmm." Montana was focused on sucking, tasting him.

"Yeah? I'd like that. I want to be inside you, to feel you gripping me tight." He had condoms and lube, everything he needed. His hands moved over Montana's back as he moaned at the way Montana tugged on his nipples.

"I'll suck you, if you want."

"No making love?" He would have pouted, but it looked silly on him.

"How bad does it hurt?"

Billy shook his head. "It shouldn't hurt at all, Tanny. Not if it's done right. I'll take my time, stretch you—I'll make you feel good."

Tanny's fingers were on his lips, his jaw, his throat. "You swear? I'm not sure I want to, but I'm not sure I don't."

"I swear. You can suck me off first, if you like. That way I can take even more time." He could take all day if it wasn't urgent.

"Okay. I like sucking you." Tanny moved down, lazy and slow, nibbling on his belly.

"I like being sucked." But what he really wanted was to be inside Tanny.

"Well, we work together, then." Montana's chin bumped his cock. He gasped softly, hand reaching to slide over Tanny's short hair. "Shh. It's okay. No biting. I promise."

Billy chuckled. "I'm not worried about you biting."

"No? I thought everyone did." Those lips wrapped around his cock, pushed all the way down his shaft.

He cried out, hips pushing automatically. Tanny was eager and hungry around him, sucking and moaning, working his cock like a starving man.

"That's so good. So very good." His legs spread; his balls drew up. Tanny didn't let him breathe, think, nothing. "Yes. More. Montana!" His hips pushed in with short, sharp jabs as his orgasm worked its way up his spine.

It felt like a dream, the heat, the suction, the way Tanny worked him.

Before long he was crying out, coming in long spurts

down Tanny's throat. He watched as Tanny took him, tongue moving, cleaning him off.

"I do love your mouth, Tanny." Was it possible to love Tanny's blow jobs after only two of them? Tanny grinned around him, nuzzling and winking up. He couldn't help but grin back, his fingers stroking Tanny's face. "Come back up here. It's about time I blew your mind."

"Okay." Montana pressed close, lips red and swollen. He touched them; Tanny's tongue flicked out to taste him.

"Do you know how sensual you are?"

"Huh?"

He grinned, nipped at Montana's lower lip. "You're very sensual. I'm thinking you'd maybe even make hedonistic under the right circumstances." And he so wanted to present Tanny with the right circumstances for that.

"What does hedonistic mean?"

"It means enjoying pleasure, succumbing to it." He pressed kisses to Tanny's lips between each word.

"Aren't you supposed to?" Tanny's body relaxed with each kiss.

"Yes, good point." He chuckled and continued plying Tanny with kisses.

It didn't take long before Tanny was relaxed and melted against him, eyes heated, cheeks flushed. Only then did Billy let his hand drift back to Tanny's ass. It made him feel good when Montana didn't flinch, didn't stiffen. It proved the man wasn't scared of being touched, just inexperienced.

He fondled and squeezed Tanny's ass for awhile, enjoying their kisses and letting things go slowly.

"You... you like to spend time. It's nice."

"Quickies are fun, but if you have the time to spend that's even nicer." He wanted to spend hours with

Tanny—no days and days, bringing Tanny to the edge and then backing him off again, making him go forever between coming.

"I guess. I usually just sorta rubbed off or played in the back seat. Kid stuff."

"I'm going to be selfishly glad that you haven't done anything else. There's something very wonderful about being able to be the one to make you feel things for the very first time." His index finger slid along Tanny's crack as he spoke.

Tanny's breath hitched, and one of those lean legs slid up along his own. Such good instincts. His finger slid down farther, finding Tanny's hole and rubbing it gently. He just wanted to let Tanny feel it.

"You don't think that's gross? I mean... dirty, kind of?" This from a man who had come to him infested with lice.

"Not at all." He grinned suddenly. "Do you know what rimming is, Tanny?"

"Yeah, I mean, I've heard of it, but... I don't know, man. That's..." Tanny's nose wrinkled.

"Shall I show you?" He licked his lips, eager suddenly for the flavor of Tanny on his tongue.

"You don't have to..."

He shifted, moving Tanny to lie on his stomach on the bed. "I want to, Tanny. This is something I enjoy."

"Why?" Look at that ass, the pattern etched into that back.

"Because I love how good it makes my lover feel. I love how intimate it is." He reached out, fingers sliding along the crease where thigh met ass.

"I don't know if... " Tanny's legs curled, ending up under the man, ass in the air, exposing that tiny hole.

He knew Tanny was clean—the man showered every day just like he did.

He put a hand on each ass cheek and leaned in to blow gently on Tanny's hole, just to see it respond. Tanny's ass clenched, the ring of muscles bunching and relaxing.

"Mmm... you can shout if you want to." Fighting his grin, he leaned in and licked the wrinkled skin.

Tanny scooted forward, a soft cry filling the air. He followed, licking again. He could taste heat and musk, Tanny.

"Is... are you... Oh, God."

Oh, God, indeed.

He lay down behind Tanny, hands spreading the sweet ass. He licked at Tanny's hole over and over again. It didn't take long at all for Tanny to start humping the air, hips moving up, pushing toward him. One hand slipped under the lean body; he saw Tanny's arm moving.

It was time to up the ante a little. He pointed his tongue and pushed it right into Tanny's body. Tanny stilled, then climbed over the mattress toward the headboard.

"Where are you going?" Billy growled, hands sliding on that lovely ass.

"I. That's sort of. Yeah. Wow."

Billy chuckled and followed Tanny. "I'm not done here yet."

He spread Tanny's ass cheeks again and went back to tongue-fucking. Montana's sounds were addictive, and Billy let himself imagine all the things he was going to do to this beautiful man. How he was going to fuck this tight hole with dildos and fingers, cock and plugs.

When Tanny's hole was dripping with his saliva, he switched from his tongue to his fingers. He lubed the first one up and teased it around Tanny's hole.

Tanny cried out, the sound ringing out. "Billy. I'm going to come."

That hand was working faster, harder.

"Go ahead, Tanny. I'm not going to stop." He kept

playing; he would let Tanny come, show his lover just how good this could be before there was any stretching with his fingers.

Sharp, hungry cries filled the air, and that hand snapped around Tanny's cock. He scraped across the wrinkled little hole with his fingernail. "Come on, Tanny. Let me smell your come."

"Billy!" There. There it was. Damn.

As Tanny came, Billy slipped his lubed finger into Tanny's little hole. Tanny's body rippled around his finger, squeezing him, letting him in. He wriggled it inside Tanny's body, circling his finger, not letting up.

Tanny unconsciously pressed back onto his finger, riding his touch. He slid his free hand to Tanny's belly, stroking it as he searched for the man's gland.

"Billy." Tanny shifted, then stopped, gasped softly. There.

He wriggled his finger, tapping the little bit of flesh again and again.

"I. I. Fuck. What are you doing?"

He chuckled. "It's called the prostate, Tanny. Feels good, doesn't it?"

"Uh-huh. Uh-huh. Don't stop?"

"No, no stopping. Not yet." He twisted his finger, and slid it in and out and kept stimulating that sweet spot.

Tanny whimpered low, moving on the bed. "I don't know what to do."

"You don't have to do anything at all." He slowly worked a second finger into Tanny.

Tanny groaned and kept moving, fucking himself and that hungry little hole. The way the scars moved along Tanny's back was fascinating, the way Tanny's hole clung to his fingers even better.

He added more lube, watching how Tanny's body swallowed him up. He knew there'd been no pain so far, only pleasure. He wanted that to continue. Working slowly, he teased another finger into Tanny's ass.

"Oh. Full." Tanny never slowed, kept pushing back toward him.

"You like it." He was surprised by the possessive, needy growl his voice had taken on.

"I don't know." Yes, he did. Tanny's body knew.

He stretched all three fingers. He knew if he got Tanny well-stretched, used to the fingers, then his cock wouldn't hurt, there would be only pleasure and his sweet hedonist would be begging for more. Pulling his fingers together, he twisted them and pushed at Tanny's gland again. Tanny shuddered, and those ass muscles rippled, squeezed him tight.

"Do you have any idea how sexy you are?" He couldn't wait to be buried inside Tanny, feeling that around his cock.

"Hmm?" Tanny looked back at him, lips parted, eyes heavy-lidded.

"I want you," he told Tanny. The proof was in his cock, which was hard enough to hurt.

Tanny nodded. "You make me feel good."

"Good. I think you're ready for the next step." He touched Tanny's gland again, to remind Tanny how good this felt.

"O...kay." Tanny groaned, head resting on his hands.

He rubbed Tanny's ass with one hand as he grabbed a condom with the other. "It's going to be good."

He didn't get an answer, just a soft little gasp. Billy put the condom on and got it good and lubed up. Then he slipped two fingers back into Tanny, to make sure everything was good and slick, and to hit that little gland one more time. Fuck, that felt good; he could only imagine how it was going to feel around his prick.

Groaning, he moved closer and let his fingers fall away.

He didn't give Tanny any time to think or to breathe. He pushed his cock against the hot little hole. Tanny was slick, and the head of his cock popped in, making Tanny groan and him gasp.

"Montana. God. Just breathe, okay?" He stroked that little bit of flesh right above Tanny's ass that wasn't scarred and that had all those little nerves in it.

Oh, fuck.

Oh, fuck, he could feel that, all through his cock.

Tanny's body rippled and shook, working his prick, milking it. A low, drawn-out moan was pulled out of him.

"Yes." He touched Tanny again. And again. And once more.

As Tanny's body rippled around his cock, he slowly pushed in deeper. He ignored the need that urged him to thrust deep, and simply filled Tanny with care.

"It... it's really big."

"But not too big." He kept touching, sometimes Tanny's ass, sometimes the scarred back.

"N...no. No. Not too big."

Groaning at the tight heat around his cock, he kept working his way slowly in.

"I don't know what to do."

"Just keep breathing and let me in." He reached around to grab Tanny's prick. Tanny wasn't hard, not after coming twice and worrying.

Billy tugged and squeezed anyway, teasing the warm flesh. He felt it in Tanny's cock when his own finally sank deep enough to nudge Tanny's gland.

They stayed still for a long few minutes, both breathing together, both of them shivering. He leaned forward and traced one of Tanny's scars with his tongue. God, he needed to move soon.

"Oh. Billy." Tanny rocked, sliding on his prick, riding

him slow and easy.

A low, needy moan came out of him, his hands finding Tanny's hips. He pulled partway out, then pushed in, both of them crying out.

He did it again, and then again, the pleasure of Tanny's tight passage huge.

His.

This was his.

He pushed in again, eyes closed, focusing on this first time. So tight. So hot. "Montana." He whispered his lover's name.

"Uh-huh. Right here."

"Me, too." He moved a little bit faster, the sensations intense, amazing.

The soft sounds got louder, filling the air, over and over. His own deeper moans met Tanny's noises and the sounds of their flesh hitting made a fiercely heated counterpoint.

"Billy." One day it would be Master. He believed that.

"Right here," he growled, his voice hoarse. His hips moved faster, his hand sliding on Tanny's cock. Tanny's prick was filling, responding to him, starting to leak on his palm. He began to press kisses along Tanny's neck, tongue flicking out to taste his lover's skin.

"I... I don't know what to do."

"Close your eyes and listen to your body. You know what to do."

"You sound so sure." When Tanny chuckled, he felt it all around his cock.

"Because I can feel it."

"Feel it?" Tanny started moving faster.

"Yes. Each ripple around my prick says your body knows." He managed to get the words out between gasps.

"Oh." Tanny's cock jerked, throbbing in his hand.

"Coming, Tanny. Coming." He pushed in harder. He slid his fingers across the tip of Tanny's cock.

"Again. Please. Please. I... Come on, damn it!"

Laughing, he pushed in harder, faster. He found Tanny's gland again and started pounding against it as he jacked the man, gave Tanny his best moves. He felt it—the way Tanny whimpered and jerked, bucked and shuddered. The man was close. He bit at the skin of Tanny's neck, and growled softly. "Come on, Montana. Give it to me now."

Tanny gave him a low, drawn-out cry, body jerking around his prick. Then heat poured over his hand. Tanny's scent filled the air and Billy bucked a few times, his smooth thrusts lost beneath Tanny's pleasure.

He moved a moment or two more, then his own orgasm hit him and he filled the condom in long pulses.

Tanny slumped to the mattress, panting, loose and boneless underneath him.

Billy followed, not quite ready yet to pull out of Tanny's ass. Making sure he didn't crush Tanny, he held his weight up with his arms. He rested his cheek against Tanny's scarred back as he panted and tried to catch his breath.

His.

Tanny was his and he was in serious, serious trouble here.

Wonderful trouble.

Now he just had to convince Tanny that right here was where Tanny wanted to be, too.

Chapter Fourteen

Sore. His ass was a little sore.

Montana stretched, feeling it all through him. He'd let Billy fuck him. He'd let Billy fuck him and it had been good.

And he'd come three times and his balls were never going to recover and they ached.

Wow.

Billy hadn't kicked him to the curb when they were done, either. Billy wanted to cuddle, to hold him. One of Billy's hands rested on his hip, and Billy patted him. They dozed, off and on, neither one saying anything.

It was a little weird.

After a couple of hours of dozing, Billy yawned and stretched, turned to him and smiled. "Hey, you."

"Hey." He didn't know exactly what he was supposed to feel.

"How are you doing?" Billy's hand slid from his hip to his ass, stroking gently.

"Is it cool if I don't know?"

"Yeah, it is." Billy kissed him softly. "There's no rules here, you know?"

"It's a little weird. I've never... I don't know how to do the lover thing." He was more of a 'let's rub off and go away' type.

"So you'll learn." Billy made everything sound like it was so easy.

"Did you like it? Fucking?" Or was it making love. No. Fucking. Making love was girly.

"I loved it. I'd like to do it again. A lot." Billy winked.

"I don't know if I'll get it up again for a week." Hell, Billy'd come twice and he was older... Well, maybe not. "How old are you?"

"Thirty-three."

"When's your birthday?" Not that much older. He was twenty... six? Seven?

"I'm a summer baby. June twelfth."

"Cool. Mine is on Valentine's Day." Twenty-six. He was twenty-six.

"Is it? How wonderful." Billy kept touching him, gentle strokes here, there.

"I guess. Yeah. It's an okay day." He let himself relax again.

"We'll have to make sure it's extra special next year."

Next year, huh? "You think you'll still want to be my friend next year?"

"I know I'll still want to be your friend and lover next year. And the year after that."

Right. "How do you know?"

"Because I'm falling for you, Tanny. I have been from the start."

"Me? No..." There was no way.

"Yes, you." Billy stroked a hand over his head and then brought him in for a soft kiss. "Yes, Montana. It's the truth."

"You're a little crazy, man. I'm a loser junkie." It was sweet, though.

Billy swatted his butt, not even hard enough to sting. "No. You. Are. Not. And I want you to stop saying that kind of thing about yourself."

"It's the truth." What exactly was Billy going to do about it?

"It is not!" Billy sat up and started ticking things off on his fingers. "You live in a nice place. You make art that sells. There's a man in your life who cares about you. You've been clean for a month."

"I still want it, and it's your house, and I made enough to take you to McDonald's." He wasn't going to let Billy blow sunshine up his ass.

"But you haven't taken it, I've told you it's your home, too, and you'll make more next time. You need to start seeing the good in things, Tanny."

"I do. I see the truth. You only see the good."

"You need someone to see the good in you, to believe in you."

"You're sweet." A little naive, but sweet.

Billy started laughing.

He popped Billy's ass. "Quit laughing at me."

"I'm sorry, Tanny, I'm just not used to being called sweet."

"Well, you are." He'd never met someone as nice. Not even his gran.

"Thank you, Tanny." Billy grinned, gave him a flirty look. "Will you still think so when I beat your ass until you come?"

He stared a second, then started laughing. Right. Like that could happen. Billy reached out and smacked his ass. "You quit laughing at me."

"Ow!" He blinked, laughter trailing off. "Careful."

"I'll always be careful of you, Tanny." Billy's fingers trailed over the skin he'd hit.

"I. You. Are you hungry?" He wasn't sure where they were going here.

"I could eat. What do you want?" Billy kept watching

him, staring at him.

"I don't care. I'm easy. I think I need a shower. I'm a little wigged out."

"Because I'm talking about BDSM, or because I'm talking about us still being together when your birthday comes around again?"

"A little of both. I mean, the BMS thing? Not my deal, but I get it." Except he didn't.

"BDSM. And I believe you could benefit from the lifestyle a lot." Billy shrugged. "But more important for now is you wanting to stay with me—our relationship."

"I'm going to disappoint you." It was what he did.

"I don't think you will." Billy had a confident little smile.

"You think I'm a better person than I really am."

"I have faith you can be the person I see inside you."

"Aren't we going to make breakfast?" This wasn't going anywhere.

"Are you trying to change the subject?" Billy was getting up, though, seeming unconcerned with his nudity.

"Yep." He headed to the little bathroom to clean up.

Billy followed, wrapping around him from behind, hands sliding over his hips. "Look at us in the mirror, Tanny."

He looked up, Billy was solid, strong. His hair was growing back. They looked good together.

"Makes a nice picture, doesn't it?"

"Yes." He liked how they fit. He liked everything about his life here.

"I'm going to warn you right now." Billy's hands tightened on his skin. "I'm going to hold onto this picture. As hard as I can."

"What does that mean?" Did that mean Billy didn't think it was going to stay?

"It means I want you to stay."

"I want to... I want. Jesus, can't we just eat? This is really intense."

Billy chuckled and kissed his neck. "Yes, Tanny. We can just eat."

"Okay. Cool. I need to wash my clothes today. Both my jeans are dirty." One of his pairs of jeans was worse than dirty; it was almost gross.

"How about you let me take you shopping for more clothes?"

"No. No more taking advantage of you." They were lovers, now. It was even more important.

"You're not." Billy squeezed his hips again. "I swear you are not."

The touch was... intense.

"Breakfast?"

Billy held his gaze in the mirror for a long moment and then nodded. "Breakfast."

"'kay." He didn't know what to think, what to do, so he... didn't.

They could just eat.

Chapter Fifteen

Billy hummed as he made breakfast. The coffee was perking away and Tanny was setting the table.

He had two things on his mind—officially inviting Tanny to move into his room from the guestroom, and Thanksgiving. He usually had an invite from someone at the Hammer who knew he was on his own, but he hadn't really been to the club since Tanny'd moved in with him, and Thanksgiving was next week. Besides, he kind of wanted to spend it with Tanny.

He dished up their food and sat, giving Tanny a smile as his lover sat across from him.

Tanny smiled back, focusing on the food, humming under his breath.

Billy decided to take the bull by the horns. "I'd like you to move into my room with me, Tanny."

"Why?"

"Because we're lovers, and lovers share a room."

"Oh." He could see Tanny working through that, thinking about it. The things that Tanny worried about were still an endless source of amusement.

"I thought you could use the guest room for your art supplies and your pieces as you finish them." The more Tanny thought of this place as home and his, the better.

"You... did you like sleeping with me? I mean sleeping-sleeping."

"I did. Did you like sleeping with me?"

He liked the way Tanny seemed like he was really thinking about it, considering it. "It was warm, safe. I don't know if I want to get used to feeling safe like that."

"Tanny... I'm not going to kick you out," he reminded gently.

"You say that, but..." Tanny shrugged. "You don't want to, right now, I know."

"I'm not going to want to later, either." He knew Tanny didn't believe that, but he did. They'd have stumbles, sure, everyone did, but people worked through the shit. He decided to try another tactic. "Besides, you should enjoy the warmth and safety while you have it."

"Do you think so? I guess so. I like how you smell, the way your heart beats."

"Those are good things." Something warm and happy curled up inside his chest.

"Yeah. Yeah, they are." Tanny ate a piece of toast, crunching away.

"It's Thanksgiving soon," he pointed out, pleased with his sort of segue.

"Yeah? How did we miss Halloween?"

They'd missed it because he'd known that, if Tanny'd gone out, Montana would have slipped. It had been easier to... ignore the holiday. As rarely as Montana left the apartment, it had been easy.

He shrugged. "We just did. We'll catch it next year, do something cool with costumes." He reached out and took Tanny's hand. "I'd like it if we could spend Thanksgiving together."

Tanny grinned, their fingers twining together. "Where else would I go? Do you have family you need to see?"

"Nope. I usually horn in on one of my friends' celebrations. It'll be nice to have one of my own." He squeezed Tanny's hand. "Is there anyone you'd like to invite?"

"Would you like to meet my drug dealer?"

"Um... not really." Like no way. Even if the man was family.

"Well, I killed my sister, my parents hate me, and you don't want to meet Mike, so, no." Tanny blinked, looked shocked. "Okay, that was mean-sounding."

Bitter.

Angry.

He squeezed Tanny's hand again. "You're allowed to be angry over what happened."

"I'm not fucking angry."

Uh-huh. Right.

"You sound pretty angry. If I was you, I'd be pissed off at myself, my parents. Have you dealt with any of that? Because if you don't, it's just going to keep on festering."

"I don't need a fucking therapist. I need..." Tanny frowned, stood up. "I'll do the dishes."

"Tell me what you need, first." Tanny kept censoring himself.

"I just need a fix, or to take a walk or something. I just... I must be tired."

"Why?" He got up and wrapped his arms around Tanny from behind. "Why must you be tired?"

"Because I'm grumpy, and I shouldn't be grumpy."

He rubbed Tanny's belly. "Why are you grumpy?"

"I don't know. I shouldn't be. I don't want to talk about this. I need to go find cans."

He pushed a little harder, trying to encourage the tension in Tanny's abs to ease. "Stop trying to run away, Tanny. I'm not going anywhere."

"Running away is what I do."

"Not anymore." Because he'd follow.

Montana's head tilted, much like a puppy's. "How do you know?"

"Because I won't let you. You run; I follow."

"That's kind of scary. I need to run, sometimes. I have to fuck things up."

"And you will. And I'll be there to help you pick up the pieces." Eventually Tanny would understand that, believe it.

"Why? Why me? Why didn't you pick someone clean? Why..." Tanny pushed into his arms, kissed him hard enough that his knees buckled, then pulled away.

He grabbed Tanny's arm to keep him from running away. "We don't get to choose, not really. It just happens."

"What? You see some stoned loser on the street and you're in love?"

"It wasn't like that, though, was it? I saw you, I invited you to dinner, gave you a warm place to stay, and then fell in love." He grinned, winked. "After you painted the turret room and didn't ruin that amazing ceiling molding."

Tanny's laughter made him grin. "And here I thought I hadn't given you anything."

"Bullshit. You've give up drugs for me. You've given me your trust. You've tried because of me. I know how hard that's been for you." He'd never once felt like this was one-sided giving.

"Is it always like this? After fucking? So... intense?"

"No. If it's just getting off, if you don't care, then no. It's only like this because it wasn't just fucking." He was explaining it all wrong

"I don't get it. Why would you want..." Montana stopped, rolled his eyes, then grinned. "Okay, you know what? I need to find cans. I'm all confused and shit. It's like having you in me scrambled something and made me stupid."

"You want me to come look for cans with you?" Did Tanny trust himself out there alone yet?

Montana didn't answer him, but he saw the bare nod.

"We can use a few of those reusable grocery bags. I'll even help you wash 'em once we get them back here." He rubbed Tanny's back; it was going to be all right, it was all going to work out.

"Okay. Let me get my jeans into the dryer to get the cold off."

"We need to buy you some new clothes." Tanny just didn't have enough yet. A change for every day, at least, was really more in line with what Billy thought was reasonable. At least Tanny had a warm jacket now.

"When I can."

It occurred to him, sort of out of the blue, that he didn't know if Montana had a driver's license, a Social Security card. He didn't know Montana's last name. Oliver would not approve.

Screw Oliver and his disapproval. Billy was following his heart.

"I still haven't paid you for the last of the painting," he noted.

"I don't want your money, Billy. I'm not a whore. I live off you enough."

"I'm not treating you like a whore!" he snapped.

"I didn't say you were!" Tanny could snap right back.

"Okay, then. All I wanted to do was pay you for the work you did." He had enough, and Tanny didn't; it didn't make Tanny a kept man if he shared what he had.

"You did. You fed me, let me sleep here. That's payment. I... I don't want to have anymore deep talks today, Goddamn it!"

"Let's go on and look for your cans, then." He would drop it for now—Tanny was clearly becoming stressed. The discussions could wait.

One day, though. One day they wouldn't wait any longer.

One day soon.

In the meantime, Billy would help Tanny hunt cans so he could make his own money to buy things with.

Chapter Sixteen

Tanny clipped the fifty zillionth can to make propellers. His fingers were blistered and bloody, his shoulders hurt, his eyes itched and... And he had ten left, and he'd be done.

He'd been working his ass off for six days, but he was getting there.

He clipped around another set of edges, then started building another one.

He'd almost gotten the wheels on when someone banged on the door. Billy was late—out at some meeting or another—so he went to answer it, wiping his hands on the towel in his pocket. There was an old dude there—somebody Montana thought he remembered, or maybe not. He'd seen a zillion people. "Yeah?"

The guy blinked. "Is William home?"

"Who?" Figured that the old dude interrupted him for the wrong house. "There ain't a William here, man. Sorry."

The guy stared. "Nonsense. I've been in this house a hundred times. I know this is his home."

"Man, there's me and..." Oh, wait. William. Billy. Duh. Right. "Sorry, you want Billy? He's at a meeting. He should be home in a second."

The man's eyebrow went up and his back went

straight—straighter. "He left you here and went out?"

"Yeah... I was working." He wiped his hands again. "You want to come back in a little while?"

The man took a step in over the threshold. "You're living here?"

"Uh. Yeah. Yeah, I'm renting the guest room. Dude, you can't come into Billy's house." He didn't know this guy.

There were footsteps on the stairs and then Billy's voice. "Oliver? Is that you?" Billy chuckled, his arms full of grocery bags. "Long time no see."

"Good evening, William. I was coming to check on you and invite you to Thanksgiving dinner." Oliver looked at him like he was slime. Okay, this just sucked.

"Oh, thanks, man, but Tanny and I are going to have Thanksgiving together." Billy nodded at his bags. "I've got a turkey and everything. You two haven't officially met yet, have you? Tanny, this is my friend, Oliver. And Oliver, this is my lover, Montana."

Those eyebrows lifted even higher. "Your lover? What a surprise."

He looked over at the guy, then took the bags from Billy. "I'll put the stuff up, man. My shit's all over the kitchen table."

"Thanks, Tanny, I'll help. Come on in, Oliver. I don't know why you're surprised."

"William. I... I must say that we've met your former acquaintances before they moved in."

Billy stopped and turned to Oliver. "So?"

"That's because he let me come in before we started fucking. And before you ask, I haven't stolen anything from him, I don't imagine I'll start anytime soon, and I don't see myself being your friend, so you don't have to worry about me stealing shit from you." He took the bags from Billy and headed into the kitchen. There.

"Oliver, I don't appreciate you coming in here and insulting my lover. This isn't like you." Billy sounded like he was pissed and hurt.

"I haven't insulted anyone, William. And you have to excuse me if I'm concerned. You disappear for weeks, you don't mention your lover, and then expect no one to worry when I discover the addict you found in an alley living in your home?"

Tanny just walked away. This was what he'd warned Billy about. What he was was fine, here in the house, but no one with a real life, with something to lose, wanted someone like him around.

"I expect you to trust my judgement, Oliver."

"William. Please, I mean no disrespect. I worry."

"You don't need to worry, Oliver." Billy's voice lowered, but Tanny could still hear it. "Tanny won't hurt me. Not on purpose, and he is not responsible for my heart."

"My friend... Please... Have you... I mean, you're taking a terrible risk—with your heart, your health."

"My heart, yes, but I haven't got a choice. My health? Not at all. We're using condoms."

"Have you gotten him tested?"

Tanny put the milk away, put the celery away, then put his shoes on. He needed to take a walk so that they could talk.

He left a note—*you talk. walking. be back later. toss the planes in the closet. M.*

Then he headed out to the beach to walk and wander. Man, it was Thanksgiving, almost.

Almost.

He needed to think about this, about what was right. About whether he wanted a normal life. About whether fucking a writer and making planes was normal. About whether or not he was willing to let Billy lose friends and all the life the man'd had.

Because that was the thing, wasn't it? He wasn't stupid—he'd seen the pictures in frames around the apartment: Billy laughing at parties, different men with him, lots of people. Billy hadn't gone out once since he'd shown up.

That was his fault, because he couldn't be trusted to go out and not use.

Fuck.

He looked out at the ocean. If he was a decent man, he'd just hitch a ride and go.

Now.

Tanny looked at his hands and sighed. This sucked.

"Whether I've had him tested or not is none of your business. And he's not an animal, if that were to happen it would be his choice!" Billy was beginning to be more angry than hurt at Oliver's attitude.

"I never suggested he was an animal, William. I'm suggesting that I care more about my friend than some unfortunate from the street, and I'm suggesting that if the situation were reversed, you'd feel the same!"

"I would trust you, Oliver. I'd like you to trust me. Tanny is a wonderful person. He just needs someone to trust him."

"I'm sure he is. Is he into the lifestyle?"

"Not yet. The potential is there." He drew Oliver to the kitchen. The groceries were put away, the table covered with cans. The only thing missing was Montana. "Tanny?"

Nothing. Nothing, and the man's shoes were gone.

"Fuck." Then he noticed the note. "Oliver, I need to go."

"There's a note here, friend." Oliver handed it over.

"I've read it. I have to go." He had to find Tanny before the man did something drastic. "He thinks you don't like him. He thinks I'm going to lose my friends if I stay with him."

"I don't like the risk. I won't lie. You are dear to me, William." Oliver sighed, patted his arm. "However, you are a smart man, if a bit of an optimist, so I trust I will learn to like your new beau. I'll help you look."

He pulled Oliver to him and hugged the man. "Thank you, Oliver. That means a lot to me. And to Tanny, too. Come on. He'll be down at the beach."

Oliver was, before anything else, an exceptional friend.

"If you'd like, I can call Jack. We could meet him for supper." They headed down the stairs.

"Thank you, Oliver. If Tanny's feeling up to it, we'd love to go."

They headed for the beach, Billy keeping his eyes open for Tanny in case he hadn't been gone long enough to reach the beach. He saw his lover, leaning on the waterwall, staring out over the water. He relaxed a little bit now that they'd found him.

"Tanny," he called out as he and Oliver approached, so he didn't startle the man.

Tanny looked over, face somber, quiet. "Hey, guys."

"Hey." He leaned in and gave Tanny a kiss. He wouldn't hide how he felt.

Tanny smiled a little. "Didn't you see my note? I said I'd be back."

"Yes, but I didn't know how long you'd be, and Oliver wanted to invite us out to dinner with his lover." And he'd been worried that Tanny might do something drastic, given he was upset.

Tanny looked at Oliver, obviously suspicious.

"Why?"

Oliver's lips twitched. "Because William is my friend. He cares for you, ergo you and I will learn to get along."

At least Oliver was honest.

"I think you'll like Oliver's lover. Jack is... a lovely man." A bit of a prima donna, but Oliver adored him and Jack adored Oliver right back.

"Is he going to look at me like I'm trash? Because I'm done with that today."

Oh, yes. Go Tanny. His lover was usually the one running himself down—this made a welcome change. "Oliver?"

"I'm his top, William, not his conscience. I do apologize for making you feel bad. I have an innate distrust for addiction."

"With reason, Oliver." He patted Oliver's arm and then turned his attention back to Tanny. "Why don't we give it a try? We can leave at any time if you're uncomfortable."

"Sure. Nowhere fancy."

"Call Jack. We can meet him somewhere." Billy couldn't help grinning. His friend making the effort should go a long way to helping Tanny realize that Billy wasn't giving up his life to be with the man.

Oliver nodded, stepped away, and Tanny looked at him. "I don't have to come, Billy. I don't fit in."

He reached out to stroke Tanny's cheek. "Of course you're going to come. I want you to get to know my friends, for them to get to know you. You can't fit in if you don't even come."

"Pizza or Chinese, lads?" Oliver was trying, Billy'd give the man that.

"Tanny?" He smiled at his lover.

"Pizza." Tanny always chose pizza, if he had a chance.

"La Luna?" Billy asked Oliver. It was great pizza, but with a very casual atmosphere.

"Perfect." Oliver turned back to the phone, and Montana looked back out over the water.

He reached out to stroke Tanny's belly. "Thank you for making the effort."

"I'm just doing it for you. I thought about leaving. It's fair that you know."

"I'm glad you didn't. I want you to stay."

"I know. That's why I didn't."

He had to lean in and give Tanny a kiss for that. Then he took his lover's hand. "So, Oliver—are we good to go?"

"Absolutely. Jack's excited. He enjoys meeting new people."

"Good." He squeezed Tanny's hand and they headed off toward La Luna.

Oliver walked with them, hands in his pockets, whistling. "So, the little planes. They look like the ones at Rainbow Artists. I bought one from there two weeks ago."

"Did you? Those are Tanny's creation. Helena was really enthusiastic about having them. She was right, too, they sold like hotcakes."

"So, you did those? Excellent. You should meet Les. He's an interior designer."

"Oh, that's an excellent idea. Tanny painted my place, helped me choose the colors. He's got a great eye. You do, you know." He smiled at Tanny. Tanny rolled his eyes, shook his head. Billy chuckled.

"No running yourself down, Tanny."

Tanny snorted. "Billy has an overdeveloped appreciation for me."

"Someone needs to."

"Bullshit."

Oliver's lips twitched, eyebrow arching.

He waved a finger at Oliver. "Hush, you." Then he turned to Tanny. "Don't swear at me."

"I didn't swear at you. That would be calling you a motherfucker. I swore."

"Semantics. You're not a loser, Tanny, and I won't let anyone call you one. Not even you." He stopped walking and gave Tanny a hard kiss.

Tanny blinked, swayed a little. "Okay."

He smiled and nodded. "Good." He started walking toward La Luna's again.

Oliver was barely holding back his laughter. Barely. Billy might have to beat the man.

They made it to the little restaurant without anyone being beaten and Jack was already there, sitting at a table with a red and white checkered table cloth. Billy waved and made his way over, still holding onto Tanny's hand.

"Hey, there! Master William!" Jack bounced up, hugged Billy tight, then kissed Oliver. "Hello, love."

Oliver chuckled. "Jack, Montana. Montana, this is Jack."

Billy waited to see what Jack would make of Tanny. And what his lover would think of Jack.

"Hey." Jack grinned, held out one hand. "Tell me you like pepperoni."

Tanny shook. "I like pepperoni."

"Excellent!"

"There we go—bonding over pizza toppings." Billy chuckled and pulled out Tanny's chair for him.

Tanny looked at him curiously, but sat, eyes going to the menu.

He took up a seat next to Tanny, hand moving to rest on his lover's thigh. "I'm in the mood for something exotic."

Oliver chuckled. "Artichokes? Venison?"

"I'm thinking the balsamic chicken, actually."

"Can I have pepperoni and sausage and olive, sir?" Jack was in rare form, bouncing and laughing, the hyperactive man in constant motion.

Oliver chuckled. "Yes. But no Coke or Mountain Dew."

Tanny looked shocked, but never said anything, eyes on the menu.

Billy smiled softly and squeezed Tanny's thigh. "What about you, Tanny? What would you like?"

"I'm easy. I'll just share with you, if you want. That and a Coke'll do me."

"That works for me." He placed their order and then smiled at his friends. "So, Oliver, what have you been up to lately?"

"Working, of course. The club's been busy preparing for holiday festivities, fundraisers, parties. You know. Jack's just recently returned from Las Vegas on a shoot."

"How did that go, Jack?"

"It rocked! I played slots and danced. I shot about a thousand images and took pole dancing lessons!"

Oliver's lips twisted.

"Pole dancing lessons?" Billy laughed. "And are you installing a pole in your dungeon, Oliver?"

"Dungeon?" Tanny squeaked, and Jack laughed.

"No! I want one in the Hammer!"

"Oh, good lord." He looked over at Oliver. "A pole? At the Hammer? Is that wise?" The twinks would have a field day.

"Perhaps in one of the larger rooms in the back..." Oliver rolled his eyes.

Billy chuckled. Oliver did indulge his Jack so. It was sweet, really, how in love the man was.

"I bought lamé hot pants, just for my Ollie."

Billy thought Tanny was going to sink into the floor.

Of course, he was blinking pretty hard himself, trying desperately not to picture that.

Thank goodness their waitress showed up with their drinks and garlic sticks.

"So, Tanny, what do you do?"

"With what?" Tanny looked over at Jack.

Billy didn't know whether to laugh or cry. He squeezed Tanny's thigh again. "I think he means what's your job?"

"I make shit out of trash."

"Oh." Jack looked a bit taken aback.

"It's called found art," Billy put in. "I believe you have a piece of Tanny's found artwork in your house, by pure coincidence.

"The plane? Oh, man. I loved that. So cute. Where did you learn to do that?"

Tanny met Jack's eyes. "When I lived on the street I made them so I could buy drugs."

Billy didn't say anything, he just waited. He knew this was Tanny's big test of Oliver and Jack. If they could accept this, Tanny might begin to believe that being with Tanny wasn't going to ruin his life.

"Oh." Jack blinked. "What kind of drugs?"

"Speed."

"Huh. Were you homeless?"

"Yeah."

Jack bounced a little. "Would you be willing to talk to a reporter?"

"Jack." Oliver's voice snapped out. "That's hardly appropriate."

Billy didn't know whether to be taken aback or to look at it from the angle that at least Jack wasn't looking at Tanny like he was trash.

"I'm sorry, Master. I just... I'm dying to do a shoot, you know? I would love to hear your stories."

Montana shrugged. "Tell you what, you give me whatever you're on, we'll do a shoot."

"Montana." It was his turn to draw his lover back.

"What?" That was a direct challenge, straightforward and firm.

"Don't be rude. Jack doesn't do drugs, and he's interested in your story."

"So, what? You get that buzzed naturally? Must be nice." Tanny pushed back from the table. "Does anyone know where the bathroom is?"

"I'll show you." Billy stood. "If you'll excuse us."

"I'll be right back." Tanny tried to smile.

He put his hand in the small of Tanny's back and led him to the little toilets at the back of the restaurant.

"Thanks." Tanny pulled away. "I'll only be a minute."

"Hey." He waited for Tanny to stop. "No one's judging you out there. Oliver is trying, and Jack genuinely likes you. And he is high on life—on his life and his love and what he shares with Oliver." The kind of life he wanted for Tanny and himself.

"Dude, your friend told him he couldn't have a Coke. The guy called you master. He's high."

"It's all part of the lifestyle I told you about, Tanny. BDSM. That's their relationship."

"Okay. Cool. Look, I have to fucking piss."

"Of course. Sorry." He gave Tanny a soft kiss on the lips and then went back to the table.

Jack was sitting, head down, quite obviously reprimanded. "Master William, sir. I'm sorry, sir."

He sat and petted Jack's hand. "It's okay, Jack. You were just reacting honestly, yeah?"

It was a lot for Tanny to take in. And maybe, just maybe, knowing someone could be as happy as Jack was without drugs was something that was going to take

Tanny some getting used to.

"I know, but... He's new. I need to learn to think."

Billy chuckled and nodded. "I won't argue with that." He gave Jack a wink to let the man know he'd been forgiven. By Billy at least.

"Is he... is he mad at me?"

"No. He thinks you're high."

"What?" Jack stared over at Oliver. "Am I acting high?"

"No, love. Just exuberant."

"Tanny hasn't had a lot of good in his life, Jack. He doesn't believe there's anything other than drugs that could make someone as happy as you are. I'm hoping to change that."

Jack sighed, shook his head. "That's so sad."

"Yes, it is. But as I said, things will change. I'm glad he saw how happy you were without drugs."

"I... is he still on them?"

Billy shook his head. "No, Tanny's clean. Has been since the night he moved in."

"Wow. Did he... I mean, I know it's personal, but... Did he have hallucinations?"

Curious man. "These are questions for Tanny, Jack. Though maybe not tonight, hmm?"

"Right. Sorry. I... Do you want me to go check on him?"

Billy shook his head. He didn't want Tanny thinking he didn't trust the man. "He'll come back when he's ready."

The pizzas came and they all started eating, the period of time stretching out. He was ten seconds away from getting up and going to check before he saw Tanny, heading their way.

He smiled and waved. "I hope you don't mind that we started."

"That's cool." Tanny sat, drank deep from his Coke. "It smells good."

"You okay?" Billy asked quietly when everyone started eating again. Tanny nodded, but wouldn't look at him. Billy frowned, the pizza suddenly not nearly as enjoyable. He'd wanted Tanny to have a good time, and that clearly wasn't happening.

Jack reached over, touched Tanny's hand. "Do you like Tanny or Montana best?"

Tanny looked up, eyes surprised. "So long as you don't call me Monty, I don't care."

"Oh, I hate when people call me Jack-O, so I get that."

Billy smiled over at Jack. Bless his heart, he was trying hard.

Montana nodded, actually smiled. "I bet."

"You want a piece of pepperoni?"

"Yeah. Thanks."

Billy took a silent breath of relief. "So Oliver, have I missed any interesting news at the club?"

"Just the normal. Are you coming to the holiday leather party?"

"When is it this year?" Tanny would look beautiful in leather pants and nothing else. Or even a leather kilt... Billy smiled at the thought, his cock starting to fill.

"The leather party is the twelfth. The bondage Santa party is the twentieth. And, of course, Jack and I are hosting our party on Christmas evening."

"Oh, that could be fun. If Tanny's up to meeting my friends by the handful instead of one or two at a time." Oliver's Christmas parties were always a treat.

"Excellent. We'll dine at six, open presents at nine, and then the party will begin." Oliver smiled, the look a touch wicked. Billy chuckled. He hoped he and Tanny would be far enough down the road by then for wicked.

"Oh, you should come. It's so fun. We dress down—jeans and sweaters—there's music and dancing and if you drink, you can stay over." Jack bubbled over at Tanny. "It will be fabulous."

"It is fun, Tanny. It might be nice to have something with people for Christmas."

Those black, black eyes met his. "Do you usually go?"

"I do, but if you won't be comfortable, we don't have to." He wanted to spend Christmas with Tanny and just being able to would make it special enough.

"You should go, then. People like to be traditional around the holidays."

"I want to spend Christmas with you. We can decide where and how that happens later." Billy chuckled. "We haven't even had Thanksgiving yet!"

"No. No, we haven't. Are you coming to our house? We're having a formal night." Jack looked like he wanted to bounce, but he wasn't.

He shook his head. "Not this year, Jack, but thank you."

"Oh, that's too bad. Manning's coming, Parker, Rich and the twins..."

"So you won't even miss me." Billy smiled at Jack and then looked over at Tanny, his smile increasing.

Tanny had finished his Coke, was looking at the glass.

"Do you want some more, Tanny? Or some dessert?" He wondered if it was getting to be too much for Tanny.

"I'm sorry. I need to go. I have to finish working." Tanny stood. "You have fun. I gotta hustle."

His lover took off without staying another word.

Jack blinked, "Oh, God. Did I do something wrong?"

Oliver patted Jack's hand. "No, Jack. Breathe."

"No, no, Jack. It's not your fault. Being... normal is

hard for Tanny. I hope you don't mind, my friends, I'm going to go home with him." He took out his wallet and grabbed some bills.

"I've got this one. You buy the next. We'll all go out, see the lights together." Oliver was a good friend.

"Thank you, Oliver. I look forward to it." He put his wallet back, gave them both smiles and a wave and headed home.

Chapter Seventeen

He'd scored in the restaurant.
He had a pill in his pocket.
One red.
One.
He hadn't taken it yet. He wasn't sure if he was going to, but it felt good, knowing it was there.

Tanny walked toward Billy's house, head down, fingers rolling the pill, over and over.

He was almost there when he noticed footsteps about a block behind him, a low whistling sounding as well. He didn't look back. He knew it was Billy. It had to be.

When the footsteps got closer, Billy called out. "Hey, Tanny."

"Hey." He sighed, pill flipping in his fingers. "I didn't mean to interrupt your food."

"I was pretty much done. You didn't eat much, though—did you have enough?"

"I don't know." He flipped the pill again. "I'm going to tell you something. I scored at the restaurant. I haven't taken it yet, but I'm going to. I need it, but I'm not going to lie to you. Once I take it, I won't be hungry."

Billy's eyes widened and then narrowed. "There's plenty of food inside," Billy told him as they climbed the stairs. "Let's flush the pill down the toilet."

"No. I need it." He needed something to make things... bigger.

"No, you don't." They stopped at the door, and Billy turned him so they were facing each other. "What is it that you really want that you think that pill is going to give you?"

"Speed. Clarity. It makes me feel special, like I'm not the biggest loser on the planet, trying to be something I'm not."

"You're not the biggest loser on the planet, and I hardly think that pill is going to give you clarity." Billy shook his head. "Come in and let me try something. We'll leave the pill on the counter in the bathroom and flush it after, when you see how good things can be without it. How does that sound?"

"Do you promise you won't flush it? You swear?" He turned the pill again.

"No. You will, but I won't."

"Okay. I'm going to trust you, all right?" Don't fuck this up.

"Just as I'm trusting you to go put it in the bathroom. I'll meet you in our bedroom, okay?"

"Okay." He nodded, headed to put the pill on the tiny shelf above the sink, next to the glass they kept their toothbrushes in. It sat there, taunting him.

Still, he'd been honest. He hadn't lied. And Billy had trusted him to go put it in the bathroom by himself. He could hear the man moving around in the bedroom.

He headed in, rolling his shoulders. "So? I put it up."

"Good. First I want a word from you that means 'stop right now'."

"Huh? Like cease?"

"Well, the word can be anything, but when you say it, no matter when or where or anything, everything stops. No matter what."

"I don't get it."

Billy wasn't making any sense.

"Just pick a word you normally wouldn't use in everyday conversation or during sex."

"Uh... armpit?"

"As long as you aren't likely to say 'suck my armpit hair', that'll work." Billy's lips were twitching, his eyes dancing.

"Oh, gag. Gross. No. No way. Nasty." Just ew.

Billy started laughing. "Okay, armpit it is." Billy began stripping off his clothes. "You, too."

"Huh? You wanna fuck? Now?" Jesus.

"You want something to make you feel good."

"Yeah, but..." He wasn't horny.

Billy stared him down.

"What?" This was weird.

"But what, Tanny? You agreed to try something other than the drugs to get you where you needed to be."

"I..." Well, he had, he guessed. "Okay. It's a little weird, though. Just getting naked."

"Then let me do it for you." Billy stepped forward, hands sliding on his arms.

"Your hands are warm." He let his hands circle Billy's waist.

"I like touching you." Billy's fingers moved to tug his T-shirt out of his jeans.

"Good." He sucked in, arms up. "I wasn't going to lie to you. I'm not ashamed of needing the pills."

"I'm glad you didn't. I think it's a good sign." Billy pulled his T-shirt off, and leaned in to kiss across the top of his shoulders.

"A good sign of what?"

"That it doesn't completely rule you."

He didn't know what to say about that.

He just didn't.

"Stop thinking and just feel, Tanny." Billy's tongue did something wicked to his nipple as warm fingers worked open his jeans.

"Okay." His fingers stroked over Billy's hair, touching carefully.

His other nipple was bitten at the same time that Billy's fingers slid across the head of his cock.

"I'm not..." He wasn't. Not yet. His cock jerked and began to fill. He was going to be, though.

"You will be." Billy gave him a wicked grin and pushed him down onto the bed. His pants were tugged down to his shoes, which were pulled off.

Then he was naked.

His hands slid over his belly, down toward his cock. Billy climbed up onto the bed and kneeled over him.

That was hot.

His hands moved to Billy's stomach, touched the fine skin. Groaning for him, Billy bent to give him a hard kiss. His lips parted, his moan surprising him. Billy licked into his mouth like it was a delicacy.

Oh.

He pushed up, happy as their bodies met, skin-on-skin. Their cocks rubbed together as the thorough, careful kisses continued. Tanny found himself relaxing, leaning into Billy and focusing on the taste of his lover's mouth.

Billy's hands slid over his skin, the touches hard compared to the light kisses. Montana shivered a little, those harder touches enough to make him shudder.

"Love the feeling of your skin." Billy's words were a little growly.

"It's... thank you." Was that right?

"Mmm... you're welcome." His right nipple was pinched and Billy's tongue slid across his lips again.

He shivered, nipple aching a little.

"You like that?" Billy asked, moving to give the other

Found

one the same pinch.

"I. Yeah. A little."

Billy chuckled softly and bent to lick at his nipple, tongue as gentle on it as it had been on his mouth. He moaned, eyes dropping closed. The light touch came again and again, first to one nipple, and then to the other.

"It's good." So good.

"I know." Billy's lips wrapped around his left nipple and firm suction started.

"Billy..." His knees got a little weak. The tip of Billy's tongue flipped back and forth on his trapped nipple. "That tingles."

So did the humming.

Then, without warning, Billy bit his nipple.

"Ow!" He jerked away, eyes wide. He rubbed the little bit of flesh. "Careful."

Billy chuckled and jacked his cock. "You liked it, though."

"I... I don't know if I did."

"No?" Billy moved to the other nipple and the sweet, soft suction started.

"I don't...." He whimpered, head falling back.

"Stop thinking," growled Billy just before biting his left nipple.

"Don't bite." His hips started rocking.

His prick pushed through Billy's hand. "Because you hate the biting."

"Uh-huh." Wait. What?

"I don't think that's true." Billy's tongue slid around his nipple once more, then Billy's lips, teeth threatening.

"Don't. I'm not lying..." He bit his lip. Billy bit him, too, sharp and short. He cried out, hands in Billy's hair. The bite was soothed a moment later, Billy sucking and gently flicking his tongue over Tanny's nipple and these little sounds started bubbling out of him. The next little bite had his whole body jerking. Before he could complain, the sweet touches were back.

His cock was hard, leaking, his fingers opening and closing, over and over. Billy just kept doing it, moving from one to the other, now biting, now licking, now sucking. He never knew what was coming next.

"Billy. They're hot. I..." He needed to... something.

Billy looked up at him, eyes dark, hand still working his cock. "You can come if you need to."

Then Billy blew on his chest. He cried out, spunk shooting from his cock, need sharp and sudden and unexpected.

"Nice," murmured Billy, pushing him higher on the bed. He went, melted and quiet, sated. Billy cuddled up, cock hard against him. "I want inside you."

"Okay." It hadn't hurt before. Billy wouldn't hurt him now.

Billy nudged him over so he was on his side, and then pushed his top leg over. A moment later Billy was curled around him, fingers toying with his hole.

"You're warm. It's nice."

"Lovemaking is supposed to be nice." Billy landed soft kisses on his neck and a slick, warm finger pushed into him.

He spread and pressed back, eyes rolling back into his head at the touches.

"You make me need, Tanny." Billy murmured the words against the skin of his neck, just below his ear.

"Good. I want to." He didn't want Billy to be finished with him. His answer made Billy growl a little. It was a good sound. The stretch in his ass got bigger, Billy putting two fingers inside him now and moving them around. That odd swelling in his chest happened again, the sensation making him gasp a little. Billy's breath slid against his skin as the fingers inside him kept making everything feel bigger and bigger.

"Fuck..." He moaned, his entire body trying to move.

"Yes. I think you're ready for that now." Billy's fingers disappeared and he heard the crinkle of a condom package opening, and then Billy was pushing into him, cock hard and hot and insistent.

He gasped, his entire body rippling, aching as he arched. Billy's hand slid around to hold his belly, tugging him back as the thick cock continued to spread him wide.

"You're big." He tried to catch his breath, tried to see.

"You can take me. Nice and easy." Billy settled and stilled once he was all the way in.

They breathed together for a few moments, Billy all around him and inside him.

Tanny moaned, almost crying, and that made him angry. "I'm not sad."

"Good tears? That's good." Billy's hand petted his belly.

"Yeah? Yeah, it's okay?" Oh, thank God.

"It's honest, and that's good, Tanny. Don't worry about anything. Just enjoy it." Billy's hips began to circle, moving the cock inside him. He felt every inch, sliding out and pushing in. It felt so strangely intimate, having someone pressed up against his back, against all his scars.

He groaned, the tears sliding down his cheeks for a minute before he could breathe and focus, lean back against Billy's chest. Soft kisses slid along his neck and shoulder, and the hand stroking his belly shifted to circle his cock and hold him.

"Can we just stay like this for a little while?" Still and quiet?

"We sure can."

"Cool." He closed his eyes, breathing with Billy.

Billy's movements were slow and sweet. It was like they were in a cocoon of peace and pleasure. He'd never felt like this, never felt like he was home.

Never.

It went on and on and he could tell Billy's focus was on him.

"Better." He couldn't help smiling.

"Mmm... good." Billy hummed and stroked his cock, still rocking gently into him.

"I. Yeah..." He moaned, caught and so fucking happy.

"Gonna move a little faster now." Billy's thrusts speeded up, not a lot, but things got more intense.

His body stretched, he took Billy in and in and in.

"So good." Billy's words were soft. "You're so tight, so hot."

"I want. I want you to... I need. This is."

"What do you need, Tanny? What do you need me to do?" Billy's words were like touches, sort of.

"I... I don't know. Help me?"

"Always." The way Billy said it sounded like a vow. Moving faster, Billy squeezed his cock, the stroking becoming rougher, almost insistent.

"Oh. Oh. Oh." The word burst out of him, over and over and over.

The gentle touches on his neck suddenly became sucking, Billy pulling up a mark on his skin. He moaned, eager and hot, his skin feeling too tight. Billy's teeth scraped over his skin at the same time as Billy's thumb pressed against his slit. He squeezed tight, balls aching as he came.

Gasping, Billy jerked inside him. The cry that followed held his name.

"Billy. Billy." He tensed, clenched around Billy's cock.

"I've got you." Billy's fingers petted his belly.
"This was good."
"It was." Billy kissed the side of his face. "It is."
"For you too?"
"Absolutely for me, too."

He gripped Billy's fingers, hanging on. They twisted with his and another soft kiss pressed onto his skin. "I'm sorry if your friends didn't like me."

"Oliver is simply overprotective, and Jack liked you a lot. I think he was rather fascinated because your life story is so very different from his own." Billy groaned, prick sliding from him. A moment later the covers were pulled up over them both.

"This is okay?" They were okay?

Billy's arm tightened around him in a one-armed hug. "Yes."

"Okay. I have to make more planes. Later."

"Tomorrow. While we plan our Thanksgiving menu."

"You think that's okay?" It was what he wanted.

"Why wouldn't it be?"

"I just feel a little la..." He yawned. "Lazy."

Billy chuckled. "Good sex deserves good cuddling after."

He chuckled, nodded. Okay.

Okay.

Chapter Eighteen

Billy held Montana for a long time. It was warm and cozy and, after their long bout of lovemaking, felt perfect.

Eventually, though, they began stirring and he kissed Tanny's shoulder. "How about we take a shower together and then we can go plan our Thanksgiving dinner, see what we can cook tomorrow and what needs to wait until Thursday."

"I don't know. We could just stay for a little while..." Tanny nodded, even though his words contradicted the agreement.

"It is a comfy spot, isn't it?" He kept his hand on Tanny's belly, holding his lover close. "We certainly don't need to go anywhere to talk about Thanksgiving. I bought a turkey. It's fucking huge."

"I like turkey. Are we going to have mashed potatoes and pie?"

"We can have whatever you like. Mashed potatoes sound good. And I've got lettuce and stuff for a salad. Carrots and beans for vegetables. What kind of pie do you want?"

"I like pumpkin if there's whipped cream. If not, I like pecan."

"Excellent. I bought one of each." He wasn't sure

about the whipped cream, though. They could go buy some if they needed to.

"Cool." He wasn't sure what Montana's family had done at Thanksgiving. Hell, he wasn't sure if Montana's family did Thanksgiving. "We've got the parade and stuff on TV and of course the eating. Is there anything in particular you want to do with the day?"

"No, not really. I usually go to the shelter. There's lots of food."

"If you wanted, we could go for a few hours and help serve." He could go out and buy a couple more pies for them to take with them, as well.

"No." The word was flat, harsh. "I can't."

He stroked Tanny's arm. "Okay. That's all right, Tanny. This is a day for us to share how we want to. There's no right or wrong."

"Maybe. Either way, I just can't. I can't go see all those people."

"That's fine." He kissed Tanny's shoulder and rubbed the slender belly. "We can make our own traditions."

"Yeah? Okay. Okay. I'm sorry." Tanny took a deep breath. "Except that's a lie. I'm not sorry."

"So don't be sorry. You need to look out for yourself, Tanny. And if that means not seeing the people from your past, then that's what it means." Billy loved that Tanny was honest with him, even when he thought it would make him look bad. Tanny nodded, chin dipped, fingers stroking his hand. "I think we should start our Thanksgiving making love. I think that would be an amazing tradition."

"You want to have another holiday with me, too? You're sure?"

"Yes, Montana. I'm sure." Thanksgivings, Christmases, New Year's Eves, birthdays: he wanted them all. He loved how Montana relaxed at his words, focusing on him.

Needing him. Wanting him.

"We'll make our own traditions for every one of them." He placed one kiss after another on Tanny's shoulders. Every now and then he'd lick along one of Tanny's scars.

"I... I don't..." Tanny groaned, stretched a little bit. "That feels funny—good, but funny."

"You've never let anyone back here." He kept doing it, kissing, licking—touching.

"No. No, never. It's ugly." And the little spots of unscarred skin between the scars were deliciously sensitive.

He licked a patch of skin and scars and then blew gently across the wet flesh.

"Billy!" Tanny jerked, pulled away a little.

"They don't scare me."

"They should."

"Why?" Just because Tanny thought they were ugly and horrible, didn't mean everyone else had to hold the same opinion.

"Because they're ugly. They're scars."

"They're a part of you, so they could never be truly ugly."

Tanny stilled, head tilting. "What?"

"You aren't ugly, Montana. You're quite striking, in fact. And your scars are a part of you."

"I'm ugly. I don't want to talk about this."

"You are not ugly, you're not a loser, and you can't run away from these conversations forever."

Tanny sure was trying to, though.

"I can too." Stubborn brat.

"You can try, but I'm going to keep coming back to them."

"No. I don't like to talk about things."

"I know. But they don't go away just because you don't talk about them." He wouldn't let Montana hide from him, drawing into himself. He tugged on Tanny, shifting his lover so they were lying face to face. "You want to go get that shower now?"

"Uh-huh." Those pretty, dark eyes were worried, focused on him, begging him to make it better.

He smiled at Tanny and then kissed the man. "No matter how much you tell me you're ugly—I won't believe you. I have eyes in my head. I see you, Montana. And seeing you, I choose to hold you in my arms."

"Why? I'm stupid and a loser and a tweaker, and I killed my sister, and I'm not good at things and..."

"Stop that." He growled at Tanny. "You're none of those things and you are so good at all kinds of things."

"Make me." Those lips went tight.

Leaning in, he kissed Montana. Hard. Their lips mashed together. Montana's eyes went wide, then Montana kissed him back with equal intensity. Billy kept kissing Montana, tongue pushing in, his lip, or maybe Tanny's, splitting. He didn't wait to see if Tanny panicked, trusting in his instincts, in what he knew about his lover.

Lapping the blood away, he rolled Tanny to his back and continued kissing. It was hard and full of growls and just what Tanny needed.

Tanny's legs wrapped around him, the man clinging like a limpet. Yes.

His thumbs found Tanny's nipples and they dragged over the little nubs. The flesh tightened, but he knew Tanny needed more. He let his nails scrape over them this time, teeth hard on Tanny's lower lip. Billy felt the cry, more than heard it. He rocked them together, Tanny's cock hard and hot against his own.

He loved how Tanny arched, how Tanny wanted him. "Yeah, like this." He pinched Tanny's nipples again.

"I don't. I don't like..." Tanny arched, throat working as a flush climbed up the lean body.

"You seem to like it a lot." Billy pinched again, twisting Tanny's right nipple.

"Don't." Montana gasped, eyes a little wild.

Bending, he bit at Tanny's other nipple.

"Billy." Montana's hands landed on his head, directing him, or trying to.

He moved from one nipple to the other, biting, sometimes hard, sometimes softly.

"Stop. Stop, it's making my belly ache."

"That's a good thing, Tanny." His hips drove their cocks together as he bit again, tugging on Tanny's nipple.

He could feel Montana's heart pounding. He'd never have this again—the first time Tanny discovered pleasure in pain, the first steps they took on this path. Billy breathed in deeply, taking in the scents and the sounds, the feeling of Tanny in this moment.

He let one nipple go and went to the other one.

Tanny tried to pull away, but that pretty nipple was right there, hard and swollen for him.

He flicked his tongue across it a few times, mixing it up.

"Oh..." Montana relaxed, moaned, tension fading. It was almost going to be a shame to bite again, break that relaxation.

Almost.

It would be worth it in the end, though.

He bit down. Hard.

Tanny screamed, seed splashing up over his abs, even as Montana tried to get away.

He wrapped his hands about Tanny's shoulders, keeping him right there as he eased the swollen nipple.

Tanny shuddered violently, trembling in his hands. "That hurt."

Billy kissed his way slowly up along Tanny's chest to his neck, his mouth. "It made you come."

"It hurt." Tanny's kiss was sweet, lips clinging to his.

"I know." He kissed Tanny back, making sure his lover knew pleasure and ease.

Tanny was shivering, only slowly relaxing.

He pushed his tongue into Tanny's mouth, fucking it gently. He kept it up until Tanny was easy under him, eyes closed, fingers gentle on his arms. Then he settled, holding his lover close.

Chapter Nineteen

The kitchen smelled good—warm and spicy and weirdly homey.

Tanny was struggling to finish airplanes before four o'clock so that Helena could come pick them up.

His nipples hurt.

Not bad, just a little, and it was a little weird and a little hot and a little tender, but.

Yeah.

Billy was fooling with the turkey—getting it ready to go into the oven tomorrow morning. Every now and then he'd come over and give Tanny a kiss.

Tanny wasn't sure what to think. The Red was still in the bathroom, sitting there. Waiting for him.

He didn't need it, not right now.

"Okay, that's everything ready for tomorrow. I thought we'd have sandwiches for supper tonight—I've got crusty bread and brie cheese."

"What's brie cheese?" He fastened on a propeller.

"It's a soft cheese that's really good. Nice and gooey—almost like butter." Billy washed his hands and came to sit beside him. "Can I do anything to help?"

"I've got three more to finish." He held out his hands, the fingers blistered and sore. "I'm almost done."

Billy made a small noise and gently touched his hands.

"When you're done I'll play doctor with your hands."

"You don't have to, but I'd love a bandage." He bent back to his work, whistling.

Billy kissed the back of his neck. "I'll go get the first aid kit while you finish up."

"'kay." He sighed and tried to finish. The second to last gave him troubles, but the last one finished easily, and he popped them in a box, leaving them outside Billy's door for Helena to pick up.

He'd done it.

He was exhausted.

"You're done?" At his nod, Billy cheered. "Way to go!" One of Billy's hands landed on his shoulder, rubbing.

"Yay." He leaned his head on his arms, his nipples hard and aching.

"That was hard work, eh?"

Billy's fingers moved on his shoulders. "Come to the bathroom. We'll shower—I can help ease your muscles under the hot water, and then I'll fix up your hands."

"Okay. Yeah." Yeah, he could get into that. "It feels good to be done."

"I can't believe you got them all done so quickly." Billy's hand landed in the small of his back, leading him toward the bathroom.

"Me either. I hope they sell." The pill was there, on the shelf. Waiting.

"Well, the orders for other stores are basically already sold and I bet you the rest sell just as well as the first batch did."

"I hope." He winced as he tried to open his jeans. He was getting fat. They were tight.

"Let me help with that." Billy grinned at him, fingers sliding on his skin. "We need to get you a new pair."

"I need to stop eating so much."

Billy snorted. "You're still skin and bones. It's going to

take a lot to make you fat."

"My jeans don't fit, though." He let Billy get him in the shower, moaning at the heat.

"So we buy you new jeans." Billy's fingers dug into his shoulder, easing the tight muscles.

"Oh." He didn't argue. He didn't care. Not right that second. He just didn't want Billy to stop.

"We'll have to make this a tradition. Rubbing you down after a hard day."

"I don't have many of those." Still, it felt good.

"I know. I'd like us to make a ton. Make them together."

"Hard days?"

Billy chuckled. "No. Traditions."

"Oh." He grinned, cheeks heating. "Right." God, he was a giant dork.

Billy's hand slid around to grope at his crotch. "Of course 'hard' days wouldn't be a bad thing..."

He snorted. "Uh-huh. That was bad." Funny, but bad.

"I know. I have never claimed to be a comedian." Billy was still chuckling, though, clearly amused at himself.

They laughed together, and it felt good to do it.

Really good.

Billy grabbed the soap then and started sliding it over his skin. Front, back, sides—it didn't seem to matter to Billy if his scars were ugly or he was too skinny or anything.

Tanny soaped back, wanting to help, to touch. Billy made appreciative noises, pushing into his touches, imitating them on his own skin. He touched until the soap started really stinging his hands.

Billy must have seen him wince or something, because the next thing he knew, he was being rinsed off.

"I...We don't have to get out yet. They're just a little tender."

"Okay. No more soap, though." Billy's arms went around his waist and tugged him in against the strong body.

He rested his cheek on Billy's chest, eyes dropping closed, just for a second. Billy held him and touched his sides, his back. Each of his scars were traced.

"That feels nice." Weird, but nice.

"Good." Billy dropped a kiss onto his head and kept touching.

Tanny surprised himself by just standing, just relaxing for a little while. At some point the gentle touches slid from soothing and exploring into arousing.

He couldn't help smiling. Billy wanted him, a lot.

Tilting his head up, Billy took a kiss. Tanny opened up, kissed the man back, tongue sliding against Billy's. One of Billy's hands dropped to his ass cheek and tugged their crotches together. Billy was hard, heavy and hot against his belly.

Fuck.

The kisses got hotter, a low groan filling his mouth.

His own cock took longer to rise, slowly swelling up against Billy's thigh.

Billy rocked them together slowly. He'd never known anyone who wanted this to last, wanted to take so much time to let it build.

"Does it feel good to you?"

"This? Oh, yes."

"Me too. You want me to suck you?" He knew Billy liked that.

"Is that what you want, Tanny?"

"I..." He stopped, thought about it. "Sort of? I'm sore—my back is sore, my hands are sore, but I want to taste you, make you come."

"How about we take it somewhere more comfortable, then?"

"Yeah, yeah. That would rock." He'd had about three hours of sleep last night, trying to finish his work. He could do comfortable.

Billy turned off the water and drew him out of the shower. He was dried off tenderly, like he was something special, precious.

"You're so good to me."

"You're going to suck me, and yet I'm the one being good to you?"

"Uh-huh."

Billy chuckled and drew him into the bedroom. "I'm thinking I won't argue with you over that."

"No? Good." He didn't even look at the pill as he left.

Billy stopped them partway down the hall. He was wrapped in warm arms, Billy taking a kiss. He wrapped his arms around Billy's waist, fingers petting.

"God, you're intoxicating."

"Is that good?"

"It is. It can be dangerous, too. I could lose myself in you, Montana."

"I'm sorry? I can try to not."

"No. No. You aren't doing anything but being yourself. And that's a good thing." Billy kissed him. "I don't think I'd mind getting lost in you."

"I just..." He kissed Billy again. "There are so many rules..."

"What rules?"

"You know—how to make things work, don't lie, don't take the pill, don't fuck up."

"I never said you couldn't fuck up. We all fuck up now and then, Tanny. It's what makes us human." Billy pushed him up against the wall and kissed him hard.

He didn't bother to argue; he just opened up, tongue-fucking Billy's lips. Billy began walking them back down the hall toward the bedroom, never breaking the kiss. Montana followed, humming, licking into Billy's mouth.

They moved into the bedroom and onto the bed, Billy's hands everywhere. He moved into the touches, almost dancing.

"Beautiful," murmured Billy.

"Am not." He kissed Billy harder.

"You are, you know." Billy looked into his eyes, wouldn't let him hide from the words.

"No. No, I'm not."

"You are." Billy pressed kisses on either cheekbone, his nose, his chin.

"I'm not." He loved the kisses.

"Are, too." Billy grinned at him, kept peppering his face with sweet touches.

"Not. I'm an ugly loser."

Billy growled. "No. You are not."

"I am too." He knew it.

Billy straddled his waist and then grabbed his hands and dragged them up over his head. "You have the most amazing dark eyes."

"They're just..." He looked up. "What are you doing?"

"I'm not letting you go until you stop denying what I know to be true."

"You... You have to." Didn't he?

"Nope. I'm way more stubborn than you."

He chuckled, just a little unnerved.

"You have a strong nose, like a hawk's. And high cheekbones." Billy leaned in to kiss each part he mentioned. "You're like an exotic prince."

"Don't. Please. I'm just a fuck up." The compliments made him uneasy.

"Not true." Billy was growling again.

"It is true!" He surprised himself by yelling. "I'm nasty

and awful and ugly and you have to STOP PUSHING ME!"

Billy shook his head. "You're stunning and beautiful, and I'm never going to stop pushing."

"You have to. You have to let up."

"No. It gives you what you need."

"No, it doesn't. I need to breathe."

"So breathe." Billy met his eyes, not backing down at all.

"What are you doing? What's going on?"

"You remember that word, Tanny? The one you wouldn't say by accident?"

"Armpit? Yeah." Although he was a little surprised he did.

"If you can't take it anymore, you can use it. Otherwise, you trust me." Billy's eyes started at him, into him.

"Take what? What do you mean?"

Billy squeezed his hands around Tanny's wrists. "This. Not being able to move." Then Billy leaned in and looked him in the eye. "And this. Me seeing you and telling you how beautiful you are."

"I'm not. I'm not beautiful.'

"You are." Billy licked across his lips. "Even more so with your lips glistening, your eyes shining..."

"You're ridiculous..." It was sweet, thought.

"Nope. I'm not at all. You, on the other hand, are stunning and arousing." Billy rolled and the hard cock slid along his belly. "See?"

"This... You're so pushy." He snuggled in, tried to pull his hands free.

"I won't deny that." Billy's lips slid along his jaw.

"I don't understand all this mess." It scared him, a little bit.

"But you're enjoying what we do together, aren't you?"

"I do. Mostly. Some of it wigs me out."

"I don't think that's a bad thing, though." Nibbling at his ear, Billy bit his lobe.

"You don't? Shouldn't it...Oh." Ow.

"You remember that I told you I was into BDSM. That's a part of it—pushing yourself, your lover. Finding the boundaries and roaring past them to bring pleasure and focus." Billy sucked on his lobe, soothing it.

"I can't do that stuff, though. I don't want to hurt you."

"You can have it done to you, though." Billy shifted, moving to tongue his nipple.

He went still.

"Do you want to hurt me?"

"Not hurt—push." Billy kept teasing at his nipple. "You liked it when I bit you here yesterday."

"No, I didn't and they're tender today, be careful." His heart was pounding, hard.

"I made you come yesterday. By doing this." Billy bit, gentler than he had yesterday, but it was still a bite.

"Billy, stop it. You're making me wigged out. This whole thing is weirding me out, huh?"

"You're only weirded out because you like it."

"My hands hurt, Billy, and I'm tired and not feeling like this is a good idea."

"Your hands hurting makes this the perfect time to have them held over your head."

Billy rolled against him again, cock hard and hot, good as it slid against his own cock.

Something built in him, something very close to anger, which he wasn't interested in. He wrapped one leg around Billy's thigh, tugged them tighter together. Humming, Billy shifted. The solid legs slid down, bringing their cocks together, and BIlly's mouth closed over his again.

He opened to the kiss, tongue sliding against Billy's—

to stop the words, if nothing else. Billy's kisses were even more intense with his hands held up over his head. His scars pulled a little, under his shoulders, and he couldn't help but moan. Billy swallowed the sound, hips beginning to rock, to slide their cocks together.

That seemed a lot more... normal, so he relaxed, eased into Billy's kisses and started rocking back.

"Sexy," muttered Billy. His lower lip was bitten and then Billy was kissing him again, hard.

He laughed a little, then his laughter dissolved as Billy's cock and his moved together perfectly, pleasure sliding up his spine. Eyes staring into his, Billy kept kissing and moving against him. It had never been intense like this with anyone else.

He closed his own eyes, hiding a little bit, protecting himself.

A low growl sounded, but Billy continued to move against him. Billy kept making him feel good.

It was easy, to breathe, to relax, to get his shit together.

To feel.

Billy transferred his right wrist into the hand holding his left, and then Billy started to touch him.

"I can't touch you..." He twisted a little, moving against Billy.

"You can touch me later, give me that blow job you offered earlier." Billy's fingers slid across his nipple, and then twisted it.

"Easy!" He jerked, tried to pull away. "God damn it!"

The next touches were gentle and Billy's hand moved down, tickling along his side.

"Why do you do that? I don't get it."

"Because it gets you hard, gets you off."

"I don't know about that."

Billy laughed softly. "Montana. There's nothing to know—it got you off yesterday."

"Not the hurting part!" Right?

"No?" Billy gnawed on his nipple. It didn't hurt, more ached.

"No..." Oh. Oh. Oh, that felt...

Yeah.

"Good thing I'm listening to your body instead of your mouth."

"Hmm?" The little ache just got better and better, his world spinning.

Billy didn't answer him with words; instead, Billy's mouth continued working his nipple. His hips moved, rolled against Billy. It felt so good. So heated. Billy eventually slid over to work his other nipple, the same slow heat building there.

Sounds started hiccupping out of him, the sensations more than he could cope with.

Billy gave his nipple one last bite and then brought their mouths together. "Come on, Tanny, let go."

"Billy. Billy..." He moaned, so fucking hard he hurt.

"Yeah, come for me, Tanny. I want to smell you."

"Billy." He arched, spunk pouring from his prick.

"Yeah. Sexy beast." Billy let go of his hands and slid down to lick the come from his belly.

Tanny couldn't answer, all he could do was moan, touch his throbbing nipples. He could feel Billy's prick, hard and hot on his thighs. It was leaking, leaving behind a trail as Billy moaned over his belly.

"I want to suck you."

"Yes, please." Billy rolled onto his back, arms and legs stretched.

He rolled over, heading for that heavy cock, wanting to taste. Maybe needing to.

Billy made an encouraging noise, fingers sliding over

his head.

"I love your cock." He moaned the words, then started licking and lapping, one of his hands between his own legs, just petting his own spent cock.

"It's all yours." Billy's voice was hoarse, needy. Hot.

"Mmmhmm." He groaned, tongue pressing the tip of Billy's cock against the roof of his mouth.

"So good." Billy's legs stretched, shifted.

He nodded, sucking harder, letting Billy feel it. Billy's cock was thick and hot, the head filling his mouth. The man's balls were soft, almost like silk. He couldn't stop touching them.

Rolling them.

"Montana." Billy said his name like he was special.

"Mmmhmm." His fingers slid behind to touch that little strip of skin that he knew felt so good.

"Yes. Oh, yes." Billy's legs came up, which gave him better access.

He kept touching, sliding his sore fingers on the wrinkled skin. All the time, his head bobbed up and down, tongue slapping Billy's prick.

"Fuck. Don't stop, Montana. Please."

He was responsible for that pleading, begging note in Billy's voice. He wouldn't stop. Not a chance. Ever. Tanny closed his eyes, going down farther, sucking harder.

"Like that. Yes." Billy's hips started to push, to rock the thick cock deeper into his mouth.

He hummed with every push in, with every arch and ache and roll of the hips. Hands holding his head down, Billy moved harder until the man was fucking his mouth hard. Oh, fuck. Hot. They rolled then, suddenly, and Billy was on top of him, fucking his mouth and he'd never felt so wanted, so much like he was where he needed to be.

"Fuck. Montana! Yes!" Billy fucked and fucked his mouth and then suddenly was coming, filling him up with long spurts.

He had his hands wrapped around Billy's ass, dragging them tight together.

One of Billy's hands slid over his head and along his cheek. "Oh, so good. So very good. I didn't hurt you, did I? Didn't choke you?"

He shook his head and hummed happily, tongue cleaning the heavy prick. This wasn't like it had been with anyone else, ever. And Billy held him after, made sure he was okay.

"Good. Good. God, you're good at that, Tanny." Billy kept petting and touching him.

"You taste good. I like that."

Billy slid back down so they were lying together. "I'm glad."

He nodded, suddenly tired. Not sleepy, but exhausted. Billy drew him in close, hands stroking, soothing over his skin.

"Mmm. That's nice." He blinked, breathing in time with Billy, their hearts beating together.

"Yes. It is." Billy kissed his forehead. "Nap for a bit?"

"Rest, yeah. I'm sore." His hands burned now.

Billy grunted and rolled way. "Stay there." He padded out of the room, obviously unconcerned about his nudity.

"Billy?" He leaned up on one elbow. "Are you okay?"

"Yeah, I'm just getting something."

Billy disappeared, then came back a moment later with the first aid kit in his hand. "I don't want you hurting unnecessarily."

"I... Okay?" Billy was so weird.

Billy sat on the bed and took his right hand. "I've got some antiseptic spray in here that should numb the pain."

"Cool. Will it sting?" His fingers curled without his permission.

"It might a little, but then it should feel better." Billy carefully uncurled his fingers and sprayed his hand.

He winced, but it was just cold, not stingy. "That's good."

"Better, isn't it? Other hand, please."

He handed his hand over easily. Billy held it gently and sprayed the stuff over it.

Looking into his eyes, Billy smiled. "There we go. Now there can be comfortable cuddling."

"Thank you, Billy."

"You're welcome."

Billy lay down again and tugged him into the strong arms.

He chuckled and cuddled in.

Happy. Warm.

It was a good place to be.

Chapter Twenty

Billy basted the turkey, double checked the temperature on the oven and grabbed a couple of Cokes.

He headed into the living room to join Tanny who was on the couch in front of TV. The parade was on. It made a good excuse to sit close, maybe get something started.

He offered Tanny the Coke.

Tanny smiled at him, patted the sofa. "Can we sit together?"

"Yeah, we can." He sat and shifted until they were touching from shoulder to knees. "What have I missed?"

"There was a big turtle and a bunch of Rockettes."

He rested his hand on Tanny's thigh. "What were the Rockettes wearing?"

"Sparkles."

"And did they kick up to here?" He let his hand slide up to the top of Tanny's thigh.

Tanny's laugh sounded happy. "They did. It sort of rocked. Look. Balloons."

"Balloons?" He turned his hand to cup Tanny's balls in his jeans.

"Uh... uh-huh. I remember the Snoopy one was... Oh..." Tanny scooted closer.

"You like the Snoopy one?" He fondled the balls he

held. God, Tanny was sexy.

"When I was little, yeah."

"Which one do you like now?" He moved to cup Tanny's cock, stroke it through the denim.

"You. I like you, Billy." Tanny's legs spread. "Is it okay to do this, on Thanksgiving?"

He chuckled. Tanny did have some strange ideas. "We're making our own traditions, remember?"

"Yeah, but... I just thought... This is supposed to be all pure and righteous and about praying."

"No, it's about giving thanks for the good things in your life." He kissed Tanny softly. "For me this year that's you."

"I don't give you half what you give me."

"You've given me everything, Tanny, how could I ask for more?" He wasn't watching the parade at all; he was far more interested in watching Tanny.

"Me? All I've done is mooched..."

He shook his head. Montana still had such a low opinion of himself. "You trusted me. You've been clean for me. You've let me love on you."

"I do love you." The words surprised him, so simple, so easy.

He felt his smile start from deep inside himself. Then he kissed Tanny, everything else forgotten. Tanny's hands wrapped around his head, held him closer. He plundered Tanny's mouth, his hand tightening on the hot cock.

"Mmm." His sweet lover spread, moaned deep in his throat.

Billy shifted and moved to lie between Tanny's legs.

"Billy." Montana moaned, tongue sliding on his lips.

"That's me." He slid his hand over Montana's head and looked into the dark eyes.

Montana looked at him, smiled. "You're warm."

"I'm hot for you." On fire, really. Montana made him

want. Hard.

"You want me? I'm yours."

"I want you. Any and every way I can get you."

"Okay." Montana's hand slid down his back, caressing his spine.

He pressed their lips together again, happier than he could remember being in a long, long time. They kissed, Christmas carols from the TV filling the air. Montana tasted good, the flavor becoming more and more familiar under his tongue. Relaxed under him, Tanny was easy, spread, happy.

He wriggled, pushing their cocks together. Tanny kept moving, rubbing against him, sliding faster. His lover was so hungry, so eager for his touches.

Montana needed to be noticed.

His Montana. His, and he wasn't ever letting this go.

He ran his hand beneath Montana's T-shirt. He found warm skin, and he rubbed and stroked. He and Montana would learn about Montana's needs, his limits and his deepest desires, together.

"Fuck. Your hands. They feel good."

"They were made for your skin, Montana."

"They were probably made for a lot of people's skin, hmm?"

"No, they did okay for a lot of people. They were made for you." He slid his index finger across one of Tanny's nipples.

"Still tender." Yes, and if he had his way, they would be tender often.

"I should kiss them better." Grinning, he pushed Tanny's T-shirt up to expose the slightly swollen nubs.

They were bruised, just barely, the tips hard and tempting. He leaned in and gave each one a soft kiss. Tanny's moan felt amazing. He flicked his tongue back and forth across the right nipple, wanting more sounds.

"Tender. Damn, Billy."

"Makes you ache deep inside, doesn't it?" He cupped Tanny's balls again.

"Yes."

Ache and want, he'd imagine. He moved over to tease Tanny's other nipple. This beat watching the parade, hands down. Tanny moved restlessly, legs shifting under him. He pushed one knee up against Tanny's ass, rubbed it a bit.

"Billy." That sounded like it felt good.

"Uh-huh." He lapped at Tanny's nipple again, and let Tanny's own movements make the friction between ass and knee.

"We're supposed to be watching the... the parade."

He couldn't resist teasing. "You can't do both?"

"No. God, no."

Billy chuckled. "I could stop if you'd prefer to watch the parade."

"Asshole." Montana laughed softly, shook his head.

He bit at Montana's nipple.

"Fuck. Don't."

He flicked it with his tongue. That made Tanny gasp. There was so much to teach Tanny: pain, pleasure, the deep aches and wants. Submission. God, he wanted to show Montana everything.

He left Tanny's nipples to take the thin lips again. Plunging his tongue into Tanny's mouth, he put everything he felt into the kiss. Tanny opened right up, fucking his lips, loving him back. Billy gently fingered Tanny's nipples.

Little sounds pushed into his lips, over and over, Montana beginning to shiver. Montana was so responsive; it was exciting and arousing. Sliding his hands down along Montana's chest, he pushed his thumbs in beneath Montana's jeans. He slid his thumbs back and forth across

Tanny's hips.

The bones were sharp, the skin smooth and warm. It fascinated his fingers. And today they had nothing to do but explore, play, make the day as good as it could be.

He sucked on Tanny's tongue. He loved the little surprised sounds, every time he showed Tanny something new. Billy slid his thumb over to Tanny's jeans' button and popped it open. He didn't try to get to his lover's cock, though. Not yet. Instead he played with the soft skin there, just above Tanny's curls.

Tanny moaned, hips arching, humping toward his touch.

"So needy," he murmured. He loved it. He teased the tip of Tanny's cock through his underwear.

"Yes, touch me? Please?"

"Mmm... yes." He undid Tanny's zipper and pulled the underwear down beneath Tanny's long, hard prick.

That pushed Tanny's balls up, making an obscene little package. He petted the tight balls, fingers working them gently. Montana reached down, fingers stroking the long, hard prick.

"No, I think you should keep your hands off yourself." He was growling a little, but at least he hadn't slapped Montana's hand away and growled 'mine', right?

"Hmm?" Tanny blinked at him, looking a bit confused.

He met Tanny's eyes. "You can touch me, and I can touch you. No touching yourself."

"I... Okay?" That hand moved to his belly, around his hip.

Good boy. He didn't say the words, though. Instead, he pushed into Montana's touches, let his lover know it was good. Montana loved touching him, enjoyed giving pleasure. That was going to serve his lover well.

"You can undress me if you want." He slid his fingers

across the tip of Montana's prick.

"I... I want. Fuck." Montana jerked, drove up toward his touch.

"Yeah, I want to fuck, too." He continued to tease the tip of Montana's prick.

"I just... I." Tanny blinked, then pulled away from his touch. "Damn, I can't think when you do that."

"You need to think to make out? I like to go with what feels good." He reached to tease the head of Tanny's prick again.

"I need to think, sure." Tanny shifted, tugged his shirt up and off.

He pressed into Tanny's hands. "What do you need to think about?"

"What do to, how to feel."

"You could do those without thinking." He took Tanny's mouth again, eager to make his lover forget everything. He swallowed Montana's argument, one hand pushing in Tanny's hair to hold him still. Kissing Montana breathless had the same effect on himself, and Billy moaned.

Tanny licked his lips, kissed him, over and over, fingers sliding down his spine. "Fuck." Tanny moaned.

He pushed their hips together. "I want you, Montana. Right here on the couch." With the damn parade on in the background.

"Perv." Montana's laugh was fucking sweet.

"Yeah? You think that makes me a perv?" He laughed, too. "I want to do you on the kitchen table, too."

"The kitchen table?" Tanny chuckled, nuzzling into him.

"Uh-huh. Every flat surface in the place." And a few that weren't flat at all.

"You can't want me that much."

"I do, Montana." And more.

"I... Why? Tell me why."

"Because you're sexy. Because those eyes draw me in. Because I love you."

"Me? For real?"

"Yes, Montana. You."

"Okay. I'm going to believe in you."

He gave Montana warm smile. "I'd like that. I'd like it a lot. And I believe in you."

"I've never loved somebody before."

"I'm glad you love me." Billy took Montana's hand and kissed his fingers, one after the other.

"What if I suck at it?"

Oh, he was going to start growling again. "What if you're fantastic at it?"

"I'm not fantastic at anything." Stubborn boy.

"You suck like a dream."

"So, I don't suck at sucking?"

He chuckled and nodded, fingers moving to squeeze the tip of Tanny's prick. "You do not suck at sucking."

Tanny's fingers brushed his, touched the turgid shaft. He pressed his thumb against the little slit. Tanny groaned and arched, teeth bared with pure need. Fuck, Montana was sexy.

Billy slid to the floor and held Tanny's prick to his mouth. He pressed his tongue into the slit this time.

"Billy..." Tanny spread, heels digging into the sofa.

He didn't answer; he simply started fucking Tanny's slit with his tongue. Filthy words poured out of Tanny, making him smile. Adding to the sensation, he stroked the tight balls with his free hand.

"I. I need. I need to come."

"Already?" Billy grinned up at Montana and this time he licked across Tanny's slit.

"Like... like it takes forever."

"It can." It would. One day Tanny would come on

command. And not come on command.

"Uh-uh."

Oh, yes. One day Montana would know control like he couldn't even imagine. "Come on, then. Let's see how long you can hold out." He redoubled his efforts of fucking Tanny's slit.

"Not. Not long if you do that..." Tanny drew his knees up, spread wide.

"You like it, huh?" Not everyone did, but Tanny was getting off on it big time. Shit, the man was just dying for attention, touch, love, to be shown everything.

"I do. It burns a little."

"Does it?" Did Tanny realize he'd just admitted to liking something on the pain side?

"Uh-huh." Tanny's fingers stroked his own slit. "Right there."

Billy groaned, a shudder moving through him. He pushed his tongue deeper. Montana's groan echoed in him, it rang out and overrode whatever high school band was on the TV. Billy started alternating between fucking the slit and sucking the head.

"Billy. Fuck. Fuck. Fuck. Please."

He didn't answer, just kept torturing his lover the best way he knew how.

"I'm going to come."

He grabbed Tanny's sac, tugged firmly. Not yet. His tongue slapped at the top of Tanny's cock, his fingers twisting Tanny's balls, just a touch.

"Billy. Billy. Billy." It was like a chant.

Yeah. He took the head between his lips and tugged, his tongue back to fucking that tiny little hole. Spunk splashed into his mouth a second after Tanny screamed out his name, pretty cock pulsing. He wrapped his lips properly around the head and sucked strongly to stretch out Tanny's orgasm.

Tanny never went soft, working through one orgasm and staying hard for the duration.

"Mmm." Billy gave the head of Tanny's cock one last suck and then kissed his way down to Tanny's balls. Still pushed up, they were hot against his lips.

"So good. So good. Billy. I can't breathe, it's so good."

He backed off some, tugging at Tanny's jeans and underwear to pull them right off. "I want you." He knew he'd already said it, but Tanny needed to hear it. A lot.

"Yes. Yes, Billy." Tanny helped him, getting them both completely naked, hands and lips on his skin.

Once they were both nude he climbed up onto the couch, lying back and bringing Tanny down on top of him. Their cocks slid together and he gasped.

"You're hot." Tanny moved again, arched.

"Uh-huh. Hot for you." He slid his hands down to grab Tanny's ass.

Tanny's muscles rippled, moving against his palm. His fingers slid to find Tanny's little hole. He wanted inside that tight heat. He wanted to fuck Tanny.

That tiny ring of muscles shifted and clenched, Tanny never still.

Soon he'd introduce Tanny to toys. A cock ring to keep him from coming so quickly, a plug to keep him filled. Little clamps to bite at his nipples. Today, though, he just wanted inside. He pressed two fingers against Tanny's lips. "Suck on them. Get them wet."

"Mmmhmm." Montana had a mouth made for sex, eager and hungry, and those lips wrapped around his fingers and sucked, hard.

Groaning, Billy dropped his head back onto the pillow. The sucking on his fingers had sensation thrumming through his body.

"Fuck." The single word slid from him. He looked

up, watching Tanny's face—the expression one of pure bliss. His cock started to drip and he could feel each suck in his balls. He tugged his fingers away before they got carried away, sliding his fingers down between Tanny's ass cheeks.

"I was sucking..." Tanny spread a little farther, letting him in.

He offered Tanny his free hand as he teased both wet fingers against Tanny's hole. Montana moaned, lips opening, eyes closing as that amazing suction started again. Using Montana's suction as a guide, he slowly worked his fingers into Montana's ass. Billy could feel each little moan, each deep cry. Tanny was right with him.

He began rocking his hips, his fingers slowly pushing deeper and deeper into Tanny's body. The suction around his fingers got stronger, harder, Tanny's tanned skin starting to flush. The fucking condoms were in the bedroom.

He pressed his fingers in deeper, finding Tanny's gland. Tanny arched, hips bucking furiously, eyes huge. Billy pushed again and then stopped, fingers dragging out of Tanny's ass and mouth.

"Billy..." Oh, fuck yes.

"Condom, beautiful man. We need one. Right now."

"Yeah. Yeah, okay. Okay. Hurry."

Laughing, he leaned up to bite at Tanny's lower lip. "You're on top, Tanny. You go get it. Bedroom, side table drawer."

"Oh. Right. Duh." Tanny chuckled, blushed. "I was busy."

"I know. I liked how you were busy." He grabbed Tanny's ass and took a hard kiss. "Now go. Hurry."

Tanny nodded and went, pretty little ass bouncing. Billy watched him the entire way, hand sliding down to stroke his own cock. He wanted so much, and he was beginning to believe, rather than hope, that Tanny would give it to him.

He kept slowly stroking his cock, waiting for Tanny to come back.

It didn't take Montana long, his lover holding a string of rubbers in one hand. "You... you have some weird things in that drawer..."

"Uh-huh. We can talk about them later." He patted his thighs. "Right now you're needed over here."

"Am I?" Tanny came over, straddled his thighs.

"Yes. You are." He slid his hands up over Tanny's legs and squeezed. "Glove me up."

"Mmmhmm." Tanny's fingers were gentle, careful.

"I should have told you to bring lube, too." He hadn't, though, so he offered his fingers over to Tanny to slick up again.

Tanny grinned, licking his fingers, then sucking them in. Fuck, that felt amazing. He pushed his fingers in and out of Tanny's mouth. Dark eyes stared down at him, so serious, so needy. He pulled his fingers from Tanny's mouth and pushed them into the tight hole again. Moving them, he made sure Tanny was nice and stretched.

He held Montana's gaze the entire time.

"I... It feels good, having you in me."

"And you're going to get to control it this time." He spread his fingers inside Tanny until he found that little bump and nudged it.

"Do it again." Tanny rocked, pushing his fingers in deeper.

A fucking natural, that's what Tanny was. He curled his fingers so they would stroke across Tanny's gland as they rocked together.

"Oh. Oh. Oh. Billy..." That pretty, long cock bobbed, slapping against his belly.

"You ready for me, Tanny? Ready to ride my cock?"

"Yes. Yes. In me, hmm?"

"Yes." He eased his fingers out and guided his cock to Tanny's hole, rubbing the tip against the hot flesh.

Tanny nodded, easing himself back and taking his cock.

"Fuck, yes." Billy held still, waiting for Tanny to be seated.

"I. I feel you." Tanny took him in little pulses, down to the root.

"Uh-huh. Yes." He nodded, his hands moving to Tanny's hips.

"More." Tanny shivered, pushed down hard onto his prick.

"Fuck!" He bucked up, cock slamming hard into Tanny's body.

"Yes." The single word was whispered, Montana staring into him.

Hands wrapped around Tanny's hips, he began to bring their bodies together, over and over again. Tanny rode him easily, heavy-lidded and wanton. He kept bringing Tanny down as he pushed up, one hand moving to Tanny's cock and pulling him off. Montana was panting for him, little short cries filled the air.

"Sexy," he muttered, words spilling form his mouth. "Hot. Tight. Mine."

"Yes." Oh, fuck. Yes. Yes.

He slammed up harder with his hips, going deep into Tanny's body. Heat sprayed over his fingers, Tanny's cock pulsing weakly. The rhythmic squeezing of Tanny's ass milked his own cock, demanding his orgasm. Billy gave it, shouting loudly as his filled the condom.

Tanny slumped forward, landing on him, panting.

He ran his hands along Tanny's spine, down to cup the amazing ass. His fingers lingered along Tanny's crack and then slipped down to touch where they were joined, where Tanny was stretched wide around his cock.

The whimper he got was an addiction.

He kept touching, kept petting. "That was amazing. You're amazing."

"Just yours."

"That's right." He kissed the side of Tanny's forehead and smiled. "Mine."

It was the best Thanksgiving ever.

Curled up in the armchair, Montana dozed, blinking at the game on the TV. He wasn't into football, really, and he'd eaten more than he'd eaten in ten years.

But he was happy and warm, and Billy was watching and laughing.

So he was happy.

The phone rang and Billy reached for it.

"Hello? Oliver! Happy Thanksgiving to you, too... Oh, yes, we've had a wonderful day." Billy smiled over at him. "I wouldn't change a thing... what? Jack wants us to have some leftovers? We can cook, you know, and have plenty of our own leftovers." Billy laughed. "No, palm them off on someone else, my friend." Billy listened for a moment longer. "Just a minute, I'll ask."

Putting the phone against his chest, Billy turned to Montana. "Would you like to go to Oliver and Jack's for dinner on Sunday? They're trying to use up all the leftovers," he added in a loud whisper.

"I..." He stopped, chewed his bottom lip. "Are you sure they want me, too?"

"They wouldn't have invited us if they didn't want us there."

"Do you want to go?"

"It would be fun, but I want to go with you, not on my own."

"Okay. I'll try." He would try a lot, for Billy.

Billy gave him a happy smile and put the phone back to his ear. "We'd love to come, Oliver. Can we bring anything? No? Okay, we'll see you around four." Billy hung up and gave him a warm smile. "It'll be fun."

He nodded, smiled back. Tanny wasn't sure about that, but it would be okay.

Billy patted the couch beside himself. "Come sit?"

"Sure." He unfolded himself and wandered over, unable to stop his smile.

Billy moved closer once he'd sat, hand sliding to his thigh. "Have you had a good day?"

He nodded. "I ate a lot. It all tasted good."

"Was that your favorite part of the day?" Billy's eyes twinkled at him.

"Mmm. No. No, I liked the dog show." They'd watched that together, wrapped up in a blanket, naked.

"Oh, that was good." Billy nibbled at the corner of his mouth. "I liked the part where I was inside you."

"I did too." He scooted even closer, wanting in Billy's lap. "Is this okay?"

"No, come here." Billy tugged him, encouraging him right to where he wanted to be.

He settled, happy, cheek on Billy's shoulder.

"Mmm, a man could get used to this." Billy's fingers slid over his back.

It was easier, with every touch, to let Billy stroke his scars. Billy absently kissed the side of his face, attention on the game. Tanny just relaxed, eyes closing as he dozed on and off.

Billy's cheering woke him up, the happy laughter moving the wide chest he was leaning on.

"Mmm. Go team?" He frowned, looked over, then stretched.

Chuckling, Billy nuzzled against him. "You were sleeping. I didn't mean to wake you."

"S'okay. Sleep too much." He hummed softly.

Billy's hand patted his back. "You've probably got years of sleeping to catch up on."

"No. I just ought to take the pills again." But he wasn't ready.

Billy snorted. "Fucking pills."

"No. There is very very little fucking when you take them."

"I know. I hate them. I don't want you taking them anymore. You don't need them."

"No. No, I don't. Not right now. Maybe later I will, though." There was still one. In the bathroom. In the medicine cabinet.

"No. You come to me if you think you do. I know what you need. I've proved that."

Tanny didn't know how to answer that, but he nodded.

"Good, good." Billy's mouth met his, the kiss lazy. He kissed Billy back, letting Billy hold him. "Mmm. So sexy, so sweet."

"Mmm. Not sweet." He chuckled. "You're missing your game."

"I've got a much better game right here."

"Game?" He shook his head, grinned a little. "You like love-making better?"

Billy kissed him softly. "I do."

"Me too." He reached up, arms wrapping around Billy's neck.

"How'd I get so lucky?" Billy mapped his face with warm fingers.

"You're not. I am. I got a home."

"But I got you, that's better than anything." He shook his head. Billy was deluding himself. Billy grabbed his head between strong hands and held him so they were looking each other in the eye. "Stop that."

"Stop what?" He couldn't look away.

"Trying to convince me you aren't worth anything."

"I'm not." He was shaking a little bit, unnerved. "Your game's back on."

"And I have you in my arms. Guess which one is more important to me?" Billy's eyes felt like they were looking right through him.

"Shh." He reached up, covered Billy's eyes with one hand. Chuckling, Billy tried to snap at his wrist.

"I said, shh." He grinned, kept Billy's eyes covered.

"You realize I talk with my mouth, not my eyes, right?" Billy kept chuckling.

"Uh-huh. I can ignore when you talk, if I have to. It's harder when you look at me."

Billy's hand took his and pulled it away from the piercing eyes. Billy looked right at him. "I don't want you to ignore me."

"Sometimes I need to." Billy needed to understand that.

"Whenever we start talking about how you matter and aren't garbage."

"Shh." He didn't want to talk about this.

"No. I won't be quiet. I love you. I love a beautiful man." Billy began kissing his hand, his nose and cheeks. Billy's eyes held his as he spoke. "I love a worthy man. You, Montana. I love you."

"Billy..." The words panicked him a little bit.

"Did I mention sexy?" Billy rolled their hips again, the hard bulge in Billy's sweats proof of his arousal.

"You're insatiable." That was easier to deal with.

"You bring it out in me. Besides." Billy's hand dropped to his crotch and rubbed. "And speaking of insatiable..." Billy winked at him.

He chuckled a little, relaxing. "Uh-huh."

Billy squeezed. "What do you think about toys, Tanny?"

"I've never made any."

"No, no. Sexual toys."

"Is that legal?" That was kinda gross... oh, duh. "You mean like vibrators. Those are for girls."

Billy blinked at him. "Legal? For girls?" He shook his head. "No, I mean adult sexual aids, and believe me, there are plenty for boys. Plenty."

"Like what? Really? I mean, I've seen vibrators and shit."

"How about cock-rings and plugs? Dildos and anal beads? Wands, nipple clamps?"

"Wands? Like bibbity-bobbity-boo?" He knew what dildos were, of course, and nipple clamps—which, ow. He didn't want to get his prick pierced, though.

"Uh-huh." Billy's hand slipped into his sweats and circled his cock. Then one finger slid across the tip and pressed gently against his slit. "They go right here."

"No way." Now he knew Billy was messing with him. "That's dangerous."

"Not if you know what you're doing." Billy kissed the side of his mouth. "Don't worry, we're not there yet. Not even close."

"No. No, we're so not."

Billy chuckled. "I bet you're ready for a cock ring, though."

"No!" He shook his head. "No way. No fucking way am I letting someone put a ring in my cock!"

"No, no. That's a Prince Albert. A cock ring goes here." Billy's hand slid to the base of his cock, to fingers circling it, squeezing. "It keeps you from coming so fast."

"Oh. Oh, God. You scared me." He actually had a little sweat going.

Billy kissed him gently. "Sorry, Tanny. I'll be sure to be clearer next time I'm talking about such things."

"It's okay. I just... Wow." He cuddled in.

Billy began to stroke him gently, free arm around him, holding him close. "I can see how one would be much more... daunting than the other. We should get out my laptop and cruise a few sites."

"Mmm. I can't use a computer, man. I never learned how."

"Oh, it's easy. I'll show you." That gentle stroking continued.

"I'm not very smart with things." Hell, he couldn't read all that well, really.

"I bet you can learn."

"You know that I'm kind of dumb, okay?"

"No, I don't know that at all." Billy's words were short, clipped.

He sighed. "Don't be mad at me. It's just what it is."

"I'm not mad at you, Tanny. You know I don't like it when you run yourself down."

"I'm just telling the truth."

"All right." Billy's hand had stilled, though it still held his cock loosely. "Why do you believe you're dumb?"

"I didn't finish high school; I fucked up every job I ever had. You met me in an alleyway scoring drugs." The words bubbled out of him. "I killed my sister. My family hates me. I can't read very good."

"You know you can still learn to read properly, right? Take your GED?"

"Right. Hi, Teach. I'm a twenty-six year old loser. Can we start with Dick and Jane?"

"I don't mean in a class, Tanny. I mean here, or in an adult course. Hell, I can help you learn to read properly. I know you're not stupid, which means you can learn."

He pulled away, shivering. "Just stop. Stop pushing.

Let me be."

"Why? Why don't you want to be the best you can be?"

"Stop it!" He wrapped his arms around himself.

"No. I want to understand and I don't, Tanny. I don't understand at all why you're working so hard to keep yourself in the gutter." Billy's arms held him close.

"Because that's where I belong!" He pulled away, standing up, fingernails scoring his arms.

Billy jumped up as well, hands grabbing his, keeping him from hurting himself. "What are you talking about?"

"I suck. Don't you get it? I suck at everything and you'll figure it out, and then I'll be alone and scared and cold and shit and the world will feel sorry for you." His heart hurt.

"No. No, I don't get it. I believe in you. I believe that you don't suck, not if you try not to." Billy wouldn't let him go.

"Let me go." He stepped closer, needing that comfort.

"No, I'm not going to do that." Billy held him in a full body hug. "I'm not ever letting you go, Tanny. You're mine."

"You promise?"

"I swear it, Montana." He'd never heard Billy sound so fierce.

"Say it again." When he was a kid, promises only counted if you said them three times.

"I'm not letting you go. You are mine." Billy's voice didn't soften.

"One more time. Please."

"Mine. You are mine, and I'm not letting you go. I swear it to you, Tanny. And one day you'll believe it."

He closed his eyes, took a deep, deep breath.

"I'm going to tattoo it on your belly. My name, right here." Billy's fingers slid across his stomach, just below his navel. He cried out, his cock filling, surprising him. Billy's mouth crashed on his, all teeth and heat. He climbed up into Billy's arms, hips bucking. He needed. Now. He needed to be Billy's.

Billy's hand wrapped around his cock, pulling as hard as that kiss.

"Please." He wasn't sure exactly what he was begging for.

"Come for me and then we'll go." Billy's hand tightened and moved faster.

"Go?" He arched, going up on tiptoe.

"Go get the tattoo."

"It's Thanksgiving..."

"Someone'll be open. I won't make you wait." Billy's thumb pressed against his slit as it slid past.

His teeth rattled with his orgasm, his entire universe spinning. Billy stroked him through it, lips on his.

"Please." He whispered the word again, clinging, holding on.

"I have a call to make."

"Okay." He nodded, swallowing hard.

"I know some people. I'm betting they'll do this for us." Billy's hand slid across his back. Then Billy grabbed the phone.

Montana didn't worry, he just leaned and closed his eyes a second, let Billy deal with him.

For him.

Chapter Twenty One

Billy pulled up in front of the tattoo parlor and smiled. Killian was already there, a light on at the back of the shop. He had some good friends.

He held onto Montana's hand and led his lover in.

The little bell over the door went off and he called out. "Killian?"

"Back here. Lock the door, dearest." The place was dark, quiet.

Billy did so, and then squeezed Montana's hand. "I think you'll like Killian. He's very passionate about what he does."

"Yeah? Is he cool?"

Billy wasn't sure what had broken through to Tanny, but there was something between them now, a fire, an electricity.

"He is." He took Tanny to the back, where the light was.

The room was clean, simple, the chair waiting for them, along with Killian. "Treat's dropping some food off at his dad's. He says hello."

"I appreciate this, Killian. Very much. I'd like you to meet my lover, Montana. Tanny, this is Killian, the best tattoo artist in town."

"Montana. That's a perfectly lovely name." The lean,

icy blond stood, shook Tanny's hand. "What can I do for you?"

"We have a tattoo we need." He smiled at Tanny, reached out to slide his fingers over the skinny belly through his T-shirt.

"You said it wasn't complex, yes?"

"That's right. My name on Montana's belly."

"Easy enough. Would you like it to be your signature or a script?"

"Montana?"

Those beautiful eyes stared up at him, and Tanny shrugged.

"My choice. Good. My signature." He reached out and stroked Tanny's cheek. "My signature on my lover."

"Oh, that's lovely." Killian nodded, smiled. "I'll need you to take your shirt off, please, Montana, and Billy, I'll need you to decide whether you want to shave the area or you want me to."

Billy didn't even have to think about that. "I'll do it."

"Excellent. The safety razors are there. Just clean the area, shave him, and sign him."

Tanny vibrated against his arm.

"Thank you, Killian. Shirt off, Tanny. On the chair."

"Yeah. Yeah, okay. Thanks, man. For doing this on the holiday and stuff..."

Killian grinned, nodded. "It's cool."

"It's going to look lovely on your belly." Billy helped Tanny take the T-shirt off.

"You're sure?"

"One hundred percent. You need to know, in your skin, that you're mine no matter what."

"I. I need to sit, before he sees."

Billy saw Killian still, but the man didn't look over.

"He wouldn't judge you for it, Tanny." Still, he guided Tanny to the chair, putting the T-shirt down first so

Tanny's scarred back wouldn't stick.

"It's just so ugly." Tanny whispered, leaning back.

"I don't think it is. I have a feeling Killian wouldn't either." He stroked Montana's cheek and then the lean belly, fingers sliding where his name was going to go.

Montana grinned, nodded once at him. "It's okay."

"It is. Now, let's shave the area." He stroked Montana's belly again and then took the shaving gel. A small squirt afforded enough of the stuff for the area in question and Billy shaved it carefully, fingers trailing behind the razor to caress Montana's fine skin.

Montana didn't tense up, didn't seem worried at all, just let him touch.

Once he had the area shaved he gently dried Tanny off. "Okay, Killian. What did you want me to use to sign my name?"

"There's a felt pen over there on the counter. You might practice on that paper."

"I think I know how to sign my name." He gave Montana a wink.

Tanny laughed.

Killian snorted. "Just remember it'll be there forever."

Billy nodded, his fingers trailing again over Montana's skin. "Yes, that's the point." He picked up the pen and leaned Montana back, stretching him a bit. He took a breath and then signed his name on Montana's belly, curving it up around Tanny's navel.

His.

His lover.

His friend.

His Montana.

He looked at it and nodded. Yes. "That'll do it, Killian. Can you work with that?"

Killian looked over, stared. "Nice signature. Yeah. Yeah, I can."

"Excellent. I'll stay here and hold your hand, okay, Montana?"

"Okay. I'm not scared."

"I understand that you can get quite a high from the endorphins the pain causes." He took Montana's hand and sat next to him, well out of Killian's way.

"Pain sucks, but I can cope."

Killian chuckled, the sound warm, fond.

"I know." He petted Montana's shoulder. His lover could cope with quite a bit of pain.

It didn't take Killian any time to get set up, then he turned to them. "I just need you to sign the waiver and I'll need a copy of your driver's license."

"Montana doesn't drive."

"That's cool. You have any kind of ID? State ID, something with a picture?"

Montana was almost gray. "No. No, I don't. Sorry. I left it in my other life."

Killian's lips twisted. "Let me have your ID, then, Bill. I'd use that." Killian gave him a look.

"I do have a license." He passed that over and patted Montana's shoulder again. "It's okay, I'll vouch for you."

"Go ahead and fill out the paperwork, then." Killian stood. "Bill, I have something for you to sign in here."

He followed Killian into a little office. "Is there a problem?"

"Well, no, because we're friends, but... Bill. You need to get him identification—a Social, something. I can help you, if you need it, but you have to... especially if you're bringing him to the Club." Those eyes were so serious. "Oliver and Xavier won't allow him in without that."

"I will, Killian. I'm working on it. One thing at a time, hmm?" First he had to convince Montana he was more than just garbage and worth having identification.

Found

"Okay. Okay. I just... We're friends, hmm? I had to speak up."

"I know, I know. He was living on the street, Killian. It's a bit of an adjustment."

"Okay. Promise me you'll look into it soon, though. Make him legal."

He nodded. "I think we've turned a corner here today and we can move forward."

"Excellent." Killian nodded and headed back, where Tanny was sitting, the paperwork filled out with large, clumsy letters. "Thanks, Montana. I appreciate it."

Billy sat back next to Montana and took his lover's hand again. "You ready?"

"It's all okay? Still?"

"Yep. It's fine." He stroked Montana's shoulder.

"Yeah?" Montana leaned back, eyes on him. "I'm sorry about the I.D. thing."

"It's okay. We can deal with it later. This now, hmm? So you always know."

"This now." Montana nodded, eyes closing. That trust was staggering, amazing.

Billy took a breath, his heart full, and nodded at Killian. "We're ready."

The actual tattoo only took a few minutes, the black scrawl over Montana's belly simple, neat, perfect.

He nodded. "Perfect. What do you think, Montana?"

"It's pretty. Thank you." Long fingers stroked the skin around it.

Killian nodded, then grinned as a horn honked. "Anytime. Well, that's not true. Treat's ready."

"We really appreciate you taking the time on Thanksgiving to do it. I owe you one."

"You owe me two." Killian held out one hand and he deposited two hundred dollars in it.

"I have a hunch we'll be back. During regular operating

hours next time." He winked.

"Sounds excellent. Happy Thanksgiving."

"You too, Killian."

With a last smile for the tattoo artist, Billy turned his attention to Montana. "You want to leave your shirt off? We don't have far to go to the car."

"No. No, someone might see..."

Killian gasped, stepped forward. "Who did that? That's amazing work..."

Billy held on tight to Montana's hand, rubbing one shoulder to calm his lover.

"It's absolutely... Oh. They're scars. They're lovely, Montana. Perfectly fascinating."

His lover shuddered, turned a little green.

"He was in an accident," Billy said softly.

"They're beautiful." Killian looked at Billy. "Can I touch them?"

"No." He nearly snarled the word out. He cleared his throat and took a breath. "No," he said more calmly.

Killian held his hands up, grinned. "Okay, boss. Breathe. Take your boy home."

Montana was vibrating, pale.

He nodded; he knew Killian understood how these things worked, even if he wasn't aware of the ramifications of Montana's scars.

"Come on, Tanny." He helped Montana off the chair and into his T-shirt, and then led him through the shop.

Tanny was shaking against him, but left, heading right for the car. "Are we going home?"

"We are. Me and my Montana. Are going home." He let Montana into the car and went around to the driver's side. Billy thought there were tears on Montana's cheeks, but he wasn't sure. "We'll be home in a few minutes. Are you okay?"

He reached out to touch Montana's thigh.

"Yeah. Yeah, I'm fine. I am."

He glanced over at Montana. "Okay." It wasn't like he could do anything before they got home, anyway.

"Can I turn on some music?"

"Sure." Billy waved at the radio.

He was curious to see what Tanny would choose. The loud rock was passed over, the country, the doo wop. The dial landed on a jazz station, Montana settling back to listen.

Interesting.

It wasn't long before they were back home. Billy pulled into his parking spot at the back of the building and turned off the engine.

"We could have leftovers, huh?" Montana sounded a little shaken.

"We could go inside and talk about what's bothering you." He squeezed Montana's thigh and then got out of the car and went around to help Tanny.

"Nothing's bothering me. You always want to talk."

He chuckled as he led Tanny up the stairs. "And you never do."

Montana didn't answer, just smiled a little.

They got in and he hustled Montana toward the bedroom. "I want to lay you out and take a good look at it." He figured it was a good place to talk, too—comfortable and warm.

"Okay." Montana slipped off his shirt, toed off his shoes.

"You might as well strip completely." He gave Montana a wink. There was no reason to be coy about what he wanted after he checked out the tat and dealt with whatever was bothering Montana.

"Yeah? You like me naked."

"I do. You've got a sexy body. It turns me on."

He toed off his shoes and left them by the door. "Once

you're naked you can strip me down, too."

"You're not broken, you know." Montana winked at him, then stared down at the ink on the flat belly.

"I know I'm not broken." He reached out and ran his fingers around the tattoo, careful not to get to close to the fresh ink. "What do you think?"

"It burns, just a little. It's dark. Do you think it's okay?"

"I think it's great. Anyone who sees it will know that you're mine."

Montana pinked, but nodded once.

"Do you like it?" he asked, curious.

"I do." Montana shrugged, swallowed. "I think... I think it's cool."

He smiled and nodded. "It is." Then Billy spread his arms. "Now undress me."

Tanny chuckled, shook his head with a grin, then worked his clothes off.

"If you're really good at it, I'll give you a reward."

"Like what?" Montana's touch was gentle, gentle.

"I'll suck you off."

"Really?" Tanny eased his shirt off, then frowned. "What does really good mean?"

"It means that you do what I ask and you make me feel good doing it." He liked that Montana didn't just jump at his orders. He liked that his lover thought about things.

"I try to make you feel good whenever we have sex." Tanny undid his belt buckle. "I'm sorry about the driver's license thing."

"It's okay. We'll need to talk about getting you some I.D."

"I... I have a social security number. I don't have a card anymore, though."

"Oh, that's good. You can get a new card. You need

I.D., Montana." He closed his eyes and Montana slid his pants down. "But not right now."

"You're hard..." Montana sounded surprised, one hand caressing his prick through his boxers.

"I watched a man put my mark on you. Of course I'm hard."

"You liked that?" His boxers were eased down, his erection stroked.

"Yes." He reached out and touched Montana's shoulders. "I liked it a lot."

"Why?"

"Because you're sexy. Because knowing that my mark is on you touches something primal inside me."

"I like that you wanted it. I mean, that you..." Montana sighed. "Hell, I don't know."

He stepped out of his pants and then tugged Montana up. "I love you," he said quietly before taking Montana's lips with his own.

Montana stepped close, then jerked, stepped away. "That stings."

"The tattoo?"

"A little. Not bad. It just... I wasn't expecting it."

"The pain'll ease and then disappear altogether." He rubbed Montana's back to distract him. "Get in bed, and I'll blow you."

"I... Can we just sit together? God, that sounds stupid, but my heart's racing a little and I'm sort of nervous and... Fuck."

"Get in bed, Tanny." He climbed in with Montana and drew his lover into his arms. "Why are you nervous?"

"I..." Montana hid his face, pulled the covers around them. "I've never had a lover before. Never been someone's. I'm scared I'll do something wrong."

"But that's the point of the tattoo, Montana. It doesn't matter if you do something wrong—you'll still be mine."

"I know. It's big. I mean, isn't it? Something big?"

"It is. It's everything." He kissed the top of Montana's head, the soft hair tickling his lips.

"Okay." Montana pressed closer, eyelashes tickling him.

He chuckled and began touching Montana. His fingers explored, running over whatever parts of Montana he could reach.

"Oh..." Montana arched a little, moaned.

"You feeling any better?" Billy knew the best way to calm Montana's nerves was to fuck them out of him.

"Yes. Yes, I am. Do. Whatever. Thank you." Montana chuckled. "I know, what guy says wait a minute on a blowjob, huh?"

"Guys who know what they need, or don't need. I like that you were able to say something." He liked it a lot.

"I just. I needed a minute."

He pressed a kiss to Montana's face. "We have all the time in the world."

"Okay. Good." Montana lifted up, mouth offered to him.

Smiling, he pressed their lips together. Montana's were soft and warm; they felt good against his own. Montana moaned, tongue slipping out, brushing against his lips. He wrapped his lips around it and sucked gently.

His lover melted, leaned right into him and held on.

Groaning, he deepened the kiss, sliding his tongue along Tanny's and then into Tanny's mouth. Montana opened, let him in, the little cry sweet as honey. He tasted Montana's mouth, the straight teeth and hot gums. Then he pressed in deeper.

Montana's cock filled, swelled, pushed, rose against him. Someone was eager now that they were back on familiar territory. Moaning, he slid his hand down Montana's body until he reached the long cock. Eager and heated, Montana's prick pressed into his hand, nearly burned his palm.

He slowly broke the kiss, his mouth staying in contact with Montana's skin as he worked his way from lips to chin to neck. Billy got harder, listening to the little moans, the heady cries. He scraped his teeth along Montana's Adam's apple, tongue following behind.

"Do it again?" Montana's cry was enough to drive him a little crazy.

He scraped again, and then again before moving on toward Montana's right nipple. That sensitive little bit of flesh drew up tight. It reached for him, Montana's body begging silently for his touch. He flicked his tongue across it and then bit down hard.

"Billy!" Montana's cock pulsed, going wet-tipped against him.

Fuck, he loved the sound of that needy cry. He touched the tip of Montana's cock, fingers smearing the drops of liquid.

"I. I. Oh." Montana's legs jerked, heels sliding on the sheets.

Fingers still fondling Montana's cock, he slowly left sucking kisses along Montana's skin. He felt Montana relax underneath him. He skirted the tattoo; soon enough he would be able to touch it, to trace the letters of his name with the point of his tongue. For now he let it be.

Still, it was there. Permanent.

His.

He admired it for a moment and then turned his face down to lick at the tip of Montana's cock. Montana's fingers shook, sliding over his temple, his forehead. Humming softly, he carefully traced the veins that ran along the hard cock.

"Oh, God. Please. So good."

He opened his mouth at the base of Montana's cock,

sucking like he was going to draw up a mark.

"Billy. Billy. Billy." Montana's hips rolled, that cock bobbing against his face.

He slid his mouth up along it and then took in the head when he reached the top. Sucking gently, he held the head in his mouth and flicked his tongue against the sensitive tip.

"Fuck." Montana moaned, stilled, almost like he was waiting to see what Billy would do.

Back and forth, he flicked his tongue; sometimes the movements were broad and covered the whole head, others they were tiny, just flicking at the slit in the middle. Montana's fingers stroked his hair, his head, the digits trembling against him. He fucked Montana's slit a few times before opening wider and taking more of the hard flesh in.

Montana arched, slid into his mouth, hips moving almost—almost—lazily. Billy wrapped his hands around them, encouraging the movements. Montana's cock tasted sweet with a hint of salt. He kept sucking, his fingers reaching up and toying with Montana's balls. Montana's cock pushed deep, nudging his throat as the lean hips punched.

He took it. He took Montana in and swallowed around the tip. Montana rippled, entire body going stiff and still, that pretty cock swelling.

He grabbed hold of Montana's balls and twisted them as he tugged them down hard enough to stop the orgasm. "Not yet," he muttered after pulling off.

"Oh." Montana groaned, looked a little stunned, a little shocked. "Fuck."

Billy smiled up at his lover. "It's going to feel amazing when I do let you come."

The lean legs shifted, slid on the bed. "I want you."

"You want me inside you?" He wanted to hear

Montana say it. He wanted to hear Montana beg for it.

"Yeah."

"Say it."

"What?"

"Say you want me inside you."

"I..." Montana blushed. "But you know?"

"I do." He licked around the head of Montana's cock. "I want to hear you say it."

"I want... I want you to fuck me."

He growled happily, pushing Montana into the mattress as he kissed his lover. Montana opened up, tongue sliding against his. He found the lube and opened it one-handed as they kissed. One of Tanny's knees drew up, cock sliding against his, over and over. It felt so good. It would be so easy to just rub off until they both came, but Montana had asked to feel him inside, and that was what he was going to do.

Getting his fingers slick, he pushed one into Montana's tightness. Montana was a little swollen, a lot hot, ready for him. He pushed in a second finger, adding lube and stretching more. Montana's face hid in his throat, soft little cries sharp on the air.

"Love being inside you." He whispered the words and withdrew his fingers.

The blush made him smile; the moan made his cock jerk, slapping against Tanny's lower belly.

He covered his prick and then took Tanny's hand and brought it to his cock. "Guide me to you, Montana."

Montana's hand moved up and down, stroking once, then rubbed the tip over his hole.

"Oh fuck, yes." Billy pushed. Montana's hole wrapped around him, took him in and in and in. He met Montana's eyes, watched them as he sank all the way to his balls.

"F... f... full." Montana gasped, fingers opening and closing, over and over.

"Uh-huh." He was going to teach Montana all about being full. Fingers, cock, toys, fist.

"You need to move..."

"I do." He could feel it in his balls. So he did, pulling away slowly and then pushing right back in. He didn't tease long; he knew what rhythm he needed, and he went with it. In and out, he drove himself into Montana's body.

Montana took him, as if the man was made for him, created just for him.

He held Montana's gaze as he pounded in. His. His. Fuck. His. Montana panted, lips parted. "Come now," he ordered as he wrapped his hand around Montana's cock.

It took Montana a few strokes before heat poured over his fingers. One day his lover would come at his command. Groaning, he pushed in harder, faster, searching for his own release. The tight muscles rippled, rocked around his body, milking his cock. He cried out as he came, filling the condom in long pulses.

Thin arms wrapped around him, held him close.

He rested on Montana's body, trusting his lover to say something if he got too heavy. Billy kissed the side of Montana's face, panting heavily.

They rested together a long time before Montana smiled. "Let's get cleaned up and go watch a movie downstairs?"

"Sounds perfect." He kissed the side of Montana's lips. "Happy Thanksgiving, Montana. I hope we have many more."

"Yeah. Yeah, me too." Montana nodded. "Me too, Billy."

He couldn't ask for anything better than that.

Chapter Twenty Two

Tanny sat at the kitchen table, drinking coffee and working, watching the sun come up. The planes had sold. And sold. And they wanted more.

Lots more.

He'd gone to bed with Billy every night for the last three nights, slept for two hours, then gotten up to work. He wanted to die.

The Red was sitting there on the table. He didn't even remember picking it up out of the cabinet, but it was there.

Staring at him.

It would help. It would help so good. He sobbed a little, fingers tracing the tablet. One more plane, and then he'd take it. He had to.

He needed to.

So bad.

Billy came into the kitchen, blinking and yawning. "Coffee?"

"I made some." He pointed to the freshly made pot.

"Oh, yes." Billy filled a coffee cup. "You need some?"

"Uh-huh." He got up, brought his cup over, the ceramic clattering a little on the counter. One more plane.

Billy's hand, warm and solid, slid over his back. "You okay?"

"Yeah. You sleep good?" He poured the coffee, splashing a little on his fingers. Damn. He drank some, then headed back to the table.

"Yeah, not bad. Still working on these, eh? Damn, you're going to need an assistant soon."

He nodded and chuckled, attaching a wheel.

Billy sat by him and watched, sipping his coffee. "When have you been doing all these?"

"Huh?" He wasn't in a place to answer complicated questions.

"You've got boxes and boxes of these done. Have you had any sleep recently?"

"I go to bed with you."

"Yeah, but you're never there when I wake up." Billy drank some more coffee. "You're not in trouble or anything, but you're starting to look pale and you look almost like someone punched you in the eyes."

"Yeah. I know." He nodded, finished the plane. "I know." He didn't want to lie to Billy. He wasn't ashamed.

"Are you almost done? I mean I know they want as many as possible before Christmas, but there's only so much you can do."

"I want to be. I. I have to take the pill." He held up his hand when Billy opened his mouth. "No. You have to listen to me. I'm going to lose it. I have to. You can be mad, if you want, but I'm not going to lie and I'm not going to be ashamed of needing it."

"Why do you think taking the pill will make a difference?"

"Because it will. I mean, it's speed. I'm tired..." Didn't Billy know what speed was?

"But wouldn't a good night's sleep help? Then you

wouldn't be tired."

He nodded. He had all these airplanes and he couldn't wait. Not for all the hours until it was night time.

"I tell you what. Let's deliver these to Helena and see how many more she needs and what kind of deadline we're looking at. This isn't healthy and I really don't want you taking the pill. You've done so well so far and I know how it works, I know that the minute you take it all the withdrawal that you've endured will have been for nothing."

He almost burst into tears. "I can't. I can't take them to her right now. If she says she wants more, I'll scream." He tried to drink his coffee, holding the cup with both hands.

"Oh, Tanny." Billy reached out and touched his hand. Then he pursed his lips. "Come on. Let's go to bed. You need sleep."

"I can't. I have ten more to do and I'm so tired and I hate this and I don't like planes and MY HANDS HURT!" His voice rose and rose until he was screaming, so tired he was seeing things in the air—ghosts. Ghosts with black dots.

"They can wait until you're not about to fall over." Billy's hand circled his arm. "Come on. It's time to sleep."

He stood up, sobbing, shaking. "I need help."

"Oh, Tanny, you need to come to me before you're this bad." Billy grabbed him around the waist and picked him up, carrying him toward the bedroom.

He held on, shaking, clinging to Billy's shoulders. "I'm sorry. My head hurts. I'm so tired."

"You need to sleep, Montana. I know you needed to get these done as well, but you should have asked for help or at least let me know how overwhelmed you were."

Billy put him down on the bed like he was something precious.

He shivered and shook, so tired and stressed and caffeinated, he couldn't relax.

Billy went to his chest of drawers and rummaged around, coming back a moment later with a small bottle. "Turn over. I'm going to give you a massage, ease those poor muscles."

He turned, the tears leaking out now. "I'm sorry."

"What are you apologizing for?" Billy straddled his thighs and oil poured over his skin.

"I don't know."

Billy chuckled at that and started rubbing his shoulders. Billy's touch was firm but not painful. "No apologizing unless you know why you're doing it."

"Okay." His eyes fell closed. "I want to be good..."

"You're being fantastic. You're working hard; you're loving me."

"I do..." The touch was hypnotic.

"Good, good." Billy's massage moved from his shoulders out to his arms, easing the muscles there.

"So tired, Billy. I can't live like normal people..."

"If you don't sleep well at night, we'll find a new routine for you." Billy spoke quietly, hands constantly working his muscles. "I don't have a job that requires me to be anywhere at a specific time."

"I just... there was so much work."

"You should have said something. You're not on your own anymore and you don't have to face everything alone."

He couldn't fuck up. Not yet. Not again. Billy's fingers slid over his back and down along his spine, and then they were digging into his ass. This sound left him, almost a pained cry.

Billy's hands stilled. "You okay?"

"Yeah. Yeah, that was... I don't know." It knocked something loose from him.

"Something good, I hope." Billy went back to massaging his ass.

"Uh-huh." He nodded, tension melting.

Billy slipped farther down his legs, fingers digging into his thighs now, insisting each muscle relax. Every so often a sound would escape him, leaving him more empty. The thorough massage continued down his legs, right to his toes. By the time Billy's hands left his skin, he was melted.

Billy lay down next to him, giving him a warm smile. "Better?"

"God, yes. So much." He blinked, barely able to keep his eyes open.

Billy kissed him softly. "Sleep, Tanny."

"Uh-huh."

Right. Sleep.

He could.

He so could.

Chapter Twenty Three

Billy had helped Tanny pack up the boxes of planes for Helena, amazed by how many had been made in the week since Thanksgiving. No wonder Tanny had started to look a little bit like a ghost; there were a crazy amount of planes here.

The boxes were loaded into his car and he drove Tanny over and helped him unload.

Helena had a customer and, while they were waiting, Margaret came and introduced herself to Tanny, leaning heavily on her cane.

"Hello, you must be Montana. I'm Margaret."

"Hi. Hi, Margaret." Tanny looked confused.

"Come sit for a few minutes. I don't know if Billy mentioned it, but I'm a book binder and I'm looking for an apprentice." She smiled at Billy when she said his name and he nodded at her.

"You make books? I... I've only done that with newspapers."

"I do. I make blank books to sell here and through some of the distributors we partner with for ridiculous sums of money. And I do special orders as well. People bring their books in to be bound. Usually authors." She looked ruefully at her hands. "These don't work like they used to, though."

He looked at Tanny, who reached out, took Margaret's hands, so gently. "Do they hurt? Mine hurt sometimes now. The planes."

"I have rheumatoid arthritis in them. It feels like it's getting worse every day." She gave Tanny a soft smile. "I'm looking for an apprentice, actually. Someone to pass my skills on to. Someone who can take over for me."

"But... I don't know how to make books... Don't you want someone that's trained?"

"No, I most certainly do not." Margaret shook her head and it almost sounded like she'd growled. "I had someone trained. The little ass thought he knew how to do things better than I did. Cheeky little bastard."

"I don't know... I haven't been an apprentice before. What do I do?"

"You come to the workshop every day and learn from me. I can't work for more than an hour or so at a time, but then there'd be a couple of hours where you practice what I showed you under my supervision. So let's say four hours a day. I usually take Monday and Tuesday as my weekends."

"I..." Tanny looked at him. "Is that cool?"

"I don't see why not. The place is close enough you can walk. It's a good place to work, to learn. And Margaret's good people." He winked at her.

She smiled, chuckled. Maggie had been in the lifestyle for years. Her partner had passed away two years ago and he thought, maybe, she was just waiting for somewhere to go.

"What do you say, Montana? Help an old woman out?"

Billy thought it was a great idea. It would get Tanny away from having to do the planes, which hurt his hands and got him too stressed out, and it would leave them plenty of time for training, playing. Loving.

He hoped Tanny thought it was a good idea, too.

"I'll try. I can try."

"Oh, that's wonderful! Thank you." She laughed softly. "Is tomorrow too soon for you to start?"

"I can come, yes. I'm not as tired today."

"Tired?" Margaret looked up at him. "What are you doing to the boy, Billy?"

He held up his hands. "Nothing, I swear."

"I was making planes."

"Yes, I heard Helena had ordered an exorbitant amount of them."

"Lots." Tanny had slept for almost an entire day; his lover still looked exhausted.

"It would be nice for Tanny to have something else to do besides the planes."

"What's this?" Helena asked, coming to the back. "You're stealing my best new artist?"

Margaret nodded, smiled, the look oddly young, wicked, almost naughty. "I am. I'm going to enjoy working with someone, damn it."

Helena pouted. "Well, I've got these boxes at least. Maybe I can talk you into making more for me."

Billy snorted. "Not too much pressure, please, Helena. They're harder to make than you'd think." And having made that many in one go really had put the hurt on Montana's hands.

"Then we'll raise the price." She nodded. "I have a check for you, Tanny."

"Can you give it to Billy?"

"Are you sure you want me to do that? It's your money."

Billy might have bristled at her words, but he was also happy that Helena was looking out for Tanny's interests. He didn't believe Tanny had enough people like that in his life. Maybe Tanny never had.

"He has a bank deal. I don't."

Helena handed the check over to him, looking a little confused. "Why don't you just get an account of your own?"

Tanny seemed to shrink a little, beginning to panic.

Margaret snarled. "Leave the boy alone, Helena."

Billy nodded, pleased with Margaret's protection of Tanny. She would be a good teacher for him. "Thanks, Margaret. What time would you like Tanny here tomorrow?"

"I like early—how does eight a.m. work for you?"

Tanny nodded. "I'll be here."

Billy was so pleased. The airplanes were making money for Tanny, had proved to him that he could make money with his stuff, that it was art. But they were a lot of work and hurting his hands and stressing him. Billy was glad there was something else he could do and he had to wonder if Tanny would have even considered it if he hadn't already had such a success with the planes.

"Thanks, Margaret."

"Oh, no, you don't need to thank me. I'm not doing this to make work for Montana. I need someone to learn the business and take if over." She met his eyes, nodded. "I'll take exceptional care of him, when he's at work."

Billy smiled and nodded as well. He knew she would. It was an ideal situation, really. Tanny would have freedom, and at the same time he wouldn't be out there all on his own.

"I'll see you tomorrow, Margaret." Tanny offered her a smile, a nod.

"I'm looking forward to it."

Billy made sure he had Tanny's check in his wallet and that Helena had signed for the delivery of the planes they'd dropped off and then they headed out.

"You feel like going to the beach for a wander? I enjoy

it this time of year—fewer tourists."

"Sure." Tanny nodded, smiled. "I have my sweater on."

Tanny had worn and washed that sweater, over and over. Billy'd decided that Santa was going to bring Montana some clothes this year.

He stopped them at the pretzel stand before they got out onto the beach. "You want one?" It smelled divine.

Montana considered it, stopping to think about it. "I could, yes."

"Two, please." Billy passed over the cash and was given two steaming hot pretzels. "You want mustard or anything?"

"No. I don't like mustard." Tanny breathed deep. "I used to steal the stale ones at the end of the night. I love them."

Billy chuckled as they started walking. "I like them just as they are, too." He took a bite and moaned happily.

The wind coming off the water was cold, but Montana was warm against his side. He thoroughly enjoyed the pretzel and, afterward, licked the salt and grease from his fingers. It was a simple pleasure, but one that was easy to sink into.

Montana ate about half of his, then broke the other half up into little pieces. It wasn't long before the stray dogs started coming, begging the treats.

"Oh, do you know most of them?" Did Montana want a pet? Did he even maybe have one he'd never said anything about?

"Almost all of them." Tanny scratched and smoothed them all, the dogs wagging and panting for him.

"Did you have any pets?"

"Before I came here, yeah."

"What kind?" Billy picked up a stick and tossed it, watching as several of the dogs went after it.

"Oh, I had dogs—my favorite was a little lab mix. She was real smart."

"Do you miss having dogs?" Not that he was going to suggest they get one...

"Sometimes. You have to take care of them, and I like that, but they take a lot of energy and time, too."

"It's a big responsibility, isn't it?" Billy tossed the stick when it was brought back to him.

"Yes, and I'm sort of a fuck up."

Billy growled a little bit. "I thought we'd agreed not to say things like that anymore."

"No, we agreed that you didn't like it."

"You aren't a fuck-up, though. So you should stop saying it." Damn it, Tanny had delivered all those planes and then he'd signed up for a job as an apprentice. That wasn't fucking up.

Tanny didn't answer; they just kept walking, moving.

"Do you want to walk home via the market and pick up some stuff for supper?"

"Sure... what are you hungry for?"

"We could do a shrimp stir fry with lots of fresh vegetables." It was easy enough and he was feeling a need to get away from the heavy stuff.

"Sure." Tanny was nothing if not easy about food.

They headed off toward the market and he took Tanny's hand, kissed it. "You good?"

"I think so?"

"Good. I am, too." He was grinning as they wandered into the market.

"Can... can we get some grapes?"

"Sure. What else would you like?"

"An apple."

They stopped at the first fruit stand and Billy pointed to the half dozen varieties. "What kind?"

"Green." Tanny smiled. "You can take it out of my money."

He asked for six green apples, a bag of grapes and some pears. "We need veggies for the stir fry and we need some seafood."

"Okay. What kind of veggies? Pineapples?"

Someone had a sweet tooth today.

Laughing, he picked up a pineapple along with some bean sprouts, bok choy, broccoli, and snow peas.

Tanny looked at the bok choy. "Cabbage?"

"Basically. From China or Japan or something."

"Huh. I like cabbage okay."

"It's lighter than regular cabbage. Tastes different in a stir fry, too." They made their way over to the fishmonger. "Oh, look at the shrimp."

"They look like bugs." Tanny leaned into his side.

He chuckled. "Underwater bugs, so they don't count as bugs. Do you like lobster? Crab?"

"I don't know."

"Oh, fun. We'll get a bit of each and throw it all in the stir-fry." He liked being able to introduce Tanny to new things.

"Isn't that really expensive?" Tanny looked nervous, worried.

"I'm paying for supper, so you don't have to worry about it."

"Still. That's your money. You could buy three whole cases of ramen noodles."

He made a face. "I don't want to eat ramen noodles. I want to eat seafood stir-fry."

"Okay. Okay, I just... I worry that feeding me is going to make you lose your house."

Billy blinked. "I can afford to feed you and keep a roof over our heads."

"But are you sure? What if the apprentice thing doesn't work? What if the airplanes don't sell?"

He tilted his head. "Would it make you feel better if

you helped me write out the budget?"

"You write it out?" Jesus, how had Tanny *survived*?

"I do. Money coming in, money going out. It's especially important because I don't have a 'regular' job."

"I... I don't know if I can." Tanny got that look, that look he was learning meant that Tanny was going to shut the conversation down.

"Montana, would you like me to teach you to read and write properly?"

Montana hung his head, drew into himself. "I...I want... I..."

"What, Tanny? What do you want? What do you need?"

"I hate being stupid."

"You're not stupid. I bet you'll learn quickly."

"I'd try." The words were whispered.

"That's my Montana." He reached out and stroked Tanny's belly through his clothes, right where he knew his name was.

Montana gasped, lips parting. He smiled and passed money over for the seafood. Tanny blushed dark red, wandered off a little, looking at the different stalls.

Chuckling, he followed slowly, admiring Tanny's ass.

Tanny picked up a little carved doll, put it down. A group of men started toward Tanny—Billy could see them, pointing and looking. He kept an eye on them and moved closer to his lover, wondering what was up.

Tanny looked over at him, smiled. "This is pretty, huh? I like the face."

The men slowed down, separated.

"It is." He tilted his head, looking at the doll as he tried to decide whether or not to point the men out to Tanny.

He didn't have to; Tanny looked up and paled. "Billy, we should go."

He nodded. Tanny could tell him what was going on later. "Okay. I have everything we need for supper tonight."

He took hold of Tanny's hand and led him toward the exit. Tanny didn't look back, just kept moving them, kept them in the crowds. He didn't like this. He didn't like it at all. At least the roads back to the car were peopled.

"I think they've found another mark. Someone easier."

"Mark? Who were they? What did they want with you?"

"I think they wanted your money. They thought I was going to steal from you and then they could beat me up, take the money."

Billy growled. "We should go to the police, turn them in."

"For what?"

"Well for..." Okay, he supposed they hadn't actually done anything yet. "I don't like them being out there," he muttered.

"Me either. They used to get me a lot."

"God, people can be such assholes." He grumbled and growled. He was beginning to see where some of Tanny's suspicions came from.

"Yeah." Tanny didn't even sound surprised.

He put his arm around Tanny and gave him a hug.

Tanny looked up at him, smiled. "What was that for?"

"Because I love you and I want to make everything better for you."

"You have."

Warmth went through him and this time he gave Tanny a kiss. "I'm glad."

"It's been a full day already, hasn't it?"

"It has. And you've got a busy day tomorrow, don't

you? Is there anything special you want to do? Anything at all?"

"I..." Tanny shrugged. "I don't know. I have a job and that's wigging me out a little, so I guess not."

He grinned suddenly. "You want to go home and make love? I hear it's a great way to unwig folks."

"Okay. Sure."

"Come on, there's the car." He opened the doors and tossed their groceries in the back seat.

Tanny walked around the car, stopping as a police cruiser pulled up. The window rolled down and a hard face appeared. "You aren't supposed to be here, kid. You turning tricks, now?"

"What? No. No, I'm leaving."

Billy was going to blow a gasket. "Excuse me, officer, but Montana works at the Rainbow Artists right across the way there."

One eyebrow went up. "Since when? This kid's a tweaker."

"Not anymore. He's been living with me for... at least two months." God damn it, no wonder Tanny didn't think he was ever going to be anything but a loser, if that's all that was ever expected of him.

"And you work there? Good to know. I'll be checking in, kid. Every day."

Tanny looked like he was going to melt into the parking lot.

"Is that necessary?" Billy asked. This was harassment.

"I don't want this piece of shit stealing from those nice ladies."

"I wouldn't..."

"What? Speak up, asshole. You have something to say?"

"No."

"Because we can take a ride downtown."

Tanny shook his head and then ran, heading right back into the market, into the crowd.

"I want your fucking badge number. Right now. And then you'll be speaking to my lawyer."

"For what? Shaking down a known criminal? An addict? Does your lawyer know you're being taken?"

"For harassing a guy who's doing his best to make something of himself. Badge number. Right now." And soon, because he had to go after Tanny before this day became any worse for his dear lover.

The cop snarled out his badge number, then asked for his license and registration.

Billy handed it over and memorized the cop's number. He was calling Watson as soon as he found Tanny and got home.

God damn it.

God damn it.

Tanny was out there, running, because of this fuck.

He waited impatiently for his license and registration back; he knew better than to leave them with this asshole. It took at least fifteen minutes for the asshole to call it in. While he waited, he called Oliver to get Watson's number.

"Oliver. It's Billy. I need Watson's number." He didn't know whether to scream or cry or both.

"What's wrong? Jack, I need Watson's number."

"Police harassment." He clipped the words out.

"Jesus. Is Montana okay?"

Oh, Oliver was a good friend.

"I don't know. He took off. I need to go after him, but this... they're running my license and registration. I need to find him."

"Took off? Christ. Do you want us to come? 919-555-9009."

"Yes, Oliver. Please. And thank you. The market at the beach."

"We'll be there in ten."

The phone went dead.

"Are you done with my stuff yet?" He glared at the cop.

"I am. Looks good. Watch that one. He has a record."

"He has a record with me, too. A good one." He grabbed his papers and shoved them into his wallet. Then, without even checking to see if he'd locked the car, he took off after Tanny.

Chapter Twenty Four

Tanny ran until he couldn't run anymore. Then he turned around and ran more. He knew it was going to happen. He knew it. It had to.

His past would find him here. He stumbled on the sand, went down hard, sobbing.

"Montana!" The shout came from down the beach. He gasped, trying to catch his breath. Billy's hands landed on his shoulders, pulling him back against the muscled chest. "Montana. Oh, thank God."

"I'm so sorry. I told you. I fuck everything up."

"No. No, not this time. You didn't fuck this up. You didn't do anything wrong, Tanny. Not one thing. Well, except maybe running away."

"Billy." He clung to his lover, shaken, so scared, so humiliated. "You're a good man. You deserve better."

Billy held onto him, held tight. "You're a good man, too, Tanny."

"No." His head hurt so bad.

"William? Did you find him?"

He hid in Billy's chest, refusing to look up.

"Yes, we're over here, Oliver." Billy kissed the top of his head. "Oliver and Jack came down to help me look for you."

"I'll go get some water, Oliver? Maybe some juice?"

Jack sounded so worried.

"That would be lovely, Jack." Oliver was close, now. "How can I help, William?"

"Your overcoat, can I borrow it?"

"Absolutely."

"Thank you, Oliver." A moment later something soft and warm surrounded his shoulders. "Do you think you can walk?"

"Yes. Do... do you... I'm so sorry, Billy."

"Shh. Shh. You don't have to apologize. I'm going to have that asshole up on charges for harassing you." Billy helped him up, kept an arm around him.

"Can you do that?" He cuddled into the coat, moaning at the warmth. "Thank you for letting me use your coat."

Oliver met his eyes, smiled. "Absolutely. We protect our own, Montana. We will not have you threatened, not after you've worked so very hard."

His tears threatened again. They'd had a meal with Oliver and Jack after Thanksgiving, had played cards and laughed, and it had been nice.

"That's right." Billy walked him back up the beach, toward a strange car. "Oliver and Jack are going to take us home. We'll come back for my car later."

"I... Is that okay?"

"Of course it is. If necessary, Jack and I will bring the car while you two connect."

"You're more important than any car, Tanny. Than anything." Billy's words were gruff, the arms around him tightening.

"I want to go home." He wanted to be in Billy's bed, warm and safe.

"Five minutes and you will be." Billy helped him into the back seat of an expensive sedan and climbed in with him.

He cuddled in, eyes closed, wrapped in Billy's arms and Oliver's coat. "Our supper. Our shrimps."

"Oliver and Jack will rescue them along with the car. I don't want you to worry about any of it, okay?" Billy held him tight, hands moving on him, warming him.

"I'm so sorry. That cop. He's mean."

"He's an asshole." Billy's words surprised him, and he laughed, drinking deep of the orange juice Jack handed him. Billy smiled and hugged him tight. "That's a good sound."

"I just... I don't want to get you in trouble." He didn't want to be something dirty in Billy's world. He'd been so scared.

"Neither of us had done anything wrong, Tanny. The only one in trouble is going to be that asshole."

The car came to a stop. "We're home."

"Do you need us to come up or just fetch the car and leave it, William?" Oliver always sounded so fussy.

"I know it's rude, but if you could just bring the car and leave the groceries by the door? We need some private time."

"We'll put them in a cooler with ice. You take your time."

"Thank you, Oliver. And you too, Jack. We'll be in touch."

"Here... here's your coat."

"You can keep it for a few days, if you'd like, Montana. There are storms coming."

"No. No, I couldn't. I... If I need a coat, Billy will help me." Billy always helped, and he had money.

"I will." It sounded like a promise.

"All right." Oliver sounded weirdly pleased. "That sounds good."

He left the jacket behind, took the juice with him. "Thank you."

Billy got them upstairs and let them in, guiding him to the bedroom.

"I. We're okay? You're not mad at me?" He was shaking, adrenaline making him shake.

"No, not at all. I'm angry—I want to knock some heads together—but not yours." Billy drew him into the strong arms and held him close. "I love you, Montana."

"I love you. I'm okay. I had to... cops scare me, Billy. Bad."

"I'm not surprised." Billy tipped his head. "It's okay. I have you now. You're home, you're safe." The words ended on a kiss.

He opened up, partially embarrassed that he was such a dork, partially needing Billy to touch him, love him. Billy moaned into his mouth, one hand slipping behind his head and tilting it. He leaned into the touch, trusting Billy to hold him up.

Billy's muscled body supported him. Warm hands slid over him, like Billy was memorizing him. His scars didn't even matter. "Billy. Billy, love."

He did.

So much.

"Good. All that matters is the love we have." Billy pushed him gently toward the bed. "I'm going to love you now. I'm going to make you feel good and hot and wonderful.

He was the luckiest man ever.

He so was.

Billy tugged at his sweater, pulling it and his T-shirt up over his head at the same time. "I like that sweater, so much."

"Looks good on you." Billy pushed him onto the bed and began working off his jeans and underwear.

He helped, wriggling out of the clothes and snuggling back into the bed that was theirs now. It smelled like him and Billy; the scent surrounded them, made him hard. Of course, that could be Billy's hands, sliding up his legs. Warm and sure, they spread him and teased along the soft skin of his inner thighs.

"Mmm." He reached down, stroked his cock, slow and easy, encouraging it to full hardness. Billy played with his balls and then reached back to stroke the skin behind them.

"Your fingers are warm." He spread a little wider.

"All the better to turn you on." One finger slid across his hole.

His body clenched, his hand working faster, thumb working the slit.

"Don't come yet," Billy murmured.

Tanny nodded, slowed down a little, hips rocking on the sheets. Then Billy pushed forward to lick at his hole.

"Billy!" He arched, knees drawing up, hips rolling.

"Yeah, that's it; show me that hot little hole."

"Billy..." He blinked, his belly going tight at the dirty whispers.

Billy chuckled, hot air sliding across his crack, his hole. "Yeah. Yeah." Billy's tongue swiped across him a few more times.

"I. I want. I need..." He laughed a little, eyes rolling. He'd gone from zero to sixty, so fast.

"Don't worry, Tanny, I'll take care of you." Billy's head lifted, eyes looking into his. "Like always."

"Is that okay? I mean..." He stopped touching himself, reached for Billy's face.

Billy nuzzled into his touch and kissed his fingers. "It's great, Tanny."

"Okay." He just... He worried. So ridiculous.

A soft chuckle sounded. "And I'm not doing a good enough job at this if you have time to worry if it's okay."

Billy's tongue pierced his hole, started fucking it. His

hands landed on the sheets, fingers digging in and holding on as pleasure flooded him. Over and over, Billy's tongue pushed into him. It was hot and slick and so good.

Tanny gasped and groaned, cock bobbing and leaking. Billy's fingers played with his balls, feeling them up and playing with them. Then they slid up along his cock, the touch light, barely there. He reached out, his fingers meeting Billy's.

That made Billy hum, which vibrated up through his ass.

"I'm gonna come."

"No, no, Tanny. Wait." Billy did that thing with his balls, grabbing them and tugging.

"Oh. Oh, Billy. That aches. So good."

"Mmm. I know." Billy chuckled softly and licked at his stretched balls, fingers still dancing on his cock.

"I..." He didn't know what to think.

Billy's fingers let him go and instead kisses pressed against his hole, his balls, the base of his cock. Crazy. Billy was going to make him crazy. That hot mouth slowly moved up along his cock, tongue dragging over his skin.

"I love you." He whispered the words, meaning them.

He could feel Billy smile on his skin, Billy's nod. He relaxed, enjoying the ache, the pressure, the way Billy's tongue felt on him. Billy's tongue teased across the head of his cock, flicking back and forth across his slit. The burn got hotter, higher, more and more fierce.

One of Billy's fingers pushed into his ass.

"Please." He moved down, rocking into Billy's touch.

"You want me?" Billy asked, chin rubbing against the head of his prick.

"Yes. No. I mean, I need you."

Billy smiled and rose up over him. A condom was grabbed and handed over. "I need you, too. Get me covered."

"Okay." He eased the rubber over Billy's cock, then started stroking, up and down.

"Mmm. Oh, careful. I don't want to go off before I'm inside you."

"You're sure?" he teased.

"I'm sure." Billy's voice was rough with strain. He'd done that.

He eased up, stroking gently.

"Your touch. So good." Billy's hand slid over his chest.

He arched, cock swelling, aching. Two fingers from Billy's other hand slid into his hole.

"Oh. Full." The stretch, the pressure, was still so new.

"Two fingers." They slid in and out and spread, stretching him.

"Mmhmm. Only three fit ever; two is full."

"Only three? I think I can manage more than that."

"Uh-uh. You can't." That wouldn't work.

Billy chuckled, the sound sexy. "Can too." A third finger slipped into him, opening him farther.

"N...no. No, you'll hurt me." That didn't hurt, though, not at all.

"I don't think so." Billy fingers wriggled and stretched.

"It would." Why were they talking?

"Would not." Billy's fingers disappeared and then came back, the lube slick and cool.

"Mmm." He arched, humming low. "Would too."

Billy's fingers felt bigger now, more somehow. "Not."

"Uh... uh-huh. I bet you."

"Name your terms." In, out, Billy stretched him wide.

"Uh... Uh... I... If it hurts, you have to stop." Was that right?

"If you give me the magic word, I have to stop." The fingers inside him wriggled. Four. There were four of them inside him.

"Uh... Shrimps. I want... I want to go have lasagna if I win."

"Deal." Billy bent and sucked at the tip of his cock. "But I'm going to win."

"What... what do you win?" He played fair.

"I get to put a ring on your cock and a clamp on one of your nipples."

"Okay..." He could handle that.

"Good. Good." Billy's fingers disappeared and a bunch of lube was pushed into him.

"That feels good, the coolness."

"Good. This is all supposed to be good." Another kiss pressed to the tip of his cock.

"Mmmhmm." His toes curled and the world went a little fuzzy around the edges.

In and out, Billy's finger pushed and stretched. Four. God.

"You're ready for more."

"Not ready..."

Billy chuckled and licked the tip of his cock again. The fingers inside him spread and twisted, one brushing across his prostate.

"Oh. Oh. Oh, Billy..." His shoulders left the mattress.

"Yeah, it's good, isn't it?" Billy kept making the same motion, over and over.

"Uh-huh. Uh-huh. Uh-huh." He was flying.

Billy kept feeding more lube into his ass, slathering the fingers that fucked him.

He almost didn't notice when those fingers curled in around themselves and Billy's whole hand started to push in. Then it got way intense way fast.

"Billy. Billy, please." He gasped, the pressure so big, so scary.

Billy's free hand slid over his stomach. "Shh. Relax, Montana. I've got you. I won't to anything to break or hurt you."

"You promise?"

That finger traced Billy's name. "You're mine, Montana. Mine to keep and to hold and to love. Mine to protect. I have you. Right here." As he spoke, Billy's hand pushed against the ring of muscles guarding his ass, and then pushed right in.

A cry pushed out of him, tears streaking his cheeks, surprising him.

Billy's hand was solid and hot inside him, fingers on the other hand tracing the name on his belly over and over again. "I have you. I have you, Montana. I'll always have you."

"I'm scared."

"What are you scared of, Montana? You're in a safe place here. You can tell me anything."

"Losing you. Hurting you. How big this feels."

"It's huge and I'm going to hold onto it, onto you, with everything I have." The hand inside him moved, fingers wiggling.

He whimpered, lips open as he gasped. Billy's free hand slipped to his cock, circling it and stroking gently. The other hand, the one inside him, curled into a fist and began moving inside him.

"Oh, God..." His head tossed, his throat working.

"You can call me Billy." He could hear the gentle teasing in Billy's voice.

He almost chuckled, but he wasn't sure he could, really. His tongue wasn't working. Both of Billy's hands continued to move, stroking him inside and out.

Tanny couldn't think, couldn't do this. Couldn't breathe. "Help me."

"Follow my voice, Montana." Back and forth, up and

down, Billy worked him. "Breathe with me. In... and out.."

It was like being high.

Oh, God.

It was like being high—waves of pleasure and Billy was right there and he was flying.

"That's it. Fuck, look at you. Glowing."

"Billy." That's all he could say.

"I have you." Billy's thumb pressed into his slit at the same time as the knuckles inside him brushed over his prostate.

Spunk shot out of him, his entire body shuddering, the room, the world disappearing. He'd never had a high that felt so good.

When he came back to himself, Billy's hand was still inside him, solid and hot. There.

"I love you, Montana."

"Love." He was sobbing now, lost and found all at once.

Billy's free hand stroked him, touching him everything as the other hand slowly worked out of his body.

"Yours." His body clenched, trying to keep Billy in.

"Mine. Always." Billy's hand stilled inside him. His lover's eyes met his, heat and love and home in them.

"I promise," Tanny managed.

A wide smile lit up Billy's face. "I promise, too. Now, take a few breaths and relax; I need my hand back."

He took one shaky breath, then another, then breathing got a little easier.

"Good. Good, Montana." Billy's hand started moving again, pulling out. "Even when it's out you'll be able to feel it for a long time. You'll be able to feel me holding you in the palm of my hand."

He closed his eyes, tears coming again.

Billy's hand was so, so huge, and then suddenly it was

gone, his hole snapping closed behind it.

"I don't know what to do. I don't know what to do. I don't know what to do."

Billy crawled up and pulled him into the strong arms. He shuddered, clinging, suddenly worn to death, exhausted, the day overwhelming him.

"I have you," Billy told him. "I have you. Now. Always."

"I'm sorry. I'm sorry. I'm not usually a weenie."

"You're not a weenie. My lover is not a weenie."

"I love you." He sighed, leaned in, eyes closing.

"I love you, too." Billy kissed the top of his head. "You'll never forget that, never forget the feeling of me holding you in my hand." Billy chuckled. "And I won the bet."

Chapter Twenty Five

Billy rescued their groceries from outside of their door. There was enough ice in the cooler that nothing was spoiled.

"It looks like our supper is safe."

Montana nodded, curled up at the table with coffee, looking a little shell-shocked, still.

He put the cooler down on the counter and grabbed a blanket from the laundry. He put it around Montana's shoulders.

"Oh..." Montana looked up at him, eyes almost bruised looking. "Thank you."

"You're welcome." He stroked Montana's cheek gently. "If you need anything, you let me know, hmm?"

"I just... I'm feeling a little... I can't believe I. I'm feeling... I don't know the words."

He took Tanny's mouth in a hard kiss. "Just breathe, Tanny."

Montana took a deep breath, responding beautifully.

"Mmm. That's better." He took another kiss and grabbed the chopping block, set out the vegetables.

Tanny watched him, cuddled in the blanket, quiet and still.

"Stir frys are easy. The hardest thing about them is all the chopping." He grinned. "Of course I kind of like the chopping. Therapeutic."

"Yeah? I used to like grinding corn for my gran."

"Yeah? How old were you when you did that?"

"Little. Maybe four or five. She had us when we were little."

Oh, lord he could just see Tanny helping out, little and sweet. "I bet you were a picture."

"I guess? I looked like everyone else."

"Was it good? With your grandmother?" Had Tanny ever had anyone in his corner?

"Yeah. She was nice. She smelled good."

"Grandmothers smell either good or bad, don't they?"

Tanny smiled at him, nodded. "I think so, yeah."

Billy got out the wok and put it on the stove, added the oil. "How long did you live with her?" he asked, looking to keep Montana engaged, a part of things even if it was only conversation.

Tanny shrugged. "For a while. My mom was in prison and Katy and me stayed with her."

Billy managed not to wince. It was a hell of a thing for a kid to grow up with. "What was she in prison for?"

"She robbed a gas station."

"Must have been hard." He threw the vegetables into the wok.

"I guess? Not as hard as when I killed Katy."

"Will you tell me what happened?"

"I... I was stupid. I fucked up on the road." Montana pulled the blanket tighter around him. "I don't remember any of it, only what I was told."

He went over and gave Tanny a hug. "It's okay, Tanny. You're safe here."

"It's just... it'll always be my fault."

"You don't actually know that, though, do you?" Not if Tanny couldn't remember and was going by what other

Found

people, who presumably hadn't been there, had told him.

"Huh?" Tanny looked utterly confused.

"Well, who told you what happened? What exactly did they tell you?" An angry parent screaming "You killed your sister" wasn't exactly an accurate picture of what had happened, was it? Billy imagined Tanny would never get over what happened if he couldn't come to terms with it.

"We were on my motorcycle. I went too fast and hit an oil slick, her head exploded."

"You weren't wearing helmets?"

"I was. She didn't like them. They messed up her hair."

Billy growled a little. "So it's your fault because you didn't force her to wear one?"

"It was my fault because I wrecked the bike."

"How do you know you were going too fast?"

"Because I had to have been. Everyone said."

"You mean they assumed that's what happened, and as you didn't remember it was easier to just let you take the blame for the accident." Billy stirred the vegetables viciously.

"I'm trouble. Everybody knows it. I wasn't using then, though."

"They made assumptions. For all you know, your sister started fooling around and that's why you crashed."

"No. It was my fault."

"I thought you said you couldn't remember what happened?" He wasn't trying to be an asshole, but it seemed that a lot of Tanny's belief of himself as a useless loser stemmed out of the motorcycle accident where his sister had been killed.

"I can't. I don't want to talk about this anymore."

He went over and gave Tanny a hug. "All I'm saying is

maybe there's more to it than just you being responsible for killing your sister, that's all."

"More? Isn't that enough?"

He looked into Tanny's eyes. "Not if the truth is that it wasn't your fault, or not all your fault."

"It'll always be my fault. I'm a fuck up."

"You're not." He stared at Tanny for a moment, let his lover know how absolutely serious he was. Then he went to put the fresh shrimp into the wok.

"It smells good." Tanny got up, wandered over to him.

He slipped an arm around Tanny's waist. "It does, doesn't it? The shrimp fries up very quickly, especially in such a hot pan. As soon as it goes pink, it's ready. And you want to take it off right away or it gets overcooked and rubbery."

"Yeah?" Tanny pressed closer to him, cheek on his shoulders.

"Yep. And rubbery shrimp is not good shrimp." He could smell the garlic and sesame sauce coming on the steam and he grabbed a couple plates for them.

"Oh, man. I could eat a bunch of that."

"That's good, because there's a lot of food and only the two of us." He bumped hips with Tanny.

"Well, you're a bottomless pit..." Tanny teased.

"Me?" That made him laugh. "It takes a lot of food to keep these muscles strong."

"It does." Tanny patted him, nodded.

He flexed a little for Tanny. He wasn't a huge muscleman with a massive ego or anything, but he liked knowing Tanny appreciated his body.

Tanny hummed softly, one hands sliding down his belly.

"Mmm... the shrimps are ready."

"Then we should eat." Tanny kept touching.

"Mmmhmm." He dished the stir-fry onto both their plates.

"I like the seed things."

"Bean sprouts. I think you're going to like the shrimp a lot." They sat side by side, close.

"Can you use chopsticks?"

"I can. I might even have some here. You want to eat with them?" He could feed Tanny with them, it could be sexy.

"I don't know how, but I think they're neat."

He got up and rummaged through the utensil drawer. "Aha!" He pulled out a couple pair of wooden chopsticks from the last time he'd ordered Chinese and went back to Tanny's side.

"You think I can?"

God, hadn't anyone taught Tanny anything?

"Sure. Here." He put one set between his own fingers and showed Tanny how to work them.

Tanny looked, watched, then bingo. Picked up a shrimp and ate.

Stupid, his ass.

"Good job." He grinned and grabbed one for himself. Oh, they'd come off nicely. "Do you like it?"

"I do." Tanny picked up more, eating happily. "I like it a lot."

"I thought you would. I bet you'll like lobster and crab, too. We'll have to try different stuff." Billy speared a snow pea and munched on it.

"Okay." Tanny nodded at him. "I like the spicy parts. We should have more spicy food."

He forced himself not to look surprised. He thought, maybe, Tanny had just made a preference known. "We can do that. All sorts of things can go into a stir-fry and it's quick, good for us."

"Okay." Tanny held up a bite of green pepper. "Want

a bite?"

"I'd love one." He'd eaten enough to satisfy the hunger in his stomach; they could play now. He leaned toward Tanny and opened his mouth.

Tanny grinned, popped the pepper in his mouth. The chopsticks were actually perfect for feeding each other, making it a fun experience, a tease. He chewed and then offered Tanny a snow pea from his own plate. They fed each other, bite after bite, the pleasure slowly growing.

At one point he snapped Tanny's tongue with his chopsticks.

Tanny jerked back, laughing hard. "Turkey!"

Grinning, he snapped the chopsticks in the air and made gobbling noises. Oh, that laughter filled the air, filled the house. He watched Tanny's face, utterly smitten.

"You okay?" Tanny's eyes twinkled.

"Absolutely." He reached out and stroked Tanny's cheek, Tanny's lips.

Tanny's lips wrapped around his finger, sucking a little. He groaned, pushing his finger in and out of Tanny's lips. Eyelids going heavy, Tanny sucked and moaned, tongue on his finger. His cock began to fill, the air becoming charged.

"Mmm." The sound vibrated around his finger.

"You're seducing me," he murmured, voice low, full of growing need.

Tanny smiled, tongue licking the tip of his finger. He was all but purring. He slid off his chair and stepped up close to Tanny. Those big eyes smiled up at him, Tanny becoming more and more confident. He kept watching, his eyes heavy-lidded as each suck of Tanny's mouth made his cock throb. Tanny worked his finger like it was his cock, head bobbing,

"Fuck, that's... that's something else."

"You want more?"

"Yes." There was no hesitation to his answer.

Tanny reached for his waistband, tugging his sweats down to bare his cock.

"Oh, yes. Please." He swallowed and smiled, watching Tanny.

Tanny licked the tip of his prick, humming a little, sounding so happy.

"Good, that's good. More, please."

He got a nod, a moan, then Tanny took him in, sucking easily. The pleasure spread from his cock, making his skin hum. Warm hands slid around his hips, petting his skin. Montana was good at this and he was only going to get better the longer they were together.

Billy stroked the short hair. That hot tongue traced his prick, from base to tip, flicking at the slit. He reached one hand for the table to keep himself upright, the other kept sliding through Montana's hair.

His cock was worshipped. Worshipped by that pretty mouth.

He groaned and let Tanny know how good it felt. Tanny slowly sank to the floor, kneeling before him, sucking harder. It was beautiful, seeing his lover on his knees like that.

"Mine," Billy growled softly.

Those eyes stared up at him, Tanny swallowing around the tip of his cock. He held Tanny's gaze and began slowly rocking in and out of Tanny's mouth. Billy was lost. Right here. Right in Montana's mouth. He hummed softly, hips moving faster, the pleasure suffusing him.

Tanny took him and took him, swallowing on each push in. It was too good to last very long and he could feel his orgasm coming, gathering in his balls. Billy pushed in deep, holding his cock in for a second, feeling Tanny swallow all around him.

He traced Tanny's lips where they stretched around

his prick. That made Tanny's throat convulse again. Moaning, Billy closed his eyes and breathed deeply. He didn't want to come right away; he wanted this to last.

Tanny's hand slid up and down his body, stroking him. Gentling him. He petted Tanny's shoulders and breathed, his orgasm backing off again. Opening his eyes, he smiled down at Tanny. Fuck the man was sexy. On his knees, lips parted around his cock, Tanny blew his fucking mind.

"Soon," Billy warned, any control he'd found disappearing beneath the onslaught of Tanny's mouth and how his lover looked.

Those warm fingers nudged his balls, rolling them in their sac.

"Yes!" He cried out and pushed deep, his balls emptying.

Tanny swallowed and drank him down, humming around his cock. He leaned hard against the table, panting. His cock was cleaned, then he was tucked back away. He sat down abruptly, his knees finally giving out, and he opened his arms.

It didn't take a second before he had an armful of Montana, who cuddled in close. He wrapped his arms around Tanny and held on.

His. This was his.

"Love you," he murmured. "Very much."

"Love." Tanny's lips were soft, warm on his jaw.

"How are you feeling?"

"Good. A little worn out, maybe?"

"I'm not surprised. A lot of stuff happened today." He stroked Tanny's ass, knowing that intimacy would be the thing he remembered the longest: holding Montana in his hand.

"It did. Do you think it would be cool to just hang out for a little while?"

"I think it would be very cool. You want to hang out

in the bedroom or living room?" They could watch some movies, or put on some music.

"Hmm. Let's get some blankets and pillows and be on the sofa."

"Sounds lovely. You get those and I'll choose us some music."

"Okay, Billy." He got a soft kiss, then Tanny headed off.

He watched Tanny go, admiring the lean body, the soft sway of ass. They were ending the day on a good note. Not bad at all, considering.

Chapter Twenty Six

He'd woken up at the crack of dawn and had been waiting at the studio when it opened. Tanny spent all morning trying to listen and learn, trying his best to remember everything he was told, everything he was taught.

Trying was the operative word.

By the time his work day was done, he was frustrated and tired and feeling more than a little stupid. He went upstairs and slid in, pouring himself a Coke and heading to the bathroom for a soak. And to touch that single pill that was waiting for him there.

Except it wasn't there.

He frowned, hands shaking a little. Where did it go? He didn't want it right now, but it was his.

He headed for Billy's office, knocking on the door. "Where is it? Where's my stuff?"

"Hey, you're home. How was your first day?"

"Hard. It was very hard and I need a shower. I think my pill fell, though, because it's gone." It was important to him, to know it was there.

"I'm sorry you had a hard day. I imagine they'll get easier. But not if you take a pill to make it through." Billy got up and wrapped him in a hug. "I'll shower with you, give you a massage."

"I didn't say I wanted to take it."

"Oh. Okay. I thought that's why you were upset, because you wanted it and it's not there?"

"I'm upset because it's not there. I need it to be there. So that I know that it is there."

Billy was quiet for a moment and then he nodded. "Okay. It's probably on the floor in the bathroom."

"Yeah. Okay." He nodded. "Sorry, I just... It means something to me, that it's there." It meant it was there, and he didn't need it.

"Then let's see if we can find it."

He squeezed Billy's fingers. "How was your day?"

"I missed you. I've gotten used to you being around all day so to have you missing all morning... Well, it was different." Billy turned on the light in the bathroom.

"Yeah. It was hard. I'm... it's hard to remember things."

"It's your first day, Tanny. Nobody remembers everything the first day. That's why most training is anywhere from two weeks to several months." Billy went to look at the shelf where the pill had been and looked to see if it had slid behind anything.

Tanny nodded, but he wasn't sure. He looked behind the toilet, around the sink.

Nothing.

"I hope it didn't fall into the toilet."

"Me too, because I'm not going there." He grinned at the idea, chuckled a little.

Billy laughed. "Yuck."

They kept looking, Billy finally shaking his head. "I don't know, Tanny. I don't see it anywhere."

"I..." He surprised himself with the anger, the loss in the center of his chest. "I think I'm going to take a shower now."

"You want your massage in the shower or after?"

"After. I... I think I need some time to just be bitchy."

"Because the pill is lost?" He knew Billy didn't understand.

"Because the pill is lost. Because I can't write stuff down. Because I'm tired."

"So bitch at me about stuff while we get wet." Billy started stripping.

Billy wasn't listening. Again. "I... I don't want to bitch at you. That's not fair."

"Why not? That's part of being partners, isn't it? The bad along with the good."

He sighed, rubbed the back of his neck. "I. I hate being stupid."

"You're not stupid."

"I am stupid." Asshole.

"I don't believe that."

Tanny was going to whack Billy with a rock. A big rock. "You don't have to." He was really getting mad.

"Don't have to what? I love you, I don't believe you're stupid, and one day you'll know you're not."

"I can't read good. I can't write good. I'm just a dummy."

"You'll learn to read and to write. And you'll stop being a dummy when you start believing you're not."

"What if I can't learn?" They got into the tub, the water hot on his skin.

"I'll be shocked."

"Ass." He sighed, leaned back into the water.

"No, this is an ass." Billy's hands grabbed his, squeezed.

"Don't make me laugh!"

"God forbid." Billy winked.

"What if I can't make this work?"

"Are you talking about the bookbinding?"

"Yeah. What else would I be talking about?"

"I just wanted to be sure that was it." Billy kissed his nose. "If the bookbinding doesn't work out, you'll find something else."

He closed his eyes, uncomfortable with this, with Billy believing in him.

"I know what you're thinking and you're wrong. My faith in you isn't misplaced."

"You can't know what I'm thinking." Could he?

"No? I've been paying attention to you, Montana. Very close attention."

"I... That makes me feel very... nervous."

"I know that, too." Billy's eyes held his. "But I held you in my hand—I've got you. You're safe."

He gasped, staring at Billy, fascinated, remembering.

"That's right. I'm not going to let you forget every good thing between us."

"You're not?"

"No, I'm not. You deserve to be here with me, Montana. I want you here. I love you."

"I've never known anyone who said that as much as you do."

"It's the truth. One you need to hear again and again to believe."

He pressed close—not looking for sex, just wanting to touch and be touched a little. Billy's fingers slid over his shoulders. It wasn't a full on massage, but between fingers and water, his aches were beginning to be soothed.

"Did you have lovers that you lived with before me?"

"No one's ever stayed longer than a weekend. Though I had lovers I could call if I needed."

"Why not? Did you not want them to stay?"

"Not to live with me, no. You're the first one I wanted to have stay."

Tanny thought about that, really thought about it. "I want to be good enough, to be the one you wanted to stay. I want that really bad. So bad that it hurts a little."

"But you are, Tanny."

He shook his head. He wasn't. Not yet.

Billy gave him a smile, strong fingers continuing to touch and ease him. "One day you'll believe it."

He chuckled, leaned against Billy's shoulder, eyes closing. Billy kissed the top of his head. He was touched wherever Billy could reach, touches so easy and comforting. They stayed under the water for a long time, up until it started getting cold.

"Come on. You need something in your belly. Everything seems better with food."

"Okay, yeah." He got out of the shower, grabbed them both towels. "I missed you today."

"I know. I liked having you to myself all day."

"You'd get tired of it."

"I hadn't before now."

"No, me either." Tanny grinned. "But it'll be good, to buy clothes and stuff."

"Yes. It'll be good for you to be able to do that." Billy started drying him.

He nodded, caught himself yawning. "Do you pick up a Christmas tree?"

"It usually depends on what my plans are, but as there's two of us, I'd like for us to go get one."

"Can we have lights?" He loved those best.

"Anything you want. It's our first Christmas together, it should set the tone for all of them to come."

"Then it should be what we want."

"Exactly."

"I... Right." He headed into the bedroom to find some clothes.

Billy followed, hands fondling his ass. "Sometimes I just can't resist these sweet cheeks."

Tanny chuckled, scooting forward out of Billy's reach.

Found

Billy followed, though, fingers pinching his skin.

"Stop it!" He laughed, scrambling across the bed.

Chortling, Billy climbed onto the bed, chasing him down.

"You can't catch me!" He hit the floor and made for the door.

"Yes, I can!" Billy's footsteps sounded behind him.

He slipped and slid down the hall, laughing hard. Billy's fingers brushed against his ass for a moment, the heat of the man's breath between his shoulder blades. His skin was tingling, awake, so alive. Billy's arms slid around his waist, tugging him back against the solid body.

"You... you caught me," he panted.

"I did." Billy nibbled at his shoulder, teeth sliding over his skin.

"What are you going to do with me now?"

"I might just have to eat you up."

He chuckled, "Are you the big bad wolf?"

"I believe I am." Growling loudly, Billy dragged him back down the hall.

His cock started to fill, the easy play exciting and fun. Billy got him into the bedroom and manhandled him onto the bed, grinning, growling, and baring his teeth.

"No biting, now."

"No? You just might like it." Billy snapped his teeth together in the air.

He stilled, gasped a little.

Oh, that was... weird.

Laughing, Billy pounced him, teeth on the skin of his shoulder. He jerked away, gasping, heated. Billy pushed him down onto the bed and grazed his cheek.

"Billy... Don't. No biting."

"You like it too much, don't you?" Billy held his gaze and bit down on his lower lip.

Hard.

The whimper escaped him and he went stiff, almost scared.

"I'm going to mark you, Montana." Licking down along his jaw and to his throat, Billy bit down on his neck.

"I. I don't know if..."

Hot.

That was hot.

Billy growled and bit down harder, mouth sucking. He was going to have a huge hickey there. Huge. His cock went from full to achingly hard. That growl sounded again as one of Billy's hand landed on his balls, squeezing and playing with them.

His toes curled, his heart beating faster. "Billy?"

"Gonna blow your mind, Montana." Billy's hand gentled, rolling his balls now, and then it slid up over his cock.

"I'm a little wigged out, man."

"Because you like the biting." Billy licked the mark he'd pulled up. "It doesn't make you weird or sick, you know."

"I just... I don't know about this." The mark tingled.

"This knows." Billy stroked his erection. "Let your body tell you what you like."

He moaned a little, and his hips started rocking in definite, sure pulses.

"Mmm." Billy's hum sounded self-satisfied. Then Billy bit at his right nipple.

"Ow." He whimpered, his nipple drawing up into a hard nub.

Billy's tongue flicked across it and then another bite landed on his skin, this one next to his navel. His skin was tingling, almost burning. Bites and licks, Billy alternated them, hand still working his cock.

"I..." He was getting so hard, starting to need it.

Turning his head, Billy licked at the tip of his cock. He reached down, stroked his cock, the pleasure building. Billy grabbed his hand and pulled it away from his cock, held it against the mattress.

Tanny blinked down, lips parted. Oh. "What?"

"Mine." Billy growled softly and then took his cock in and went down on it.

"Oh." Yeah. Yeah, okay. His.

So his.

Billy's head bobbed, taking him all the way in before pulling back up. His hips rolled and he tried to keep the heat of that mouth.

That's when Billy came right off and laughed. "You're not running this show, Tanny."

"I'm not? You're sure?"

"Oh, I'm very sure." Billy smiled at him, eyes twinkling. His wrist was squeezed.

He found himself smiling back. Billy looked down again, slapped his prick with a hot, wet tongue. He groaned, confused, just a little lost. Surging up, Billy kissed him, bringing his focus to their mouths, to the hard push of Billy's tongue between his lips.

He wrapped his arms around Billy's neck, held on tight. Kissing he understood, he got.

"You have to trust me," Billy told him as their lips parted.

"I do." He did.

"Then trust me." Billy kissed him hard on the mouth and then began to kiss down along his neck.

"What... what does that mean that I need to do?" Oh, he loved that.

"Let me take you to the places you're not sure you want to go."

"You... you promise it'll be okay, though, right?" Not that he was scared, because he wasn't. Just a little weirded out.

"I promise. I want to blow your mind, to make you feel so good and push you to higher and higher pleasure." Billy grinned suddenly and slid out of bed. "Let me get something that might make things easier for you."

He rolled over on his side, watching. "Easier?"

"Uh-huh. Something to help you trust me completely." Billy took two silk scarves out of one of his drawers and came back to the bed to trail the silk over his skin.

Oh, that felt good. "Soft."

"It is." Billy let the silk slide up over his back.

He shivered, the different sensation overwhelming.

"Put your hands over your head." Billy's words were softly spoken, but he could hear something strong in them, too.

"Okay..." He turn onto his back again and reached up, hands stretching out.

"Good job." Billy straddled him, cock and balls hot and soft against his chest. Then Billy leaned forward and wrapped the silk ties around his wrists.

He watched, a ball of excitement growing in his belly.

The silk scarves were then tied to the headboard. The material didn't feel tight or painful around his wrists, but he definitely couldn't get his hands free.

"There," murmured Billy, hands sliding on his arms. "Now you have no choice but to lie back and let me have my wicked way with you."

"You'd untie me if I wanted you to, though." Right?

"Of course. Your word is armpit, remember?" Billy grinned and bent to lick and nuzzle into his right pit, breath hot as it moved over his skin.

"Uh-huh. Armpit. I remember."

"Good. Use it if you need to." Billy kissed his pit and then licked over to his nipple, tongue-tip teasing across it.

He arched, the touch making him tingle. Billy wrapped

soft lips around his nipple and hummed, the vibrations making the tingles increase.

"Billy. That feels..." Good? Intense? Amazing...

Billy's answer was to hum louder, which made the vibrations even stronger. He moaned, twisted a little. The suction became stronger, Billy's teeth grazing his nipple now, too.

"I don't... That..." He didn't know about the biting.

"Just feel," murmured Billy.

"I don't know how."

"Should I gag you, too?"

"Why? Do you want me to be quiet?"

"No, I need you to stop second guessing yourself and me."

"Let me up." This was weird and he didn't like it.

"No." Billy's fingers danced along his cock.

"Now. I don't like this. I feel... like I'm disappointing you."

"Stop that, you're not disappointing me at all." Billy licked at the tip of his cock, and then nuzzled his hip.

"You swear?" He loved Billy's lips.

"I swear, Montana." Billy's mouth wrapped around his hip bone.

"I'm so... Oh." He wasn't sorry. He wasn't sorry.

Billy sucked on his hip until the skin was so sensitive he thought he might scream. Then Billy moved to his other hip and did the same thing. Weird little sounds were hiccupping out of him, but he barely noticed, he was so focused on Billy's mouth.

Tongue hot enough to burn, Billy slid his mouth to the crease where Tanny's thigh met his torso. Licks and nips were followed by scrape of teeth and then more sucking.

He found himself relaxing back, drowning in those touches. The skin behind his balls was next, Billy spreading his legs and nosing aside his balls. He couldn't breathe, couldn't quite think, and his knees drew up.

Billy's tongue slid up and down along the soft skin between his balls and hole, teeth following. He whimpered, nodded, his eyes rolling back in his head. Billy bit and licked and sucked and drove him out of his mind.

"Billy. Billy, I. Please. Can't breathe."

Billy's tongue flicked at his hole. "You're allowed to come."

"I don't know if I remember how." He laughed a little bit, gasped.

"Then don't. Either way, I'm not stopping." Billy's tongue pushed into his hole and then disappeared. Teeth scraped along his navel.

"Billy! Billy. I..." He twisted, hips bucking up, rolling, his cock slapping his belly.

Billy bit and sucked and licked, mouth moving over every part of him.

He wanted to touch himself, to stroke himself off. "I need to touch..."

"No, you want to touch. There's a difference." Billy's teeth threatened on his right nipple again, the touch turning into licking instead.

Tanny tugged at the scarves, heart pounding, breath coming faster. "It feels like need."

"I'm touching you." This time Billy did bite his nipple.

"Fuck! Don't!"

Billy's mouth gentled, a low hum vibrating Tanny's nipple. Huffing, panting sounds pushed out of him, and he tried to reach down, stroke Billy's hair. Billy rubbed a cheek against his breastbone, and then licked at his other nipple. There were no teeth this time and Billy headed back down toward his cock.

"I love you. I want you, so much."

"You've got me, Montana. I'm right here." Billy gave

him a happy, shit-eating grin, and then the tip of his cock was treated to a good tongue-lashing.

Tanny let his head fall back and sank into the sensations that washed over him in waves. So good. So... Oh, God, he was going to shoot.

Billy's tongue soaked his cock, licking and lapping at him like he was a candy. Then Billy took his cock in, sucking strongly.

He shot hard, shaking and calling out, the room spinning a bit.

"Look at you. So hot." Billy licked the come from his skin.

He nodded. He was. So hot. Burning up.

"I'm gonna fuck you now." Billy slowly licked his way back down to his balls.

"Yes." Yes, he could get behind that.

Billy's hands spread his legs wide and rolled his ass up, exposing his hole to that questing tongue. Still boneless, he didn't even bother to tense; he simply let Billy have him. Billy tongue fucked him until he could feel the saliva sliding from his hole over his skin. Then Billy covered his cock and lined up with Montana's hole.

He wanted this, possibly needed it. Deep and hard and... "Yours."

"You are." Billy sounded so very sure. Then Billy's thick prick pushed into him, opening him wide.

He groaned, his body accepting, taking Billy in and in and in. Billy filled him so full, cock finally seated deep, Billy's balls resting against his ass.

So good. That felt so good. He arched, hips rolling and working, riding that heavy prick.

"So eager." Billy growled, the sound pleased and began to thrust, working with him to fill him over and over.

"Eager." God, he hoped that was good.

"Yeah. So good." Billy brought their mouths together

and kissed him hard.

He opened up, relaxed now, easy, ready to give Billy what the man needed.

"Beautiful," murmured Billy, hips working hard.

"Mmm." If he was, it was because he was happy now.

One kiss followed another, and Billy began to sweat, body shining. He wanted to move, to let his hands slide down Billy's body, trace the muscles, pull the fine bastard closer. Billy thrust harder, tongue matching his cock now, pushing into Tanny's body over and over.

His cock threatened to fill again, but didn't quite make it, didn't quite get there.

"Love you." The words whispered against his mouth and then Billy stilled, eyes rolling back in his head.

"Love..." Oh, look at that.

Billy collapsed onto him, panting hard.

He moaned, loving the pressure, the weight, the closeness.

Soft kisses pressed against his neck, his cheek, Billy's touches lazy and sweet.

He let his eyes close. He let himself just stay, just for a little while.

Stay here with Billy.

Chapter Twenty Seven

Billy lay curled around Tanny, dozing idly. Every now and then he would stroke or kiss the nearest patch of skin. He'd gotten rid of the condom and undone the silk ties from around Tanny's wrists and then kept them close.

He wasn't ready to let go yet.

Tanny stayed right there, pressed against him, nose against his throat. One of his hands drifted down to land on Tanny's ass, to hold it, to squeeze it. Such a great ass. Tanny murmured softly, arched for him.

"You liked that." He meant the ass squeeze, but also what they'd done; he knew Tanny was a sub, knew the man would glow for the right master. For him.

"Hmm?" He could feel Montana's blush.

Billy chuckled. Tanny hated talking about anything personal; he'd come to know that. Bad things were to be ignored, good ones enjoyed until they disappeared.

"I'm going to do it again sometime."

"Do what?"

"Blow your mind."

Tanny chuckled. "Are you? Aren't you worried I'll lose my mind?"

"Only in a good way." Only in the way Tanny needed to lose it.

"Is there a good way? For real?"

"Yes. You, for instance, need to be shaken up, made to see how amazing you really are."

Tanny shook his head. "I don't need to. I don't like shaking."

"But you need it." He licked his tongue along Tanny's lips. He loved how Tanny's lips opened to him. Billy spent his time exploring Tanny's mouth with his tongue, his fingers remapping the shape of Tanny's chest.

"Mmm." Tanny's nipples were hard and tight, reaching for his fingers.

He was constantly amazed by just how sensual Tanny was. And by how no one had discovered this before him.

He was a lucky, lucky man.

Maybe it was time to start pushing, to keep Tanny's body occupied. With more time away from home, and with more stress, Tanny was ripe for falling off the wagon. Billy would just keep him too busy to have time for worrying about taking drugs.

"I'm going to make you hard and I'm going to put a ring around the base of your cock and I'm going to make you wear it until after supper, until after we're back in bed again."

"Why?"

"Because we'll both enjoy it."

"Oh." Those pretty dark eyes met his, and Tanny nodded once. "Okay..."

He reached down and danced his fingers across Tanny's cock. "Okay, then."

"I don't really understand all this."

He knew that. "You don't need to. All you need to know is that you like it. That I love you. That I do this because we both need it, crave it."

Tanny leaned up, whispered in his ear. "But what if I don't? I don't know if I do, yet. Will I... If I don't, will you still want me here?"

"I want you here, Tanny. Always." He was confident of that, even more than he was sure that Tanny was a sub through and through. Tanny needed to be seen, to be loved and cared for and made the focus. He needed to be the one to do it.

"You sound so sure." Tanny wrapped around him, hugged him with arms and legs both.

"Because I am. I don't give my heart lightly, Montana. But I do give it completely." He started touching Tanny's prick and balls with a feather-light touch, in love with the heady little gasp he got.

"I'm so glad."

"Good, good." It would totally suck if his feelings made Tanny unhappy. He kept touching, gently encouraging that sweet cock to fill.

Montana's legs began to move restlessly, a sure sign that the man's desire was starting to grow warmer.

"I'll just get the ring." He dropped a kiss on Montana's belly and slid out of bed.

When he got back, Montana was stroking himself, long, lazy touches, from base to tip.

"I might have to forbid you to do that indefinitely." While Montana had obviously never had a lot of partners, or been very adventurous with them, Billy was pretty sure he'd never denied himself either. When Tanny wanted to touch himself, he did.

"Huh?" That look was so honestly confused that it was adorable.

"Hands off your cock, Tanny. That's mine." He climbed back onto the bed, ready to knock Montana's hands away if he had to.

"Uh-uh. I'm sharing it with you." Tanny grinned at him, winked.

Billy laughed, pushing Tanny's hands away as he

wrapped his own around the long cock. "Mine," he said again, squeezing.

"Okay." Tanny reached for his cock, one hand cupped his balls. "Mine?"

Billy tilted his head, but he didn't need to think about it, not really. He pushed his hips so his prick slid along Tanny's palm. "Yours."

That seemed like the right answer, because Tanny smiled, fingers caressing him, just right.

Smiling, he jacked Tanny some more, enough to have that cock hard, just barely beginning to leak.

"Feels good." Tanny shifted, trying to get closer.

"Hold on. We can get close and take our time exploring each other in a minute." He wrapped a black leather cock ring around Tanny's cock, separated Tanny's balls and then wrapped them up, too. A simple click of the snaps and Tanny was bound.

"That... that's sorta obscene, Billy."

"If by obscene you mean incredibly sexy, then yes, I agree." He gave Tanny a wink and ran his hand over the hard flesh, right down to the black leather and back up again.

Montana shuddered, hid the hot face in his shoulder.

"Your body is beautiful. It turns me on." He was going to keep telling Montana these things until Montana believed them.

"I want to. I want to make you want me so bad."

"I do, Montana. We make love and I still want you. You fascinate me. You make me need and want and feel like a teenager again—all hormones and wanting."

Tanny chuckled. "But without the zits."

He blinked and then laughed. "Yes. Exactly." And Tanny said he was stupid. There was nothing stupid about that quick mind.

Tanny's hand started moving, sliding up and down his shaft.

"Feels good, Montana." He closed his eyes to half-mast and spent a few minutes simply enjoying what Tanny was doing for him. Those soft lips found the vein in his neck, the suction steady and rhythmic. He soon was thrusting his hips in time with every suck on his skin.

Montana responded beautifully, sucking and rubbing, giving him what he needed.

"That's it. Yes, please." He kept moving, Montana working to get him off.

Teeth scraped along his throat, and that made him jerk, make him whimper. "Montana!" Beginning to pant, he reached out to touch Montana's skin.

"Mmhmm." That was a happy, satisfied sound.

"Gonna make me come." It wasn't a warning; he had a hunch it would make Montana feel good to hear.

Montana's response was another, slightly harder bite.

Shuddering, Billy came. His spunk poured over Tanny's hand, the pleasure going all through him.

Tanny moaned, rocking against him, humping his thigh. He chuckled and let Tanny hump. He wasn't going to let his lover get off just now, but with the ring on, that was just fine, wasn't it? He spread his come over Montana's body.

"I'll smell like you." He was absolutely sure that wasn't a complaint.

"I know. Until I let you shower." Which wouldn't be for awhile.

"You know, I know how to turn the faucets on..." Tanny hummed, cheek on his shoulder.

He chuckled. "Yes, but you can't do it from bed."

"Nope. I can't." Tanny kissed his jaw, blinked a little. "Man, it's been a long day."

"Yeah, and it's only about supper time. You started early this morning." Billy pondered what they might have for supper.

"I did. It was so hard, Billy, trying to be smart and learn all the things."

"It'll get easier the longer you're there, the more you know." He was so proud of how far Tanny had come. And in just a few months, too.

"You think so? I mean, I feel like a little bit of an idiot."

"Yeah, because everybody knows exactly what to do on their first day at a new job." He smacked the side of Tanny's ass. "Nobody is perfect their first day."

"No swatting!"

"Says who?" Laughing, he tugged Tanny over and swatted him in the middle of his ass.

"Fuck! No. No spanking!"

"Your mouth is saying it." Billy smacked Tanny's ass again, watching his lover's physical reactions closely.

"I mean it." Tanny's hips rolled back, ass pushing toward his touch.

Uh-huh. Billy was sure a part of Tanny meant it because he thought he shouldn't be into it. Tanny's body knew, though. Billy kept spanking, hand hitting a different spot on Tanny's ass with each swat.

"Billy. Billy, stop." Tanny met his eyes, the look scared and surprised and aroused, all at once.

"It's okay, Montana. You're allowed to enjoy it." He pressed his lips to Tanny's in a quick, hard kiss, and then resumed the spanking.

"Please. Please, I'm scared."

"I know, but I have you." He held Montana's gaze. "I'm right here and I'm not going anywhere."

"I don't want you to hit me. That's wrong."

"I'm not hitting you, Montana." Not the way Tanny meant.

"But... Then what do you call it? What... what do we call it?"

"Spanking works, love. Or warming your skin." Theirs. Necessary. Hot. He had a lot of words for what they were doing.

"You won't tell anybody?"

"I won't tell anyone." Not now. Not until this was a part of Tanny's life that he accepted, understood he wanted.

Billy began spanking again.

Tanny hid his face, sweaty cheek on Billy's shoulder, nose in the curve of his neck.

"So good, Tanny. You're doing great. Enjoy it, enjoy the heat." His hand was beginning to burn, the heat between it and Tanny's ass beautiful.

"I'm scared." He knew that, but he also knew that Tanny was hard, wet-tipped. The ring was only serving to add to Tanny's excitement, keep it going.

"I've got you," he told Tanny again, watching the way his lover's ass rose to meet each slap.

He could feel Montana's tension, ratcheting up, Tanny trying to decide whether to scream or run.

He put his mouth to Tanny's ear. "I have you."

Tanny reached for him, holding him tight instead of pulling away. Fuck, yes. Yes.

"That's right. You hold on. Ten more. We can do it. Together." He started counting down from ten as he swatted.

At three, Tanny's shivers turned into full-out tremors, Montana close to losing it.

"We're almost there, love. I'm so proud of you." He did the last three in quick succession and then tugged Tanny closer, wrapping his lover tight.

"I can't... I don't..." Tanny hid in his arms, shuddering.

He held onto Tanny, humming and soothing. "You did so well. So good."

"This is so weird."

He slid one hand down and spread the liquid leaking from the slit in Tanny's cock around the hot flesh. "This turns you on. It turns me on. Forget weird or what you think other people might say. They aren't here. We are."

"Still." Tanny moaned a little, shifting on his thighs.

"Hush. Just let me hold you and enjoy it."

"'kay." Tanny cuddled in, shifting and sliding until he found a comfortable spot, then he melted.

Billy simply hung on and sank into the moment with his lover.

This was a place they would share together whenever they could.

Chapter Twenty Eight

Cleaning.
He was cleaning up and working and thinking very hard about not thinking about his butt.

Margaret kept looking at him, though.

Staring at him.

Like she knew.

But she couldn't know, right?

Margaret finally broke the silence. "Is everything okay, Montana?"

"Huh? Yeah. Yeah, I'm good. Fine. You... you ready for Christmas?"

"I'm going to visit some friends in San Francisco."

"That's nice." He shivered as his butt brushed the counter.

Margaret gave him another look.

"What?"

"Did you get your ass busted last night?"

"What?" Oh, God.

Oh, God.

Oh, God.

"You've got ants in your pants, and you jump every time you sit down."

"I'm sorry." He wasn't going to freak out.

He wasn't.

Margaret gave him a close look. "Did anyone do something to you that you didn't want?"

"I... I don't think so?"

She smiled and patted his hand. "Well, then. Let's find you a pillow, hmm?"

"Thank you." He whispered the words, cheeks so hot they burned.

She chuckled and found him a cushion, putting it down on his stool. "Okay. Back to work."

He nodded, head bent back to his desk, the back of his neck so hot.

It was quiet for a while before Margaret broke the silence again. "You're doing really well today—I can see a big improvement over yesterday."

"I. Thank you. It's better."

"I threw a lot at you yesterday. I like doing that, though." She gave him a grin, her eyes twinkling. "Toss you into the deep end and see if you can swim."

"Did I? Swim?"

"You stayed, didn't you? And you came back. I'd say that was dog-paddling at least."

Tanny blushed dark, but laughed. "Glub, glub, glub."

"There you go!" Margaret cackled and passed him the glue.

He had no idea how much time had passed when a hand patted his shoulder. "Looks like the two of you are hard at work."

He looked up into Billy's eyes, smiled.

Margaret chuckled. "We were. You two had focus training last night. I approve."

Billy simply grinned and rubbed his shoulder. "Is it quitting time yet? If it isn't, I can come back later."

"He's done. In fact, he's off until after Christmas. I'm feeling tired and I need a day or two to pack before my trip."

"Oh, that'll give Tanny and me time to plan and shop for gifts and stuff."

Margaret smiled at Billy, and they seemed to share something. "He's so quick, Billy."

Billy beamed. "I had a hunch you'd think so. You have a good time on your trip." Billy gave her a hug.

"You have a lovely holiday yourselves." She leaned in, whispered something into Billy's ear.

Billy chuckled and squeezed her elbow, gave her a wink.

Tanny cleaned up his area, his cushion falling to the floor. He scooped it up, handed it over to Margaret. "Thank you."

"You're welcome. Next time don't hesitate to ask, hmm?" She gave him a hug. "Have a good holiday, sweetheart. And be ready to work your ass off in the new year."

"I'll be here. I promise."

She patted his cheek and smiled at Billy, whose hand slid around his elbow and led him from the store.

"I thought I'd take you to lunch."

"Okay. I could eat. Margaret said I did better today."

"That's great. She also said you were quick." Billy squeezed his arm and gave him a smile. "I think we'll go somewhere with padded booths."

"Billy!" Tanny stared over at Billy, stunned. He did not just say that.

"What? Do you really want to sit on a hard wooden chair?"

"I... No. But. I. Just don't."

"Don't what?" Billy looked genuinely confused.

"I don't know that we want to talk about it. About my... my butt."

"Oh, I know that I want to talk about it, but this isn't talking about it, this is me being nice, considerate of how you might be feeling."

"Oh. Oh, God. I'm sorry." His cheeks heated.

Billy patted one cheek, thumb lingering on his lips. "We can talk about your butt when we get home."

He chuckled, grinned. "Margaret talked about it today. My butt."

"Did she?"

"Yeah." He blushed, squeezed Billy's hand. "How was your day?"

"Oh, no, I think your day was much more interesting. What did she say? And how come Margaret gets to talk about your butt and I don't?"

"Because she's my boss and do you know why she knew about my butt?"

"I'm guessing because you were having a hard time sitting." It didn't look like Billy was at all bothered to be talking about his butt.

"She said it made me better at my job..." he whispered.

To his surprise Billy nodded. "Made you focused."

"I..." He didn't know what to say to that.

"Oh, here, how about IHOP. They've got padded booths. You feel like pancakes for lunch?"

"I love pancakes for lunch. You know that." He bumped shoulders with Billy.

"I do." Billy grinned and they went in. They settled, ordered coffee and juice, both taking a menu.

Billy put his menus down. "I'm going to have the steak and eggs with the short stack on the side. If we have leftovers they can be supper."

"I just want pancakes and sausage."

They ordered and then Billy's attention focused on him. "You're looking happier today."

"I think I am? I mean, I'm a little wigged out about yesterday, but... I don't know." He didn't want to think about it.

"We can talk about yesterday if you want. Here or at home."

"Here might be... easier." They'd have to be quiet here.

"All right." Billy smiled. "Tell me how you're feeling about it, then,"

"Nervy. A little ashamed of myself."

Billy's hand slid across his on the table, squeezed it for a moment. "Ashamed? We haven't done anything to be ashamed of, Tanny."

"But I did better today. After you. You, you know."

"But why would that make you ashamed?"

"Well, because it's not very cool, huh? I'm such a pussy man that I do better at my fucking job because I got my ass whipped?"

Billy snorted. "You did better at your job because the spanking made you focus."

"But why?" That was what he really wanted to know.

"Because your butt hurt, you had to be careful of it, and that made you pay more attention to what you were doing, too."

"I don't understand. That's stupid." Did that mean he was stupid?

"It's not stupid. And you don't need to understand, do you? It's a great side effect, isn't it? I mean we did it because you liked it, because I liked it. If it makes you do better at work, too, that's a plus."

"I don't want to like it, though."

"Why not?"

"I. I don't know. Because I feel like I shouldn't?"

"You have to stop worrying about the outside world. All that matters is what you and I think."

"Wait... does that make sense? I mean, that's not like...

Using that logic, if you were cool with tweaking, then it wouldn't matter."

"No, spanking isn't illegal, so they're not comparable."

He tilted his head, trying to deal with things.

Billy went on. "If it's not illegal, and everyone is getting what they want out of it, then it's all good, isn't it?"

"I miss the buzz sometimes."

"Some of the stuff we've done together's been as good as the buzz, hasn't it?"

"Yes." That was an easy question. "Some of it's been better."

"Good." Billy waited as the waitress put their food down on the table. He leaned forward again once she'd left. "It's all right to still miss it. The important thing is not giving in."

"I'm going to buy another one, though. To have it."

Billy stopped with his food partway to his mouth. "You need that, hmm? To have it there."

"I do. I need to know it's there. To know that I didn't take it. If there was another way, I'd do it." He knew Billy hated having it there. "But there's not."

Billy nodded slowly. "I'm not sure I understand, but if you tell me that's what you need to stay off it, then that's what you need."

"I don't understand either. It's like a... A cross, or something. Like a promise if things get too bad, it's there." Did that make sense?

"As long as you come to me first if you decide that things have become too bad, okay?"

He nodded. "I told you I would. I don't lie to you."

"Okay." Billy frowned at his pancake. "The part I really don't like about this is how you're going to have to buy an illegal drug."

"Well, what else do I do?" He wasn't awful, right?

"I don't know. I just worry someone like that cop is going catch you buying it and take you down. I don't know how to get past that."

He didn't have an answer.

He just didn't.

Billy sighed. "I'm sorry. I don't mean to be an asshole about this."

"I don't mean to be awful. I just don't know how to make it right. I'm just not strong enough..."

"You are, though. You are."

He ate a sausage, shook his head.

"You made it this long without taking anything. And hell, for awhile that pill was there to take and you never did."

"But I wanted to. I held it. A lot."

"But you never took it. It was right there, in your hand. And you never took it."

"No. There was once, but you... We... You know."

Billy smiled, looking well pleased. "I told you I knew something that was better than being high."

"Yeah, well..." He chuckled. "It can't always work."

"Is that a challenge, love?"

"I... Is it? Sure. Sure, I guess." He didn't know how Billy would answer the challenge, though.

"Then I accept. I will always make it work when you need it to." Billy pointed his chin toward their plates. "Now, let's eat before it all gets cold."

"Okay."

It tasted good.

Really good.

They talked about easy things as they ate, Billy teasing him and telling him stories. Tanny relaxed, finishing his meal, accepting another cup of coffee.

When they'd finished, Billy asked for another cup of coffee for them both. "So, you don't have any ID"

"No. You know that." He'd left what little there was at the res.

"I know. But you need something. It doesn't have to be a big deal, just a state ID or something like that."

"I don't know how."

"I can help you with the process. We'll look it up online, find out what we need to get you one. Are you interested in renewing your driver's license?"

"No. No, I. I. I killed her. I can't. I won't. It's like a... crime." He couldn't breathe, all of a sudden, and it scared him.

Billy reached across the table and squeezed both of his hands. "It was an accident, Montana. If you don't want to get a new driver's license, that's fine, but what happened was an accident."

"You don't know that..." He let his fingers grip Billy's. "But I didn't mean to do it. I loved her. She was my sister."

"If you didn't mean to do it, that makes it an accident, love."

"It was my fault."

"That doesn't mean you murdered her, Tanny." Billy stared right him, eyes intense, hands holding his tight.

"I wish I could believe that."

"I wish you could, too."

He sighed, rubbed the back of his neck. Was there ever going to be a day where there wasn't something big to deal with?

Billy squeezed his fingers again. "All right, you've worked, we've eaten and done the serious discussion bit. You want to do something fun with the rest of the day?"

"God, yes."

That had Billy chuckling. "What do you want to do?"

"Anything. Dancing. Walking. Let's just go."

"It's a little early in the day to find dancing, but sure we can just go."

"Okay. You can use my money to pay for it. I just..." He spread his hands. "I've been good for weeks."

"You mean lunch?" Billy put a couple bills down by their plates.

"Lunch. Gas. Whatever."

"Why don't you save your money for Christmas gifts?" They got up and wandered out of the IHOP.

"What do you want for Christmas?" Tanny asked.

"Honestly? I'd like a new laptop bag."

"Yeah? Okay." He could figure that out. "You want straps? Handles?"

"Something for over the shoulder, I think."

"Okay." That worked. Something soft and comfortable.

"We should also get together and find something nice for Oliver and Jack, as we're going there for Christmas Day dinner. And what would you like?"

"Me? I... I need another pair of jeans and briefs." He had three pairs of briefs, but they were wearing out from washing.

"We can buy you those because you need them, but they aren't Christmas presents."

"They are." When he was a kid, his annual new shoes and jeans had been eagerly awaited.

"No, clothes don't count as Christmas presents, I'm sure." Billy sounded very sure.

"You're a little weird, Billy. What do you get for your friends here?"

"Wine, cheese, art. I hunt around for interesting ornaments. Something always comes up."

"Ah." Wow. Sometimes he looked at Billy and knew they lived in two different universes.

"Ah?" Billy raised an eyebrow at him.

"I just... That's... cool." It was easier to just not go there.

Billy shook his head. "You know you can tell me anything."

"I know. You and me, we just live in different places, is all." One day Billy'd figure that out and things would be over. He got that.

Billy chuckled. "You mean we come from different places, because we live at the same one."

"Yeah. Yeah, I guess so."

"No guessing about it. It's our home. Not mine, not yours."

"You said no more talking."

"About big things that wig you out. This isn't something like that. Is it?"

"No. It just worries me. I mean, my mom's house doesn't have lights or running water, man, and you give friends gifts that would have fed us for a month and I don't know how to feel about that."

Billy was quiet a moment. "Okay, I can see how that's highlighting the differences between our immediate backgrounds. I didn't have a good life growing up and like to indulge now. But we're still here, in the same place right now, loving each other. And I like to think that's what counts."

He nodded. "It does. I just feel like I'm out of my league with you, a lot." He took Billy's hand, squeezed it. "That doesn't mean I don't like you or anything."

"I don't think you're out of your league. I think you're right where you belong." Billy stopped and pulled him in for a quick kiss, not seeming to care who might see them. "And you can talk to me about it when it's happening, you know. So I can do something about it—I don't want to make you feel that way."

"Let's go play, Billy. Let's just go be."

Found

"Okay. Anything you want."

He kissed Billy's fingers. "Thanks, man."

He just wanted to play.

Chapter Twenty Nine

Billy whistled as he wrapped one obscene little present after another.

He put each one under the tree. He couldn't wait for Montana to open them. In fact, he thought they should start tonight. After all, they'd be spending the bulk of the day tomorrow at Ollie and Jack's.

So tonight would be best for playing.

Though, frankly, the thought of going to Ollie's with his warmth, even metaphorically, still inside Montana, held there by a plug... that made him moan. One day.

Margaret had complimented him on Tanny's focus, on his new sub. It had made him proud, had made him want to take Tanny to the Hammer, show the man off.

He hadn't—Montana wasn't ready—but he'd wanted to.

Tonight he would put a ring on Montana's cock and put the man over his knee. He would fuck Montana with a dildo, make them both need so badly.

Well, if Montana opened the right gifts. Of course, he could assist there. Assuming Montana ever came home.

He put the ones he wanted open near the front and pushed the rest around the base of the tree.

Turning on some Christmas carols, he poured himself an eggnog, pulling a second glass down for Montana. He stood there, looking at the glass, trying to decide whether or not to just pour it.

He heard the front door open and then close.

Smiling, he filled the second glass.

"I brought tamales." Tanny walked in, wearing that sweater. Again.

"The ones from that little stand?" Tanny loved those. A lot.

"Yes. Chicken and pork."

"Cool. I have eggnog. Let's eat in the living room. By the tree."

"Okay." Those pretty dark eyes stared at him. "Is everything okay?"

"Everything's fine, love. Why?"

"You just looked weird, you didn't kiss me. You always kiss me hello."

"I do. Come here." He smiled and opened his arms.

Tanny came to him, face lifted for a kiss.

He wrapped his arms around the slim body and brought their mouths together. He let the kiss linger, loving the way Tanny tasted and felt. Tanny moaned, opened up for him and started fucking his lips with that soft tongue. Someone was hungry. He slid his hands down to grab Tanny's ass, fingers squeezing.

Those tight little muscles shifted, slid in his fingers.

"There's gifts under the tree."

"Are there? Aren't we supposed to wait until tomorrow?"

"We are." He grinned. "It would be very naughty to open some of them tonight."

Tanny chuckled. "I have two or three for you."

"Are they under the tree? Because I'm serious—we should get a head start on stuff."

"They are, yeah."

"Come on then." He grinned and tugged Tanny along,

feeling like a little kid.

Tanny laughed, followed. "You're not hungry?"

"I might have gotten into the cookie tray," he admitted. And the chocolates.

Not to mention the several glasses of eggnog.

"Oh, you're cheating!" God, look at his Montana laugh.

"It's Christmas—there is no cheating." There was still plenty left for Tanny, but he wasn't exactly hungry at the moment.

"No?" Tanny kissed his chin. "No cheating. Good to know."

He chuckled and sat on the couch. Pointing at the presents, he nudged Tanny. "Go on. Pick one to open. Unless you're hungry." Tanny had brought home supper after all.

"I had a couple of tamales on my walk home." Montana picked one of the presents from the front of the pile.

Billy wasn't sure if that was the nipple clamps or the cuffs. Either worked. His prick was filling, getting in on the excitement. He kissed the side of Montana's neck.

"Mmm. Billy." Montana's fingers clenched, the paper crinkling.

"There's more where that came from."

He smiled against Tanny's neck and then backed off a little, eager to see which of the toys Montana had and what his reaction would be.

The cuffs were sturdy, metal, would hold his Montana tight.

"Oh."

Oh, indeed.

"See how they're nice and thick, almost flat at the bottom. They won't dig in and cut your skin."

"They... I don't. They're... sturdy."

"Mmmhmm. Open another one." They needed more than just the cuffs to play.

"Another one?" Tanny chose another, this box bigger.

"We'll use whatever you unwrap tonight."

"I... Use?" Those dark eyes were huge.

"Yes." He leaned in to nibble and lick at Tanny's neck again.

"I. Oh. I... That makes me flutter inside."

"Fluttering inside is good. Open the other gift." It was the plug, he was sure of it. A nice, fat soft plug to fill his lover up, stretch him. "It's going to be fun and exciting. We're both going to come so hard." He took Montana's hand and put it on the gift. "Come on and open it."

Montana nodded, fingers trembling over the paper.

He pressed his mouth to Montana's ear, whispered. "What do you hope it is?"

"I don't know. I don't know what to hope for. What... what do you want it to be?" As if he didn't know.

"Something for us to have great fun with." He bit at Tanny's earlobe. "Open it and find out what it is."

The box was opened, the fat plug lying there. "Billy. It's... big."

"It's just what you need to stretch your hole. We can put it in after I've fucked you." One day they would be able to put it in after he'd come inside his lover, the plug keeping his seed there.

He watched the shock and arousal climb up Montana's face. "Billy!"

"I'm right here." He leaned in and kissed Montana, opening his lover's mouth with his tongue.

"You want to open one more or just head back to the bedroom?"

"What... what else is there?" Montana shivered, pressed against him.

"You'll have to open them to find out. Just one more

tonight, though. The rest are for Christmas." He slid his hand along Tanny's spine.

"Uh...uh-huh..." Tanny stole another kiss, moaning into his lips. Humming, he pressed his tongue into Tanny's mouth. The cuffs clanked as they fell to the floor, Tanny moving into his lap.

He grabbed Tanny's ass, pulled him closer. "Lean back and pick them up."

Tanny looked at him in surprise, then leaned back, arching, following orders. Fuck, it was sexy. He ran his hands along Tanny's belly as he arched, traced the signature on Tanny's skin, his signature.

"Billy..." Tanny grabbed the cuffs and rippled as he pulled himself up.

"Yeah, Tanny?" He stroked that amazing belly.

"I don't..." Tanny blinked slowly, lips parted. "I don't know what to do next."

"I take you to bed and make love to you." He bit Tanny's lower lip. "Bring the handcuffs and the plug."

"Okay. Okay, Billy..." Tanny grabbed the cuffs and the box.

"Good man." Billy stood and followed Tanny into the bedroom, watching the way his lover moved. There was an unconscious grace in Tanny's movements that made him so hard.

Tanny kept looking back at him, making sure he was there.

"Don't worry, love. I'm not going to leave you hanging."

"I just... Merry Christmas Eve..."

"Yes. Merry Christmas Eve, my Montana." Billy pushed Montana toward the bed, taking the cuffs and plug from him. Billy pushed Montana's sweater up, his name right there, inked onto that pretty belly.

He traced it with his fingers. "My Montana. Mine."

"Mmmhmm. Yours." Montana shivered a bit, lips parted for him.

He kissed Montana, tongue pushing into the sweet mouth. "Hands over your head."

"Like... Like this?" Montana stretched his hands up.

"Mmm, yes. Perfect." Montana was perfect, his sub. He took the handcuffs and slid them over the tattoo. Those pretty muscles jerked and tightened, shifted for him.

"Look at you." He put the cuffs around Montana's wrists.

"I... Billy, you have the key, right?"

He took Montana's chin in his hand and looked into the dark eyes. "I would never cuff you without having a way to get you out of the cuffs."

Those dark eyes searched his, then Montana nodded. "This is real new for me."

"I know. But I tied you up before and you loved it. I made you fly. I'm going to keep making you fly, Montana. That's a promise." He leaned in, kissing Tanny hard, sealing his vow.

Tanny's cuffed hands came down, arms wrapping around his neck. He kept kissing, his tongue lapping at Montana's. Montana's legs came around his waist, his lover holding on. Billy slid his fingers down, finding Montana's left nipple and pinching.

He felt Montana's moan, the little gasp.

"Put your hands up over your head." He took one more kiss and then wriggled down to kiss the nipple he'd pinched.

Montana whimpered, tried to push into his lips. He bit Montana's nipple again. He was in charge. Him.

"Ow." That little nipple was red and starting to swell.

Chuckling, he licked at it, letting his tongue flick back

and forth over it.

"You... you're obsessed with those..."

"I'm obsessed with all of you." He did like Montana's nipples, though.

"Is that healthy?"

He raised an eyebrow and licked again. "The licking?"

"Ob...obsession."

"As long as it's not one-sided."

"No. No, it's not one-sided. Not at all."

"Good." He bit Montana's other nipple.

"Billy!" Montana jerked away, sliding on the sheets.

"There's nowhere to go, love. I have you."

"I don't... I don't know what to do."

"Just lie there and let me love you, Montana."

Montana looked a little worried, his lover so focused on doing things right, being right for him.

"Let me love you, Montana. Enjoy it. Enjoy every second of it."

"Is that fair to you?" Only his lover would worry about that, worry about him not getting off on this.

"Yes. Yes." He started stripping. "Look." He undid his trousers and pulled them down, his cock pushing out eagerly.

Montana moaned, licked his lips. *Yes. Yes, look, Tanny.* "You want it?"

"Yes. I want."

"You'll have to wait. You'll have to earn it." He stroked himself a little, until a drop of liquid beaded up. Then he wiped it with his finger and painted Montana's lips with it.

Montana's tongue slipped out, lapped the taste away.

"Mmm... sensual man."

He slid his finger along Montana's breastbone, down past his navel. Montana arched for him, thighs parting a bit.

"I know what you want." Every part of Montana was begging for him, for his touch, his kiss, his cock.

"Do you? What? What do I want?"

"You want me to make you fly."

"Yes." The admission surprised him, and it must have shown, because Montana looked uncertain. "Is that okay?"

"It's perfect." He kissed the side of Montana's mouth. "Absolutely perfect."

Montana turned his head, brought their lips together. Chuckling, he let the kiss happen, slid his tongue into his pushy bottom's mouth. Montana opened, kissed him back, tongue sliding against his. He bit at the tip gently.

Montana jerked, blinking at him. God, that was hot.

He bit again, a little harder this time, and then pulled Montana's tongue into his mouth, sucking on it. Montana's hands came down again, wrapping around his neck.

He shook his head and let go of Montana's tongue. "Keep them over your head, love."

"I... I'm sorry. It's instinct."

"I know. The real trick is obeying me even when you don't want to."

"It's not about not wanting to. It's... it's remembering, more."

"I want you to remember, though." He licked at the inside of Montana's elbow.

Montana's arm buckled, soft chuckles filling the air.

He nibbled on down along Montana's inner arm and then over to his neck. He wished Montana had opened one of the nipple clamps, but he supposed that could wait. For now he could just play with his fingers and lips and teeth. Make the tiny bits of flesh swollen and sensitive.

He began to do just that, working the right nipple first. He loved the way Montana's body jerked and pushed into each bite and lick and pinch. Tanny cried out for him, each bite making things a little louder, sharper, more focused. He murmured sweet nothings to Montana, telling his lover how good he was, how sensual and sexy and lovely.

"Billy. Billy, I... I can't breathe, it's so good."

"You can breathe. I promise." He nuzzled into Tanny's belly, tongue playing with the sweet indentation of Tanny's navel.

"I can't. I can't remember how."

He surged up and pressed their lips together, pushing air into Montana's lungs. Montana's cry vibrated his lips, the sound making him harder than ever. Billy gave Montana a couple more breaths and then made his way down again, teeth nipping at skin.

Every bite made Montana a little wilder, move faster. He reached up for the cock ring he'd left on the bedside table earlier; they were going to need it. His beautiful lover didn't even notice he was moving, Montana was so focused on his mouth. He kept alternating bites and licks as he slowly worked the ring down over Montana's prick, carefully, fingers barely touching that hard cock.

He could smell Montana's need, the male musk filling his nose.

"Billy..." Montana arched and twisted, begging for him.

"You need something?" He grinned, fingers rolling Montana's balls.

"I... I want to come. That feels so good."

"You don't get to come yet. Not for awhile." Not for a long time. Maybe not until tomorrow morning.

"Why?"

Sweet baby. "Because I said so. When I say you can come—that's when you get to." He licked the tip of Montana's prick, loving the taste of the clear liquid beading there.

Montana twisted, the chain on the cuffs jangling.

So pretty. So sexy.

Billy moaned, let Montana hear how turned on this made him. Then he scraped a fingernail along the soft, smooth skin between Montana's balls and his hole.

"Oh!" Montana's legs pulled up, exposing that pretty hole.

He loved how eager his Tanny was for every touch. Billy pressed his finger against Tanny's hole. Tapped it. The little ring of muscles clenched, twitched. He tapped Tanny's hole again. He couldn't wait to be inside there.

"What... what do you want?"

"I want to spank you and then fuck you and put in the plug. Leave you with feeling of me inside you."

Those pretty eyes went wide. "Billy!"

He grinned. "Yes?"

"I... You say things..."

"I do. And you like them." He scraped his fingernail gently across Montana's hole.

"I. I." Montana's wrists twisted again.

He chuckled and bent to lick at that sweet hole.

"Oh. Oh, God. Hot."

Yeah, it was. Groaning, he licked again, loving the scent and the taste and the way Montana reacted. Montana arched, heels digging into the mattress. He pointed his tongue and pushed it into Montana, loving the way that little hole fluttered around him.

"More. More, please. Love you. Fuck. Fuck."

He bit at Montana's ass, hard enough to leave a mark.

"Fuck!" Montana jerked away, hips bucking.

"Where are you going?" He pulled Montana back and licked over the bite before nipping at Montana's skin again.

"You. You bit me."

"Yeah. I'm going to do it again, too." He bit the other ass cheek this time.

"Fucking shit!" Montana rolled away from him, sliding across the mattress.

"Hey!" Billy grabbed Montana's hips and tugged him back.

"You bit me." Montana was trembling, bound cock leaking.

"Twice. We can make it three." He nibbled this time, mouthing Montana's skin instead of biting it.

"No. No biting. It stings."

"Stings so good." He bit the inside of Montana's thigh.

"So... it's big." Montana's arms started to move.

"It's huge." He pushed his face against Montana's ass again and gave another bite.

"Please... Please, Billy. I don't know what to do to make you happy..."

"Feel, love. All you need to do is feel."

"I'm a little wigged out, man."

"Trust me, Montana. You've been wigged out before and I took care of you, made you fly."

It took Montana a minute, then his lover nodded, once. Billy licked his thumb quickly and then worked it into Montana's ass. That sweet body let him in, Tanny moving, accepting him, needing him.

"I want you." The words growled out of him, pure truth.

"Yours."

Fuck, yes. He pushed his thumb as far as it would go and then bit Montana's hip.

"Stop fucking biting me..." Montana's ass clenched around his thumb.

He would stop when Montana gave his safe word.

Humming, he licked and bit, mouthing Montana's skin, occasionally biting down hard.

"Motherfuck..." Montana tried to turn, tried to pull away.

Billy wrapped his hands around Montana's thighs and held him in place, his mouth moving over chest and hips, belly.

"Billy... I can't. I can't do this. I'm all... help me?"

"You need something solid to focus on, hmm?"

"I don't know. I don't know what I need." That honesty pleased him, bone deep.

He sat up and pulled Montana into his lap, giving Montana a hard kiss that would steal his lover's breath, his lover's thoughts. Arms and legs wrapped around him, Montana diving into the kisses, tongue fucking his lips. He stroked his hands down along Montana's spine, humming softly.

His sweet sub relaxed, lost in him, in their kisses. He could do this until morning, winding Montana up and then bringing him back down again.

"Love you..." Montana looked debauched, heavy-lidded and wanton.

"Good." He bit at Montana's swollen lower lip, pulling it between his teeth and scraping along the tender inside.

That sound was pure desire.

"Gonna put you over my lap, Montana. Gonna make your ass red."

"Why? I haven't done anything wrong."

"It's not a punishment, love. It's to make you fly."

"And... and I can stop it, if I want to?"

"You have the control—you can stop it any time you need to."

"That's what I said, right?"

"You said want. There's a difference." He waited for Montana to work that out.

Montana's lips twitched, that smart brain working on it. "That's a really tiny difference."

"There is a difference, though."

"How will we know?"

"You'll know. You'll want to call it off, but you won't. If you need to, then you will." Montana would know. He trusted that.

"I don't like it, when you spank me."

Liar. "That's not true." Montana didn't like that he liked it.

"It is. I was so... weird the next day."

"It'll be sexy tomorrow." He grinned and leaned in to whisper into Montana's ear. "You're going to have a sore and filled ass for Christmas. Every time you move you'll think of me and what we're doing tonight."

"Billy..." He waited for the nod, the little gasp and agreement. Then he took Montana's mouth in yet another breath-stealing kiss.

Montana moaned, opening for him, offering him everything.

He worked Montana's cock for a moment and then broke off. "Over my lap, love."

Those dark eyes looked panicked for a minute, but Montana moved. Billy kept his hands moving on Montana's skin, not letting his lover freak out. Montana's belly was soft against his thighs, the cock surprisingly hard, heated.

Billy moaned and slid his fingers over Montana's ass. He traced his bite marks, the skin unbroken. They made an interesting counterpoint to the scars that covered Montana's back. The muscles jumped and leapt under his touch, Montana's legs moved restlessly.

"It's okay to enjoy this, Montana. It's good to enjoy it."

He let his hand fly.

The hand print was white at first, then bright pink. He hummed and rubbed the handprint before spanking Montana again.

"Billy..." Montana's legs started kicking, over and over.

"You can take it, love. You need it."

"No. No, why would I need it?"

"Help you focus, help you know I see you, I want you, I can give you what you need."

"I don't... "

"You do." He put his hand down on Montana's ass in a different spot with each smack.

"N...no...oh." Montana's knees curled up under him.

"Your cock is leaking all over me." Hot and growing slicker with every swat, Montana's cock felt amazing against his legs.

"My balls ache."

"Get used to it." Montana wasn't going to get to come until he was done with the spanking and the fucking and the plugging. Maybe not until after that. One day Montana's need would be focused on him, on what his touch could give. He kept spanking, hand loving Montana's skin.

"Please... I want you to stop." Montana's thighs parted, hips beginning to meet each one of his blows.

Billy loved how Montana's body knew the truth even as his mind fought it. "Not yet."

"Billy, please." That sweet ass danced for him, the rhythm fascinating and sweet as fuck.

"I love the way you beg for it." He spanked Montana's ass from the top of his thighs to the small of his back, just at the point before the scars began.

"Fuck. Fuck. Hot." Montana whimpered, back arching for him.

"It is. You are." He rubbed at Montana's skin and then spanked it again, mixing up the sensations.

"Stop..." That pretty cock was sawing against his thigh, moving steadily.

"Not yet," he said again.

"Billy..." That was a sob, soft, needy.

"Not yet," he whispered. He would push Montana, push him just past where Montana was sure he couldn't go. He pressed two fingers of one hand into Montana's hole, even as he spanked again.

This time the cry rang out. "Again!"

He pushed them deeper this time, hit a little harder.

"Fuck. Fuck me. Billy. Billy, please."

"When I'm good and ready, Montana." Beautiful, sweet, pushy bottom.

"Need you. Fuck."

He loved this, loved that desperation, that need. "You'll have me." He spanked Montana again. "I'm going to take you. I'm going to feel the heat of your ass with every thrust. Then I'm going to fuck you. Then, when we're done I'm going to put the plug in so you're full all night." In the morning he'd take out the plug and clean Montana before they went anywhere. The plug would go back in, though, before they left.

Montana rubbed harder against him, fighting to come, to get enough friction.

He spread his legs. "You can come when I tell you that you can." Which wouldn't be until morning.

"Motherfucker." The curse was bitten out, gasped.

"Montana!" He smacked Montana's ass. He did not like being called names.

"I... Sorry. Sorry." Montana stilled, shivering.

He rubbed his lover's hot ass. "It's okay. It's okay."

"Yeah?" Montana's breath was huffing out of him.

"Yeah. No name calling, love. It's not nice."

"Okay. Okay. I didn't mean to."

"You'll think twice next time." He rubbed Montana's

ass. "Now let's see if we can get back to where we were, hmm?" He began to lightly smack the reddened ass, flicking his fingers over the sensitive flesh. It was all about timing, raising and lowering Montana's level of need.

He built them back up slowly, starting with the gentle taps and working up to the harder smacks. Every now and then he'd stop again, rub, play with Montana's hole. Montana made the most amazing noises, his lover begging prettily, moaning, arching against him.

"I want you." He spread his hand wide to cover as much flesh as possible.

"I'm... I'm yours. Please. It burns."

"It does, doesn't it?" He rubbed, slipped a finger inside Montana's body.

"Yes. It fucking burns. I need... I have to move."

He pulled Montana up to straddle his lap. Tears streaked Montana's cheeks, his lover flushed, shuddering. He licked and kissed the tears from Montana's skin. "So good."

"Help me."

He pressed their lips together, taking Montana's mouth. Hot and swollen, so soft, those lips fascinated him. He licked and lapped at them, tongue slipping in, slipping out. Billy could feel Montana's cuffed hands, sliding down between them, fingers on his cock, on Montana's.

He groaned. "Did I say you could touch?"

"You didn't say I couldn't."

Billy had to laugh. "You're wearing handcuffs!"

"I am." Montana's laugh joined his.

He took Montana's hands in his, kissed the knuckles. That sigh was a happy, warm sound, let him know he was doing it right.

"Put your arms around me, love. I'll take you like this. Let you ride my lap."

Montana nodded, licked his own lips. "I can do that."

"Good." He waited until Montana had looped those bound arms around his neck and then reached for lube, slicking up his fingers.

"Is this good? You want me?"

"All the time, Montana. I want you. I love you. And this is just right." He slid his fingers along Montana's ass, rubbing, rubbing.

Montana leaned forward, resting against him and letting him hold on tight.

"Sexy. You are so hot." He pushed two fingers into Montana's body.

"Billy... I need to come." That cock was rocking, riding against his belly.

Soon there'd a sheath for it so Montana couldn't do this, a little cock cage for a sweet, heady punishment. "No. Not until I say so." He spread his legs, making it harder for Montana to work that prick against him.

"Please. What the fuck do you want?"

"I want you to enjoy my touch. To focus on the now, on the here."

Montana groaned. "Everything is so big..."

"Then stop worrying about what's coming next, and just take in as much as you can." He slid a third finger inside, stretching Montana wide.

"I. I. I... Oh, fuck. Full..."

"You'll be fuller in a few minutes."

Montana's arms tightened, and a hot, wet tongue slid on his ear. So pushy, so sweet. He stretched and scissored his fingers, opening Montana up. Every move he made got him another cry, another moan, another shiver.

Billy finally let his fingers drop away. "You're ready for my cock now."

"I've been ready. I swear. Please, Billy."

"You're ready when I say you are." He kissed Montana as he rolled the condom on, hands moving the sweet ass into place.

Montana was vibrating for him, shaking, shuddering.

"I've got you, love. Let go and trust me."

"I do. I do. Billy, please."

He settled his cock at Montana's hole and slowly let his lover drop down onto it. Montana shook, entire body arching with the pressure. Billy bit his own lip; it felt so good and he didn't want to go off too fast. He wanted to spend his time making love.

Montana's ass clenched around his cock, body milking him. Groaning, he rested their foreheads together, his hands opening and closing on Montana's hips.

Montana moved, just barely, breathing shallowly, eyes burning. He licked at Montana's lips, little touches that matched the little movements they made to bring their bodies together. The drops of pre-come slipped from the tip of Montana's cock, splashing on him.

Gasping, he moved them a bit faster. It felt so good, all the scents and sounds and feelings wrapping together.

"Need you. Need you. Need this." Montana moaned the words, over and over.

"I know. I've got you." And he wasn't letting go.

Montana's body worked him, muscles fluttering, squeezing madly.

"You're getting too good at that." He planted his feet on the ground, using them as leverage to drive him up into Montana's ass.

"Can... can you be too good?"

"Yes. Makes everything happen too fast." He smiled, and then groaned, pushing deep. Billy felt the ripple, the jerks around his cock. He moved faster, wanting to make sure Montana would be able to feel him all night long.

"Mmm. More. More, love."

"Pushy, pushy." He wasn't complaining.

"I just need you."

"You've got me, love." Montana so had him.

Montana started moving faster, bucking on him, moans beginning to fill the air.

"Remember, you can't come."

"I have to. I have to. Billy."

"No." He reached down, tugging on Montana's balls, adding that to the tight hold of the cock ring. Montana couldn't come until tomorrow.

"Billy..." Montana sobbed, fighting him, ass driving him crazy.

"You come when I say so." Billy tugged harder and then he shifted, rolling Montana onto his back on the bed and driving into him.

Montana went wild, sobbing and fighting, pushing back to meet each thrust. Billy held on as long as he could, moving hard and fast. It felt so good. He pushed in deep, eyes on Montana as his lover screamed. Hips jerking, he came. He filled the condom, his orgasm going on and on.

The cuffed hands fought to get to Montana's cock, to get Montana off.

He grabbed hold of the cuffs and dragged them up over Montana's head. "No."

"Billy... Billy, please..." Montana rubbed and struggled, moaning for him.

He pulled out and rolled to the side. He kissed Montana's neck and shoulders. "Not yet, love. Not now."

The moans turned into soft sobs, Montana pushing into the curve of his body. He ran his hands over Montana's skin, soothing and comforting and loving.

"I don't get what you want..."

"I want you to enjoy what we do together for what it is, not for the end result." He kept touching, kept gentling Montana until the panic passed. "I've got you, love. I've got you." He pressed kisses to the top of Montana's head.

Montana started to relax, started to melt against him.

He wasn't done with his lover yet, though. "You ready to play with that plug, Montana?"

"Oh, God. Billy. You can't be serious."

"I am." He slid his hand down and touched that tanned ass.

Montana jerked away, whimpered softly.

"Focus on me, love."

"I'm trying. I need you. It burns. I can't do this."

"Yes, you can." He rolled Montana onto his belly and began to kiss his way along the scarred skin.

"Oh, God. Oh, God. Billy... Please."

"Feel my touch, Montana." He traced one scar and then another with the tip of his tongue.

"Oh..." Montana stretched out, cuffed hands reaching up.

"There we go, that's better." He kept it up, kissing and licking.

Slowly but surely, Montana relaxed completely, going boneless beneath him.

He murmured happily. "There we go. Beautiful. Love you."

"Love." Montana was dozing now, fading in and out, shivering when he found a sensitive spot. He slid his tongue over one of Montana's ass cheeks. It was burning hot and licking it made him moan. He felt the low groan he got in response, Montana's hips shifting, rubbing the bound cock against the sheets.

Carefully spreading Montana's ass cheeks apart, he licked at that sweet little hole. Montana murmured softly, hips shifting again. He kept licking, pushing in to wet his lover.

"Billy..." That soft little sound made him smile.

He tongue-fucked Montana with more enthusiasm, face pressed up against the hot ass. Montana groaned, knees drawing up underneath the lean body.

"Good." He growled the word and slid his hands over Montana's balls. Heavy, full, sac drawn up tight—Montana was close again.

"Gonna fuck you with the plug now and leave it there." He pressed a kiss to one ass cheek.

"Oh, God. I... I can't. Billy..."

"Of course you can." He reached for the plug, lubed it up. It was heavy, fat, would keep Montana well-filled and needing him.

"Just relax, love." He kissed Montana's other ass cheek and then started to push the tip of the plug in.

The tiny ring of muscles clenched, Montana's body trying to fight him. Billy leaned in to lick at the little hole again. Montana groaned, leaned back into his face. He went back to fucking the sweet hole for a few moments, and then moved his face away, slipping the plug in its place.

The tip went in, Montana accepting it about halfway before rocking forward.

"You can't escape it, love." He kept pushing.

"It's big."

"You can take it." He knew it. Billy rocked it, in and out, pushing a little deeper each time. "Good, Montana. That's it. So good." He kept crooning, soothing and encouraging.

His thumb stroked the tiny strip of skin behind Montana's balls, caressing his lover in time with the motion of the plug. Soon it was all the way in. He twisted it, pulled it partway out and pushed it back in again.

Montana cried out, a flush climbing up the scarred back.

"Beautiful, love. You're amazing." He moved the plug

faster, beginning to fuck Montana with it.

"Need. Billy..." Montana pushed up on his hands, meeting his thrusts.

"I know." He stroked the small of Montana's back as he slowed the thrusts of the plug.

"Billy? Why? Why are you doing this?"

"Because when you come tomorrow it's going to blow your mind."

"I ache."

"I know." He seated the plug, making sure it was comfortable, and then settled with Montana in his arms. "It's not a bad ache, though." He knew that, too.

Montana moaned, hips still moving restlessly. He gently patted Montana's ass, murmuring, kissing the top of Montana's head. When Montana dozed off, he removed the cuffs, replacing them with soft fur-lined ones that had only a two-link chain between them. They'd nap, they'd eat, and Montana would let him feed them both.

Then he'd let Montana suck him off and they'd go to bed. In the morning, Montana would be allowed to come.

Merry Christmas to them both!

Chapter Thirty

Cocks. Mouths. Asses. Something. Anything.

Sweat, come, hunger, need. Tanny moved, cock throbbing as he was touched and licked, bitten. Fucked.

"Tanny." Someone was calling him. "Tanny."

"Shh." He reached for his cock, legs drawing up from the wonderful pressure inside him.

A soft chuckle tickled over his skin. "You need, love?"

"Billy..." He shuddered. "Please."

"You want me to make love to you?" Billy's voice whispered in his ear, Billy's hand on his ass.

"Yes. Yes, I need you." He nodded, still warm under the comforter.

"Are you actually awake yet?"

"I think so?" He wasn't one hundred percent sure.

Billy chuckled, body sliding along his.

"You're warm." He pushed back, stretching.

"That's because I've been snuggled up against you." Billy dropped kisses on his neck, on his shoulders.

"Is... is it Christmas yet?"

"It is! Merry Christmas, love."

"Merry Christmas. Make love to me."

"That'll be the best present ever." Smiling, Billy kissed

him and then nudged the plug inside him.

He gasped, his body going tight. "I don't know if it'll come out. It'll come out, right?"

Billy's tongue licked a line along his neck. "It'll come out."

"Promise?"

"I promise. It will come out."

He decided to trust, to nod. "Okay. Okay, that feels good."

"Good. I want you to feel good." Billy kept licking his neck, fingers sliding down to jostle the plug inside him.

"I..." He turned, started licking Billy's throat.

Billy moaned for him, head dropping back, hands still playing with his ass, with the plug. Focusing on the taste, the pleasure, he licked and nuzzled Billy's throat.

His lover.

Salty, sweet. Good.

One of Billy's hands slid around, touched his bound cock.

"Love." He moaned, then started sucking a mark up on Billy's neck.

"Your love, Montana." Billy jacked him a few times, fondled his balls. It actually just felt good, the ache sweet, deep.

"Love touching you. So hot. Silky." Billy's voice rumbled around him.

He felt so warm, lazy, happy.

Billy pushed the plug deeper and it nudged his gland. "Billy!" So much for lazy. Electricity shot up his spine and he arched, fingers digging into Billy's shoulders.

"Mmm. Very good." Billy jostled it again.

"That. I." Oh... He blinked up, trying to focus.

Billy's mouth closed over his, the kiss hard, bringing his focus right there. Opening up was his only option, his entire body jerking, rocking against Billy.

"Yeah. So hot, love. Best Christmas ever."

That plug rocked inside him, pushing into that spot inside him over and over again.

"Love. Love, I need. I need..." He turned, got on hands and knees, making a clear offer.

Billy groaned and rolled up to kneel behind him. He could feel his lover playing with the plug, wrapping thick fingers around the base. Then Billy started fucking him with it, gently pulling it out and pushing it back in.

He dropped his forehead on the silky-soft cuffs, whimpering softly, pushing back into each thrust.

So good.

"Look at you. Just look at you."

"Yours." He made the offer, easy as pie.

"Yes. Mine." The plug was pulled out, leaving him so empty, then he heard the crinkle and crackle of the condom wrapper.

"Yes. Please." He bucked, trying to get to Billy.

Billy pushed slick fingers into him. "Need to make sure you're ready, love."

"Please." He arched, pushed down onto the touch, riding hard.

"I have you. I won't leave you hanging." Billy pushed those fingers into him a few more times and then they disappeared and the thick heat of Billy's cock started to push into him.

His sounds pushed out of him, the pressure perfect, just what he needed.

"So tight. God, Tanny. You feel so good." Billy kept pushing until the thick cock was all the way in, spreading him wide open.

He nodded, soaring with it, cock so hard he could feel each and every heartbeat. As Billy started fucking him, one hand reached around to hold his aching cock, stroking it.

"This time I'll take off the ring. Let you come."

He sobbed softly. "You promise?"

"I promise, Montana. When I say something, I mean it." One hand stroked his cheek, his jaw, and he turned his head, kissed the palm.

"Love you." Billy went back to thrusting, movements long and slow.

"Love. Love." His eyes got heavy-lidded, his body on fire.

"Yes." Billy's hand slid down around his hip and grabbed his prick.

They moved together, strong and steady, and he drove his cock into that warm touch. He almost didn't notice when Billy's other hand got involved, opening the cock ring. Tanny whimpered, almost pulling off Billy's cock. His lover followed him, though, cock pushing back in deep.

Shudders moved over him, his balls heavy and sore. "Please."

"Yeah. Hold on and enjoy it a few minutes first." Billy thrust faster, rocking into him and pushing him into the tight hand.

"I'll try. I swear." In and in and in... so fucking good.

"Okay, love. You're allowed to come now."

He groaned, fingers curled into his palms. His balls drew up and he fought to come, but... It wouldn't work.

He couldn't come.

Oh, God.

"Shh." Billy whispered and spanked his right ass cheek.

"Billy." His ass clenched, his stomach so tight.

"Come for me. Now." There was a thread of steel in Billy's voice; he wasn't asking.

"I..." Tanny couldn't.

He couldn't.

But he did. He shot so hard that the world went gray.

"Yes!" Billy roared behind him, thrusting a few more times before coming himself.

Tanny started crying, overwhelmed, embarrassed by his reaction.

Billy slid out of him and did something with the condom. Then his lover was pulling him close, wrapping him in warm arms. "Shh. Shh. I've got you."

"I'm sorry..." He couldn't breathe, he couldn't see. He held on.

"For what?"

"Being stupid."

Billy growled. "You are not stupid."

"I can't stop crying."

"So? It moved you."

He nodded, relaxed.

"It was beautiful. You were beautiful." Billy kissed his forehead and then his nose and his lips.

"Love you." He took a deep breath, the relaxation moving through him.

"Mmm. Good." Billy grinned. "Merry Christmas, love."

"Merry Christmas." He closed his eyes for a minute, breathed deep.

Billy pressed kisses over his face. He lifted his chin, following the kisses. Chuckling, Billy kept it up, leading while he followed until finally Billy's mouth closed over his. He opened up, let Billy's tongue fuck his lips. The kiss was long and rather lazy, lasting for a good long time.

When their lips parted Billy rubbed their noses together. "So far this is my favorite Christmas ever."

"You haven't even opened your presents yet."

Billy's eyes met his, looking very serious. "I woke up with the best present I can think of already in my arms."

His cheeks went fiery, but he was pleased.

Billy smiled and kissed him again. "You wanna go make pancakes and then open presents? Jack and Oliver aren't expecting us until three or so, dinner's not 'til six."

"Okay, Billy." He blinked, lazy now.

Billy chuckled, goosed him. "Come on, lazy bones. You can keep me company while I do the pancakes."

"Not lazy. Turkey." He sat up, handed over his bound arms. "Take them off?"

Billy tilted his head. "Are you going to let me feed you if they're off?"

"What?" His cheeks heated; he liked the cuffs, sort of.

Chuckling Billy shook his head and got out of bed, helping him get up as well. "I think we'll leave them on a little longer."

"I'm going to forget how to use my hands." He pressed close, leaned against his lover.

"I'll make sure you don't." Billy draped his robe around his shoulders.

"I could put on my sweatpants." He'd come home last week to a bag of sweats and slacks, jeans, and a half dozen shirts.

"But then I wouldn't get to see you sitting around half naked." Billy winked, patted his ass.

He stopped, the sting surprising him. Oh.

"A little tender, hmm?" Billy grabbed one of the pillows and led the way out to the kitchen.

"Uh-huh. You did it."

"I did." Billy hummed, the sound happy, sexy. "I'm going to do it again, too."

"Maybe." He shivered, maybe moaned.

"No maybe about it." Billy put the pillow down on one of the kitchen stools for him. "You want chocolate chip or blueberry pancakes?"

"Blueberry, please." He settled, watched, chin on his bound hands.

Billy moved easily around the room, putting together the ingredients, warming the grill, and humming Christmas carols.

"What do you want me to do?"

"I want you to sit there and enjoy the pancakes I make."

"That's easy. I love the way you make pancakes."

"Thank you." Billy smiled at him, came over between flipping to give him a kiss.

He pushed up, tongue sliding against his lover's. Billy hummed, hand sliding to the back of his neck.

Oh.

Oh, his Billy.

Billy's tongue pushed deep, fucking his mouth. Tanny forgot about the pancakes, Christmas, anything. Sweet sounds pushed into his mouth, the hand at his neck tightening. His fingers curled, reaching what he could, all cuffed. Billy's free hand grabbed the cuffs and pulled his hand over Billy's right nipple. He pinched the little bit of flesh, trying to make Billy feel good. That had Billy gasping and pushing closer, almost knocking him off the stool. He wrapped one leg around Billy's thigh, dragging them tighter together.

"You're hungry this morning."

"I... Last night was..." He blushed dark. "You know."

"Arousing?"

"The pancakes are burning."

"Shit!" Billy hurried over to the griddle and pulled off the pancakes. He shook his head, and wiped the griddle down before putting on more batter. "I think I should stay over here this time."

Tanny chuckled, then the chuckles turned to laughter.

Billy grinned at him. "Laugh all you want, I'm staying here."

"Only until the pancakes are done."

Billy shot him a look that nearly set him on fire. "Only until they're done."

"Uh-huh." His cock was starting to swell.

Billy flipped the pancakes. "They'll stay nice and warm in the oven while we..." Billy winked.

"Are you wanting to? Already?"

"Why not? You are." Billy piled the pancakes onto a plate and put them in the oven, then covered the rest of the batter and turned off the grill.

He didn't know what to answer, so he didn't. Tanny just watched.

Billy finished putting away the pancakes and turned to him and waggled his eyebrows. "How do you want it?"

"However you need."

Billy growled at that, stepping between his legs and pressing their mouths together. Oh. Oh, God. That must have been the right answer. He brought his cuffed hands up, held on tight. Billy's hands slid around his back and tugged him in close, his cock rubbing against Billy's belly.

Billy. He rubbed harder, tongue fucking the hot, parted lips. One hand found his ass and squeezed. His gasp pushed into Billy's lips. Burned. God, it burned.

"Want you." Billy squeezed his ass again, other hand coming around to grab his cock.

"Yours." Anything. More.

Billy wrapped both hands around his ass and lifted him up. He wrapped his legs around Billy's waist, squeezed hard.

"Yeah, just like that." He could feel Billy's cock, rubbing against his ass with every step.

"Love you." Where were they going?

Billy took him back to the bedroom, setting him on the edge of the bed once they were there. The kisses never faded, never lost their power.

He clung tight, tongue-fucking Billy's lips.

Billy fumbled with the package of condoms on the bedside table. "Gonna take you."

He nodded, already slick and ready, open for his lover. Billy's mouth took his again, tongue pushing in even as his ass was pulled to the edge of the bed. Billy's cock nudged at him. He bore down, body stretching, spreading over the hard prick.

"Fuck, yes." Growling, Billy pushed in the rest of the way. That fat cock sank so deep.

His eyes rolled and he rode, moving up and down.

"Yes. Fuck." Groaning, Billy thrust in again and again. Tanny nodded, using his own strength to meet each thrust. Billy's forehead leaned on his, their breath mingling as they both panted.

"W...wow."

"Yeah. Yeah, wow." Billy nodded, thrust again. "Big wow."

"Uh-huh." He nodded, moaned, drew his cuffed hands down to pet his cock.

"No touching!" Billy growled, teeth bared.

"What?" He blinked up. "That was for yesterday."

"Your hands are still cuffed today."

"So that's for as long as they're cuffed?"

"That's right." Billy grabbed his hands and looped them up over Billy's neck. "You can hold me."

That made him moan a little, nod. This was better than touching his cock. Billy began thrusting again, and his moans filled the air, surrounded them. Dragging them closer, Tanny took Billy's mouth, tongue pushing in, fucking it. Billy held onto his hips and humped up hard into him.

Billy. His Billy. Fuck, he loved this. He arched back, shuddering. "More. Harder."

Giving him what he wanted, what he needed, Billy took him harder, pounding into him. Fuck, it was so good. Tanny let himself open, let himself fly, the pleasure making him soar. Billy's fist wrapped around his cock, hot and hard and so much better than his own hand.

"Yes. Fuck." He clenched, squeezed hard, and rode the feeling out.

Billy met his eyes. "You're allowed to come when you need to this time."

"Oh. Oh, thank you. God, I love you. Fuck." His head tossed, throat working.

"I love you, too, Montana." Billy's mouth closed over his neck, hand working him hard.

Everything inside him rejoiced as he shot; spunk spurted out of him in waves.

"Love!" Billy gave a half a dozen rapid thrusts and then froze deep inside him.

He made some sound that was supposed to be a wow or a yay or something, then slumped back onto the bed. Billy slid out of him and slumped on top of him, hands stroking, petting, touching him.

"Mmm. Sexy man."

He murmured happily. Sexy. Christmas. Good. Yeah.

His stomach growled and Billy chuckled. "I think we need to go have those pancakes, hmm?"

"Mmmhmm." He nodded, smiled. Pancakes, orange juice, and presents.

"I still want to leave the cuffs on until after breakfast, as long as your arms aren't aching."

"No. No, I'm okay." He was surprised, but he was okay. The smile Billy gave him made him feel even better.

"Good. I want to hold you and feed you."

"That sounds okay." He nodded, took another kiss.

"You can have your hands back for gifts—ripping off the packaging is more than half the fun."

"You think so?" He was so ready to find out.

Chapter Thirty One

Billy finished throwing the dishes into the dishwasher and headed to living room where he'd sent Tanny to wait on the couch for him. Breakfast had been fun and sticky and he was looking forward to releasing his lover's hands from the handcuffs and opening gifts and simply enjoying the holiday together.

"Hey, love." He waved the key as he joined Tanny on the couch.

Tanny held his hands up. "No more playing, huh?"

He grinned. Tanny had taken to the cuffs even better than he'd expected, clearly enjoying them.

"It's time. Don't worry—we'll play with them again."

"I'm not worried." Tanny chuckled.

"Oh, good." He took Tanny's hands and opened the handcuffs. He massaged Tanny's wrists once they were free. The fur-lined cuffs were gentle and had done their job without straining his sub. He set the cuffs down on the coffee table and sat, cuddling Tanny close. "Open your presents, love."

"No, it's your turn." Tanny leaned and reached and brought him two packages.

They were brightly wrapped and he turned them in his hands, weighing them, checking them out and trying to decide which one to open first.

One was large enough that he knew it was the laptop bag he'd asked for. The other was much smaller, light. Billy decided to draw out the suspense, and opened the laptop bag first.

He put the other one aside and ripped at the paper. "Oh, Tanny, it's lovely!"

The bag was simple, masculine, and the scent of leather was heady. The edges and handles were braided, the entire piece solid and rich.

"It looks handmade." And unique. Personal. He beamed at Montana. "Thank you."

"You like it? I did it myself. Well, mostly. I had some help."

"Oh, man. Montana. It was awesome to start with—that you did it yourself makes it that much better." He tugged Tanny into his lap and hugged him tight.

Tanny leaned into him, kissed his jaw. "Next year, I'll be able to buy you one."

He turned his head to bring their lips together for a proper kiss. "This one is better than anything you could buy."

Tanny kissed him thoroughly, tongue sliding on his lips.

"It really is wonderful, love." He gave Tanny another kiss and then pointed to the little presents under the tree. "Go on, open one of yours before I do my second one."

Billy got to watch Tanny stretch and arch, body rippling as his lover pulled himself back up. He murmured happily, utterly fascinated by Tanny's movements. The clever, long fingers worked the paper open.

Oh, the cock cage—they were starting at the extreme end. Billy wondered if Tanny would be able to figure out what it was.

Tanny stuck his finger in the rings, stroked the leather. "It... pretty."

"It is, isn't it?" He stroked the rings, Tanny's fingers. "You could wear it while we're at Jack and Oliver's."

"Wear it?" He got a worried look.

"Yes. Do you know where it goes?" He grinned. "It's very sexy."

"I... It's sort of small, isn't it?"

"Not for what it's meant for. It keeps you from getting hard."

"I don't get it." He got a confused, almost hurt look. "I thought you liked to make me want you."

"I do, Montana. Very much. But remember how good your orgasm was this morning, after being denied overnight?"

Montana's cheeks turned a deep, dark red, but his lover nodded.

He leaned in and lowered his voice. "Just imagine how it'll feel if you haven't been able to come for days. If every time you started to get hard, you were stopped. You'd come or not on my whim."

"Billy..." Look at those eyes.

"Intriguing, isn't it? I bet we couldn't get the cage on your cock now. I bet you're hard." He didn't check, though. Instead, he held his lover's gaze.

"Billy, please."

"Please what, love?"

"Open your other present?"

He chuckled. "Are you trying to distract me from the cock cage?"

"Yes." No matter what, his Montana wouldn't lie to him.

Laughing, he took the second gift, shook it. "So what's this?"

"Open it."

He opened the gift and found a lovely rose with a thorny stem made of burnished metal. The petals were perfectly formed, the little piece breathtaking.

"Oh. Wow. This is amazing. Truly." He was touched that Montana would make something like this for him.

"It's from cans."

"Cans that we used—our cans?"

"Yeah. The ginger ale from Thanksgiving."

"It's perfect. I love it." It was the best gift he'd ever been given.

"Yeah? I thought you'd appreciate it on your desk." Montana looked so proud.

"Yeah, it's going to get place of honor." He cupped Tanny's chin and leaned in, kissed his lover.

Tanny cuddled in, hands on his cheeks. "I'll have more for you next year. I promise."

"I'd like that. Anything made by your hands." He took another kiss.

"Yeah?" Tanny was relaxed, beaming, settled in his arms.

"Yeah." He just held Tanny, smiling back at his lover. God, he was stupid in love.

They basked like huge lizards, just hanging onto each other, smiling.

"You have some other gifts under the tree, love."

"I do?" Tanny wasn't moving.

"You do." Billy chuckled. "Trust me, the cock cage is the most kinky of them."

"Well, that's good..." Tanny leaned in. "Is there more kinky? I mean, really."

"Oh, there's so much more kinky. Trust me on this one." He gave Tanny a wink, pressed their lips together again.

Those eyes went wide, but Tanny kissed him, tongue just flicking out to wet his lips.

"Come on and open your presents." He wanted to see Montana's face with the rest of them.

"You bought so much... Pick the next one for me?"

"I couldn't choose," he admitted. "So, I just got it all."

"Just for me?" Tanny looked stunned. "Okay, which one next?"

He picked the little package that contained nipple clamps and a chain.

Tanny opened it up, groaned softly. "I know what those are."

"Yeah." He stroked the mother of pearl that decorated the tiny clips. "They'll look beautiful on you."

He loved Tanny's blush. "What next?"

He grabbed one that he was pretty sure was a vibrating dildo. The vibrator was opened, checked out, and turned on, Tanny laughing out loud.

Billy grinned. "You like that? Imagine how it'll feel inside you."

"You like putting things in my ass, Billy."

"I do. Very much." He slid his hand beneath Tanny's ass, squeezed one cheek. Then he leaned in and whispered. "You like it when I put things in your ass, too."

"We haven't done it much..."

"There's another dildo and plug in there; we'll have plenty of opportunity to do it a lot in the future. Plus there's always me." He pointed to his own crotch, his cock taking a definite interest in the proceedings.

"I like having you." Tanny liked being plugged, filled, fucked. Taken.

"I know. My sexy little bottom."

"Am not... Am I?"

"Mmmhmm, you are. The operative word there being 'my'."

"I know I'm yours."

"I like saying it." He tugged Tanny close, took a kiss. Tanny nodded, moaned. "I like hearing it."

"Good." He reached around to feel the heat of Tanny's ass, squeeze it a little.

"Still stings."

That didn't sound like a complaint. "We need to put the plug back in before we head off to Jack and Ollie's."

"We do?" Tanny scooted closer, wriggling against him. "Why?"

"Because I want to know, every time that I see you shift or wriggle or stand because you just can't sit any longer, that it's because of the marks I left on your ass and the plug I filled you with." He held onto Tanny's ass and encouraged his lover to keep wriggling, to rub. "And I want you to be aware of them—of me—every second that we're there."

"Billy." Tanny was hard. God, the man had fabulous recovery rates.

He glanced at his watch. "We have an hour. We can go play." He picked up the nipple clamps. "Your nipples could be aching, too, little sharp bursts every time they brush against your shirt." Between his ass and nipples, Tanny would move so gracefully.

"I don't... Aching is bad, isn't it?"

He picked up the cock cage, grabbed the packages that held the little paddle and the ball gag. "Does it feel bad?" Billy countered, squeezing Tanny's ass again.

What would Montana think of the last two presents?

"I. No. No, it doesn't."

"No, it doesn't at all." He brought their mouths together, kissing Tanny thoroughly.

Montana arched into him, leaned into him.

"Come on. Bed. Now." He stood and tugged Tanny up with him, making sure he had all the toys, wrapped and unwrapped, with them.

"We just got out of bed." Tanny followed him, though, eagerly.

"It's Christmas—we're supposed to indulge ourselves, right?"

"I don't remember any 'have lots of great sex' carols..."

"That's because they're all couched in metaphors." He drew Tanny back to their bed.

"What does that mean?"

"A metaphor is using one thing to speak about another. For example, if I tell you how much I like cream with my breakfast, that's a metaphor for your come in the mornings." He pulled the covers down to the end of the bed and pushed Tanny's robe from his shoulders.

Tanny's head tilted. "Like saying that somebody's eyes are like jewels?"

"Yes, although technically if you use the word 'like' or 'as' it's a simile, which is the same thing. There's another one too, but I don't remember how it works."

And Tanny was worried he was stupid. He so wasn't.

"Huh. Cool."

He'd bet that Tanny wouldn't forget that, now. "Yeah. You want to open these or just make love?" He held out the two last presents.

"I'll open them, I guess. I feel bad that I only had two for you."

"Are you kidding? I only bought mine—yours were handmade by you, which makes them really amazing gifts. Mega amazing." He could tell that Tanny didn't believe him, but the sight of the ball gag sort of derailed... everything.

He watched Tanny's face closely. "What do you think?"

"It's... does it... it's really sort of big."

"It doesn't go in your ass." It wasn't too big, really. Not for the mouth. He'd seen much bigger ones, but had started small.

"It's a gag, huh? Do those make you all hard?"

"No, actually, but I want to be sure to explore all our options. What if it makes you wild?"

"I don't think it will."

Then it would be a lovely punishment. "And what about this?" He handed over the last gift. This would be the first of many different paddles they would use, he was sure.

The paddle made Montana whimper. "I... that's harder than your hand."

"It is." He took it from Montana and rubbed it over his lover's palm.

"I'm already sore."

Billy chuckled. "I'm not going to use it today, love. We'll save this for New Year's Eve."

Today would be the nipple clamps, and would end with the plug going into Montana so he was sore and aching and focused on that and on him during their time with Oliver and Jack. Of course, if Montana happened to end up over his lap and his ass got re-warmed, he couldn't be blamed...

He took the paddle and put it with the pile of other toys on the corner of the bed and then took Tanny's mouth, tongue pushing in. Montana wrapped around him, arms and legs, lips parted to let him in. He slid his hands over Montana's shoulders and down along Montana's back, fingers tracing the scars.

His Tanny shuddered, pressed close to him and shook. He let one hand trail down to Tanny's ass, grabbing it, squeezing and feeling the heat.

"Yours."

Yeah. Yeah, he knew. He reached blindly toward the pile of toys, searching for the nipple clamps with their lovely little chain. Billy found them, fingers wrapping around the cold metal. He wanted Montana's nipples to burn, to ache with every touch of shirt for the rest of the day. Breaking the kiss, he slid his mouth down to Montana's right nipple, licked at it, bit at it.

"Billy." The little bit of flesh swelled, pushed against his tongue.

"Mmm." He hummed, knowing Montana would be able to feel the vibrations. Then he flicked his tongue back and forth, making sure the little nub was as hard as could be.

When he took it between his teeth and tugged, Montana arched, cried out, and he knew his lover was ready.

"First clamp," he murmured, setting the little teeth on either side of Montana's nipple and releasing the pincher.

"Fuck! Fucking shit!" Montana bucked, hips rolling against his leg as Tanny reached for the clamp.

He slapped Montana's hand away. "No touching!" No taking it off.

"Ow!" Montana moaned, protesting even as his hips rolled.

"Hurts so good, doesn't it?" He hunched and licked at Montana's clamped nipple, and then blew.

"Billy." Montana's head fell back, throat working, fingers digging into his shoulders.

"Right here, love." Right here and making his beautiful sub crazy. He repeated the licking and blowing several more times and then moved over to the other nipple.

Montana shivered, pulled away a little. He chuckled and licked and nibbled—Montana knew exactly what was coming now, was anticipating it.

He bit down.

"Billy... Please." That little bit of flesh throbbed, so he bit again. Then he blew on it and flicked his tongue across the tip.

"Oh..." Montana arched so hard he pulled away.

He pinched Montana's free nipple with his fingers, making sure it was nice and hard. Then he slipped on the second nipple clamp, the chain strung from one to the other. Billy grabbed Montana's hands, making sure the clamps stayed put.

He held them behind Montana's back, which arched his lover's chest toward him. Perfect. Licking and blowing, he kept the skin around the clamps sensitized by heating and then cooling it. Tanny shivered and rocked, leaning toward him, then pulling away, over and over.

It was a sexy dance and Billy loved it, loved watching.

"I don't know... I can't think..."

"Stop thinking." Billy grinned at Montana, leaned in and nipped at his lower lip. "We're making love, and that's no place for thinking."

"The clamps... they burn."

"That'll ease," he promised. The real shock would be when the clamps came off and the blood rushed back.

His cock lurched as his lover nodded, trusting, fucking believing him, just like that. He took Tanny's mouth again, hands finding the warm ass and squeezing. His. His. He was going to take Tanny to Oliver's, plugged and happy and sore and know that every sensation was his.

He reached back around with one hand and tugged lightly on the chain connecting the two little nipple clamps. Montana arched, arms and legs clenching. Billy'd bet that tight ass squeezed, too.

He was going to bury himself in there, fuck Montana. Again.

Jesus, Montana made him feel like a kid again.

He gloved up and then applied slick to his cock. "Are you ready for me?" he asked. Montana would still be stretched from last night and this morning.

"Yes. Yes, fuck me."

He pushed Montana down onto the bed and followed. He pushed with his hips, cock nudging up against Montana's hole.

"I can't believe... That you want me. Again."

"Not again, Montana. Always." He grinned and grabbed hold of Tanny's thick cock. "What about you—you want me again."

"How could I not?"

Warmth shot through him and with a low groan he sank into Tanny's waiting heat. Fuck, that felt good; the fact that Tanny wanted him just as badly only served to make it so much better. He moved slowly this time—the urgency had eased up and they had time. Billy kissed Tanny's lips. He licked at the swollen, clamped nipples. He sucked up a mark on Tanny's neck. And all the while he thrust into his lover's body again and again and again.

Montana's hands traveled over his skin, petting him, loving on him. He met the dark eyes and smiled, let his love show, let Montana see how much he felt, how big this was for him, too. Their movements slowed even more, both of them just touching, feeling, riding the sensations. This moment could go on forever, right here, right now.

Montana's fingers tangled in his hair, tugged their mouths back together.

"Mmm..." He sucked on Montana's tongue, pulling the flavor into his mouth.

He felt Montana's ass ripple around his cock with each suck. It felt so fucking good that it was going to make him come. He wrapped his hand around Montana's cock, wanting them to tumble together. Montana groaned, bucked against him. Billy sucked harder on Montana's tongue, hand and hips moving together now.

He was going to come and he could feel Montana jerking around him, close.

"Come for me now, love."

"Yes. Yes. Yes!" Heat sprayed over his fingers.

Groaning, he jerked a few times and let Montana's ass milk his orgasm from him.

Montana slumped to the bed, panting, shuddering. Billy slid out and got rid of the condom before nuzzling into Montana's neck. He had to take the clamps off, put the cock cage and plug in. Such hard work, being a Top. His thoughts made him chuckle.

"I love you," he reminded Montana. Then he took the first clamp off.

Montana's cry was shocked, pained, a little scared.

"Shh, shh, shh." He wrapped his lips around Montana's nipple, sucking to counteract the pain of the blood rushing through the little bit of flesh.

"Oh. Oh. Oh." Montana was wild under him.

He kept sucking, fingers sliding over Montana's belly.

Fingers were in his hair, tugging. Montana wasn't hard again, which was good, if he wanted the cage on, but those hips still jumped and jerked.

So beautiful, so sexy. He loved how responsive Montana was.

Soon Montana relaxed, panting softly, melted into the sheets.

"Next one now."

"No... No, please." Montana covered it with his hands.

"I have to." He took Montana's hands in one of his and undid the clamp.

This time Montana just gasped, fought for air. Billy licked and sucked, soothing the hurt again. Then he blew over the swollen nub. The nipple was red, swollen, hard. Lovely.

"Perfect." He smiled up at Montana and reached for the cock cage.

Montana's eyes were closed, his lovely one breathing slowly.

"So sexy," he murmured, his hand sliding along Montana's belly before he took hold of Tanny's cock and began to work the rings of the cage on it.

"I... That's, uh... I don't know."

"But I do. This will keep you from getting hard. You'll only get hard when we get home and I take it off, and then all the aches and fullness of the day will find their way to your cock." He bent and kissed the very tip of Tanny's cock, which looked beautiful with the rings climbing it.

"But..."

Mmm. Yes. Butt. He grabbed the plug. "Grab your knees and roll up for me." He lubed up the plug; his fingers stroked it like it was Montana's cock.

"Roll?" He loved that Montana grabbed his knees immediately.

"Yeah, just pull up enough to expose... yeah, like that." He rubbed a slick finger over Tanny's hole.

"I... I don't know if... I'm getting a little sore."

"I'm not going to fuck you with it, just fill you." He placed a soft kiss on the hot little hole. The tiny ring of muscles jerked, clenched against his lips. He licked once and then backed off, pressing the tip of the plug at Tanny's opening.

"Billy..."

He hummed softly, kept pressing the plug in. Little by little it went in.

"It's big..."

Yes, and Montana was ready for it. "It's just right. You'll feel it when you're sitting, when you're walking. All the time."

"I don't know, Billy."

"I do, though." He seated the plug, patting Montana's ass to test its sensitivity.

"Billy!" Montana jerked, pulled away, gasped. "Oh, God."

Mmm. Sensitive. "Perfect." He leaned back to look. Montana's nipples were swollen, his cock caged and ass red, the plug end peeking at him. "Just perfect."

It was going to be a lovely, lovely Christmas.

Chapter Thirty Two

"I can't go to see them, Billy." Tanny was standing by the door, shivering. Every nerve was awake and on fire.

Billy frowned and shifted the pie he was carrying to his other hand. "What? Why not, love?"

"They'll know."

"If they know it'll only because they're in the same state."

"I'm... I won't be able to sit still." He wouldn't be able to do anything...

"Don't be so sure about that. Besides, I'm sure you could stand." Billy grinned suddenly. "Or kneel by my chair."

His hands shook so hard that he almost dropped the sack of gifts. "They'll laugh at me. They already don't like me."

"Now, that's just not true. In fact, Jack likes you a lot. And no one is going to be laughing. If they aren't all in the same state, they're going to be jealous."

He noticed Billy didn't tell him that no one would know.

"I can't. I'm sorry. You go. I'll stay here and..." And what? Walk around in circles?

"No, you're coming with me. It's Christmas and we're going to go—together—to visit with our friends."

"You won't... you won't let them laugh at me, right?" It was important to him.

"I will not let anyone laugh at you, love. If they do, they aren't our friends. But I know them—no one will laugh at you." Billy stroked his cheek. "You're my lover, and they'll be happy for you, for us, that I have your focus."

He reached for Billy's hand, squeezed tight. "Okay."

Billy leaned in and kissed him, and then they gathered their stuff and headed out to the car. He walked carefully, each step making him ache a little. Billy's arm came around his waist once they were down the stairs and slowed down for him.

"I..." He didn't know if he could do this. "I don't feel like this is my body."

"Ah, but it is totally your body—you're just more aware of it right now than you ever have been." Billy held the passenger door open for him. "Trust me, Tanny, this will be fun, it will be good."

"I'm trying to." He slid in, goosebumps coming up all over his skin.

"Oliver has very hard chairs. He also has very soft chairs and you may sit in one of them." Billy stroked his cheek before going around and getting into the driver's side. "And it's only a short trip to get there."

He nodded, fingers twisting together. His heart was racing, pounding, almost like he was stoned.

Billy's fingers trailed softly over his thigh and then they were off. Billy drove carefully, going around bumps and potholes as they drove toward the ritzy part of town. Tanny jittered and shook, fingers smoothing his new sweater, his soft, khaki slacks—both presents from Billy.

Every time they stopped at a light, Billy's fingers would touch him, sliding on his skin.

The streets were quiet and it wasn't long at all before

they were pulling up at a huge house. A huge house.

"I don't belong here." Not even a little.

"Yes, you do. This is our friends' home and they have invited us."

"Your friends." God, he was scared. What if he broke something? What if something went missing and they blamed him?

"No, love—our friends. I swear." Billy's hand was back on his thigh. "You'll see."

"Okay. Okay. This is... it's hard, huh?"

"I know. I do, love. I get it. I'm asking for a lot from you."

He met Billy's eyes, just to make sure he wasn't being teased.

Billy's eyes were full of love, no teasing, nothing negative. "Come on, let's go in."

He nodded and slipped out of the car, grabbing the bag of presents. Billy took the pie that was their contribution to Christmas dinner and led him up to the front door. Billy gave him an encouraging smile and rang the bell.

The door opened, Jack's huge smile greeting them. "Guys! Come in! Manning and Les are here, Dawson and Banner. Harrison and Giles."

"Merry Christmas, Jack." Billy gave Jack a one-armed hug.

"Merry Christmas!" Jack kissed Billy's cheek, then hugged Tanny tight. "Please, come in. It's very casual, Tanny. Whatever your mas..." Jack's eyes cut to Billy. "I mean, there's no formality."

"I hope you and Oliver didn't go overboard with the tree this year..." Billy grinned and turned to him. "A couple of years ago the tree had to have been twenty feet tall. And we were all sitting there, opening presents, when it came down on top of us."

"Oh, no." Twenty feet tall. Tanny tried to smile, tried

to not look like he felt like the world's biggest poser, biggest liar.

God, his last Christmas at home, they'd all gone to the food bank, had been pleased to get a turkey that would feed them for a week.

"It was crazy," Jack said, and took the pie from Billy and the bag of presents from him, and Billy wrapped an arm around his waist, guiding him into a large room with a tree that was not twenty feet high.

The room was full of music and laughter and people having fun. Tanny kept his attention on not looking like an idiot, not letting it show, how his body was being. They were warmly greeted by everyone and Billy drew him over to a love seat with soft, fluffy cushions.

He sat and did his best to stay still and quiet, tried not to let his nerves show.

Jack came out of the kitchen and bounced over. "What do you guys want to drink? We've got alcoholic and non-alcoholic stuff."

He looked to Billy. He wasn't sure he could handle a drink, not right now.

"Have you got cranberry juice?" Billy asked.

"I do! How about with some sparkling water so it fizzes?"

Billy chuckled. "Sounds good. Tanny?"

"That sounds good, thank you."

"Two blood-red fizzy drinks!" Jack was bouncing around like he was high himself.

"Are you sure he isn't a tweaker, Billy?" he whispered.

Billy chuckled and whispered back. "How are you feeling right now? Do you feel like you're high, out of your skin?"

"I already told you that."

"Well, Jack is high on what he and Ollie do. Plus the

man takes an insane amount of joy in playing host."

"I... Okay." He didn't know where to put his hands, what to do.

Billy took his hands and gave them a squeeze. "Just relax, Montana. We're all here to have a good time. You included."

He finally relaxed enough to look around. There was a couple sitting together in a large chair, looking at a book. He recognized the man who'd given him his tattoo, both him and his partner looking pale, a little sad. On the far side of the room, a long, tall dark-haired man was sitting on a pillow on the floor, head on a muscled thigh, sound asleep.

Manning was telling a story and Les was listening animatedly, while Oliver and a big, bald man chuckled.

Billy leaned over and nodded at the man on the pillow. "I imagine he's been whipped or caned, which is why he's on a pillow."

"He looks exhausted..."

Jack came up, glasses in hand. "That's Giles. Don't worry. Master Harrison says he had a rough night."

"It looks like he's managed to find some peace." Billy patted Tanny's knee, stroked it.

Jack nodded. "So does Master Harrison."

Tanny took his drink, sipping the bubbly juice. Oh. Tart.

Ollie looked over at Jack and patted his knee. Jack beamed at the older man, hurrying over to sit with a happy laugh.

Oliver raised his glass. "I'd just like to make a toast. To good friends and good times. Merry Christmas everyone."

They all raised their glasses—even the sleeping Giles lifted his head and smiled.

"Merry Christmas."

"I hope everyone is hungry. Jack has spent the last two days cooking. I believe we'll be eating buffet style, so if you'd like to go help yourself..."

Billy turned to him as some of the couples got up. "Would you like to come choose or would you be happier if I shared my plate with you?"

"I'll just share, if that's okay." The sweet concern made him glow a little bit, made him smile.

"More than." Billy kissed the corner of his mouth. "I'll be right back."

When Billy had gone, Montana realized that a lot of the couples present had broken into two, with one of the pair going to the kitchen, the other staying behind.

Giles smiled over at him from the floor, dark circles almost painful under his eyes. "You're new? I am too. Giles DeSante."

"Montana." He offered over a smile. "I. Are you okay?"

Giles nodded. "I've been working. I can't sleep. Harrison helps, you know?"

No, not really.

Well, maybe.

"You both look happy—well-taken care of." Jack bounced. "Oliver made me scream last night. He's such a wonderful master."

Giles chuckled and tossed a throw pillow over. "You always scream."

Tanny just swallowed, watched.

Jack tossed the pillow back. "When I'm lucky, yes."

"What about you, was it Tanny? Are you a screamer?" Giles looked at him, and he blushed dark.

Jack bounced. "Tell me you are!"

"No. No, I don't think so..." God, where was Billy?

"No, you're very new to all this, hmm? I remember those days. It's okay." Giles reached over, patted his hand.

"Billy's a stud." Jack gave him a wide smile. "You're very lucky. Did you get something wonderful for Christmas?"

"I did. He was real nice. Generous. What about you?"

"Oliver is always generous. Even better were the presents in the bedroom, if you know what I mean." Jack winked.

Giles chuckled. "We're opening ours tonight. Last night, I was getting... help."

Help? What did that mean?

Jack laughed. "Oh, details!"

"I couldn't sleep, man. Haven't in days. Harrison worked my ass until I came, then made me come three more times. The last time almost hurt, but I slept. I slept so hard, man."

"Why couldn't you sleep?" Jack asked.

Giles shrugged. "I start thinking and it just won't stop, you know?"

Tanny found himself nodding. "I used to do that." He used to like it.

"Yeah? I hate it."

The man who'd been with Giles came back. "What do you hate, G?

Those huge eyes looked up at the massively muscled man. "Not being able to sleep, sir. Not being able to stop."

The big man smiled. "I think we've figured how to help with that, though. A fine Christmas gift."

"Yes, sir." Tanny watched as Giles stared, completely caught up in the man. "Thank you."

Billy wandered back a moment later with a plate full of food. "Jack, you've outdone yourself this year."

"Thank you, Master William." Jack kissed Billy's cheek. "I'm going to go sit with Ollie."

Billy sat next to him and offered him a fork. "Unless you'd like me to feed you?"

"No..." He ducked his head, a little unnerved. Ollie was feeding Jack, though, and the big man—Harrison—was binding Giles' hands behind him.

Billy looked him in the eye. "We're all different, love. What works for them, isn't necessarily what works for us."

"I just... I'm a little nervous, I think." Once he said the words, the tension eased a little bit.

Billy nodded. "We haven't spent a lot of time socializing. I've wanted you all to myself." Billy sat next to him, drew him close, and they started to share the food—turkey and ham, mashed potatoes and salad and rolls. The food was wonderful.

There was a little conversation as they all ate, but it was light and easy. Everyone was focused on their partner, on eating.

He ended up leaning on Billy, all of them laughing at one of Manning's hospital stories. The whole thing was normal and silly and...

He didn't belong here.

He didn't belong here.

He didn't belong here.

His heart started pounding violently, his body starting to tremble.

Billy put their plate on the coffee table and turned to him. "Montana?"

"Don't. Don't talk to me."

"What's the matter?"

He leaned close. "I don't belong here. I'm a junkie, a freak. This is all so... normal."

"You are not a freak, you are an ex-junkie—so just stop putting yourself down. And you are my lover, which means you belong here with my friends and their lovers."

Billy growled the words out.

He stood, suddenly unable to take it. "Jack? Where's your bathroom?"

"Right down the hall, second door on the left. Are you o..."

He nodded and ran, closing the door behind him.

Moments later a soft knock sounded. "Montana? Let me in?"

He reached behind him with shaking hands. "I'm okay."

"Love? Please?"

He opened the door, needing Billy's presence more than he needed to hide. Billy came in without saying anything, arms open for him. Tanny pushed in, took a deep breath that was all full of the scent of home for him.

Billy's hands stroked down along his back, fingers warm.

"I'm sorry."

"What happened?" Billy didn't sound angry.

"It's like a TV show or something out there. You get the feeling that nobody knows about sleeping under the bridge or eating charity or nothing. I feel like a faker, like my gran's gonna pop out of the floor and start screaming at me." Once the words started, they wouldn't stop. "I'm just a nasty old reservation dog, and I ain't never had stuff like this, Billy, and it scares me. All this. Like I'm gonna get used to it and then it'll be gone and that ain't about you either." He took a deep breath. "I know you have me, but that isn't always about you. I can fuck stuff up, all by myself."

Billy kept holding him, all though his long speech and after. His concerns and worries weren't poo-pooed or belittled.

Finally, Billy spoke. "We can all fuck stuff up, love. One minute you've got the whole world in your hand, the next—nothing. You can't live in fear of losing the good stuff, though, because then you'll never enjoy it, never be happy. I just want you to be happy, Montana. I want to be happy with you."

"I know. I know all this." He sighed. This was why he didn't want to talk about things. "My heart just... You know?"

"Just what, love?"

"I don't belong here. This house cost more than my parents and grandparents made in their whole lives, all together."

"I don't have anything like this in my life, either, Tanny. But Jack and Oliver are our friends and they invited us. That means we belong here."

"You're my friend." He didn't have any others.

Still.

He felt better now. Like he could breathe.

Billy nodded. "I am. And Jack would like to be if you'll let him." A soft chuckle shook Billy's chest. "I think Giles would very much like to be friends as well."

"I like Giles." The man got it, he thought. Sort of.

"Then we should arrange to get together after the holidays, maybe go out to dinner or have them over for an afternoon one weekend? Watch movies, eat, get to know each other?"

Tanny nodded. "Okay. Okay, Billy." He took a deep breath, squeezed Billy's hand. "Okay."

"Let's go back now. There's presents." Billy waggled his eyebrows.

"I've had a lot of presents." One was hard, filling his ass.

"I know." Billy's hand drifted down and patted his ass. "But I'm pretty sure Jack and Oliver have presents for everyone. And we have ours to give out."

"No touching." He chuckled a little, though.

"That's my line." Billy's fingers stayed on his ass, tickling over his hole.

"Don't..." His cock jerked and he shivered, the metal around it weird and wrong.

Billy kissed him. "Come on. Let's go see if Ollie and Jack bought everyone sex toys again this year."

"You're joking."

"No. No, I'm not." Billy chuckled. "It was... a very interesting Christmas."

"Are people going to have sex here? I mean, at the party?"

"Possibly."

"I... Are you going to have sex with other people here?" It was very important that he know.

Billy growled. "No. And neither are you. I don't share."

"Okay. Okay, good, because... I don't. I don't share either."

Billy nodded. "No, you don't." Billy's mouth descended on his.

He pressed closer, lips opening, the weight of Billy's passion sorta stunning him. Billy's tongue pushed right in, flickering through his mouth and filling him with Billy's taste. Tanny pushed up, crawled into Billy's arms, his caged cock aching.

Leaning back against the door, Billy kissed and stroked him. Warm fingers pushed his shirt against his nipples, making them ache. He whimpered and shifted, fingers sliding down to his cock.

"No touching." Billy grinned at the words.

"I'm not cuffed."

"No, you're not, but you're caged." Billy's fingers slid down and stroked his cock.

His cock jerked and he gasped. "Don't. It aches."

"See? No touching." Billy gave him a wink and another

hard kiss. "Come on, before they send a search party."

He nodded, met Billy's eyes. "I'm sorry for freaking out."

"Thank you for letting me in, letting me help."

Tanny managed to smile, to kiss the corner of Billy's mouth.

Billy patted his ass again and then settled with an arm around his waist, guiding him back into the living room. Six pairs of eyes met him, but Billy's arm was warm, solid behind him.

"I understand there are presents," Billy said, bringing him over to the couch.

"I knew you'd be the first to ask!" Jack clapped and laughed. "And thank God—it's about time!"

"Sorry, guys." He said it softly.

Giles smiled. "It happens. Are you okay?"

"Yeah. Yeah, I just... " He shrugged. Freaked out.

"Needed some alone time with Billy." Jack winked and leaned into Ollie's swat.

"Yeah." He nodded, cheeks pinking.

"Yes, I'm a very lucky man." Billy grinned and tugged him down to sit close.

Giles was still kneeling on the floor beside Harrison, Les was in the doctor's lap, looking happy, relaxed.

He wasn't relaxed, but Tanny thought he could be happy.

"You want to sit in my lap?" Billy asked as Jack went to the tree and began distributing gifts.

He nodded before he thought. He wanted to be close. The smile Billy gave him made him feel good, and those arms opened immediately for him. He moved into Billy's lap, cheek on one shoulder.

"Mmm." Billy kissed his forehead and they sat and watched as Jack passed out the gifts.

There was even one for Billy and another for him.

"Thank you." He couldn't quite believe this, but it was sweet, like a commercial.

"Open it," Billy insisted. "And then you can help me with mine."

The paper was fancy, with lots of ribbons. His fingers were a little shaky, but he got the paper open, the little friendship bracelet falling into his lap. "Oh, look."

"Oh, that's pretty." Billy took it. "Shall I put it on?"

"Do you like it?" Jack asked.

"It's beautiful. Did you make it?"

"I did. Although I had to redo it about four times before I got it to look like a real bracelet."

"It's fucking cool."

"Yay!" Jack laughed and bounced and came over to give him a hug. "I'm so glad you like it."

"I did. Do. It's cool. Thanks."

"You're welcome."

He and Billy had picked things from Rainbow Artists for everyone they knew was going to be here, and a few extras in case there were more.

Several of the other couples had done the same thing and they wound up with gift cards for a fancy restaurant, a bottle of champagne and an expensive-looking basket of cheeses.

One of the last gifts opened was to Billy from Oliver. Inside was a beautiful paddle made of several different woods, inlaid and beautiful. His and Billy's names were inscribed on the handle.

"Wow, Oliver. This is lovely, thank you."

Tanny just stared.

He.

Uh.

Wow.

"I hope it'll bring you closer," murmured Oliver.

"Oh, it's lovely..." Giles smiled over, the look on the

man's face... fatherly, somehow.

"It's truly lovely. I'm sure we'll put it to good use." Billy tucked it next to the bottle of champagne.

Harrison and Giles had given Jack and Oliver a huge pink ball gag, which had the whole room laughing, and Harrison unwrapped a... a...

"What is that?" he whispered to Billy.

The thing looked like a steel tube with a long, smooth piece of metal poking down through the center.

"It's a cock cage with a sound. The sound is that extra piece." Billy's voice dropped even lower. "It goes inside your cock."

His eyes were going to bug out of his head and fall into Billy's lap.

Plop.

His own cock tried to swell, but couldn't, the metal pressing into his flesh.

Billy smiled at him. "We'll work up to something like that."

No fucking way.

Ever.

Not in a million years or after a bajillion beers.

Billy patted his caged cock.

"Don't," he whispered, hiding his face.

"Shh. Everything is fine, Tanny."

"He's so pretty, Master." Tanny thought that was Giles' voice, but he wasn't going to look at make sure.

"He is," growled Billy. The strong arms wrapped around him, made him feel safe. He heard someone moan, then he heard someone kissing. Billy simply held him, hands warm through his clothes, breath even warmer as it brushed over his head.

Soft chatter filled the room, along with the periodic moan. Tanny stayed put, letting himself hold on.

"I've got you," murmured Billy, hands soothing on his

skin. "I've got you."
 And Billy did.

Chapter Thirty Three

Billy made sure the champagne was sitting in a bucket of ice. He had a bunch of ready-made hors d'ouevres warming in the oven. A brand new year was coming and he was going to start it with Montana.

Billy thought that was something to celebrate.

Humming, he made a quick sweep through the living room, putting away a few DVDs, making sure they had lube and condoms within easy reach. He wanted to get rid of those, actually. He figured tonight was the night to bring it up.

He knew Montana was his, knew he didn't want anyone else ever. He only hoped Montana would believe in them enough to take the test so they could stop using the rubbers.

"The bathroom's all clean, man. We're good for the New Year."

The one thing Tanny'd been insistent about was cleaning the entire apartment for the New Year, top to bottom.

It was adorable.

Dear.

"So we can stop cleaning and start celebrating, hmm?"

"We can." Tanny was wearing some of the new sweats

he'd been buying and sliding into Tanny's dresser. He'd found a brand that was sinfully soft on the inside. He was sure they felt wonderful against Tanny's ass when it was warmed from his hand.

"There's food and champagne in the kitchen when we're ready for it."

"Do you want me to dress up, or is this okay?" Tanny looked comfortable and the clothes were easy access.

"I'm happy with comfy and casual if you are, love." They didn't have anyone to impress but each other.

That smile was all the answer he needed.

"Any other traditions you'd like to follow for New Year's?" He wrapped his arms around Tanny's waist, taking a hug.

"No. No, this is perfect."

"It is, isn't it?" He tilted Tanny's chin and took a kiss.

Tanny's tongue slid against his, pushing almost lazily.

"We're supposed to be ending the old year as we'd like to start the new one. I think an evening of celebrating and making love would be perfect, don't you?"

"That's your answer to every holiday." That wasn't a no.

"It's a good answer." Billy took another kiss. "Did you have something better to do?"

"Not one thing."

"Good." He pushed his hands into the back of Tanny's sweatpants and cupped the fine ass. It was warm, the skin soft, an addiction. "Love your ass." He squeezed, his fingers moving toward the hot little crease.

"No spanking it." Tanny nibbled on his bottom lip.

"No? How about testing out the paddle Ollie gave us?"

Tanny shook his head. "It'll hurt."

"It'll be deeper than with my hand, but it won't hurt more than that."

"I..." Tanny lifted his face for a kiss, eyes focused on him.

"You're mine." He granted the kiss Tanny wanted, fingers squeezing, digging into Tanny ass. He liked being able to admit it now. To say it aloud.

His.

His lover. His man. His sub.

"Couch. I have some things laid out," Billy added.

"Mmmhmm." Montana let him walk them back toward the sofa.

"Including that paddle." He watched Montana's face as he said it. He did love to push. It didn't hurt that Montana took to it like the pure natural sub he was.

That cock cage had come off when they'd gotten home Christmas Day and Tanny'd been wild. His lover had let him fuck the sweet, tight ass with the plug until Montana had screamed.

He was hard and leaking just thinking about it. "Come on," he growled suddenly. He moved them faster, eager to get Montana naked and bent over the couch.

Montana moaned, followed him, those dark eyes heated and focused.

When they got to the couch, he pulled off Montana's T-shirt. He let his fingers glide along Tanny's ribs as he did, fingertips sliding on the warm skin. Then his fingers dipped down, touching his signature.

"Mine," he said again. It bore repeating.

Tanny nodded. "Yeah."

Leaning into Tanny's neck, he began to pull up a mark. He was going to leave a lurid bruise for them to start the New Year with, so that every time he looked at Montana he would see it.

"I. I have to work next week..."

"Maggie's not going to be upset if you come to work marked."

"You're sure?"

He almost laughed. Maggie had been a big, bad top, once upon a time. She'd love it. "Absolutely." He went back to making his mark. He loved the way sucking on Montana's skin brought the taste up.

Montana moaned for him and they stretched out together, filling up the couch. He slipped into Montana's waistband, feeling for the heat and silk of Montana's prick. The sweet flesh was getting hard, pressing against his palm. His lover was so responsive to every little touch. It aroused him all the more.

Montana traced his nose, his jaw, fingers petting him. Murmuring happily, he turned his face, following those fingers. He bit at them as they slid past his lips. That made Montana chuckle, tap at his lips. He loved these playful moments as well as the intense ones. Billy opened up and took Montana's fingers in. He sucked on them, bit at the tips.

"Bitey man!" Montana pulled away, tapped his nose.

"You like it better when I'm swatty, hmm?" He grinned and gave Montana's ass a slap.

"Ow!" That wasn't true; he could see it in Montana's laughing eyes.

"Say it again after the fiftieth one."

"Fifty? No..." Montana stilled. "No, Billy."

"You don't think you've already had fifty, love? You've never counted them."

"I haven't. There's no way. You'll hurt me, Billy."

"Montana." He waited until he Tanny's full attention, their eyes on each other's. "I would never do anything to you that would damage you. Never."

Montana searched his eyes, really looked, and then he could see his lover relax, hands cupping his face. "I know."

"Good." He turned his face to kiss Montana's palm.

"While we're talking—there was something else I wanted to discuss."

"Is it a bad thing?"

"No, not at all. Come, sit." He pulled Montana down into his lap and took a kiss. He thought all discussions should start with one.

Montana settled easily, chuckling into his lips.

"I'd like us both to get tested."

"Tested? For what?"

"HIV. AIDS. I want us to get rid of the condoms. I want to feel your silk and your heat tight around my prick. I want to come inside you and then plug you, spend the day knowing my come is still inside your body."

Montana's lips parted, the soft gasp so sweet.

"I don't want anyone else, love. Just you."

"Just me? For real?"

"Yes. And I would like you to make the same commitment to me."

"I don't want anyone else. I didn't before you."

He beamed at Tanny, the words making him warm. "Then we'll go see Manning. Have the tests done and then we can dispense with the condoms."

"Okay. Will it hurt?"

"There's a pinch when the needle goes in, but it doesn't hurt much or for long."

Montana nodded, then kissed his jaw. "No problem."

He laughed and hugged Montana close. "That's great. I can't wait to feel you without the rubber, to know my come's inside you."

Montana's cheeks burned bright red, hot against his throat.

"You're thinking of it, too, aren't you?" He slid his hand along Montana's back, the scars so very familiar now.

"Yes." That was his lover. Always so honest.

"Patience. It shouldn't take too long to get the results back once we take the test. It won't be easy, though, knowing it's so close." Billy cupped Tanny's prick through his sweats.

"I'll wait, to make sure you're safe."

"That we're both safe." He brought their mouths together, the kiss deep, heartfelt.

Tanny hummed, moaned into the kiss, tongue sliding against his.

"We're wearing too many clothes." They always seemed to be. He should keep Tanny naked and ready while they were home. The thought made him groan.

"We're always getting naked." Tanny teased him.

"I like you naked."

"I've noticed that. I like you naked, too."

"That works out well." He slipped off Montana's T-shirt, mouth going to one of the sweet little nipples. They were still bruised—not from Christmas, but from all the nights and attention since. He licked them gently and breathed on them, pressing kisses and licks on the swollen skin.

The deep sounds he was getting used to were filling the air.

"We should get these pierced."

"What? No. No way..." The tight little bits of flesh pushed against his teeth.

Uh-huh. Tanny just hated that idea. He bit down on the hard little nipple.

"Billy!" Those hands landed on his head and pulled him closer. Such a sweet pain-slut.

He kept playing with Montana's nipple. It tasted so good, Montana's skin and sweat delicious.

"Aches. Aches. Don't stop."

He had to stop for a moment because he couldn't contain his smile. Then he was back at it, sucking hard, playing the nipple with the tip of his tongue. Then he bit down, rolling Montana's nipple in his teeth. Each cry made his cock throb.

He left it only to move on to the other one. He worked the left nipple as hard as he had the right. Oh, yes, a little barbell in one nipple, to give Montana different sensations in each.

"Please." Montana was beginning to shudder, to shake.

"You could come just from this, couldn't you?" He didn't need to touch Montana's cock to know it was hard, leaking.

"I don't know. It burns. I..."

"Love it. You love it."

"I don't know."

"I do." He pushed Montana down onto his back, pushing his thigh into Tanny to give him something to rub against.

Montana's hips rolled up, rubbing immediately. Montana's body knew.

He continued to lick and suck and bite as their hips moved together. His Montana went wild, rocking and slamming up into him, rubbing furiously. Fingers taking over for his mouth on Montana's nipples, he kissed his way to his lover's neck. "Come," he whispered into one ear.

"Oh. Oh..." Montana shuddered and shot, coming at his word.

Fuck, yes.

He covered Montana's mouth, kissing hard and deep. Montana was everything he'd ever wanted in a lover, in a sub. Billy let their lips drift apart and smiled down into the dark brown eyes.

"I want to make love to you now."

"Mmm. Now is okay with me."

He found the lube and passed it to Montana. "I want to watch you open yourself."

"Billy…" He loved that shocked look.

"Yes. I'm going to watch." He tugged Tanny's sweats the rest of the way off and undressed himself as well. Then he settled close, so he could touch, encourage Montana.

"Don't you want me to touch you?"

"There will be plenty of time for that, love. Go ahead, slick up your fingers and spread yourself open." He wasn't going to let Montana distract him out of this.

Montana's fingers trembled as he worked the top of the slick open. Billy slid his hands up and down Montana's legs, watching closely. He loved every effort, every tremor.

"It's weird, with you watching."

"I always watch you. Always."

"Not always. Sometimes I'm not here."

Smiling, he pressed their lips together. "I mean while we make love."

Montana chuckled for him, deepening the kiss, even as those slickened fingers disappeared. He pulled away enough to watch. Montana was stretched, arched, fingers moving.

"Fuck." He groaned and shifted right back so he could watch the long fingers go right into Montana's hole. The wrinkled skin stretched around them.

Montana tried to hide from his eyes, head ducked down.

"No, love. Be proud. You're beautiful, and I love looking at you."

He could feel Montana's cheeks heat. "It's the truth." He slid his fingers down along Montana's breastbone, heading for his crotch.

"I…I'm ready for you."

"Are you?" He slipped one of his own fingers in with Tanny's.

A sharp sound pushed into his lips. Oh, yes.

He slipped on the condom and settled between Montana's legs. Montana groaned, shifted and tried to bear down on him.

"No, no, love. I'm running this show."

"I..." Montana shifted under him, barely moving.

He pushed just the tip of his head into Montana's body. Montana tried to push down onto his prick again. Billy pulled back, his cock slipping free once more, and he placed a kiss on Montana's nose and another on his lover's lips.

"Billy..." Montana followed his lips.

"Yeah, love?" He licked this time, the corner of Montana's lips fascinating his tongue.

"I. Mmm. Love you." Montana was distracted now.

Billy nodded. "Yes. Yes. Love." He kissed Montana, tongue slipping in between the sweet lips. He nudged that hot little hole again with his cock. Montana moaned for him, lips parting easily, body heated and yielding under him. He pushed in a little further and then pulled out again, teasing Montana's body and stretching out the pleasure.

"Tease." The single word was whispered against his lips.

"Yes." He didn't deny it. He was teasing his lover, but it would be worth it. Tanny would know pleasure, long, slow pleasure.

"Are you happy, Billy?"

"I am, Montana. I am so very happy." He pushed in a little again, his cock resting just inside Montana's hole. "Are you?"

"Yeah. More than ever."

"Good." He drove in hard.

The little gasps and moans became cries—sharp and happy, Montana taking him, in and in. Groaning, he stopped only when he was in as far as he could go. Montana was so tight, so hot around his prick. He held perfectly still, watching Montana jerk and slide, try to fuck himself.

It was hot, how much Montana wanted him.

He waited until Montana had stopped moving and then he slid slowly out, right out. This was good now—it was going to be amazing without the latex between them.

"Billy..." Montana panted, eyes questioning, a touch unsure.

"It's okay, love. I just want to take my time. I want to make it last." He wanted Montana to want him more than anything else ever.

"Oh." Montana offered him a husky chuckle, a wink. "Last and last, hmm?"

"Yes." He leaned in and whispered, "I want you to be desperate for it."

"I already came." Montana nuzzled his jaw. "What if I can't be desperate?"

"Then we'll make love all night long." He was pretty sure he could make Montana desperate for it, though.

"So long as you kiss me at midnight..."

"I'll kiss you now and just before midnight and at midnight and right after midnight." He pushed slowly back into Montana as he spoke.

Montana's laugh had a definite hiccup in it.

When Billy was all the way back in, he circled his hips.

"Mmm. Feel you." Montana's hands slid up his arms, over his shoulders.

He nodded and pulled slowly out once more. Then in again, just as slowly. It felt fucking amazing. Montana tried to tug him in closer, pull him deeper. He didn't let his beautiful sub set the pace, though. He kept it nice and slow.

"Billy..." Montana lifted up on his elbows, mouth sliding on his skin.

"Yes, love?" He arched, giving Montana more skin to play with.

Something unintelligible was murmured against his throat, then Montana started sucking.

"You going to mark me, love?" He started making little tiny movements. In and out and in and out, an inch at a time.

"Yes. You're mine." The words were soft, but fierce.

He growled in response. "I am."

Montana's teeth scraped over his skin, burning him a little. He thrust in all the way, slamming up against Montana's ass. Montana cried out, teeth sinking into his skin. He pulled out and did it again, one hand reaching to tweak a nipple.

"Oh. Oh, fuck. Billy."

"That's right, Montana. Fuck."

"Harder. I want it harder."

"That sounds like a demand instead of a plea."

"Huh?"

Fuck, this was fun. "You're supposed to be begging me, remember?" He started taking it slowly again, long slow movements that slid his cock out and back into Montana's body. A snail would have moved faster.

"Billy..." Montana's nails pushed along his back.

"Yes, love?" They were going to do this all night if they had to.

"You're driving me nuts."

He knew that. "That's kind of the point." Grinning down at Montana, he slowly pulled all the way out.

"Bastard. So mean."

That had him laughing. "I can be much meaner than this."

"No way. Meanness is bad for you." Tanny was

laughing, too.

He pushed back in and circled his hips again. Both their laughter faded into moans.

"Oh, there. Again, love."

"This one right here?"

"Uh... Uh-huh..." Montana's eyes rolled up into his head.

He circled again, and then did a slow in and out, groaning at the way Montana's body clung to his cock.

"Yours. Billy." One day it would be Sir. He knew that.

"Yes. Mine." He continued the slow pace, though he did move a little faster.

They settled into the rhythm, Montana moving with him. He sped up slowly, almost imperceptibly. It felt so damn good; he could die doing this. Soft little sounds started filling the air, Montana right there with him, watching him. He started tweaking Montana's nipples, adding to the sensations.

"I. I. Billy..." Montana's nipples were dark red, hot to the touch, swollen and sensitive.

"Right here, love. I've got you. I really do."

"I ache."

"You're going to feel me all day tomorrow. All day long."

"I am. I... I'm not sorry. I'm not."

"Neither am I." He picked up speed then, punching his hips.

"I. I need to touch my cock."

Sweet baby. "No, you don't."

"I do..." Montana whimpered, fingers digging into his shoulders.

"You'll come without a touch to it this time." He reached for Montana's nipples again, twisting one and then the other.

"No..." Jesus, every touch made Montana's ass clench around him, so tight.

"Yes." He shifted, nailing Montana's gland. "Yes."

Montana arched, hands stretching up above him.

That's right, love. You know what you want, what you need

He leaned in and nosed Montana's pit. Montana arched, fingers digging into the couch cushions. Billy mouthed his way over to Montana's nipple and teased it with the tip of his tongue as his hips kept punching in hard, pinging Montana's gland every time.

"Billy. Billy. Billy..." His name rang out, the sound filling the air, over and over.

"Yes, love. Yes." He worked Montana's nipples, the little gland inside Montana's body. "Give it to me."

"Love..." Montana twisted and he bit down, teeth sharp on that poor little bit of flesh. Heat sprayed over his stomach.

The smell of it was intoxicating.

Groaning, Billy slammed in a few more times, and then came long and hard. He shook with the power of it, gasping and grunting with the pure pleasure. Collapsing onto Montana when he was done, he lay there panting against his lover's neck.

"Love you." The words were sweet to his ears.

"Me, too. For real."

Tanny chuckle filled him up, top to bottom. "Yeah. Yeah, Billy. For real."

"Yeah." He smiled, staying right where he was.

Chapter Thirty Four

"What happened to your arm?"

Tanny stopped on his way out of the shop, head turning as he tried to figure out who was talking to him.

"You shooting up again?"

"I never did." Who was that?

That cop who had been hassling him was leaning against the wall, scowling at him. "Sure. What's that then?"

"Blood draw. From the doctor."

"Bullshit."

"It isn't. And... and it ain't none of your business." Asshole.

The guy stepped forward. "I'll make it my business."

"No." He took off, heading straight for the house, for safety. He heard the cop's laughter, following him.

Billy was at home, smile fading as he charged in. "Montana? What's wrong?"

"Nothing. Nothing. I don't want to talk about it. I'm going to take a bath." He headed straight for the bathroom, feeling dirty.

Billy's head popped around the door. "Love?"

"I just need a bath, okay?" Please, just don't ask.

"Something's wrong, Tanny. You can tell me, you know."

"I don't want to talk about it." He tore his clothes off, tore the bandage off.

"You want me to join you? Give you a massage?"

"Yes. No. Fuck. I don't know. I just... I just need to..." Think. Stop and breathe.

Billy started stripping. "Get in the tub, love."

"I just..." He got into the bathtub and pulled the curtain, hiding for a second as he turned the water on hot.

It seemed like no time at all when Billy pulled the curtain back again and slipped in behind him.

"Hey." He turned his face into the water, let it pound down against him.

Billy's arms went around him, the touch easy, good. Billy didn't say anything, though. He leaned back and closed his eyes. Warm. Billy was warm. Billy didn't push or question him. His lover was just there, holding him.

He let Billy do it. Hold him.

Make it better.

Soft kisses began to pepper his neck and shoulders.

"Love you," Tanny said. That was the truth.

"Good. Because I feel the same way."

"I'm not using. I'm not. I didn't even buy another pill."

"I believe you."

He almost cried, but he didn't. He nodded. "It's the truth."

"I know." Billy's fingers stroked soothingly over his belly.

"Okay." He smiled as Billy traced the inked signature on his skin.

"You want to talk about what set this off?" There was no pressure in the words.

"No. Someone was mean and asked if the bandage was because I was using, even when I never did that."

"Asshole."

"Yes."

The warm tracing on his belly continued and the soft kisses resumed.

"How was your day?" he finally relaxed enough to ask.

"Eh. My current article is proving to be a bitch to write. I can't wait to be finished with it."

He leaned back harder. "I made a book all by myself."

"Really? That's very cool! Did you bring it home so I can see or shall I come down to Rainbow Artists tomorrow?"

"It's still drying. You could come down and see." Maybe that bastard would leave him alone.

"If I come down around the time you sign off we could have a late lunch." Billy's fingers wandered away from his belly, one going up, the other going down.

"Okay. That would be good. We haven't gone out to lunch in a long time."

"We've been too busy with holiday stuff. I mean, I like the holidays, but it's nice now that they're over and we can get back to normal."

He nodded. Of course, he wasn't sure what normal was really.

Billy's hand wrapped around his cock, jacking him slowly; he could feel the heat of Billy's want against his ass. He spread, head falling back as he enjoyed the touch. Hand sliding down to cup his balls, Billy rolled them, and teased a finger or two along the patch of skin behind them.

"Yours." He loved that, the feel of his nuts in Billy's palm.

"That's right. Mine." Billy pressed more kisses along his shoulders, fingers tugging and feeling up his sac.

"Oh..." His knees buckled a little, his heart thrummed in his chest, and he thought he might forget how to breathe.

Billy's other arm wrapped around his chest, holding him up against the strong body. That made him feel so... He didn't know if there were words for the ache in his belly. A rumbling sound vibrated up along Billy's chest and sounded like a moan against the skin of his shoulders. The gentle play around his balls slid away, Billy stroking his cock again instead.

That was more familiar. Easier to cope with.

"There's a silver ring in the soap dish," murmured Billy, still stroking. "I want you to put it on."

"I..." His cock jerked in Billy's hand, and he nodded. "Okay. Okay, Billy."

He reached for the ring, the metal cool and smooth to his fingers. Billy continued to stroke, making sure he was fully hard, and then the big hand disappeared, leaving him to do as Billy had asked. He slid the ring down, then carefully slid one ball through, moaning as his cock throbbed. Damn it.

Billy leaned over his shoulder, hands on his hips, and watched.

"I..." He moaned, wanting... something. God, this was all so much. It took him a minute, to slide his other ball through, the ring tight, holding him out.

"Perfect," murmured Billy, cock sliding along his ass, hand coming back to stroke his hard-on.

"It's tight." His balls ached.

"Yeah. It's meant to be." Billy turned him, fingers on his nipples.

"I... I want... Billy..." His eyes were rolling in his head.

Found

"You're going to get Billy." He got a wink and then Billy turned him, started sucking on one of his nipples, hand drifting down to play with his cock-ringed prick.

His nipples were perpetually swollen, tender, teased by that mouth.

"I want these pierced, Montana."

"What?" Oh, God. Those teeth.

Billy bit and nibbled, sucked on his tit. Then those amazing eyes looked up at him. "I said. I want these pierced."

"Billy..." His stomach muscles went so tight they burned.

"Yes, love?"

"Why?"

"Oh, there's more than one reason. They'd be sexy. They'd drive you crazy. It would be so easy to tug and work your nipples with them."

"You... you work them now." Over and over. It was maddening.

"Yeah, but when they're pierced, I'll be working them even when I'm not with you."

This noise pushed out of him, his hips bucking like he was fucking the air.

"Mmm, that's right, love." Billy pinched his nipple and then slowly slid down onto his knees in front of Montana.

He stared down, swaying a little. "Billy?"

"Right here." Billy leaned in and traced his name with a pointed tongue. Oh, that was so hot, but sweet, too. The tracing turned into sucking kisses.

"Love you." He was swaying; he couldn't help it.

"Yes. Me, too." The kisses turned into bites, Billy's teeth on his skin.

"No... no biting." He stepped backward with a moan.

"But you like the biting." Billy bit him again.

"Don't!" He didn't.

Not really.

"You like it when I mark you." Another kiss pressed against the spot where Billy had bitten.

Tanny couldn't deny that. He just couldn't. Billy's hands landed on his thighs and turned him, that bitey, kissy, hot mouth staying on his skin.

"I don't know what to do." He reached down, tangled his fingers in Billy's hair.

"Feel, love. Enjoy. Listen to your body."

"My body's lost its mind."

Billy stopped, his head tilted, and then those dark eyes flashed up to his and Billy started to chuckle.

He grinned down, tickled. "It's true."

Billy bit at his hip and then stood, bringing their mouths together for a laughing kiss. He stepped in, tongue against Billy's. This was a good thing—him and Billy and laughing. Billy's strong hands grabbed hold of his ass and squeezed as they kissed.

The water was getting cold, so he reached to turn it off, get them some towels.

"Bed. I'm going to tie you down and drive you insane and not let you come until you'll go crazy with it."

"Billy!" That wasn't helping him focus.

"I do love the look on your face when I tell you what I'm going to do to you."

"I... I don't have a look..." Did he?

"You do! Shocked and turned on all at the same time. It's very sexy."

Tanny chuckled. He didn't know about that.

Billy tweaked one of his nipples. "I'm serious now."

He whimpered, went up on tiptoe. "Oh."

"You're beautiful and sexy and everything about you makes me want, need."

"I. I don't know what you want me to say."

"Thank you? I love you? You're sexy, too?" Billy grinned, winked. "Or you can say nothing and just keep giving me the look."

"I love you. You're the most finest thing ever."

Billy leaned in to kiss him hard, fingers trailing down his belly to grab at his bound cock. He bucked up into the touch, hips rolling as he tried to take more.

"Always so eager." Billy bit at his lower lip and then tugged on it with his lips.

"I can't help it."

"It wasn't a criticism."

"No? Sorry. God, I'm just all... is it called defensive?"

Billy nodded. "It is. I imagine it's because of what happened with the asshole, earlier, hmm? We should just go to bed and I'll fuck it out of your mind."

"Okay." He could handle that.

Taking his hand, Billy led him back out and to the bedroom. He followed, holding on, each step making him feel more relaxed. Billy moved them right into the room and pushed him onto the bed.

"Pushy." He laughed as he bounced.

"Yep. I am."

Thank God. He reached up for Billy, knowing his lover would make it better.

Chapter Thirty Five

Billy had dinner sitting in the Crock-Pot, so they wouldn't have to worry about it. He had a new tube of lube in the living room, one in the kitchen, and one in the bedroom, so wherever they wound up, they'd be ready.

Lube but not condoms.

He chuckled again, well pleased about the phone call he'd had earlier.

Now all he needed was Montana.

Montana came in, waved to him and headed toward the bedroom. "Hey. Gonna get clean."

"You already are," he called out as he watched Montana make for the hall.

"Uh-uh. I smell like glue."

Grinning, he followed. "You might smell like glue, but you're still clean."

"No. I've been working. How was your day?" Montana was already naked, heading for the shower.

"It was great. Wonderful, in fact." Billy stripped down as well and got in with Montana.

"Cool." Montana leaned under the water, reached for the shampoo.

Chuckling, Billy took over the shampooing. Montana's hair was growing out quickly.

"Mmm." Montana's hands wrapped around his waist. "Hey."

"Hey. How was your day?" He was itching to tell Montana, but he could wait. At least a few moments.

"Okay. I worked hard. I didn't leave the store. I did a book and a half."

"That's great, love. What has Margaret said about your progress?"

"She hasn't fired me. She didn't even come in today."

"That's great sign of confidence in you." He kissed Montana's nose and ran his hand through the short hair, getting the shampoo out.

"You think so? I want it to be good."

"It is. If she didn't trust you, then she wouldn't be comfortable leaving you there on your own, doing the work on your own."

Tanny smiled. "That's kinda cool, huh?"

"Very." He grabbed the soap and began rubbing it over Tanny's skin.

"Mmm. Did you have plans for supper?" Tanny stretched up, back and shoulders popping.

"There's food in the Crockpot. So we don't need to worry about it. And yes, I have plans."

"Cool." He got a quick kiss.

"I got a call from Doc today."

"Yeah?" Tanny's eyes caught his. "It's good news, right? I mean, you'd tell me if it was bad."

He grinned. "I've already told you the results."

"You did?" He saw Tanny frown, saw the way that mind worked—so quick, so fucking smart. "You did. I'm clean."

He laughed. "I did—you are—we both are."

"For real? Oh, damn. Damn. That's rocking cool."

"For real. We can dispense with the condoms." He couldn't wait to feel Tanny's silky heat wrapped tight around his prick.

"Oh, wow. I can... Wow."

"Let's go to the bedroom and explore all the things we can do."

"All of them?" God, he loved that laugh.

"Well, we'll start with one or two."

"Okay. Which two?"

"We're going to bareback. And then I'm going to plug you with my come still inside you."

"Oh." Tanny stared at him, lips parted.

Oh, he did love that look.

He leaned in and kissed those parted lips. He slid his tongue right into Tanny's mouth. Tanny stepped up, brought their bodies together, the long cock hot against his thigh. Groaning, he rubbed against his beautiful, wet lover.

"Mmm. Billy."

"Right here. With you. Come on. Let's get to bed. I want to be inside you."

"Hungry lover." Tanny smiled at him, kissed him.

"Yes. I want you. I want this. I have for a long time."

"I'm all yours. I promise."

"That goes both ways, love."

"I know that." Montana chuckled, kissed his nose.

"Good." He tried not to manhandle Tanny to the bed, but he was so hard, so eager.

"Is it going to feel different, do you think?"

"I think so, but I don't know for sure. I never have before—not with anyone." It was important that Tanny realized that, realized how special he was.

"But you want to with me, huh?"

"I do. It's important."

"Yeah. Yeah, it is to me, too."

"Good."

They went into the bedroom and Billy nodded at the

bed. "Sheets are clean, too."

"You're spoiling me."

"I want it to be special." Maybe he was making too much of it, but it felt like their first time all over again.

"I do, too. I promise. I want this. With you."

Cupping Tanny's cheeks, he brought their mouths together. Sealing it with a kiss, so to speak. Tanny's lips parted easily, letting him in, tongue sweet and hot. He pressed them closer together, feeling all Tanny's warm skin pressed up against his own.

Tanny moaned, the kiss going deep, Tanny's full cock against his hip. Billy rubbed and slid against Montana, teasing them both. He loved the way Tanny's body felt—smooth on one side, rippled on the other.

"I'm going to be inside you. Just me." He whispered the words against Montana's lips.

"Just you. Your cock. You trust me, huh?"

"I do. I always have, Montana." Right from the start. Something in Tanny had called out to him.

"Always. I don't deserve you." Tanny cupped his cheek.

"Shh. You're mine and I'm yours and that's the end of it."

Tanny's smile warmed him, hit him, deep in his belly. He lowered Tanny down onto the bed, their lips pressed together in a kiss. They started moving, slowly and he focused on the way Tanny's skin slipped against his, how his lover fit against him. He found Tanny's hands and twisted their fingers together, holding on as he kissed all over Tanny's face.

"Love you, huh? So bad." Tanny's voice was gaspy, husky.

"So good." There wasn't anything bad about the way they loved each other.

"Uh-huh. So much."

He gave Montana another kiss and then reached up under the pillow where he'd left a tube of lube. "We'll get you ready together."

"You like to watch that, huh?" Montana stayed close.

"I do." He nipped at Montana's right nipple. "You start with one and then I'll join in."

Montana moaned a little and he bit again. He was going to get them pierced—both little nipples for him. Montana was going to protest the entire time, but he was going to love it, too.

"Come on, now. Get your fingers slick and put the first one in." Billy was a little eager.

Montana took the lube, slicked his fingers quickly.

"Here, slick mine up, too." He held his hand out. They got their fingers slippery, both of them chuckling.

"God, I love you." He kissed Montana hard.

"Love. So much." He could feel Montana reaching down, slicking that tight little hole that was his.

He shifted so he could watch, moaning at the sight of Montana's finger disappearing into his body. Reaching out, Billy slid his own finger in next to Tanny's. Those long, lean legs spread for him, one knee bending for him.

He watched for a moment and then met Montana's eyes. "I'm going to feel this heat and silk around my cock."

"I hope it's good for you."

"It's going to be good for both of us, love. That's the goal." He slid another finger in. "Another one from you, too."

"That... that's four..."

"Yes. But your fingers are long and slender." Much like Montana himself.

"Yours aren't."

"That's why it's just two of mine." He winked and leaned in to bite at Montana's nipple again.

Montana cried out, that sweet hole jerking around his fingers. Groaning, he bit again. He could imagine that action around his cock, and it made his balls ache.

"Fuck. Fuck, Billy. That burns."

"I'm going to get you pierced." He licked at the reddened nipple, teased it with his tongue.

"N...no..." Oh, he could feel how much Montana liked that, all around his fingers.

"Yes. Maybe a ring and a barbell. Or two rings so I can attach a chain and let it swing between them." He pushed with his fingers, finding Montana's gland.

"Fuck..." Montana grunted, bore down, whimpered.

"Mmm... yeah. Okay, love. Fingers out. I don't want to wait any longer." Not to mention that Montana was more than ready.

"Good." Montana nodded, clinging to him, legs coming to wrap around his hips.

He shifted his hips until his cock pressed against Montana's hole, and already he could feel the difference doing this without the condom made.

"Yours. I promise."

Those soft words made him shake a little bit. Billy brought their lips together, his tongue pushing into Montana's mouth as his cock pushed into that tight, hot hole.

Oh, fuck.

Fuck yes. That was hot, perfect.

He could feel every inch of Montana's body grasping at his cock, pulling him in deeper, as he kept pushing.

"Oh, fuck. Oh, you feel so good."

"I know. God." He was nearly whimpering, the heat burning him up. He breathed against Montana's lips and moaned as he finally went as far as he could. Montana was looking at him, staring into him, and it was so fucking hot. He held on for a few moments and then began to move. He pulled slowly out and just as slowly pushed back in again.

He could feel everything—each muscle rippling and dragging against his shaft.

"So good," he whispered, body forcing him to move faster, to push in harder.

"Uh-huh. More. More, Billy."

He gave Montana what he wanted, what they both wanted. His hips pushed harder, his cock gliding in and out with more and more speed.

Oh, fuck. He'd never be able to give this up. Never.

He got one hand loosely wrapped around Montana's cock and began to tug on it as he pushed in over and over.

"Mmm. Good. So good." Montana's body worked him like a fist.

He wanted it to last forever, but knew it couldn't. When he felt himself beginning to go over, he held Montana's cock tighter and jacked his lover hard and fast.

"Yeah. Yeah. It's good. We're good. Please..." Montana arched, feet banging on the mattress.

"Come for me, love. Let me feel you around my cock."

"Yes..." Montana stilled, ass muscles milking him, jerking around him as heat spread between them.

Holding off as long as he could, Billy watched his lover's face as Montana came. Then he came as well, seed pouring into Montana's body.

Into Montana's body.

He shuddered again.

Montana kept moving around him, jerking and shifting.

"Love. Fuck." He leaned his forehead against

Montana's, panting hard.

"Uh-huh. Love. Wow."

"Yeah. There's a plug. Under the other pillow. Can you reach it?"

Montana's forehead creased, but he reached under the pillow.

"It's just a little one. Just enough to keep my come inside you."

Montana nodded. "I... I kinda like those. The plugs. Kinda."

"What do you like about them?" He took the plug from Montana, fingers lingering on his lover's.

"I... The feel. The pressure."

"And now you can add the way they keep my come inside you to that list." He slicked the plug up with lube.

"Uh. Uh-huh." Montana's eyes were fastened on him.

Billy nodded. "Uh-huh." Then he slid the plug down to Montana's ass. He'd have to come out first, of course. Just as soon as he could give up the amazing feeling of Montana tight and hot and silky around his cock.

Montana squeezed him again. Hard.

Groaning, he leaned their foreheads back together. "I could become addicted to this feeling."

"Yeah." Montana's ass started working his cock.

He wasn't going soft at all, and wasn't going to, not the way it felt. "Love. Love."

"Uh-huh. You... you like that." Montana was going to drive him out of his fucking mind.

"Yeah." He couldn't deny that, he wouldn't even try.

His lover kept moving, working his prick, making things wild. He stayed where he was, breath coming in faster and faster until he was gasping.

"You're going to? Again?"

"Don't stop," he ordered, because yes, he was.

Montana groaned, nodded. "Yeah. Yeah, okay, Billy."

"So good. You're so good." Billy started taking soft kisses. He rubbed their lips together and fucked Montana's mouth with his tongue.

This time the build up was slow, steady, something he could focus on.

Billy eventually added his own movements to the mix. Each time Montana's ass squeezed him, he pulled slowly out and then pushed back again. It felt like he was going deeper, though that had to be just an illusion.

Montana started panting, body sheened with sweat.

He got his hand back between them, fingers stroking Montana's cock.

"Oh." Montana's body moved faster.

"Uh-huh." Yeah, "oh", and also "oh, my God" and "wow", and "more, more, more." He began to squeeze Montana's cock every time Montana's body squeezed his and the two of them moved faster and faster.

Montana's shoulders left the bed, body rocking furiously. Billy's lover was magnificent.

Holding on as long as he could, Billy finally had to let go. "Now," he told Montana. "It has to be now."

"Uh. Uh-huh..." Montana's eyes rolled back in his head, a sharp cry sounding as heat spread between them.

"Yes!" His own cry came from somewhere deep inside as he filled Montana with more spunk.

Sweet Montana. Sweet, well-fucked lover.

He grabbed the plug, still slick from earlier, and slid out. As quickly as his cock came out, he pushed the plug in.

"Oh..." Montana's stomach jerked.

He twisted it and then seated it, not playing—he figured they'd both had enough for now. "Now I'm inside you until the plug comes out."

"When? When will you take it out?"

"I don't know." He grinned evilly. "Next time I want

to make love to you."

"Billy! You can't!"

One of his eyebrows went up. "Why not?

"I... Because."

"It turns me on, knowing my come is trapped inside you."

Montana's lips parted, the soft gasp perfect. Groaning, he slid his tongue inside Montana's mouth to taste the heat there. His sub. God, he wanted to just push and push.

"I want to go soon and these pierced." He pinched one of Montana's nipples.

"I... But..." Montana shuddered, scooted closer.

"No, I'm not piercing your butt," he teased.

Montana swatted his butt.

"Oh, ho! That's my job!"

"What? You spank yourself?" Montana whapped him again.

"You know what I meant!" He rolled them and smacked Montana's ass with his hand.

"Stop it!" Look at that well-fucked, plugged ass with his handprint on it.

"No, this is too pretty." He smacked Montana's ass again.

"Billy!"

He rolled Montana over his lap, fingers jostling the plug before he spanked those tight little ass cheeks. He kept it up, his hand and Montana's ass both going red, getting hot.

"Billy. Billy, stop." Montana was beginning to shift, pant.

He caught the base of the plug with his fingers, jostling it.

"Billy, stop! I can't..."

"Can't what, love?" He didn't stop, he could feel

Montana's prick growing hard and hot against his leg.

"I can't... not again." One day Montana would learn that his cock wasn't always the point.

"You don't need to come. In fact... "

He held Montana in his lap with one arm and reached for the side table drawer with the other. He managed to get a cock ring out without losing his grip on his lover.

"Billy." Montana moaned, kicked for him.

"Mmm... yeah, that works. See? No coming. Just feeling my come inside you and feeling my hand tanning your ass."

"I..."

He kept touching and Montana kept moaning, bucking for him. "God, you're beautiful, Montana."

"Am not."

"Yes, you are." He hit Montana's ass again and nodded. Yes. That was beautiful.

Beautiful and all his. He hit again and again, loving the rhythm, the sound.

When he couldn't possibly smack Montana again, he stopped. He panted, hand resting on top of the reddened ass. Soft little sounds filled the air, Montana fighting to catch his breath.

"So beautiful." He whispered the words, repeated them. "So mine. Love you."

"I... Love, huh?"

"I know." He bent and kissed the back of Montana's neck, his fingers tracing the scars he knew by heart now. "I know."

"They're ugly."

"No, I don't think so." The strength they represented was huge, the ability to heal, to continue, to transform into something new...

Montana beamed at him, cuddled in.

"I'm glad we did this. I'm glad it was you."

"Promise?" Montana stole another kiss.

He lingered on Montana's lips for a moment. "I do."

"I'm glad it was me, too."

"Good." The word was almost fierce as it left him and his kiss was hard, tongue pushing into Montana's mouth to take and taste.

His sub. His Tanny. His. He couldn't help saying it out loud. "Mine."

Montana stared at him, nodded. "Yours."

His fingers went automatically to the tattoo on Montana's belly and he smiled all the way to his toes. "Yeah."

Montana was his.

End